It's all in
the mind, you
know...

OCTOPUS' GARDEN

By

Aaron Mermelstein

Salami and Eggs Publishing LLC

Second print edition, Copyright © 2014
Salami and Eggs Publishing LLC
P.O. Box 9104
St. Louis, MO 63117-9998
All rights reserved.
ISBN-10: 0989771016
ISBN-13: 978-0-9897710-1-6
OCTOPUSGARDENBOOK@GMAIL.COM
Twitter: @OctopusGrdnBook

For the girls.

And the boy.

Second and third generation
Beatle fans.

Or would have been.

OCTOPUS'
GARDEN

OCTOPUS'S GARDEN
By Richard Starkey

I'D LIKE TO BE UNDER THE SEA
IN AN OCTOPUS'S GARDEN IN THE SHADE

HE'D LET US IN, KNOWS WHERE WE'VE BEEN
IN HIS OCTOPUS'S GARDEN IN THE SHADE

I'D ASK MY FRIENDS TO COME AND SEE
AN OCTOPUS'S GARDEN WITH ME

I'D LIKE TO BE UNDER THE SEA
IN AN OCTOPUS'S GARDEN IN THE SHADE

WE WOULD BE WARM BELOW THE STORM
IN OUR LITTLE HIDEAWAY BENEATH THE WAVES
RESTING OUR HEAD ON THE SEA BED
IN AN OCTOPUS'S GARDEN NEAR A CAVE

WE WOULD SING AND DANCE AROUND
BECAUSE WE KNOW WE CAN'T BE FOUND

I'D LIKE TO BE UNDER THE SEA
IN AN OCTOPUS'S GARDEN IN THE SHADE

(INSTRUMENTAL BRIDGE)

WE WOULD SHOUT AND SWIM ABOUT
THE CORAL THAT LIES BENEATH THE WAVES
(LIES BENEATH THE OCEAN WAVES)
OH WHAT JOY FOR EVERY GIRL AND BOY
KNOWING THEY'RE HAPPY AND THEY'RE SAFE
(HAPPY AND THEY'RE SAFE)

WE WOULD BE SO HAPPY, YOU AND ME
NO ONE THERE TO TELL US WHAT TO DO

I'D LIKE TO BE UNDER THE SEA
IN AN OCTOPUS'S GARDEN WITH YOU
IN AN OCTOPUS'S GARDEN WITH YOU
IN AN OCTOPUS'S GARDEN WITH YOU

DEAR SIR OR MADAM
WILL YOU READ MY BOOK?
IT TOOK ME YEARS TO WRITE.
WON'T YOU TAKE A LOOK?

After all these years, I'm tired of being dead. I've been dead for more than forty years now and I'm sick of it. Hell, I've seen 60 come and go and for all I know I'll be dead for real someday soon and I've got to get this story out.

I'm pretty sure John Lennon is actually physically dead and gone, though I'm still not one hundred percent on this. I've seen his horrific eyeglasses with blood on the lenses at the Rock and Roll Hall of Fame, the ones he was wearing when he was assassinated—yes, "assassinated" is the right word, not "murdered." But knowing what I know, I still can't say for definite. I am, however, completely certain George Harrison is dead if only because bad things happen to good people. And I'm positive that as of this writing Paul McCartney is still alive, even though he was once seriously thought seriously dead, but that's another story. Actually, no, that's *this* story. I paid big money a few years ago to sit in the nosebleed seats to see Paul in concert but he didn't recognize me among the fifty-thousand other fans. And Ringo? I especially wish Ringo a long and happy life. And Paul too, now that I think about it. That's just the right thing to wish for.

I'd like to say "hi" to Paul. And hello, Ringo.

And now the jig is up.

Sorry.

No. I'm not really sorry. I'm not sorry at all. It's time.

<u>CAN</u> BUY ME LOVE

It all boils down to this: in the spring of 1970, construction was completed on a massive steel and glass geodesic-domed Atlantis on the floor of the Pacific Ocean. It was fully pressurized to sea level and located approximately one hundred miles east-northeast of the coast of the Jarvis Islands, south of Hawaii, almost on the equator. Because it was built on a volcanic shelf on the seabed, the highest point of the dome was only fifty feet below the surface of the water.

Then it was successfully occupied by humans for more than eighteen months.

It was conceived, planned, authorized, constructed and populated under the auspices of the Beatles.

Is that clear? Underwater dome. The Beatles. That's what this is all about. That, and how I—*we*—got there and why.

It was Pepperland. An *Octopus's Garden*. It was "the Glass Onion." It was a genuine place of perpetual love, music, serenity and beauty. It was Utopia. It was Shangri-La.

While it was quite obviously a monumental engineering achievement, it was also a spectacular success as a great example of worldwide secrecy and deception.

And it also was a tremendous failure.

I know all this because I saw Pepperland. I experienced Utopia. I lived in "the Glass Onion" from the late summer of 1970 until the autumn of 1971, right before the roof both figuratively and literally fell in on the place.

I got there via two private planes, one boat (not a *ship*), all of which were "presumed lost" by the U.S. Navy and one real, live yellow submarine. Also "lost."

Through an elaborate hoax invented by agents of the American CIA and other international intelligence agencies, I was personally "lost" too. My disappearance from The World was backed up by official government reports that I fell overboard into the Mississippi River while on a late-summer cruise aboard a reproduction side-wheeler excursion boat at St. Louis. "Eyewitnesses" quoted in these reports (mostly people who were "dying to take you away—hoping to take you today"), said I was leaning over the rail of the boat photographing the Gateway Arch when I fell head-over-heels into the dark water. They feared I was bonked by a tree floating in near-flood stage river water and my body was quickly swept away by the strong current of the Mississippi's waters.

Units of the United States Coast Guard and the St. Louis Fire Department searched three days for my body. I would like to thank those Coast Guardsmen and fire department personnel for their genuine and sincere perseverance in a cause they did not know was futile and I would like to tell them "hi" and that I'm really okay, at least as okay as somebody who's been dead so long can be.

Many members of the intelligence community who planned my disappearance and the disappearances of three hundred and fourteen other Pepperlanders were also in The Onion with us. We called them "Meanies," after the villains in the animated Beatle movie *Yellow Submarine*. Their original purpose was supposed to have been pure, empirical observation of the place and its inhabitants. They regularly filed top-secret reports about the successes and failures of Utopia (especially the technical and psycho-social aspects), reporting anything that might be important for any government information-gathering needs regarding the totally supervised, isolated lives of a carefully chosen group of select people. They were instructed not to interfere with any events that took place nor were they to actively participate, that was all part of the deal with the Beatles that led to the agency's involvement in the entire Pepperland project.

Quickly though, as John Lennon predicted, many of the intelligence agency people "showed their bloody intelligence," fell into the ambiance and spirit and soul of the place, forgot their assignments and became residents like the rest of us. Some were taken out of The Onion by other Meanies and some remained. We assumed the who-stayed/who-left decisions were made on the basis of the specific importance to the Company of each particular Meanie (and they *all* seemed "particular," now that I think about it). One former CIA man even became "Musicmaster," the chief disc jockey responsible for ensuring a variety of live and recorded music played inside The Onion at all times. He was always held in some suspicion, however, since we never knew whether he took the Musicmaster role to truly become part of Pepperland or if it was simply another one of his job assignments. Since the CIA considered music as much of an experimental drug as the genuine chemicals they made freely available, it is possible he could have been motivated by either reason.

According to the *St. Louis Post-Dispatch* microfilm I found at my public library, many of my high school and college friends attended a lovely memorial service for me after my tragic loss. A page 1B story carried a picture of my girlfriend deep in mourning, her hand covering her grieving eyes. I would like to thank all those people who attended for their friendship and for their grief, real or feigned, and I would like to tell them "hi." The newspaper headline read "Services Held for River Victim."

A later *Post-Dispatch* article reported that my parents collected one-point-eight million dollars from the boat operators, claiming a higher railing would have prevented my fall into the Mississippi. In truth, the boat railing was the perfect height and absolutely nothing would have prevented my fall overboard, if only because I never fell overboard. The boat company raised the railing on the excursion boat anyway. I sincerely apologize to the boat company, its insurers and those workmen for their unnecessary labor and troubles. I would like to tell them "hi, I'm okay," and that I hope they got overtime.

While cruising through the old microfilm, I also read my father's obituary for the first time. He passed away in 1993, probably wondering why I did not personally meet him in heaven.

My mother still lives in our old house in University City, a St. Louis suburb. I learned this by checking the phone book, though I did not call her. She is 89 years old now. As far as she's concerned, I've been dead since 1970. It's been a long time. You might ask how I have resisted calling or visiting her after all these years. Habit, maybe. But also out of fear of hurting her, maybe shocking her to death, who knows? She's been better off not knowing the truth. I would hope that no one tells her now, that she simply continues thinking I'm long gone.

To this day I deeply regret beyond human imagination every part of the sham I perpetrated on the people I loved and who loved me. I am deeply pained by any grief, pain or inconvenience I caused my parents, my friends, my former girlfriend, the United States Coast Guard, the St. Louis Fire Department, the workmen who built the new railing on the excursion boat and anyone else.

But as much as I want to be alive again, I still don't regret the experience, not even the tiniest smidgen.

Until this writing, none of the three hundred and fourteen permanent residents of The Glass Onion have betrayed it to anyone.

Because, dammit, *it was Pepperland.* It was Utopia.

Until it failed.

And now I need to tell the truth.

LOVE ME DO

It seems ridiculous to me to have to explain that the Beatles reshaped culture during the 1960's. Unfortunately, it *is* necessary if only to help explain how something like Pepperland could possibly happen, not necessarily as merely an incredible engineering achievement but also— and most importantly—as an *idea*. Though the throng of second and third generation Beatle fans is huge, only those of us who were at that special age and of that special generation at that special time can really understand—and can still *feel*—the impact the Beatles had on us. Only we can truly comprehend how they positively changed everything.

For us, the screaming adrenaline rush of the alleged mass hypnosis of Beatlemania was as important and as a defining event as the Depression or World War II were to our parents. We became, by deprogrammer textbook definition, a cult. We worshipped the same gurus, wore the same sacramental garb and hairstyles, sang the same music, chanted the same mantras and lost control of our emotions when the Holy Ones were on TV. We eagerly bought each new vinyl addition to the gospel according to John, Paul, George and Ringo.

When John Lennon said the Beatles were "more popular than Jesus," everyone knew he told the truth. Even the protesters knew it was true while they burned their Beatle records and held pray-ins to prove Jesus still had fans of His own.

The protests were a mystery to me. I never understood how anyone would or could burn Beatle records. One high school friend confided to me that she put Johnny Mathis records inside Beatle album jackets for her church Beatle bonfire. I felt sorry for her, knowing Beatle album jackets were always beautiful and interesting. A few years later, I learned how truly interesting Beatle album jackets could be.

As far as my own story goes, I was a 15 year-old high school sophomore when the Beatles first invaded the United States and the earth near the beginning of 1964. I enjoyed their music, but wasn't quite as crazy as lots of other people my age. I liked the Beatles just like every other teenager, but I certainly didn't go overboard, at least not until a few years later when I *really*, literally, went overboard for them.

But from the beginning, I enjoyed using the Beatles to irritate my father, a full-time job for most 15-year-olds anyway. And I was good at my job. "Vat are you, a Biddle?" he'd ask in his immigrant accent when my hair got shaggy around the edges. He considered it a huge insult to call me "a Biddle" and appalling to have a son who looked like one. I was, of course, flattered to be connected to the Beatles even if it was only to annoy my father when I was too lazy or didn't have the three bucks to get a haircut, which he would have given me gladly. If I had either the courage or the money, I would have bought a collarless suit and "Biddle Boots," just to annoy him even more.

Before I was a real Beatlemaniac, I was a Kathy Powell maniac.

My secret, deep and totally unrequited crush on her began in the fifth grade. To this moment, I can still visualize her, exactly as she looked then. She had long, arrow-straight auburn hair, phenomenal brown eyes and the hugest leg-to-torso ratio I'd ever seen on a human. Even in fifth grade, she was already the kind of long-legged beauty I'm sure she became even better at being as an adult.

She was tall. I was short. She was as rugged and tough a fifth grade jock as most of the boys on the playground but she was certainly much more graceful. I was always the kid picked last for teams. She was beautiful. I wasn't. She seemed incredibly smart and phenomenally wise in the ways of the world to me. I was stupid.

She was the classic All-American *shiksa*, the perfect cover girl for *Modern Goy* magazine, if such a magazine actually existed.

It was a given, then, that it would have been forbidden by my Jewish, Holocaust-survivor parents to have anything to do with her. Had they known about my simple, normal, adolescent feelings for Kathy, they would have instantly assumed that she and I would marry and *that* was absolutely unthinkable.   Still, with her incredible looks, intelligence, humor and long fifth grade legs, she made my hormones rage like the Mississippi River in flood stage.

By the time we reached eighth grade, she had only grown smarter and cooler and even more beautiful. She seemed to have gained even more of a sense of worldliness that told everyone she ran with a much cooler crowd than I could ever compete with—high school kids.

But my biggest problem, starting the instant I first saw her in the fifth grade—hanging all other obstacles—was that Kathy Powell scared me totally and completely shitless.

By the time we reached high school, my fear of her lessened but never went away. Besides, our universes seemed so different I could still never think of much to say to her that didn't make me sound totally dorky.

But then, I had such an incredible idea that I was certain it would melt all ice between the two of us.

I assumed from the stickers and doodles on her notebooks and from her conversations on which I intentionally eavesdropped whenever possible, she couldn't love me because she was head over heels crazy in love with Paul McCartney. I knew she never ever had such dreams of me.

I developed an intense jealousy of McCartney, knowing that if he walked into our algebra class, my one true love would abandon theorems and run off with him immediately. I became determined to take the hand of the beautiful Kathy from him.

Purely as a survival mechanism then, and to win Kathy's heart—or at least to win her minimal interest for even a moment—I began to take the Beatles as something more than a group whose music and popularity I simply enjoyed and used as a tool to piss off my father.

Ultimately, it didn't work.

Kathy Powell wasn't with us in Pepperland.

I'm sure she wasn't there because I looked for her every time the submarine came into the Pepperland dock. My vigil became less obsessive as time passed, but I never stopped looking for her subconsciously, hoping that her love for the Beatles had paid off.

I don't know where Kathy Powell is now but I would truly like to know, just to find out how she turned out and if she still loves Paul McCartney and the Beatles. Or ever thinks of me.

"Hi Kathy."

I resolved to become an expert on all things Beatle to win her heart and mind. Failing that victory, I would have been happy to simply get her attention. It was my only hope of creating any sort of link between Kathy's world and mine. I'm still amazed at what the raging hormones of a lazy teenage boy can motivate him to do.

But I learned that learning to love the Beatles was easy.

I looked forward to each new Beatle single and album, buying each one the first day it was released. I listened to them constantly to memorize the new songs to be able to sound like an expert. "Yeeeeeeeeeaaaaaahhhhhhhhhh, I got *Hard Day's Night*," I remember telling her in my coolest possible attitude, "I especially like 'Ringo's Theme.'" The cut was an instrumental version of the vocal 'That Boy.' I would lock myself in my room and listen to it over and over, singing the words along with the instrumental:

> **...this boy would be happy, just to love you,**
> **But oh my-yyyy-yyyy-yyyy-yyyy.**
> **That Boy won't be happy**
> **'Til he sees you cry-yyyy-yyyy-yyyy-yyyy.**

That I was the first one in our class to see *A Hard Day's Night* impressed even Kathy. I made sure she knew how I suffered for seven hours in oppressive St. Louis heat waiting to buy the ticket, but she never knew it was strictly to stir her interest. She would never have understood how I wanted to give up the wait a thousand times but the desire to have her interest was more powerful than my desire for air conditioning. She was full of questions about the movie, wanting to know every detail. We even developed a little inside joke when I called our math teacher "a clean old man." After she saw the movie the second weekend it played, she quickly lost all further need for me.

Sometimes, I guess, the love you take is not equal to the love you make.

When I told Paul McCartney the details of this story while we were in the Glass Onion, he enjoyed this saga of my first Beatle adventure and swore that if he had known, he would have gladly relinquished Kathy's love to me.

In 1966, the announcement came that the Beatles would play a concert in St. Louis' Busch stadium. I waited sixteen hours in line to buy the five-dollar ticket, besting my *Hard Day's Night* record.

The concert was on a stormy night in August and from the moment "the boys" took to a covered platform at the top of the infield, no one could hear anything but the screaming, screaming, screaming. I learned recently that they only played eleven songs that night but the music was irrelevant. What was most important was the *experience*, that we were *there*. We saw *them*.

For years, whenever I saw a televised baseball game from the now genuinely dead and demolished Busch Stadium, my eyes wandered to second base as I remembered that was the spot where the Godhead once appeared to us upon a makeshift pulpit, where they preached before righteous multitudes of pilgrims in a holy revival unlike anything anyone had ever seen before or since. Most important, it was unlike anything any of us had seen or been a part of or *felt* before or since.

Looking for Kathy on the first day our high school junior year, I learned she had moved away during the summer. I doubt if she ever thought of me again.

I would have liked to have seen her in Pepperland if only to know whether she stayed as crazy about the Beatles as she forced me to become, to tell her that my life was totally rearranged by her crush on Paul McCartney, my crush on her and my love for the Beatles.

After all that, I still feel the need to explain that the Beatles were an incredible phenomenon to those of us who lived Beatlemania. They created a lot of Kathy Powells of both sexes.

The summer after Kathy moved away I found a real girlfriend to replace the one in my ambitions.

Everything about Mara was right; her looks, her personality, her humor, her easy laugh, even—by God—her religion. My parents loved her.

The only thing even remotely wrong with Mara—and admittedly it was a biggie—was that she was a Dave Clark Five fan.

I didn't hate The Five but never thought their music was anything special, certainly not as special as The Fab Four. Magazine and newspaper articles at the time worried me when they asked whether DC5 might "become more popular than the Beatles" and it upset me that Mara could contribute to this type of sacrilege, this pop culture Golden Calf. But I also felt that these religious differences—the Fab Four versus the fake Five—could be surmounted. At least she wasn't a Stones fan.

Mara made me feel glad all over.

Mara was the unidentified girlfriend crying in the newspaper photo that was taken at my memorial service.

We saw *Help* together during the third or fourth weekend after it opened and I never felt the urgency to impress Mara like I would have wanted to impress Kathy. Of course it was thrilling to see the Beatles on screen again, in color, but I controlled my excitement lest Mara find it unusually overabundant.

The best thing about Mara was the way she always smelled of Chanel Number Five. As our relationship grew, I bought her more for birthdays and holidays so she would always smell like Mara. Even today, so many years and so many lifetimes past, whenever I'm near a woman wearing Chanel Number Five, my nose and my mental memory automatically take me back to Mara and to those times. It is still the scent of when I was the most in love in all of my life.

A few years ago I used the internet to find her parents. Pretending to plan a high school reunion, I called them, fearing that any moment they might recognize my long-dead voice. Her father told me her married name and where she lives. He told me she has three daughters.

Until now, I have been too afraid and embarrassed to call or communicate with Mara.

Even if she reads this book and learns how I hurt her so long ago—and why—and how I deceived her all these years, I doubt she'll want to talk to me.

"Hi Mara."

I'm still me. At least I'm the me that I became.

I'm sorry about the memorial service and the picture.

I did what I had to do.

I didn't think you would have understood.

WHEN I WAS YOUNGER, SO MUCH YOUNGER THAN TODAY

Mara and I were a definite "couple" by spring, 1967. That was the year we graduated high school. It was also the year of *Magical Mystery Tour* and *Sgt. Pepper's Lonely Hearts Club Band.*

Our friends were amazed when I enrolled at the University of Missouri at Columbia and Mara attended a small college in St. Louis. Everyone assumed we'd go to college together, but Missouri's journalism school seemed the right place for me and Webster College was what she wanted.

I headed for journalism school because of one of those life-flukes that change everything. In my junior year, I became photographer for my high school newspaper.

While I worked invisibly on the paper's circulation staff, one day the staff photographer announced he couldn't take pictures of a Saturday night basketball game. It sounded like fun so I volunteered to substitute.

He said shooting the game would be easy. Since the lighting would be constant in the gym, he said, he would pre-set the camera to the proper shutter speed and aperture, all I'd have to do is focus and shoot. "It ought to be simple, even for a geek like you."

I loved sitting at courtside, right under the basket—in front of everybody. It was the best game I ever shot in all the games I ultimately worked. I popped the shutter at exactly the right instant, catching every jump shot the microsecond the ball left the shooters hand, every rebound at its elbow-swinging peak. I was excited about seeing my photo credit in the paper.

When I returned the camera to the regular photographer, he asked me for the film. I told him it was still inside the camera. But when he opened the camera, I could only shrivel up and whine, "I thought *you* loaded it!"

Two weeks later, he gave me a second chance and assured me he definitely pre-loaded the camera. I shot like crazy again. After the game, certain I had spectacular pictures, I opened the camera to remove the film myself. Instantly, I got another important photography lesson: unless you rewind thirty-five millimeter film back into the cassette, when you open the camera the film is out in the open, in the ruinous light.

Twice burned third degree and after as many stupid mistakes as I thought were humanly possible, I kept trying until I got it right.

Ultimately, I became the regular relief man whenever the photographer couldn't make an assignment. When he graduated, I got his job.

Quickly, I decided photography was the job I wanted for life.

I loved photography and how it put me on the sidelines of every big game and I especially reveled in seeing my photos in the paper. I relished catching one five-hundredth of a second of life that had never existed before and that would never exist again, capturing it forever on film and paper. The idea of seizing the moment was an attitude that I would use again later, the moment I captured one single solitary moment of opportunity that I have lived for so many years ever since.

I decided to major in photojournalism in college.

There were no St. Louis programs that could compete with Missouri's world-class journalism school. Besides, it was cheap, in state and Columbia was only one hundred and twenty miles away from Mara.

I enrolled at Missouri, pledged a fraternity and left for college with some high school buddies at the end of August, 1967.

The first weeks were torture. While I was by no means homesick, I'd never known the actual hurt in the chest that comes from being away from someone.

Mara and I talked on the phone often, me using a communal phone in a booth in the fraternity house hallway. These were the days long before cell phones, even before every student had a phone in their room. The other men in the house knew that if I was talking to Mara, the hallway phone would be unavailable for a long time.

We wrote letters every day.

Octopus' Garden

She always sprayed her letters with Chanel Number Five.

When the mail arrived, I snatched her letters and ran to my room. Then, I would lay on my bed with the envelope over my nose, smelling Mara and her perfume, lining my nose and memory with her scent. When I couldn't stand the masochistic agony of the wait any longer, I eagerly ripped open the envelope and devoured every word. It was a ritual of self-denial, tinged with scent-induced pleasure, memory and pure lust. I always wrote back immediately.

We never wrote about the Beatles or the Dave Clark Five. Neither group mattered.

Neither of us dated other people while we were apart.

But in December of that freshman year, just a few weeks before finals, I did fall in love.

I was reborn.

It was that rebirth that led to my death.

I saw the light.

SOMEBODY SAY, "AMEN, HE SAW THE LIGHT!"

The light was on a wall next to a heavy door. It glowed with the words "ON AIR."

Larry Goldberg was a fraternity pledge brother and high school buddy. One lazy Saturday afternoon, he asked if I wanted to go to "the station" with him. I didn't know what he was talking about. For all I knew, he wanted to go pump gas.

He was a disc jockey at KMZU, the on-campus dormitory radio station, a station I'd neither heard nor even heard of.

While I really would have preferred lolling around the fraternity house on a gray winter day, wallowing in my loneliness, Larry hit a nerve of fraternity brother guilt when he begged me to take some pictures of him "at the board" in front of the microphone so his parents could see him at work.

Even though it was truly just a small, dark hole of a few rooms in the basement of a dormitory cafeteria building, I instantly thought "the station" was the most wonderful place in the world. The equipment was old and nearly obsolete, discards from "real" stations looking for tax deductions. Larry said the control board had a tendency of giving mild electrical shocks if you completed a circuit by touching the wrong two places at the same time, but he could never exactly predict which two places those were.

But the machinery, the buttons and the quivering meters were all absolutely fascinating to me.

Once, he patronized me and asked what I wanted to hear. Accepting his patronization gladly, I asked for Beatles. "Easy," he said. We went into the hallway outside the studio, he searched a card catalogue and he quickly pulled a 45-rpm copy of *Eight Days a Week* from some tightly-packed shelves. It was exciting to hear it on the air, knowing that during those few minutes, people all over campus were listening to what I chose for them to hear.

But what was most amazing of all was that I knew that while Larry was on the air he was talking to lots of people without ever seeing them, choosing and playing music they were hearing, all without knowing if anyone was even listening. He worked feverishly on simple faith, talking and playing music, hoping somebody appreciated or noticed his efforts, that somebody was "out there." I don't think Larry understood the metaphysical and even spiritual idea of it all, I think he just wanted to be on the radio. But I was converted. I wanted to have that faith too.

That same silly, blind faith haunted me again later at that instant when it, coupled with my desire to capture a never-again moment, made me reach for the heavens.

SOMEBODY GIVE ME ANOTHER AMEN!

After a brief, but pressure-filled audition for the station chief announcer, I was duly given a DJ shift. Wednesday afternoons from one to two o'clock were mine. It was a tiny airshift that was available because the student who had it before was fired for not showing up one day and making the DJ before him stay on the air, forcing him to miss a class. I knew it wasn't much. Most students were still in class or somewhere on campus at that hour and there wasn't much of an audience, but I treasured my time on the air.

Larry Goldberg was my teacher. He taught me to "cue" records, shifting the turntable into neutral and channeling it into an off-air, closed circuit on the control board, turning the record back and forth by hand to hear the first grooves of the music and then wiggling it backward, leaving a small gap before the stylus hit the first note. If done correctly and professionally, the record started cleanly with no silence before the music, at-speed and the music didn't "wow" when it began.

I "wowed" a lot of records.

I learned the intricacies of the "cart" machines that played plastic tape cartridges of commercials and fever-pitched station jingles that were stolen from "real" radio stations and re-edited by creative student geniuses so that the singers sang our station call letters.

And most of all, I learned that the tight Top 40 format demanded that there be no dead air. Music or jingles *had* to be playing at all times. Never, never, never, never, never, NEVER dead air. We had to run "a tight board," never allowing the bobbing needle of the VU meter to hit zero. *NEVER NEVER NEVER DEAD AIR.*

Except for newscasts, talking was never allowed "in the clear," between two songs, only during the fade-out ending of one record and the instrumental lead-in of the next. Jocks were never to talk over the vocal portion of a song, only up until the very split second the singing began. To talk over singing was "to walk on the vocal." "To walk" was not as great a sin as dead air, but reinforced a DJ's amateur status.

Something had to be playing at all times.

The air had to be filled always.

There was no dead air.

"Walking on the vocal" was forbidden.

Format was to be strictly followed, playing the right kind of songs at the right times, hitting the newscast at exactly the right time.

It was a huge mess of rules, discipline and instructions that seemed overwhelming. Still, I wanted to feast on this banquet of regulations in one-hour bites, a buffet of music and jingles and "no walking on the vocals" every Wednesday afternoon. I wanted my board to be tight and I wanted to be loose.

I renamed myself "Jeff Scott," a name that I thought sounded snappy enough and WASPish enough for a hot disc jockey who never allowed air to die. Besides, I thought it would be cool to call myself "Great Scott" on the air, but Scott Roberts, another DJ, already took that nickname. So "Jeff Scott" it was. My parents were very upset when I told them my new name, never understanding how or why I could change my name for something as trivial as an hour on the radio. "Show business," I told them.

I learned that KMZU, owned by the Residence Halls Association, was a "carrier current" radio station. Its ultra-weak AM signal was carried from the station via telephone lines to a shoebox-sized transmitter in each dormitory basement. Then the building's electrical wiring carried the puny signal up to the audience. Unless you were inside a dorm with a radio close enough to a wall where the "current" was "carried," you couldn't hear the station. As a frat rat living in Greektown, I never heard "The Great 58." And at first, I hoped no one else did either, at least when my little show was on the air.

My beginnings in radio were as depressing as my start in photography: I not only "walked on the vocals," I stomped them. I murdered the air, strewing corpses of dead air all over my hour. I "wowed" records instead of wowing the audience. I shattered the format, playing the wrong songs at the wrong times and always hitting the newscast early or late—if I remembered to turn on the newscaster's microphone at all.

But like photography, with practice, I got better at radio too. In fact, it wasn't long before I got radio down cold. No more dead air. Vocals were untrodden-upon. I got comfortable and I got good at being on the radio.

I stopped taking pictures.

I changed my major to "Radio/TV."

When Mara came to visit, I dragged her to the radio station and played tapes of my most recent hour of fame.

She acted impressed.

The next year, as a sophomore, I was named chief announcer. It was my job to lay on the pressure when new people auditioned for airshifts and by God, I laid it on thick. I wanted them to want their precious time on the air as much as I did.

One new freshman I auditioned had an incredible "set of pipes," a deep bass voice that seemed to rattle the feet in my socks when he spoke. We put him on the air immediately, giving him two hours of airtime two days a week. There would be no bush-league, one-hour-a-week startup crud for this talent.

I guess my decision about him was correct, he's now a news anchor for the CBS radio network. I want to say "hi" to him too. I'm the guy who put you on the radio for the first time. I hear you on the radio all the time now. I'm not on the radio any more because I was dead for a while. But I'm not dead any more. Now there's a piece of news you can use.

As chief announcer, I won the 5-7 p.m. air shift Sunday through Thursday, a huge promotion. Though I had to miss my own dinner at the fraternity house, there was a relatively large potential audience for me that was coming and going from their own meals and just beginning their evening study routines.

And always, *always*, I played Beatles music whenever I could.

At the start of my junior year—the 1969-'70 school year, the years of *Yellow Submarine*, *Abbey Road* and *Let it Be*, I became station music director. It was a big jump in station hierarchy and I worked the 9-11 air shift, Sunday through Thursday nights. It was deep into the hours when students studying or loafing in their rooms had the radio on. It was the beginning of free time when they turned the volume up. It was Prime Time.

As MD (an abbreviation I used often to impress my parents), I listened to all the records that came into the station, choosing which would make the KMZU playlist and which would fall into KMZU oblivion. Sometimes I was right in my choices and the songs I picked made the national top 10. Sometimes I was wrong and the music I chose went nowhere.

It was a position of incredible power and incredible potential for failure. I was crazy about the job.

As music director and prime-time DJ with experience, I could exercise executive privilege and disregard the tight format, playing new records, entire albums or whatever I damn well chose. I pompously named my nightly two hours on the air "The Music" (pronounced on the air *"The Meeeewwwwuuuuuusic"*), and often introduced new artists or songs that would never get played during the tight format of the rest of the day.

As I over-exercised my own executive privilege on the 9-11 airshift, the station program director also used his and gave himself the 11 p.m.-1 a.m. shift. That was *real* Prime Time in campus radio, perfect downtime when most studying was finished and relaxation and radio were campus-wide activities. It was the best time of the night for all-purpose bullshit sessions in blacklight-lit dorm rooms, for pizza delivery and air guitar.

The program director used the air name "Mark W. Richardson."

His real name was Mark William Frick, but he thought that didn't sound quite right for a tightly-wound DJ on a tightly-formatted rock radio station so he took his father's first name for his own last name, becoming Mark W. "Richard's son."

He was a real radio man, a top forty heavyweight. He ran the tightest board of all. Boa constrictor tight. No dead air ever. To watch him run his board was to watch a concert pianist in action, his long, thin fingers flying from button to button, turntable to cart machine, always with a wide full-arm follow-through. In passionate rock jock style, he hit the last letter of his name hard: "Mark Dubble-YOU RichardsoNNNNNNNN*uh*!"

Long and lean with a tightly curled, nappy, white-boy Afro hairdo that would have made any black man of the '70s jealous, his face was a perfect, inverted isosceles triangle, the point of the long end forming his chin. Framed by his round hair, he looked like some sort of warning sign, a circle with a triangle inside.

He was a year older than me, from St. Genevieve, Missouri—"St. Jen"—a small, flood-prone Mississippi River town about an hour south of St. Louis with a deep French heritage. One summer day between my sophomore and junior years, he visited me in St. Louis and insisted we spend the day driving around looking at radio and TV towers. To me, they were only red and white metal towers. To such a dedicated radio man as he, each "stick" was a story. "There's an FM on that one...they share that tower with TV...that array is purely directional..." When other people visit St. Louis, they go to the Arch or tour the Budweiser brewery. Mark and I road-tripped through antenna farms and he was one happy visitor.

He used his experience at KMZU well. Today he is president of a chain of radio stations. I will not tell you the name he uses in his current life.

As the 11-1 man at the station, Mark "mangled the heavyweights," as he put it, for two prime time hours Sundays through Thursdays. Then he flicked off the transmitter that sent the station signal to the dorms, turned off the lights and locked up until the morning man arrived.

I don't need to tell Mark W. RichardsoNNNNNNN*uh* "hi" here. I tell him "hi" all the time.

IF I AIN'T DEAD ALREADY,
GIRL YOU KNOW THE REASON WHY

It was spring, 1970. It was my junior year in college. I was twenty-one years old. If I could see myself now as I was then, I would tell myself "hi."

One Thursday morning over bitter coffee and grease-dripping eggs prepared by Mort the fraternity house cook—a man for whom the French translation of his name was also the perfect description for his cooking—I read the now genuinely dead *St. Louis Globe-Democrat*. A tiny item caught my eye.

Above a dark, obscure photo was the headline "Rumors of Beatle Death Rampant in Europe." The article described persistent rumors that claimed Paul McCartney was dead and that his demise kept secret while he was replaced by a look-alike.

I carefully tore the small article from the paper and intended to mention it on the air that night. Just a mention, I thought.

When I arrived at the station, Mark was already in the small office we shared, doing whatever program directors do. Our so-called "office" was really a filthy storage room cluttered with equipment that was actually crappier than the stuff that actually kept the station on the air, old magazines and boxes of discarded records—duplicates and duds not even a packrat like me wanted to add to his record collection.

When I mentioned the article, Mark said he saw it too and that he also intended to mention it on his show.

My airshift ran normally for most of that night. About ten-thirty, as the Jeff Scott show wound down, Mark came into the studio to get ready for his time on the air. I held up the article as I "outro'ed" a record and motioned him toward the microphone. "Mark Dubble-You RichardsoNNNNNNNN*uh* is here," I said, "ready to mangle the heavyweights from eleven 'til one, so keep your radio here on 'The Great 58.'

"Mark, did you see this article about the late, great Paul McCartney?"

From off-mike, a deep, loud voice came through my headphones, pretending to be shaken. "Indeed I did, Young Jeffrey." He often called me "Young Jeffrey." I think it was because it had a better rhythm than just "Jeff." He still calls me that sometime too. "How I miss Paul already," he added.

"Take a seat, Mark," I told him. "Let's talk about this."

The studio was barely big enough for one person to sit comfortably, so he had to maneuver his skinny body past my chair to rest his bony butt on the countertop under the control board. Listeners could hear the creak of the spring-loaded microphone arm as I moved it between us. I pushed my chair back and stood so I could be on the same level, the same microphone plane, as he. "So what do you make of this? What's this about?"

He laughed and said he didn't know, that he thought the article was pretty bizarre but come to think of it, it had been quite a while since Paul had called him to make an on-air request. Then he gave the "request line" number for Paul or any other listeners to call. What a genuine, through-and-through radio man.

The article said that people in Europe had gotten "clues" about Paul's death from various Beatle albums, especially *Sgt. Pepper*, *Magical Mystery Tour* and "*The White Album*." It said that when they played "Revolution Number Nine" backwards, they heard someone saying something about Paul's death. That undescribed weirdness was proof enough for some to believe that one of the most beloved performers of the largest generation in history had died without anyone knowing it, that a grand cover-up was in effect that fooled people around the world. "Why would anybody play it backwards?" I asked. "Even forward it's nothing but noise."

"Riiiiiiiiight," Mark said.

Immediately, we both knew what we had to do. "We gotta try this," I shouted, running out to the hallway shelves where we kept the albums. Mark held the door open so listeners could still hear my voice. "I'm looking through the 'B's," I yelled…Joan Baez, Beach Boys, Beatles. Got it!"

I ran back into the studio and put the "D" side of the album on the turntable. It took only an instant to realize the turntable wouldn't spin the record backwards at all, much less at normal speed. Mark instantly knew if we were ever going to hear this, it had to be done the hard way. "Put the turntable in neutral, between the notches for 33 and 45," he said quickly. I did as he said. "Put the needle at the end of the cut and turn it backwards with your finger. We gotta do it by hand."

Pushing down the green Apple graphic on the label with my index finger, I turned counter-clockwise, trying to maintain a speed that at least looked close to thirty-three-and-a-third rpm, but a backwards thirty-three-and-a-third.

Maintaining a standard play speed in the forward direction on these ancient, held-together-with-spit-and-voodoo turntables was hard enough for our staff of student engineers. Playing a record backwards, by hand, was impossible.

All we heard was "Revolution Number Nine" backwards. Just like it was when played forward, it was just sound effects and noise, but this time it was sound effects and noise in reverse.

And then, like that, there it was.

.saw ti ereht ,taht ekil ,neht dnA

"Turn meyon deadmun. Turn meyon, deadmun. Turn meyon deadmun."

I stopped turning and had to stop myself from blurting out "shitfuck!" so near an open microphone.

There was dead air.

I ran the record forward with my finger.

"Number niyun. Number niyun. Number niyun."

And then backwards again.

"Turn meyon deadmun. Turn meyon, deadmun. Turn meyon deadmun."

There was no denying it. It was there.

.ereht saw tI .it gniyned on saw erehT

STEP UP TO THE MYSTERY TOUR,
STEP RIGHT THIS WAY

We must have played it back and forth twenty times. It was the same every time.

"Number niyun. Number niyun. Number niyun."

"Turn meyon deadmun. Turn meyon, deadmun. Turn meyon deadmun."

My knuckle ached from pushing the record backwards so many times. We played the entire nine-minute cut forward and hand-turned it backward, listening for anything else that might be hidden. Forward, there was only noise, odd pieces of miscellaneous racket, strange sounds and voices. Backwards, the "turn meyon" segments were too clear and too strange to be coincidence.

There was absolutely, positively no reason in the universe that a backwards "number nine" should sound like "turn me on dead man" even in a British accented "number niyun." We figured maybe it should have sounded like "nnnuhhheyennnn rrrubmun." Granted, the "mun" part was there, but not the "turn me on dead…"

At first, we certainly didn't suspect anything sinister or conspiratorial. We thought it was simply weird that someone was so clever with audio production, a normal thing for radio men to think. We appreciated such a masterwork of tape editing craftsmanship by whoever was responsible for turning "number niyun" into something unique when played backwards. We complimented the unknown tape editor for even thinking that anyone anywhere *might* ever play it backwards. We suspected it was all something John Lennon did on a silly whim.

Then the whimsy ended abruptly.

The participants in all those post-study hour, in-room and all the late night bullshit sessions came awake and alive. Our phones lit up. While audience call-ins were always encouraged on the station—music requests mostly—the quantity and intensity of what was just beginning is still amazing to Mark and me.

"Play 'Strawberry Fields!'" one listener insisted. "Listen all the way to the end and don't talk over the ending like you always do! Let it go all the way to the end without saying anything!"

"Why?" we asked. "What's at the end?"

"Somebody says 'I buried Paul.'"

"What?"

"Just play it and keep your mouth shut!"

Shut my mouth.

It's there. It says "I buried Paul." We didn't know whose voice was saying it but we thought it sounded like John Lennon, but slowed down. We debated on the air about whether it really might have said "I'm very cold" (which, of course, would also have been significant relative to a dead man), but in the mindset we were in, "I buried Paul" quickly won out.

The number and excitement of the phone calls increased quickly as each bit of rumor spread, each new discovery was made. Everybody spoke with exclamation points at the ends of their spoken sentences. "On the back of *Sgt. Pepper*, John, George and Ringo are facing the camera but Paul's turned away! He's different! He must be dead!"

"Play 'I am the Walrus!' Somebody says something at the end. I don't know what it is, but it's weird!" We played it and absolutely heard something weird at the end. Someone is talking through the slow outcue fade-out, the part we usually talked over and covered up. We could definitely hear the words "my body." Playing the last minute or so of the record a second time, we could still hear talking, but couldn't make out any more words. A third time we definitely heard the word "death." Finally, listening carefully, studio monitors turned up the maximum, we heard the words "*untimely* death."

The first batch of calls spurred other calls. As cool and hip and in as Mark and I fancied ourselves to be, it seemed we were the last people in America to know about the rumor, that our listeners were more in on what was happening than we thought. Whenever we turned off our microphone while the "clues" played, we talked about how dumb we felt and how, as radio men, we obviously weren't the centers of the entertainment universe we thought we were.

So many listeners called to give us clues, our on-air session seemed to be the first time so many people put so many pieces of the Beatle puzzle together in so large a group, an entire on-campus community. "There are twenty guys in my room," one caller said. "Everybody's got their albums out, looking for clues." As he spoke to us on the phone, we could hear "Revolution Number Nine" playing backwards on a hand-turned stereo turntable in the background.

"Look at the cover of *Abbey Road*," another caller insisted. "Look how they're dressed and how they're crossing the street."

"What's there?" Mark asked, grabbing the record from the stack that had built up in the studio. Our jaws dropped as the listener described what she saw and what she interpreted from the back of the record. "It's a funeral procession! Look how they're dressed! John's first and he's wearing white. He's the priest! Then Ringo's in a black suit, he's the undertaker! Get it?"

"Riiiiiiiight. Go on," Mark said demandingly.

"Paul's next in line and he's wearing a suit too. But he's not wearing shoes!!!! He's the corpse!!!"

"Cool! George is last in line and he's wearing..."

"George is wearing jeans and a denim work shirt. Don't you see? He's the gravedigger!!!" We saw it clearly.

With each call and each clue it all got more and more astonishing.

The next caller embellished the *Abbey Road* interpretation. "Paul's carrying his cigarette in his right hand!" We both knew where the caller was headed and intoned together "...and Paul's left-handed!"

"Exactly! The guy in the picture is a fake! He's the replacement they put in when..."

"When Paul died. Riiiiiiiight."

And then the rumors of Paul's death got terminal.

"Look past the Beatles at the cars parked along the street on the cover of *Abbey Road*. Look at the white Volkswagen parked at the curb. Read the license plate!" In astonishment, I almost said "Oh shit" live and on the air. "The license plate says '28IF.'"

"Paul would have been 28 years old if he'd lived!"

It was not only amazing to me that it was there but frustrating that I'd never noticed the license plate in all the times I'd played the album on air and at home. Of course, until the rumors began flying, I never had a reason to look or to put it in this kind of context. For these clues, as perhaps with all conspiracies, context is everything.

"What kind of car is it?" the caller asked.

"Good catch," Mark said. "It's a Volkswagen *beetle*."

"Paul died in a car accident," another caller insisted. "There was a huge fire and he was burned horribly and they covered it up."

"How do you know that?"

"Well first of all, my roommate told me."

"Great, that's definitive."

"But listen. It's possible. "On 'Don't Pass me By,' they sing 'you were in a car crash and you lost your head...or is it hair? I don't know for sure. But then in 'A Day in the Life,' they do it again."

"Do what?"

"They talk about a car crash. The line is...I'm reading this from the words printed on the album...'he blew his mind out in a car, he didn't notice that the lights had changed'—see? It must have happened at an intersection or something."

"Riiiiiiiiight."

"'A crowd of people stood and stared, they'd seen his face before...' That's it! Get it? And after Paul died in the car accident he was replaced by a look-alike."

"Thanks for the call."

We were both still together in the studio at 11:30, already a half-hour past my airshift and into Mark's regular time. Each of us felt as if we were just getting started and agreed to stay on the air together as long as our listeners and we kept coming up with what we assumed were clues to solve some sort of mystery. We were working toward a solution even though we didn't know what the puzzle was.

Hearing us on the air in their dorm rooms, other station staffers started coming in. There were a few news people, some secretaries, even a one-hour-per-week DJ or two hoping to get a place next to our Prime Time microphone. They were all eager to help in our search. At that hour Mark, a newsreader and I were usually the only ones in the station, but that night the small place grew crowded.

We played "number niyun" again and again in both directions.

"Okay, let's stick with the 'funeral' idea from the *Abbey Road* cover," another listener began. "What's the first cut on side one?"

Everybody knew it was "Come Together."

"That's right," he said. "It's the first cut on the first side because it's the most important, right?"

"Who knows? But okay, let's go with that."

"And it's first because of the whole idea of 'come together, right now, *over* me.' Over me! Like people standing at a grave, understand?" We understood.

"And then you've got the line 'he wears no shoeshine' and Paul's barefoot on the cover, remember? He's a corpse! Then you've got the line 'hold you in his armchair you can feel his disease.' He got a disease. He died!"

"Riiiiiiight. Good one."

"And in the same song, it says 'one and one and one is three.' If Paul died, there are only three Beatles left."

"Geez Louise."

"'Got to be good looking 'cause he's so hard to see!' Well if he's dead and buried, you can't see him!"

The ideas were getting truly chilling.

"Listen to 'Revolution Number Nine' again. You can hear the car crash, you can hear fire and you can hear Paul screaming."

It seemed to be there too.

We played everything again, listening for anything that might have meaning. There were so many calls we didn't need faith to know there were people listening. "It's crazy in Lathrop Hall," one caller told us. "I just walked down the hall and you guys were coming out of every room! Keep it up!" We promised we would.

"Look at *Magical Mystery Tour!*"

We didn't have a copy of *Magical Mystery Tour*. Record theft was a chronic problem at the station and it was never more frustrating to me as music director as at that moment. "What about it? What do you see?"

"In one of the pictures inside the jacket, they're all wearing white suits."

More with white suits like John was wearing on the *Abbey Road* cover. "Are they all priests?"

"No, it's not the suits, it's the flowers! John, George and Ringo have red flowers in their lapels, okay?"

"Okay. Go on."

"Paul's flower is black!"

A few minutes later, a dayside newsman brought us his personal copy of *Magical Mystery Tour*. He had run to the studio with it from his dorm when he heard we needed it. He said he never lost track of what we were doing, that he heard us continuously as he ran down his dorm hallway and even outside through open dorm windows all the way to the station.

Sure enough, Paul—or whoever was pretending to be Paul—was wearing a black flower in the photo.

Once we had a copy of *Magical Mystery Tour*, I inspected it carefully and quickly made another discovery: on the first page of the "booklet" inside the album jacket, under a drawing of the Beatles dancing in a circle, it reads "AWAY IN THE SKY, (sic) beyond the clouds, lived 4 or 5 magicians." "Would that mean John, Paul, George, Ringo, that's four—and then when you add the replacement? That's five."

It built and built and became weirder and weirder and weirder.

We were definitely starting to believe that just maybe, this rumor thing might be more than a rumor.

We played the end of "Strawberry Fields" again and "I am the Walrus." We still heard "I buried Paul" and "untimely death."

There was nothing in "Something."

"Bang bang Maxwell's silver hammer came down on his head. Bang bang Maxwell's silver hammer made sure that he was dead."

"I found it!" another caller shouted. "I found it!"

"Found what? What did you find?"

"I found the end of 'I am the Walrus!' It's from *King Lear*! It's Shakespeare! It's act four, scene six, starting at line 252! A character named Oswald says it, as in Lee Harvey Oswald! Get it?!"

"Yeah, an assassin. We got it. What does he say?"

"Listen: *If ever thou wilt thrive, bury my body, and give the letters which thou find'st about me to Edmund Earl of Gloucester. Seek him out upon the British party. Oh untimely death! Death!'* And then," the caller added, "Oswald dies."

"Wait a minute! Hold on! Read it again!" We cued up "I am the Walrus" to the end and played it as the caller read along. It was a dead match. Turn me on deadmun.

"You think the flower thing on *Magical Mystery Tour* is weird?"

"Yes."

"Find the picture of Paul—or whoever it is that looks like Paul— sitting at a desk in an army uniform. Look at the nameplate!"

I could barely stop myself from saying "oh shitfuck" again. Usually, a desk nameplate merely displays the name of the person sitting behind it. The nameplate in front of Paul McCartney in the *Magical Mystery Tour* booklet, right there for all to see, in capital letters and subject to no possible misinterpretation, says "I WAS."

HERE'S ANOTHER CLUE FOR YOU ALL
THE WALRUS WAS PAUL

There were too many "clues" for coincidence. "Somebody's messing with our minds," Mark said with confidence. "Somebody *wants* people to find this stuff."

I finished his thought. "But we can't say they're really 'clues' to anything, can we? Maybe they're just clever little things somebody put in to see if anybody noticed."

Mark knew. "John did it," he said with absolute certainty. "If anybody would do it, John would. He's got the kind of mind that gets jollies from messing with people's heads."

One of the truly unfortunate things of the age of downloaded internet music and compact discs is that record album art has been eliminated or at least reduced from a major, well-thought-out part of an album release into what seems like an afterthought. And worse, even on CD reissues of old Beatles albums, any small booklets inside the compact disc box aren't as extensive as the larger ones that came with long-playing albums. There are no photos inside the CD version of *Magical Mystery Tour*, only song lyrics. There are no "I WAS" clues to be found, nothing to mess with our minds even a little, no trace of the mind-fucks that came with the vinyl versions of the albums and their paperboard covers.

The calls continued to come into our studio.

"On the *Abbey Road* cover, Paul's out of step with the others."

"On the inside of *Sgt. Pepper*, Paul's wearing a patch on his arm that says 'O.P.D.' That stands for 'Officially Pronounced Dead.'" Later, someone said the patch was a gift from the Ontario Police Department, that Paul simply liked it and put it on his *Sgt. Pepper* uniform. Either could have been true, of course, but the "Officially Pronounced Dead" explanation fit the mood of the night so much better.

Nobody ever logically explained "I WAS," "28IF" or most of the other clues, especially the ones that were so blatant they had to be intentional.

"John, George and Ringo are standing around a trunk on the cover of *Yesterday and Today*. But Paul is inside the trunk. It's a casket! Plus, this was the album with the 'butcher cover!'"

The 'butcher cover' is a fine bit of Beatles trivia. The original cover of *Yesterday and Today* showed the Beatles wearing bloody, white "butcher" coats and holding pieces of chopped-up, bloodied toy dolls. After it was allegedly deemed "too disgusting" by whoever deems things "too disgusting," the more innocent "trunk" photo replaced it. The rumor spread that the new cover photo was literally pasted over the old one on thousands of copies, that anyone who could strip off the replacement photo to reveal the original would own a high-priced collectors item. Almost everyone who owned *Yesterday and Today* had peeled off at least one corner of the cover to see whether the original "bloody" cover might be below. I never knew anyone who found an original cover underneath.

The "butcher cover" caller continued, making even stronger and more ridiculous claims about the three allegedly remaining Beatles. "They were dressed as butchers because they killed Paul themselves! Then they chopped him up!"

The phone lines kept blinking.

"How come *Revolver* is printed in all black? Maybe that's how he died—he was shot with a revolver!"

"Paul's the only one wearing a tee-shirt on the back of *Help*. The others are wearing regular shirts or jackets. And on top of that, Paul's tee-shirt is black! And his arms are folded like a corpse!"

Help me if you can, I'm feelin' down.

"Think of the lyrics that say 'living is easy with eyes closed, misunderstanding all you see.' Paul's dead, his eyes are closed and we all think the replacement guy who is *playing* Paul is actually Paul, so we're misunderstanding everything! Get it?"

We got it.

"On the eight-by-ten pictures that came with 'The White Album,' everybody's well-groomed except Paul. He looks awful, like he just got out of bed. Or like he died."

"On the back of 'The White Album,' there's a thank you 'to all at Number 9.' What's that?"

"Number nine. Number nine. Number nine. I don't know what it is, but it must be important!"

Some of the calls from listeners were totally non-speculative and completely convincing: "What is everyone standing behind on the cover of *Sgt. Pepper*? It's a grave! The flowers that spell out 'Beatles' are on top of a grave!

"And look at the yellow flowers on the bottom right corner of the *Sgt. Pepper* cover. What do they make?"

"A guitar?"

"Look again! It's a *left-handed* guitar!"

"Riiiiiiiight."

"And if you *really* look, the yellow flowers spell out P-A-U-L, then a question mark!"

I-t w-a-s d-e-f-i-n-i-t-e-l-y t-h-e-r-e.

When we got calls like that one, calls that seemed to cast so much light into the darkness, it was not only fascinating but also tremendously spooky. Talk of graves and "P-A-U-L?" written in flowers must have made the studio air conditioning work harder because I remember how cold I suddenly felt.

"A walrus means death."

"It does?"

"That's what I heard, and if it's true, listen to 'Glass Onion.' It says 'here's *another clue for you all*, the walrus was Paul!'"

"Who sang 'I am the Walrus?'" I asked.

"John," Mark answered quickly, "it's his kind of song. Even though it's a Lennon-McCartney credit, I'll bet John wrote it by himself. He definitely sang it."

"But he says '*I* am the walrus.' If he's the walrus, how can Paul be the walrus?"

"Then who's the egg man?"

It was getting silly. We were nitpicking semantics of a nonsense song.

As the walrus, Paul is wearing a black costume on the cover of *Magical Mystery Tour*. The other three costumes are white.

At some point in the call-in process, we realized that if something mysterious was truly going on, it had been going on for a long time on albums that were released over a number of years.

Between midnight at 2 a.m., it all stopped being fun and games and became a genuine quest for truth. Mark and I felt a genuine connection to our listeners, a deep sense that something important was happening and we passionately wanted to figure it out. Whatever it was, we wanted to know and we wanted to be part of it. It was tremendously important for us to find out what it was and why.

"'Sexy Sadie broke the rules...and made a fool of every one.' There must have been somebody named Sadie who was involved in the cover-up."

"That's a long shot. Got anything else?"

"Yeah. 'Nothing is real.'"

"You got that right."

"And don't forget 'half of what I say is meaningless.' It sounds as if they're telling us that some of the clues are bogus."

"But it's the meaningful half of what they're telling us that's so interesting!"

"But which half is meaningful, and which half is meaningless?"

"Maybe nothing really is real."

"In 'Nowhere Man' they actually tell us we're stupid if we *don't* see the clues: 'He's as blind as he can be, just sees what he wants to see.' Get it? They're saying some people see the clues but don't recognize them. They even come right out and ask 'Nowhere Man, can you see me at all?' It's their way of saying Paul is dead because you can't see him. He's nowhere, man! They even say that the clues are visible and that they're hidden in the music: 'Nowhere Man, please listen, you don't know what you're missin!'"

"In Scandinavian countries, a hand over somebody's head is a sign of death."

"I thought a walrus is a sign of death."

"Let's say that it is, too. And there's definitely a hand over Paul's head on *Sgt. Pepper*. It means he's the next to die." As farfetched as this idea was, we accepted it as fact since neither of us were experts on Scandinavian folklore. In fact, we disputed almost none of the claims our listeners made as long as they seemed reasonable in context. Context was everything. After all, it was all beyond reason and the hand-over-the-head/next-to-die clues were as reasonably unreasonable as everything else.

Maybe we didn't question it because we started finding hands over Paul's head almost everywhere. There was a hand over his head on the cartoonish cover of the *Yellow Submarine* soundtrack, a black-on-white hand in the illustration on the cover of *Revolver* and a contorted hand reaches out to Paul in the lower-right corner of the poster that came inside "The White Album." On the same poster, there is a photo of Paul looking as if he's climbing a pole—behind him is something unrecognizable. We interpreted these as "ghost hands" reaching toward him.

We beat the hell out of "Glass Onion" and foolishly came up with very little even though later we would know it was all there. Everything. "Here's another clue for you all, the walrus was Paul." The idea of a "glass onion" itself was the most obvious, but we simply didn't have enough information to understand. There was no such thing as a "glass onion." Besides, why would they put a cut on a record that so blatantly gave clues about the clues? It must have all been nonsense. We threw it off as gibberish. In an interview years later, John would say that they did it to throw off all the Bozos looking for clues.

People in dorm rooms started looking at the large poster that came inside "The White Album" jacket as if it were the Dead Sea Scroll of Beatles, something that would reveal deeply hidden secrets. "There are no accidents on that poster. Everything on it is planned." There is a series of overexposed photos of the Beatles sitting around a table. In the fifth picture in the series, Paul is the only one looking away from the group.

"The shot of Paul in the left-center edge of the poster has him looking off of the edge of the poster. I'm a graphic arts major and I know that people are never supposed to look off a page, always in! Everybody knows that! He's the only one looking off the cover of *Revolver* too! And look at the eight-by-ten pictures that came in inside *Sgt. Pepper*, everybody else is nice and clean, Paul looks like homemade shit and on the..." Having no kind of tape delay, the "homemade shit" comment went over the air and we laughed as we clicked the caller off air too late. It was a nice tension-breaker in the middle of what was already very tense.

"Okay caller, what have you got? And watch your language please, you can get us all in trouble here."

"Okay. On the poster, top left corner, Paul's in a bathtub, his eyes are closed. It looks like he's in a coffin."

"Look at the picture in the lower left corner of the poster, between the photo of George and another one of John and Yoko. Who the hell is that?"

We didn't know. "It looks like Paul with a mustache and glasses."

"He's the replacement! They've actually got the balls to show us the guy who's impersonating Paul!"

Another caller was more excited than most of the others. "It's Billy Shears! The guy with the mustache is Billy Shears!"

"So?"

"Who's Billy Shears?"

"Billy Shears won a Beatles look-alike contest a couple of years ago and now they've replaced Paul with him!"

"I know that name from somewhere," I said.

"Of course you do!" the caller screamed. "It's the last line of 'Sgt. Pepper's Lonely Hearts Club Band!' It says "So may I introduce to you, the one and only Billy Shears AND..." I finished the lyric. "...*AND* Sergeant Pepper's Lonely Hearts Club Band. John, George, Ringo are the band and they're introducing Billy Shears! It's Billy Shears *and* Sergeant Pepper's Lonely Hearts Club Band—it's Billy and the three Beatles!"

"Riiiiiiiight."

If Billy Shears was, indeed, Paul's replacement, it made sense that the "Billy Shears" line led directly into the next song on the album, "A Little Help from my Friends." It makes sense that Billy "gets by" disguised as Paul but needs a little help from his friends to pull off the charade. He's faking his way as Paul while John, George and Ringo help.

Even his name was spooky. Pronounced one way, it was "Billy Shears." Said another way, it was "Billy's here."

The next caller sounded like another non sequitur and changed everything. "It's a telephone number! The word "Beatles" on the *Magical*

Mystery Tour album! Everybody knows it's a telephone number! Call the number! Call the number!!!!!"

For the sake of honesty and simplicity here, many other books have been written listing every detail of the clues, there are dozens and dozens of websites dedicated to them, just Google "Paul is dead." Listing all the clues isn't my purpose here. My job here is to explain what happened to me. That's all.

The best of the books are *The Walrus Was Paul* by R. Jeff Patterson (Simon and Schuster/Fireside Books), and *Turn Me on Dead Man* by Andru J. Reeve (Popular Culture Ink; expanded version, AuthorHouse). The Reeve book was originally published in 1994, the Patterson book came out in 1998, almost twenty-five and thirty years after all these clues were so passionately revealed and discussed on our radio station. I suspect both books are out of print now, but you can probably find them on the internet. I wonder whether either of these guys was listening that night. I bought the Patterson book a few years ago, opened it and couldn't read it because reading the clues again was so powerfully painful. I gave it to a friend without explaining why. Maybe I'll try to borrow it back now.

At the urging of that caller back in 1970, we did call the number. That was when everything began to change for us, though we certainly had no idea anything had changed at all.

Nothing is real.

WHEN I CALL YOU UP, YOUR LINE'S ENGAGED
(you won't see me)

On the *Magical Mystery Tour* cover, the word "Beatles" is spelled out in stars. All previous album covers said "*The* Beatles." This one just said "Beatles." Looking further, we discovered that the word "the" wasn't on the *Sgt. Pepper* cover either. We interpreted the omission of the word "the" to mean that the people on the record were Beatles, but not *the* Beatles—*the* Beatles included Paul McCartney.

It was absolutely clear to us that Paul must definitely be dead.

The "it's a telephone number" theorist told us "if you hold the cover of *Magical Mystery Tour* upside-down and in a mirror, the stars that spell 'Beatles' become a phone number. 'Beatles' has seven letters...*the* Beatles would have too many numbers! It's a phone number!"

The numbers that should have jumped out from the album cover didn't jump anywhere when we looked directly at the jacket. While Mark kept answering calls, I ran down the hall to a restroom to look at the cover in a mirror. But numbers were still not obvious. Despite turning the album in every direction, I had no blatant success in determining the mystery phone number and trudged back to the studio.

"It might be 837-1438," but admitted, "I'm not sure."

Even if it was a phone number, whose number was it?

"It's not a phone number, it's just letters and stars."

What the hell? What's stopping us? We dialed the phone number live, on the air and in the wee hours of the Mid-Missouri morning. "We're sorry, the number you have dialed cannot..."

And then another caller gave us what we thought was a breakthrough. "Look at the back of *Sgt. Pepper*! George is telling you when to make the call!" Instead of complete sentences, the callers were speaking in clues. "George is pointing!"

"Okay, what do you think he's pointing at?"

"He's pointing at the line! He's pointing at the line that says when to call! He's pointing at a line from 'She's Leaving Home' that says 'Wednesday morning at five o'clock.' That's when you're supposed to call the number, that's when you can get the answer!"

We didn't know the question, but suddenly we thought we knew how to get the answer, at least *when* we *might* get an answer.

It would be sometime later when we learned that the whole idea of "leaving home" was not only a significant clue, but the most significant part of the most significant question of all.

Based on nothing more than a call from a listener we didn't know, we suddenly and absolutely believed the time reference on the song was the definite key to making a magic *Magical Mystery* call. We were completely convinced that if we called the right number at exactly the right time, we'd find precisely what we wanted to know—even though we had entirely no idea what we specifically wanted to know, other than generally everything. The call had to be made at five o'clock, Wednesday morning, London time.

"What time is that here? Is it still Tuesday night here?"

"No, it'd be some time Wednesday afternoon. Our Wednesday is still their Tuesday. Or is that backwards?"

"The earth turns to the east, they're later there than here."

"Aren't they?"

We had listeners who could make sense of nebulous photographic clues, interpret the literature of music then successfully match it with the works of William Shakespeare, put together esoteric signs pointing to a specific phone number at a specific time on a specific day, listeners who seemed to be experts in Scandinavian folklore, but none who understood simple time zone geography.

We couldn't wait until Wednesday morning or even Tuesday night. The intense energy in the studio demanded immediate answers. That the price of the call was probably prohibitive on the station budget and that the call would probably be fruitless made no difference. We dialed O for Operator and asked her to dial a number in London.

A man answered. The connection was scratchy, but audible. "Uh, may I speak to Billy Shears, please?"

"Beg pardon?"

"Is Paul there?"

"Who? Paul? Paul who?"

"This is KMZU radio in Columbia, Missouri. In the United States. We were told to call this number to find out about…"

"The United States? California what?"

"Not California! Columbia! Columbia, Missouri! KMZU radio! We're calling from a radio station at the University of Missouri! In the United States!"

"United States? Yes."

"We're calling about the clues on the Beatle albums and…"

He hung up.

It was another path that led absolutely nowhere, but it was exciting and real and good Lord, it was fun.

Listeners continued calling as dormies from all over campus kept looking and listening for anything that might have asked, or even hinted, "listen, do you want to know a secret?"

"In 'When I'm Sixty-Four,' Paul is 'yours sincerely, *wasting away*."

"Who's Mister Kite?"

"I dunno."

"Maybe he's the replacement and they did a concert with him, just to prove he could get away with pretending to be Paul." Of course, the Beatles had long stopped playing concerts. "The line says, 'for the benefit of Mister Kite there will be a show tonight…' See? It's for his benefit, it's to help him! Then they sing that 'the band begins at ten to six when Mister K. performs his tricks *without a sound*.' Maybe this replacement guy can't play a note and he's lip-synching to tapes of Paul!"

A different caller put that fake-Paul-at-the-concert idea together with an earlier element: "As the replacement is singing along 'without a sound' to 'get by with his friends,' the tapes are the help his friends are giving him so that he gets by!" He'd stitched two songs from *Sgt. Pepper* together, weaving an even deeper and seemingly more ingenious shroud of mystery.

Another caller: "They 'get by' in another song, in 'She's Leaving Home." What is it? 'We struggled hard all our lives to get by," is that it?

We were struggling hard to get by and decipher a mystery we couldn't say for sure existed.

From the moment we first brought up the subject of the rumor, the lights on the request line phones blinked constantly. Everyone seemed to be listening and taking part, searching their albums and their brains to make logical connections to the unconnectable.

Even though we knew we must have had the largest audience in KMZU history, at 3 a.m., two hours past "regulation" signoff, we decided to put an end to the clue-finding.

Thoroughly convinced something was going on, we promised our listeners that we would keep Paul's death alive. We thought we must be close to solving the mystery, maybe even closer, we thought, than anyone in the world had ever been before.

After we said our goodnights and played the signoff tape of Jimi Hendrix playing "The Star Spangled Banner" at Woodstock, Mark flipped the switch that turned off the transmitter. We sat silently in the studio, physically exhausted, emotionally drained and filled to overflow with adrenaline and afterglow.

Mark spoke first. "Let's call Clark Clifton."

I'M GONNA WRITE A LITTLE LETTER AND MAIL IT TO MY LOCAL DEEJAY

Clark Clifton was the all-night disc jockey on WUND, an Atlanta AM radio station.   One of the original "underground" DJs, his station bombarded fifty thousand watts of clear channel signal all over the eastern half of North America. His low key—no key—style made every on-campus radioman aspire to be like him. My two-hour show, "The Music" was an unabashed ripoff of what he did all night every night.

"That was..............(long pause, dead air)...................It's a Beautiful Day...............(audible sip of coffee)..........and "White Bird"......(audible puff of cigarette)..........(audible exhale)..............next............Led Zeppelin." (long pause, dead air again) Music starts. No talking-over-the-instrumental intro.

"Underground radio" was all about dead air. Even Mark, an avowed enemy of dead air, thought Clark Clifton was very, very cool.

WUND still exists, but the late-night underground format is genuinely dead. The station still bombards fifty thousand watts of clear channel radio signal all over the eastern half of North America, but instead of Clark..........Clifton..........fundamentalist preachers*uh* talk*uh* about*uh* the fire*uh* and*uh* damnation*uh* of*uh* hell*uh* and*uh* please*uh* support*uh* our*uh* radio*uh* ministry*uh* with*uh* generous*uh* love*uh* gift*uh*. Amen*uh*! Halleluiah!

We knew Clark Clifton took calls from all over the country and we figured if anyone knew anything about the Paul mystery, he would be the one.

To save what little money KMZU had, there was a firm no-long distance policy except for major news stories that were of major interest to our college student audience. Not only did we figure this was a major hard news story of major interest to our college student audience, but what the hell? We'd already called England at station expense. We vowed that if our station manager fought us, we'd find the money to repay the phone calls ourselves though neither of us knew where.

We got the WUND phone number from the Atlanta information operator.

Remarkably, Clifton answered the phone himself.

With Mark on a phone in our office and me on a phone in the now-silent studio, we gave him a full explanation of who we were and what had happened on our air that night. To save phone time, we didn't go into each detail but limited our description to the basics, the "I was" photo, the black flower, the *Abbey Road* funeral procession, and then some.

"Did you get the *Sgt. Pepper* cover?"

"The grave?" I asked. "The P-A-U-L-question mark?" Marked asked simultaneously.

"The pointing finger?"

"No, this one's a lot better," Clifton answered. "I gotta tell you about this one...wait a minute." We heard him drop his telephone onto his tabletop and we could hear his studio monitor go silent as he opened his microphone.

"Geez, he's going on the air," Mark said to me through the phone.

"Shhhhhhhhhh!"

"That was..........(sip of coffee)..........Jethro Tull..........from *Aqualung*.......... (drag of cigarette)..........you're spending the night with Clark Clifton," ("Can you fucking believe that? He actually said 'you're spending the night!'" I whispered into the phone to Mark, afraid my voice would carry from the telephone onto his air and secretly hoping it would. "How can he get away with...?") "..........on WUND, the underground voice of the planet Earth."

His studio speaker clicked back on as he turned off his microphone a full ten seconds into Emerson, Lake and Palmer's "Pictures at an Exhibition." Even though he hadn't talked over the instrumental open, he also didn't turn off his mike until deep into the song. He was probably taking another drag of cigarette, I figured. I wondered if he was smoking a "hand rolled" cigarette and whether the coffee he was sipping might have been something harder.

"Okay, I'm back," he said as he picked up the phone. I was amazed at his conversational voice and that he didn't speak..........to......us...... as..........we..........assumed..........he..........would. Frankly, I was disappointed. "So what did you find? How far did you get?"

We told him the clues we found and interpreted as absolute truth, giving him details on a few. He asked for more. "When you saw George pointing to the line on the back of *Sgt. Pepper*, did you notice which finger he was pointing with? Was it his index finger or thumb?"

"I dunno, index finger?"

"No," he replied quickly, "look again." I rifled through the stack of albums and 45's we'd left in heaps on the studio and floor until I found *Sgt. Pepper*.

"His thumb! He's pointing with his thumb!"

"Right. He's giving a 'thumbs up.' Did you get the phone number on *Magical Mystery Tour*?"

"Of course."

"Okay, here's one I'll bet you didn't get. Get *Sgt. Pepper* again."

"Got it."

"Now get a mirror."

"There's one in the restroom down the hall," I said from experience.

"No, you need a small one, like a woman would carry in her purse." Obviously, neither of us carried a purse and the women who came into the station to help when we were on the air had long gone home. "You need a mirror with a flat edge, not a round one."

"Wait a minute," Mark said excitedly. I could hear him moving equipment. I heard a crunch. He came into the studio with a chrome cover he had taken off a piece of machinery, a metal mirror the size of a toaster oven. "Use this." I told Clifton "Okay, we've got a mirror." Mark scurried back to the office to listen to the conversation.

"Good. Put it across the album jacket sideways so that the mirror cuts the drum in half, right across the words 'Lonely Hearts.'"

"Do I want the shiny side pointing up or down?" The chrome piece was longer than the entire album and I wanted to do exactly whatever was necessary to find this superclue.

"Good question—the top, the shiny part needs to reflect the top half of the album. Hold the mirror so that it cuts 'Lonely Hearts' in half. What do you see?"

"Uh, I see just the top half of the album cover."

"And?"

"Uh, that's it."

"Go to the mirror, boy!" I knew that was the line from the rock opera *Tommy* by The Who, the line that changes Tommy forever. "Hold on, let me get my album cover," he said, "it's always easier to describe if I do it with somebody." He came back to the phone quickly. "Put the mirror almost to the very top of the middle line of the letter E in 'Lonely' and the E in 'Hearts.' Look *over the top* of the mirror. Look at where the album jacket itself meets the reflection. Now what do you see?

"Okay, now I see the top half of the album reflected up into the metal…and I see…uh…" I was getting frustrated because I felt like The Nowhere Man, "do you see me at all?" "What am I supposed to be seeing?????"

"You're getting it. "Look right at the bottom of the reflection. Look at the drum. Look just at the words 'Lonely Hearts.' You may have to move the mirror up or down a little…"

I wiggled the metal, moved it slightly, moved my head up and down, back and forth. Then I hit it. It was the ultimate, perfect combination of album photo and impossible reflection. I audibly registered my sudden astonishment, not caring at all whether the words carried onto Clark Clifton's air: "ohhhhhhhhh shiiiiiiiiiiiit." Clifton laughed aloud. "I guess you found it." Mark dropped his phone and ran back into the studio to see what was there.

Reading half in the words 'Lonely Hearts' printed on the album cover and half in their reflection, it clearly says "ONE HE DIE." Clearly. It couldn't be more clear.

Clifton could hear Mark say, "oh shit" through the telephone and laughed again and asked, "Isn't that the coolest fucking thing you've ever seen in your life????"

"No," I said after a moment staring at the picture on the album cover and the reflection in the chrome. "No. This is scary as shit."

AND THOUGH THE NEWS WAS RATHER SAD
WELL I JUST HAD TO LAUGH
I SAW THE PHOTOGRAPH

"But why? Why is it there? Why are all of these things there?"

There was a long hesitation before Clifton answered. "Boys, you're gonna have to figure that one out for yourself."

Unconcerned about the expense, we talked with Clifton for more than an hour, comparing clues and speculating on possible motivation, interrupted only when he went on the air. He told us he thought we did a good job and that we knew a hell of a lot more than some people who had been working for a much longer time. His compliments made us feel tremendously cool and self-satisfied. But there was obvious hesitation in his voice when he finally ended the conversation. "I probably shouldn't tell you this, but I got a call like this last week from a radio kid at Notre Dame," he said, "a guy named Steve Handy. He did exactly the same thing you did and wanted to know what I knew."

"Yeah?"

"He told me he called the phone number, Wednesday morning at five o'clock, London time." Later, Mark told me that his first thought at this point in the conversation was not curiosity about the phone call, but how embarrassed he was that the quality of football teams wasn't the only difference between the University of Missouri and Notre Dame—radio guys there were obviously smart enough to know what time and day it was in South Bend when it was "Wednesday morning at five o'clock" in London.

"And he called me again last night," Clifton said.

"Yeah?"

"He got a call back."

"What!!!!???" Now we were speaking in sentences that ended in multiple exclamation points and question marks.

"All I can tell you—and maybe I shouldn't tell you this…I…aww, what the hell?—is that he's supposed to be in the rotunda of O'Hare airport in Chicago at nine o'clock tomorrow morning. I guess that'd be *this* morning now."

"Why? What's at O'Hare?"

"The guy who called said Handy would meet a contact and catch a flight to New York. From there he'd get a flight to London."

"Oh shit. Why? So is Handy gonna be at O'Hare?"

"He's planning on it as far as I know. That's all he said, that's all I can tell you. That's *really* all I can tell you."

We gave Clifton our phone numbers at the station and at home, asked him to call if he heard anything, thanked him profusely and said our goodbyes.

It was 4:30 a.m. Mark and I both had classes in a few hours. "Let's go to Chicago," he said with adventure in his voice. "I want to see what happens to the Notre Dame guy."

"Are you nuts?" Even though I eagerly accepted any so-called clue or hint of a clue as truth on the air while Mark was the skeptic, I was the one who doubted the common sense of a Chicago trip. "What if nothing happens? What if this guy Handy lied to Clifton? Besides," I added, "it's impossible. We'd never get there in time." Even at 90 miles per hour, it would take us five hours to make the four hundred and fifty miles to Chicago in Mark's clunker of a 1964 Ford. "That puts us there at 9:30 even if we leave right now," I insisted. "And that's if the cops don't stop us and if we don't careen off the highway from lack of sleep." The speed limit across eastern Missouri and southern Illinois was 70 and I knew I could neither afford to pay a speeding ticket nor spend the night in jail in some Podunk.

"Why don't we just work the phones?" I suggested. "Let's call Steve Handy or the radio station at Notre Dame."

"Nope." Mark folded his arms and stood his ground. "This is damn important. We've got to do this for our listeners and we've certainly got to do it for us. We're gonna fly to Chicago and see who Mister Handy sees."

"Fly? Are you kidding?" My uncertainty was becoming certain. "If I can't afford to pay for half a speeding ticket, how the hell can I afford a plane ticket to Chicago?" I couldn't believe Mark was serious. It just wasn't done.

"I've got some money," Mark flipped, "and the station will pay us back." That Mark had enough money to buy not one, but two round-trip plane tickets astounded me. He usually had to borrow money for vending machine coffee. We also had no idea whether the station would pay us back. "There's probably no budget for wild goose chases," I said.

"They'll pay us back," he persevered, "they have to. We gave them an audience that's all of a sudden desperate to hear every word we have to say about this." He was right, of course. "And even if you forget all that, I don't know about you but I'm *dying* to keep this up. Aren't you?"

"Hell yes," I responded quickly, "I *have* to know what this is all about. But..."

"But what?"

"I've never done anything like this."

"Who the fuck has?"

Speaking recently with Mark about these illogical moments in those early hours of a Thursday night and Friday morning in 1970, he confessed he's not nearly as free with money for the radio stations he manages today as he assumed our station management would have been toward us then. But he laughed when he admitted that if two small-time late-night disc jockeys gallivanted off for some unknown reason at station expense like we did, "I'd chew those puppies a couple of new assholes. I'd threaten to fire them right there for gross irresponsibility. Then I'd pay them back every penny. Then chew 'em out again. And then I'd give 'em a damn raise."

There were no flights from the tiny Columbia airport at that hour and wouldn't be for hours so we called TWA to get flight schedules from St. Louis, only one hundred and twenty very familiar miles away. The next flight to Chicago left at 6 a.m. We knew we'd never make it. But here was also a seven o'clock flight that arrived at O'Hare at 8:15. It had empty seats. We could make that flight. We could be in the rotunda of

O'Hare airport to watch whatever happened to Steve Handy at nine o'clock.

We could solve the mystery.

Mark and Isaac Newton were right. Simple inertia forced us to keep going.

Despite the hour, quite a few lights were still on in the dorm rooms outside the station. We flattered ourselves and assumed there were still groups of people scouring Beatle albums and talking about our show. In reality, we knew the lights were probably people who fell asleep with the lights on or people pulling all-nighters to cram for tests.

"Oh, shiiiiiiiiiiiiiiit!" Mark yelled as we hustled to his car in his usual spot in a no parking zone. "I don't have any gas."

"So we'll get gas."

"Do you know how hard it is to find an open gas station this time of night? Plenty of nights I've gotten off the air at one o'clock and worried I wouldn't be able to get to my apartment. There are no gas stations open at this hour."

"On the highway," I rushed in, "we'll find someplace open on the highway."

"Maybe."

Heading east on Interstate 70 toward St. Louis, we slowed at every exit, hoping to see an open gas station.

Adrenaline flowed into our bodies as quickly as the gas drained out of the tank.

Finally, after thirty anxious miles of wondering whether we'd travel even one more mile, an island of light blazed against the dark sky. We pulled into the self-service bays of a Union 76 truck stop.

Because it was the only open gas station for miles, the pumps were busy, so many through-the-night drivers taking advantage of the chance to gas up. We got in line behind a single car, the driver pumping gas, hand on the pump handle, looking as if he were almost finished. He topped off his tank, taking forever for every last drop of 29-cents-per-gallon gas to drip into his tank.

"Come onnnnnnnnnnnnnnnn!"

We kept waiting as he went into the station to pay.

A driver two gas islands over finished filling, went into the station, came out and left, all while we waited for our man to return. The next car pulled up two islands over and began to fill as we continued to sit and wait for our man who must have paid for gas, gone to the bathroom, asked directions, eaten breakfast and hit on every waitress in the café.

"Shit!"

The driver of the second car at the two-islands-over pump finished filling and went inside to pay.

Just as we were about to back up and try another line, our I'm-in-no-hurry-because-it's-the-middle-of-the-night driver came back to his car. He started the engine. In the bright light of the pump island, we could see him unfold a map.

Mark laid on the horn.

The man looked in his mirror, waved an apology and pulled away.

At 29 cents per gallon, Mark only needed to pump three dollars worth of gas to get us to the St. Louis airport and halfway back to Columbia.

We flew through the darkness toward St. Louis.

At High Hill, about halfway between Columbia and St. Louis, my eyes got heavy. "You okay?" I asked Mark. "I'm starting to feel the all-nighter."

"I'm okay. I'm fine. I'm pumped."

I could barely keep my eyes open. So I didn't.

Mark shoved me with his full weight when we hit Wentzville. "Another twenty miles."

It was 6:30.

We were going to make it.

The highway was crowded. To this day, I can't figure out why some people go to work so early. Nine, nine-thirty always seemed like a reasonable time to start the day to me. But in St. Louis, on that Friday morning in 1970, there were lots of people who had to be somewhere at 6:30 in the morning. And they were all driving slowly.

Mark wove in and out of traffic, pushing as hard as he could.

We could see planes taking off into the skies ahead of us.

"You go in and get tickets while I park," Mark said.

"Okay, gimme the cash for the tickets."

"I don't have cash, I'm gonna write a...shit."

We decided that in fairness, we would park the car and make the run inside together. We'd gone this far together and we'd make the final dash together too.

It was 6:50 a.m.

Most of the people on the crowded highway must have been headed to the airport too. We couldn't find a place to park. We ended up on the upper deck of the garage and stampeded like frightened, crazed animals toward the terminal.

Directed down the long concourse to gate 24, in those golden days of pre-Homeland Security screening, we got to the gate just in time to watch our last possible flight to Chicago taxi away. Collapsing into two chairs, there was nothing we could do. As we watched the plane take off, we crashed. The adrenaline that filled us drained quickly and was replaced by total emptiness.

Mark dropped me off at the fraternity house in Columbia and went home to his apartment. It was after ten o'clock, twelve hours since the adventure began. I should have been in my "Life and Literature of Shakespeare" class. Sitting on my bed to undress, I could only manage to take off one sock before I keeled over and fell asleep.

OH YEAH! ALL RIGHT!
ARE YOU GONNA BE IN MY DREAMS TONIGHT?

My right sock was still in my hand when I woke up at 7:30 Friday night. I'd slept on my side, across the bed, unmoved from where I'd passed out that morning. My left sock was still on my foot. All my classes were far past over and I'd long since missed lunch and dinner.

I went to the hallway phone booth to call Mark. When he answered I asked if I awakened him. A disc jockey who was always "on" even when he wasn't on the air, he said, "no, I had to get up to answer the phone."

"Did we really do that?" I asked.

"Yes. Now let me go back to sleep."

I needed to tell Mara the story.

She listened to every detail with polite interest but obviously couldn't understand why I was so excited. She couldn't relate to the perverse and obsessive passion of the hours on the radio trying to solve a mystery we only imagined existed. She sounded pleased it had happened and proud I did something that sounded so amazing, at least to me. But I knew she couldn't possibly have understood.

After I called Mara, I showered and dressed.

A fraternity pledge knocked at my door. "Phone, east booth."

"Hello?"

"I learned something that I've got to tell you." It was Mark.

"After I got back to my place this morning, I called TWA in St. Louis."

"Why?"

"I don't know, just a hunch, a wild hair. You know?"

"A hunch about what?"

"I asked about flights from Chicago to New York then connecting to London."

"Yeah?"

"They didn't have any."

"Then why the hell are you telling me this?"

"Because then I called United Airlines."

"And?"

"TWA isn't the only airline in the world, you know."

"I know, asshole. What did United tell you?"

"That they had a flight that left Chicago at ten, and then connected to a B-O-A-C flight to London out of JFK in New York."

I still didn't know what Mark was leading to, but I could feel the hair on the back of my neck starting to stand up, knowing he was probably leading somewhere. "Yeah? Go on."

"And then I asked if there was a Steve Handy on the flight from Chicago to New York."

I could sense he was getting perverse pleasure out of giving me information in slow motion. "Keep going, why are you dragging this out?!"

"Because I'm really enjoying this."

"Fuck you! Go on, dammit! What did they say??"

"What did who say?"

"Fuck you! What did they say???!!!"

"They didn't tell me anything. They said who's on a plane is confidential information."

"Shit." The hairs on my neck fell as quickly as my hopes.

"So I told them I was Handy's brother and gave them a bullshit story about how there was a family emergency and there was some concern about whether he'd make his flight because we didn't know if he'd make it to the hospital in time and…"

I cut his wonderful lie short. "Get to the point! I've had enough clues and enough bullshit to last me forever."

"The point is that they checked the computer and there was a reservation in that name on the flight from Chicago to New York." He paused for a beat, just to build the suspense. "And that reservation went on to London."

I didn't say a word as the hair on my neck stood at attention again.

"Finally, they told me Handy was indeed on the flight from Chicago to New York and so was his companion who paid for the tickets."

"Okay, so who was the companion? Was it another Notre Dame kid?"

"Might have been but I doubt it."

"Godammit, who the fuck was the companion?"

"They said his name was 'Mister Kite.'"

There was a long chunk of dead air on the telephone.

Mark finished the story in a quiet, frustrated voice, much more subtle than the draw-it-out teasing tone he'd used before. "The guy said Handy and Mister Kite used the tickets from Chicago to New York but were *not* on the flight to London. They didn't cancel their reservations, they didn't ask for a refund, they just didn't get on the plane. The guy at United thought that maybe they'd fly later."

"So that's it?"

"That's it, young Jeffrey. And I'm happy we know that much."

"Well I don't know if I'm happy or not. What's the point? I feel like we've been prick-teased again. Why didn't they catch the flight to London? Where did they go?"

"Ask Mister Kite. It's for his benefit."

"And who the hell is Mister Kite?"

"Beats me, just another clue."

"Wait a minute, Mark, wait a minute." I quickly whispered the words to *For the Benefit of Mister Kite* very quickly. 'ForthebenefitofMisterKitetherewillbeashowtonight-ontrampoline...'"
Finally I got to the line I wanted. "Remember this: 'The Hendersons will dance and sing as Mister Kite *flies* through the ring, don't be late.' Handy and Kite flew, I guess."

Neither of us could add anything more toward the solution or to the mystery so neither of us said anything more for a long time. "I'll talk to you later," Mark ultimately said. "I thought you'd want to know."

"Yeah. Thanks. I did want to know. I guess. Hey Mark, 'nothing *is* real.'"

"'And nothing to get hung about.'"

"Thanks for calling. I guess."

After the conversation, I sat in my room for a few minutes wondering what to do. Unable to think of anything constructive, I walked slowly across campus to the radio station, went straight to my office and tried to work.

Mark arrived ten minutes later, claiming he was drawn to the station too.

We both puttered around our office pit, not doing much of anything useful, but that was certainly a major part of working in campus radio. I read a week-old copy of *Billboard* magazine, Mark pretended to clean his desk—an impossible job. It was obvious neither one of us cared about *Billboard* magazine or clean desks. We were both thinking of the same thing but were both afraid to bring it up.

After a few minutes, Mark left the room without a word. "You gonna get a soda?" I yelled after him. He didn't answer. I studied *Billboard*, jotting down a few song titles, thinking I might listen to them as possible additions to my next station playlist. My head wasn't in the magazine or the playlist. Mark came back into the office after about ten minutes. "Where'd you go?"

"I called the campus radio station at Notre Dame."

"You made another L.D.? Dryden's gonna shit!" Mike Dryden was the student station manager, as tight with his budget as Mark Frick was with his board operation.

"Don't worry about Dryden. I made the call in his office on his line. He'll think he made it himself."

"So what'd they say?"

"I talked to the news guy who confirmed everything Clifton told us. He said Handy called them from O'Hare and said he'd call later."

"Did he call?"

"They haven't heard from him since."

"Shit."

"Riiiiiiiiiiiiight. And the Notre Dame guy told me something else."

"What?"

"He said they think their phones are tapped."

"Bullshit."

"That's what he said. And I don't want to talk about it any more."

"Fine. Great. Perfect."

We both knew that by missing the flight to Chicago we had missed the opportunity to see something big, whatever it was. Neither of us wanted to admit our frustration.

I DON'T REALLY WANT TO STOP THE SHOW BUT I THOUGHT YOU MIGHT LIKE TO KNOW

As we stewed silently, one of the news people came into the office. "There's somebody here for one of you guys."

"Which one?"

"He said he didn't care who he talked to, he just wants 'one of those Beatle guys.'"

I looked at Mark. "Mister Kite?"

"Naaaaah, Billy Shears."

We walked into the newsroom. The man waiting for us was a hairy person—long, unwashed and greasy blonde on his head, scraggly and unkempt all over his face. He held a cigarette between his clenched front teeth instead of between his lips, maybe for style purposes and maybe to keep his beard from going up in flames.

Since I started thinking about telling this story, I've asked Mark what he remembers from the earliest days of our adventure. It was amazing how much we each remembered, how fresh each little detail, even after all this time. We agreed on most things and argued only a few. He remembers our visitor as clean-shaven. But we both remembered how he held cigarettes in his front teeth instead of in his lips. It's odd that despite our disagreement on how he looked, we would both remember the unusual way he smoked cigarettes.

"I hear you guys are working on this Beatles thing," the visitor said. We didn't answer. After all, if he was Mister Kite or Billy Shears or somebody important, we didn't want to look too stupid so early. When he finally introduced himself, we knew he wasn't anybody important. But we didn't want to look stupid to him anyway. "I'm Lou Flowers."

I always thought Lou Flowers was a wonderful name for a disc jockey in the hippie age, especially an "undergrounder." Unfortunately, Lou never had the chance to be an undergrounder. He worked for the competition, KUMC—a tightly formatted, over-the-air top-40 rocker. Even though his show was on real, broadcast air and our shows were carrier-current, we still considered him second-class. He worked weekends. While we might have been at the piddly little campus station, at least we were on the air in prime time on weeknights and somehow that put us a notch above a KUMC weekend man—at least in our own very nearsighted eyes.

He spoke with resentment in his voice. "I dunno why I'm tellin' you guys this. I oughta use it on my own show…"

"Yeah? What?"

"But the bosses say talkin' about it on my show would be too much dead air, it'd break format." I was sure Mark was going to tell Lou how format should not be broken nor air allowed to die. "So fuck 'em," Flowers said angrily. "If you guys can use this, great. The hell with those assholes. Fuck 'em." He crushed out his cigarette on the newsroom tile floor.

"So what's the story, Lou?"

"The story is," he continued, seemingly happy to get the information off his chest, "I know for a fact that four unmarked cargo planes leave Miami every day filled with building materials, supplies and food."

"For what?"

"Where are they going?"

"It's goddamn *Pepperland*, asshole! They're building Pepperland for real!" We obviously didn't know what to think and it showed. "Gimme a fuckin' break. No wonder you guys work in this dump! Don't you even fucking even know what Pepperland is?"

We looked down our weeknight, prime-time KMZU noses at him, refusing to allow a KUMC weekend man to insult us. "Of course we know what Pepperland is."

"Well they're no shit building it for real, man. The Beatles bought an island somewhere in the Caribbean and they're building Pepperland, just like in *Yellow Submarine*! It's this cool fantasy place, see, where everybody just hangs out and gets it on and plays music and…"

"Wait a minute, Lou..." I interrupted. "Where did you get this information? Who told you?" I doubted Flowers had the same inside track to Clark Clifton that we did. "What on earth makes you think this is real?" I omitted the classic rejoinder.

Mark joined into the Pepperland debunk, obviously greatly offended by the "still in this dump" remark. "The Beatles didn't have anything to do with *Yellow Submarine*. The guy who wrote *Love Story* wrote the script. It wasn't even their voices in the movie."

Even as the hostility grew, I figured we should at least listen to what Flowers said, no matter how unlikely it might have been. "Where'd you hear this, Lou?"

"I was home in Florida last weekend. My Dad's sick and I went to visit him. A buddy told me about it."

"I'm sorry about your Dad. How did your friend know about this?"

"He knows somebody who knows somebody who works at the airport in Miami and that guy said..."

Mark challenged him again. "Wait a minute! You don't even know this stuff first-hand, do you? This is friend-of-a-friend-of-a-friend stuff, right?"

"Look," Flowers snapped at Mark, "I told you what I know, I got it off my chest and that's that. Do whatever you want with the information. If you don't want it, then fuck the both of you." Flowers jammed another cigarette into his front teeth and started to turn away. I convinced him to stay.

He told us the planes were leaving from a small, private airport outside of Miami. None of the planes had any kind of airline markings, he said, and huge crates were loaded aboard them inside a hangar. Some of the crates held building material, others carried tons of canned food, dried meats and other non-perishables.

Flowers said that the buddy who told his friend about all this speculated the Beatles bought an island that had been used as a nuclear testing site, already built up with fortifications and places to live. I jumped into challenge. "First of all, if it was used for nuclear testing, wouldn't it still be radioactive? And why would it have places to live or be built up if it was for weapons testing?"

"I don't know about that shit, man!" he defended. "All's I know is that's what I heard. Maybe it was some other kind of weapons or something." He stood up and headed toward the door again. "I just heard that you guys were getting close to this shit and I wanted to be part of it too. I don't know what you can do with the information, but I wanted to get it off my chest and that's all I fucking know." He grudgingly wished us "good fucking luck" as he walked out the door.

"Hi" Lou. You were right about the Pepperland thing, you just didn't get the details quite right.

Mark and I went back to our office re-ignited with a new way to pursue the clues and started poring over the albums again, putting everything into the context of the Pepperland idea, starting with *Sgt. Pepper.*

"Listen to this: 'You're such a lovely audience, we'd like to take you home with us, we'd love to take you home.' It's perfect. 'Home' means Pepperland."

"'Picture yourself in a boat on a river.' Is the river the ocean?"

"Beats me. I'd think 'the river' was a river and the ocean is the ocean."

"Get this one: 'I used to be angry young man, hiding me head in the sand.' Islands have beaches, beaches have sand, right?"

"'I'm fixing a hole where the rain gets in.' The island was a real hellhole and they're fixing it up to build Pepperland.'

"'She's leaving home.'"

"And she's leaving home to get 'the one thing that money can't buy,' she's leaving home to find some fun. She's going to Pepperland."

"Get this one: 'we can rent a cottage in the *Isle of Wight*.' I can't believe it. The Isle of Wight! An island! It's all here!"

"Okay, how would you get to an island like that?"

"Boat?"

"No."

"Plane?"

"No."

"Helicopter?"

"No, asshole. By yellow submarine! Listen. 'And our friends are all aboard, many more of them live next door.' Where's next door to an island like that?"

"I don't know, but the song says 'and the band begins to play.' The Beatles are the band!"

"Planes from Miami make sense. Miami is 'next door' to the Caribbean, the United States is next to the Caribbean. It's the perfect place for Pepperland."

"Did they do nuclear testing in the Caribbean?"

"How the hell should I know?"

Then Mark started going through each song lyric of *Sgt. Pepper* and "The White Album." There seemed to be a clue in each of the songs that fit perfectly into the Pepperland logic.

"'Take these broken wings and learn to fly, all your life you were only waiting for this moment to arise.'"

"If you were building Pepperland, you'd definitely need a 'little help from your friends.'"

"But other than that, 'Little Help from my Friends' doesn't seem like much."

"The friends are the people doing the construction and flying in food and stuff. If you were building Pepperland, you'd need lots of help from lots of friends."

"On 'Glass Onion' they talk about 'trying to make a dove-tail joint.' Is that like a joint that two people can smoke at the same time? You know, 'cause it's dovetailed?"

We were proving the theory that under pressure, absolutely anything can be rationalized from total illogic into reality.

"Here's a good one from 'I'm So Tired': 'You'd say I'm putting you on...'"

"'Half of what I say is meaningless.' Does that mean some of the clues are no good or that not everything is a clue?"

"I think it means that 'half of what I say is meaningless.' That could apply to anything or anybody. The trick is figuring out the half that means something."

"You know, maybe this isn't about the Beatles. Maybe this is just about learning a lesson in life. If you figure out which half means something, you can just sigh and say I've learned my lesson, all is happy with the world. 'And so, as you new graduates go forth, you should remember always that the trick is figuring out the half with meaning.'"

"Fuck you. Keep going."

"'He's a real Nowhere Man, sitting in his nowhere land.' Is Pepperland the nowhere land? Is Pepperland nowhere?"

"I don't know. Could be. Nobody knows where it is, so it's a 'nowhere land.' But it's got to be somewhere."

"Then it goes on: 'Nowhere Man, the world is at your command,' then what's the line?"

"'Doesn't have a point of view, knows not where he's going to.' If you're going to Pepperland and you don't know where it is, you 'know not where you're going to.'"

"You ended a song lyric with a preposition."

"Okay, 'know not where you're going to'...asshole."

"Thank you. 'Got to admit it's getting better...' 'Man I was mean but I'm changing my scene...' They're all gonna change their scene and go live in Pepperland!"

"Wait a minute! Let's go back to the Isle of Wight thing. Maybe that's where Pepperland is at."

"This time you're the one who ended a question with a preposition."

"We put forth the preposition that all assholes are created equal. Where is the Isle of Wight? Is it in the Caribbean? "

"Beats the hell out of me."

Good Lord we could have used the Internet. Once again, our Midwestern senses of geography got the best of us. Unless a place was between St. Louis and Kansas City, we were never exactly sure of its location.

"SHIT!" I yelled, not caring who heard my exclamation. "What's the very first line of the very first song on the first disc of 'The White Album?'"

"Shit," Mark agreed. "'Back in the U.S.S.R.' 'Flew in from Miami Beach...'"

"Then there's this from 'Honey Pie?' 'Sail across the Atlantic to be where you belong.'"

"'Dear Prudence, won't you come out to play...the sun is up, the sky is blue...look around 'round...' It's Pepperland all right. The sky is blue, everything is always perfect in Pepperland. Except for when the Blue Meanies come. I just can't figure who Prudence is."

"Was that another preposition?"

"Once I was prepositioned by a hooker in downtown St. Louis."

"St. Lou...is ends with a preposition."

"Listen to this from 'Glass Onion,'" I declared in the middle of our Groucho-like reverie as I made another discovery. "'Here's another place you can go, where everything flows...' Water flows. Pepperland would 'flow.' Remember how cool the animation was in the movie? Remember the colors? You can say the color flowed."

"I actually knew people who got totally shitfaced before they saw that movie."

"Noooooooooooo."

"Yeah, no shit. Let's keep going."

"Then there's the 'here's another clue for you all, the walrus was Paul,' but we've already got that."

"How about 'standing on a *cast iron shore*?' If they did weapons testing there, the island might be covered with iron bunkers and iron reinforcements and stuff."

"A dock can be made of iron."

"A dock where a boat or a submarine could land."

"And shit! Down at the end of the song they're 'fixing a hole' again! And it's not just a 'hole,' they're 'fixing a *hole in the ocean!*' Shitfuck. A fucking hole in the ocean!"

But still, so what? After all the work and interpretation, what was the point? "What are the clues for? If they're really building Pepperland, why would they want to tell everybody?"

"Mark looked at me hard. "It's a game. They want to find people crazy enough to put up with all the shit, to read through the clues, to figure 'em out."

"But why?"

"To find people crazy enough to live in Pepperland."

I nodded. There were a few seconds of silence. Then I had to smile. "The Magical Mystery Tour is coming to take you away."

Mark sighed and then smiled back. "Coming to take you away, take you today."

There was a pause in the repartee. Finally, I added "all the lonely people, where do they all come from?"

THE SINGER'S GOING TO SING A SONG
AND HE WANTS YOU ALL TO SING ALONG

Whatever I did for the rest of Friday night or Saturday, I was never far from the Pepperland business.

Since the story of our on-the-air adventure spread all over campus, everybody in the fraternity house was eager to learn what I knew. Since the radio station broadcast via telephone wire to transmitters in dormitories only, anybody in a Greek house or off campus was unable to hear our show themselves, so the guys in my fraternity house demanded a personal tour of the magical mystery. I was happy to repeat the clues for hours, passing Beatle albums around, sharing my vast wisdom of how Paul died, how he was replaced by a look-alike and how we were all fools for not recognizing it earlier. I repeated the whole bit over and over, group to group.

I told them about Pepperland.

Everybody believed and everybody, to a man, agreed it was too weird to be coincidence. It made too much sense to be pure chance.

Someone finally asked a very simple question that took me by such surprise I had no answer. If it was all true and I won the Pepperland lottery, would I go? It was the first time the question was raised and I gave the only answer that came to me: I didn't know.

Other than the sharing and clue swapping, I have no recollection of anything I did in that time, no memory of eating or sleeping or studying or watching television or anything except dealing in presumed Pepperland trivia.

I'm sure that somewhere during the day I thought of Kathy Powell.

"Hi" again, Kath.

And, more realistically, I'm completely certain I thought of Mara. I wondered what would happen to our relationship if I went to Pepperland.

Would she be able to go with me? Would I stay behind if she couldn't? I'm also certain that I didn't call her that day, not even once. I was afraid that she would think the whole stupid thing had gone too far. Of course, she would have been right.

While I'm not sure of any other details of that Saturday—other than I was dateless, as usual—I do remember vividly when it began anew with a new intensity.

It was about eleven o'clock Saturday night.

Beth Johnson was one of the station secretaries who volunteered to come in and help in the crush during the Thursday night marathon clue session on the air. Listening from her sophomore dorm room, she was sharp enough to figure we might need some sort of administrative or organizational help. Or maybe she just wanted to be at the station when something hot was happening, it doesn't matter. She came to the station.

She flitted around while we were on the air, busy but inconspicuous. She wasn't anyone we executive privilege guys with swollen egos would ever have noticed. We privileged guys considered ourselves far too important to pay attention to secretaries as they filed away records or answered phones or ripped news copy from the United Press International wire—unless they were really cute. But Beth Johnson wasn't really cute.

When she called the phone number on the station list, she asked for Jeff Scott. The fraternity pledge who answered told her there was no one in the house with that name. She argued she was calling the number listed on the radio station phone list. Until someone walked past the phone booth that knew Jeff Scott's real identity, she might have gotten nothing more than an argument from him. The pledge found me in my room, going over the clues again with a few other dateless-on-a-Saturday-night fraternity geeks.

"Hello?"

"Jeff?"

"Who's this?"

"It's Beth."

"Beth who?"

"Beth Johnson. I thought you knew me. I'm a secretary at the station...at KMZU?"

Oh yeah, sure." I had no idea who she was. "What's the problem?"

"I'm about five-six, a little overweight? I was at the station Thursday night."

Even with her description, I only thought I might know who she was. "What can I do for you, Beth?"

"Jeff, I didn't know who else to call."

"About what?"

Her voice reflected her nerves. "Jeff, I have a brother in the Army in Germany and he calls home every month."

"Yeah?"

"So I know how trans-Atlantic phone calls sound. They're staticky, noisy…"

"So?"

"So I just got one. At the station"

"Your brother called you at the station?"

"No, listen! I think this is important!"

"What going on, Beth?"

"I've been here about an hour, putting away records. It's my regular shift."

"On a Saturday night?"

"Yeah, somebody's got to do it."

Because she was available to work that particular shift, it was obvious Beth was also a member in good standing of the dateless-on-Saturday-night club. Besides, it wasn't as if I was doing anything more productive or more exciting. In fact, sitting around the fraternity house was what I did most Saturday nights when Mara wasn't there. To be sharing the clues was a big time Saturday night for me, at least I wasn't alone in my room or plopped in front of the communal television in the living room with the other dateless losers. "Okay, Beth, what's going on?"

"About ten minutes ago, the phone rang and I answered it. A man asked if this was KMZU and I said yes."

"Uh huh."

"Then, and I swear to God this is true, then he asked me 'do you want to try for the first plateau?'"

"The what?"

"'The first plateau!' I didn't know what he was talking about, but I said 'sure, I'll try.'"

"Sure, why the hell not? Then what, Beth?"

"Then he asked me 'who is Sergeant Pepper?'"

"What?? Reeeeeaaaaaaaalllllllyyyyyyyyy?"

"Yes, really!"

"So what'd you tell him?"

"I didn't know what to say. So I guessed Paul McCartney—it was the first name that came to me—and he said no. So I guessed John Lennon. No. Billy Shears? No."

"Keep going Beth, I'm listening."

"Then, and I don't know why, I asked if it was Brian Epstein."

"And what did he say then?"

"Then he asked me if I wanted to try for the second plateau."

"And what did you say?"

"I said of course I wanted to try for it."

"Then what?"

"He said if I wanted to try for the second plateau, I should be in the rotunda of O'Hare airport in Chicago at two o'clock tomorrow afternoon. Then he said I should also bring the people who called the number. He must have meant you and Mark." There was silence on the line. "Jeff?"

"I'm here."

"Why would he want us to be at O'Hare Airport?"

"What did you tell him?"

"I told him we'd be there. But why…"

"You did?"

"I didn't know what else to tell him. I thought that if…"

"You stay right there at the station, Beth. Don't leave. I'm coming over."

"Okay. Jeff?"

"Yeah?"

"What's this all about?"

"I'll tell you when I get there. Just don't leave."

"I'm not going anywhere. But do you know what else?"

"What?"

"A little while ago, before the phone call came, I called my roommate to tell her I'd be late. While we were talking, I heard something."

"What? What did you hear?"

"Clicking. The phone lines were clicking. It was really noisy so I called her back. But every time I called back, I still heard the clicking."

"I'll be right there."

I called Mark at home. Usually, he went out on the prowl Saturday nights, but he said he was still winding down from the days before. "Meet me at the station right fucking now," I said, not trying to be weird but being exactly that. I said I'd explain when he got there.

I ran across campus to the station.

Beth was close to tears when I arrived, her hands visibly trembling. "I know what a trans-Atlantic phone call sounds like," she repeated. "My brother calls every month and I know it's staticky and…"

"I know you do, Beth. Let's just be quiet until Mark gets here, okay?"

When Mark arrived, she repeated the story. "Did he say anything about going somewhere after O'Hare?"

Beth didn't hesitate with her answer. "No, he just said that if we want to try for the second plateau, we should be at the airport in Chicago."

"We have to go to O'Hare," Mark said. I absolutely agreed. "And Beth has to go with us. She got the call." I absolutely agreed again.

"How did you know Sergeant Pepper was Brian Epstein?" I asked.

"I don't know, it was a guess! I was running out of names and his was the only other one I could think of. Is Brian Epstein really Sergeant Pepper?"

"Beats me," Mark shrugged. "All of this beats the hell out of me."

We totally believed that the call was real. Beth's confidence, based on the sound of her brother's calls, was the convincer that the call didn't come from across campus.

While we had no idea who called or why, we could only assume it must have had to do with our call to the *Magical Mystery Tour* number in England. Maybe somebody at that number noticed us. Maybe we didn't dial a wrong number after all. "We gave our phone numbers to Clark Clifton, too," I noted. "Maybe he gave them to somebody else."

"Maybe."

Beth asked the question Mark and I already considered. "But what's with the clicking?" I picked up a phone and dialed the fraternity house phone booth. As it began ringing, there was a distinct loud click on the line. I hung up before anyone answered. Beth was insistent on finding out what she had so suddenly found herself in the middle of. "What's going on? What's this all about?"

We told her everything.

We told her about calling Clark Clifton and about Steve Handy and O'Hare and Mr. Kite. We told her about our frustrating trip to the St. Louis airport. We told her about our visitor from KUMC. When the tale was told, all she could say was "wow." She believed everything. "But why would they do that?"

"As best as we can figure it's to get people to go to Pepperland."

"Why would anybody go to Pepperland?" she asked. "Why would anybody go someplace they didn't know?" Her questions were sincere, but Mark and I were incredulous that she had to ask them.

"Because!" Mark answered. "It's the Beatles! It's Pepperland! Didn't you see *Yellow Submarine*? That's what this is all about. Don't you want to know what's happening?"

"Yeah, I guess so."

"Then you'll have to go to Chicago with us."

"Okay. I'll go. Just let me call my roommate and tell her what's happening."

We didn't let her call anyone, especially on a clicking telephone.

We decided to give ourselves plenty of time this time. No missing flights. We would be in the rotunda of O'Hare airport at two o'clock absolutely.

"What's the deal with O'Hare?" Beth asked. "It's so busy, so public. If they want to do something secret, why in such a public place?"

Mark and I knew why.

"It's in the middle of the country, it's central to everybody. And even more than that, you can fly anywhere in the world from O'Hare."

We wanted to call Clark Clifton to tell him what was happening but he wasn't on the air Saturday nights. Weekends were for Lou Flowers-type second stringers.

We agreed Mark would pick me up at seven the next morning, then pick up Beth at her dorm. We would be at the St. Louis airport by nine, nine-thirty latest for the 10:30 flight that arrived at O'Hare at 11:45.

Plenty of time.

Mark agreed to fill his gas tank before he got home.

Just like the earlier, aborted plan, Mark would somehow find the money to pay for his ticket and mine. Beth would buy her own ticket.

We called Mike Dryden, the student station manager, from our office, figuring that if anyone was eavesdropping on the station phones, we wanted them to know we were on our way to Chicago.

Dryden was as close to a true Southern Gentleman as we were likely to meet in such a remote outpost of gentility as Columbia, Missouri. He would always introduce himself to people in a classic, smooth Southern accent, pumping the hand of the person he met like some smooth but not-quite-sleazy politician: "Hah, Ahm Mahk Drahden, D-R-whyyyy-D-E-N from Valdosssssssssta, Geee-oh-jahhhhhhhhh." It was no surprise that he was able to politic his way through the campus bureaucracy into the station manager job. I have checked over the years and as of this writing he is not yet a member of Congress.

"Y'all go," he said in an instant. "We'll pay y'all back. Ah don't know how just now, but we'll find the money somewheah."

Bless him.

"Hi" Mike.

Bless you.

And I don't mind that it was your arm over Mara's shoulder in the newspaper picture taken at my memorial service. It was a nice gesture. You were just being a just-barely-less-than-sleazy Southern Gentleman. I understand.

Then Beth asked the question we all knew needed to be asked. "How will they know us? How will we know them?"

Mark gave the obvious answer. "They'll know."

Beth had work to finish at the station, she said, records to file. Mark offered me a ride back to the fraternity house. "I don't want to go home yet," I told him.

"Where do you wanna go?"

"I dunno."

We stopped at a filling station across from the journalism school buildings and Mark filled the tank. We drove through "the white campus," buildings made of white stone. Then we cruised through the "red campus," buildings made of brick, and then Greektown, trying to see what we could spot through any open sorority house windows. We sat outside a dormitory complex to see if we could hear the KMZU signal bleeding outside its regular parameters, willing to sit in the car monitoring any Saturday night second-stringer on the air. The signal didn't reach the car and for a few minutes we sat and listened to static on the 580 spot on the radio dial, hoping to hear something that sounded more like radio than radio noise. But there was nothing. Finally, our circles widening, we headed away from campus, away from Columbia and out into the boondocks of rural Missouri. In all that time, we never spoke of the radio station or Beatles or Pepperland. We just drove.

"How much do you pay for your apartment?" I asked, making smalltalk.

"One-fifty. Seventy-five each. Plus utilities."

"That's a lot for that little shithole."

"Riiiiiiiight. But it's *our* little shithole." Mark shared the two-bedroom apartment with Edward Abbott, the station morning man. Because Mark worked the late-night sign-off shift and Abbott did the early-morning sign-on, they almost never saw each other except during classes, whenever either of them bothered to be awake enough to go to class. They learned to tiptoe around one another since one always seemed to be asleep.

"I'm thinking about moving out of the fraternity house next year."

"That'd be good."

"Maybe get my own little shithole somewhere."

"Shitholes are good."

Then we'd go miles without saying anything.

Mark stopped the car. We got out and leaned on a wooden fence, staring at cows in a field, lit only by the moon and a few dim lights from a nearby barn. Mark mooed at the cows. None replied. Breaking the stillness, I said what was on my mind. "You know what's going through my head?"

"The wind?"

"Screw you."

"Then what?"

"Let's say we get to O'Hare and Paul McCartney himself is standing there in the rotunda. We say hello..."

"And he says goodbye. Ahhhhhh, another clue."

I continued on, totally serious. "So Paul or Mister Kite or whoever it is congratulates us for reaching the second plateau."

"Yeah?"

"Then what? What if he says 'let's go?'"

"I've thought of that too. So?"

"So? What do you think, *so*? Would you go?"

"You're damn right I'd go! I'd go in a fucking minute! Hell, I grew up in Saint Jen thinking Columbia was the big city! There's a whole world and I want to see it!"

I was impressed at the speed and conviction of Mark's answer. We stood at the fence, staring into the night.

A cow finally mooed at Mark and it inspired him to speak. "Wouldn't you go?"

"I don't know." Going to Pepperland wasn't my biggest concern, leaving Mara was.

Mark didn't reply. Finally, after a long pause, he admitted he understood my indecision. "I don't think you could take Mara with you. She's not going to O'Hare with us. She didn't find the clues. She's not into this."

"But I don't know if I could go without Mara. They'd take that into some kind of consideration, wouldn't they?"

"I don't know."

"They'd have to know that people have special people they'd want to take with them, wouldn't they?"

"Ask Paul when we get to O'Hare. But when it comes right down to it, how could you *not* go? How could you turn down an opportunity like that?"

"I think I might have to."

"Buuuuulllllllllllllllllshiiiiiiiiiiiiit."

Mark turned toward the car and I followed. As he opened the door and plunked himself into the driver's seat, he said what we both knew was probably the ultimate truth. "Look, nothing's gonna happen. Paul won't be there. There's no Mister Kite. There are no tickets to London. There is no Pepperland. Hell, I don't even know what 'the rotunda' is! It's all bullshit and that's that. We'll come home and spend the rest of our lives working in campus radio and sleeping through class and trying to graduate and wondering what the hell happened back in the good old days of poor old dead Paul and Pepperland. We'll be showing people fucking Beatles clues for the rest of our fucking lives. It'll make us famous in bars all over the world. Two forty-year old, broken down, alcoholic campus radio Bozos. 'Hey, I'll show you Beatles clues for a beer!' Riiiiiiiiiiiight. That's what's gonna happen. Nothing else, so just fuck it."

We drove on for another few miles, contemplating the idea of sharing clues forever, saying nothing.

Finally, I said I didn't know what 'the rotunda' was either. But we were smart guys, I said, and we'd figure it out.

"Riiiiiiiiiiiiiiiiight."

Then Mark drove me home.

I didn't call Mara to tell her what was happening or where I might be going.

In my room, I took a bottle of Canadian Club left over from the last fraternity party from my dresser drawer. Mara had come for the party and between the two of us, even mixing the booze with soda, we barely finished half the half-pint. I took a long gulp straight out of the bottle. It took a full second for the liquor to cross my tongue, go down my throat and for the taste to hit my brain. My face contorted. I ran to the bathroom, put my hand under the sink spigot and drank a long tepid bathroom water chaser.

Back in my room, I put the bottle back in the drawer for the next party—or for when they sorted my stuff after I was whisked away by Paul McCartney or Mister Kite or whoever whisked people away. It would be the post-whisk whiskey.

I managed to undress, wound two alarm clocks and set them both for 6 a.m. I set two clocks because the last time I covered Edward Abbott's sign-on shift, I whacked one clock off the nightstand and went back to sleep. I didn't sign on the station until 6:30 after a rookie newsman called to wake me. Dormies all over campus overslept because I wasn't there to wake them. I bought the second clock as backup, keeping it on the other side of the room so I had to physically drag myself out of bed to turn it off.

It wasn't easy to sleep. My mind raced.

I finally bored myself to sleep by concentrating on the non-synchronous clocks. Tick. Tick. Tock. Tock. Tick. Tock. Ticktick. Tocktick...

ALL THE WAY THE PAPER BAG WAS ON MY KNEE MAN I HAD A DREADFUL FLIGHT

As soon as I got into Mark's car, I could tell immediately that he was as tired and as tense as I was. We said nothing more than muttering a simple "hi." As we turned the corner toward Beth's dorm, she was waiting under the driveway canopy, a small suitcase on the sidewalk next to her.

"Why did you pack a bag?" At first I was politely curious, then quickly angered that she had assumed she needed to pack anything. "What makes you think we're going anywhere except O'Hare?" It offended me that she assumed we would make the New York/London flights. Mark and I agreed to assume nothing.

Beth got into the back seat, opened the suitcase and pulled out the station copies of *Sgt. Pepper*, "The White Album," *Abbey Road* and the *Yellow Submarine* soundtrack. "I thought we might need them."

"What the hell for? You're not the one who's been stealing records from the station, are you?"

Beth stayed calm. "No, I'm the one who puts away the records the thief leaves behind that you can't seem to put away yourselves. I just thought we might need them. I also brought these." She pulled three plastic-coated nametags from the bag. She had stamped "KMZU" on each tag with the huge rubber stamp we used on records in a vain attempt to deter the station thief. "So they know who we are."

Mark smiled and half-turned toward her as she drove. "Good work, Beth, good thinking. And if you look in the trunk, Jeff," he added, "you'll find some clothes I packed too, just in case."

Then I felt stupid that I hadn't packed a bag too. "Well I'm not wearing a fucking name tag."

Beth smiled and said, "fine. It's here if you want it."

Exactly as Mark and I had done two mornings earlier, the three of us headed north on Providence Road, then east on Interstate 70. It started to snow, one of those short-lived, barely-stick-to-the-pavement late spring snows for which mid-Missouri is famous.

I asked Beth for the albums. We reviewed the obvious clues. Beth found them scary and wondered aloud how weird it was that we found ourselves mixed up in something that seemed so enormous and important.

"Look," Mark threw in, keeping it all in perspective. "Jeffrey and I have already talked about how nothing's going to happen, that it's all gonna be a big bust and that we're all just imagining things that aren't there."

I added, "He's only saying that to keep us from being disappointed, you know." Beth laughed. Then I turned to Mark. "I still can't believe you packed a fucking bag."

"You're damn right I did! If we prepare for nothing and nothing happens, then fine. If something does happen, it's just gravy and I've got clean underwear!"

There was a pregnant pause in the conversation and the anger until Mark finally added, "I'll bet you're surprised I actually change my underwear, huh?"

I scanned the record jackets, looking for any clues we might have overlooked. "Look at this," I nearly shouted, "look how the words are divided up on *Abbey Road.*" The words "Beatles" and the album title are written on a wall in ceramic tiles. "The wall is cracked through the word 'Beatles' and the crack divides it up. If you read it like that, it's three words: *'Be at les Abbey Road,'* like it's in French!"

"Maybe you have to meet somewhere on Abbey Road before the trip to Pepperland," Mark figured. "Maybe it's some sort of departure point."

"Maybe that's where you go after O'Hare," I added. "Maybe Abbey Road is where it all begins." All of us were silent again, considering how well the non-pieces of non-information were starting to fit together.

"But why would they have a clue in French? German maybe, because of the Hamburg days. But why French?"

"'Michelle' has French in it."

"Good enough for me. Here's another one from *Sgt. Pepper*. In the lower right corner of the back of the album, after the credits for the photos and the wax figures, it says in small print 'a splendid time is guaranteed for all.' That kind of thing doesn't belong there. It's weird." In the context of what we were doing and what we anticipated, the guarantee of a splendid time made me happy. But the omen of where and what the splendid time might be made me apprehensive again.

We arrived at Lambert Airport in St. Louis according to plan, just after nine, going straight to the TWA counter to buy tickets for the 10:30 flight to O'Hare. "Round trip or one way?" the ticket agent wanted to know. We looked at each other, genuinely wondering if we would need the return ticket. Mark made a command decision. "Round trip please."

As the tickets printed, Mark whispered, "If we need the round trip, fine. If we don't, what the hell difference will it make?"

Then the ticket agent demanded another command decision. "When will you be returning?" We looked at each other again, not sure what to answer. Then the agent saved us another command decision. "How 'bout I leave it open? That way you can come back on any available flight." Perfect. When the agent asked if we had any luggage to check, we each said no. Beth carried her bag of records and nametags. I had obviously embarrassed Mark enough about his suitcase that he left it in the car, clean underwear and all.

Mark wrote a check for his ticket and mine, Beth paid cash for hers. To this day, I do not know whether Mark's check bounced or not. All I know is that the agent gave us the tickets, thanked us and wished us a good trip.

We arrived in Chicago at noon, with time to kill. Obviously eager for two o'clock, we decided it was important to find the rotunda where we expected to meet somebody we didn't know. Refusing to admit we didn't even know *what* the rotunda was, we asked a skycap where it was. He pointed us toward a circular, central area that connects the airport concourses, the central hub of the spokes of the O'Hare wheel. Mark said the domed ceiling reminded him of the Capitol building in Washington. "Ahhhhhhhhh," he reveled, "the Capitol *rotunda*."

It's all been reconstructed now, but the old O'Hare rotunda was a two-story circle with long concourses approaching from three directions.

There were snack bars and gift shops on the lower level, escalators ran up and down to a second-level bar. We decided that when the time came, we would position ourselves at the top of the escalator to have a panoramic view of the comings and goings to and from each concourse, all the snack bars below and the round open area into which it all converged. We didn't know what we'd be looking for, but when it arrived we'd see it.

Until then, we decided to wait in the main terminal, not wanting to establish our beachhead in the rotunda too conspicuously early.

Mark bought a Sunday *Chicago Tribune*. We shared sections as we sat. We each secretly hoped to find a headline that revealed the truth about Paul McCartney's death and Pepperland. There was nothing.

I read the comic pages, the front section, "The Arts," sports, even scanned the "society" section—looking with interest at each of the wedding and engagement photos.

At 1:30, I ultimately got flat out bored and impatient. "Let's go," I said, standing up from my chair and grabbing Beth's suitcase. There were no arguments. Mark and Beth were equally eager to get it done, to find out what awaited us in the rotunda of a strange airport far from home.

Beth grabbed the KMZU nametags. "Do we want these?"

"Sure," I answered. During the flight to Chicago I'd decided that no matter how goofy, I'd wear a nametag. "If they're not too blatant." They were blatant.

We took the escalator to the second level. Mark and I took positions on either side of the "up" escalator. Beth stood by the "down" escalator.

We looked, we scanned, we examined every moving and unmoving person anywhere near the rotunda. Throngs of people passed through the central midpoint of the world's busiest airport as each of us looked at each of them, hoping to find someone looking back for us.

No one looked back.

A half-hour passed.

It was finally two o'clock.

We waited.

My heart thumped so loudly I could feel it echo in the veins of my neck.

Another half-hour passed.

Occasionally, we took turns circling the rotunda floor, going into snack bars and rest rooms, shoving our chests and name tags forward so they couldn't be missed by anyone. No one was impressed by either our chests or radio identities.

It was after three o'clock.

Finally, I asked Beth to stay in position at the top of the escalator and asked Mark to come downstairs. "Did you see the two people just inside the bar?"

"Who?"

"There's a man and a woman sitting on the first two stools inside the bar, right smack inside the door. They're both very well dressed, very attractive, very hip."

"Which one do you find the most attractive," Mark leered, "the man or the woman?"

"Not now, Mark," I snapped, "but if you notice them—well, both of them are attractive actually—but they've been sitting there since before we got here."

Mark turned serious again. "Maybe they're just a couple of drunks."

"All I know is that they're not at a table, they're not at the fifth and sixth stools—they're at the first two right at the door—and..."

"And what?"

"Do you know how you can get a feeling when someone's looking at you so you look at them and then they turn away or pretend they're looking at something else? It happens all the time at stop lights."

"Damn, you're weird. What about it?"

"Come on! You know you can *feel* it when people stare at you."

"Yeah?" Okay. You can feel it. What about it?"

"These people never turn away. When I look at them, they look right back at me."

"Riiiiiiiiiiiight."

"I'm not kidding! Try it. It's so weird, it's painful."

We went back upstairs. The couple was still sitting at the first two stools just a foot or two inside the door of the bar.

We made genuine eye contact with them.

They made genuine eye contact back.

This conspicuous inconspicuousness went on for another twenty minutes.

Mark took the Beatle records from Beth's bag and gave one to each of us. We held them at our waists, as if we were showing them off. I feared someone would offer to buy them.

The couple inside the bar continued looking at us.

The three of us went back downstairs for another conference. Mark told Beth the "people at the bar" secret.

"I've noticed them too," she admitted. "I thought they were just sitting there for a long, long time and that it was odd. People in airports have planes to catch. People don't just sit at a bar for that long a time." I knew Beth had never been out with Mark socially before, but he didn't disagree aloud with her assessment about people's abilities to sit in bars. "He's wearing a very European-looking suit and she's very well dressed," Beth pointed out. "They look like the kind of people who'd be here to meet us."

They were *exactly* the kind of people we'd expect to meet us.

We decided against going into the bar to talk to them and agreed the direct approach would have to be only a last-ditch act of desperation.

We decided to give it another half-hour.

We went back up the escalator.

We stared. They stared back. Maybe people in bars were different from people at stoplights, I figured, maybe bar people stared back.

Then Beth saw the impossible. "Oh my God!" she whispered, holding her hand in front of her mouth.

"Whatwhat*what*??? What did you see?"

"It's not *what*, it's *who*." She pointed to four girls in the lower level of the rotunda. One pointed back and ran toward the escalator. "They're from my dorm!"

"What the fuck are they doing here?"

"I don't know!"

As the girls reached the top of the escalator, we looked back inside the bar. The people inside looked back at us. They watched as we met the girls and immediately hustled them back downstairs. "What the fuck are you doing here?" Beth asked in an uncharacteristic, whispered shout. "Are you trying to ruin everything? How did you get here?"

The seven of us, three of us wearing stupid KMZU nametags, hurried down a concourse toward the terminal away from the rotunda and away from the couple at the bar. One of the girls eagerly and proudly told their story. "We left the dorm at five! Nancy drove. We were afraid we'd miss it! What's happening? Who'd you meet?"

Beth could see anger in our eyes. "Beth, how did they know?" Mark asked. "Why did you tell them? Why?"

She was genuinely apologetic. "I was so excited after I got back to the dorm last night I couldn't sleep. They were all in Joanie's room so I went in."

"And?"

"They heard the radio show Thursday night and asked me what I knew."

"And?"

"And..."

"And what?"

"And I told them everything."

Mark accosted Nancy, the one who drove. "You drove nine hours just to spy on us?"

"Ten and a half," she said. "We stopped twice for gas and for bathrooms. We want to see what happens. Besides," she added confidently, "this is a public place and you can't make us leave."

"But this is a private event," I joined into the scolding. "Get the fuck outa here!"

Mark and I knew she was right. "Look, nothing's happened and nothing's gonna happen," Mark told her. "We've been staring at some people who have been staring back and that's absolutely everything, all right? It's a stare-down, that's it. Okay?"

"Okay."

"And the fact is, if they're the people we're supposed to meet, you hanging around might ruin the chances of anything ever happening if you haven't ruined it already. So get out of here!"

Nancy was quiet, but she looked like she understood. "Okay, we'll stay away."

"Thank you."

"But promise you'll tell us everything when it's over."

"Riiiiiiiiiiiight. Now get the fuck outa here."

Nancy took the others aside to discuss our offer of full disclosure. There was lots of visible head shaking, arguing and shoulder-shrugging before the group gave us a collective disappointed look and headed back toward the terminal, looking back over their shoulders as they walked away.

"I can't believe you told them," Mark hissed at Beth.

"I didn't think they'd come in the rain and snow."

"She's right, Mark. It's not her fault," I said. "They're just being immature assholes."

"Yeah, yeah, yeah. I know. It's just so irritating that…"

"Besides," I added, "we tried to come here to see what happened to Steve Handy."

"Riiiiiiiiiiiight. I already thought of that."

I also realized that instead of four dorm girls, it could very well have been fifty of my fraternity brothers storming the rotunda to watch us. I told plenty of them the same things Beth told the dorm girls. The girls simply had more chutzpah and a greater sense of adventure than the brothers.

We decided to accost the man and the woman in the bar directly.

But when we got back to the rotunda, they were outside the bar, standing beside the top of the "up" escalator, exactly where Mark and I had stood before.

"Shit," I whispered to Mark.

"Shit is right," he whispered back.

We stood on the side of the escalator opposite "the couple." We looked at them and they looked back. They scanned the rotunda as if they were looking for someone, the same way we looked over the crowd until we noticed them sitting inside the bar.

Beth nudged me and shook her head toward the concourse. Standing just inside the rotunda were the four girls from her dorm looking up at us. Once we saw them, they hurried to escape back toward the terminal. Mark grabbed my sleeve and said, "Let's go." I grabbed Beth.

"Excuse me," he said to the couple on the opposite side of the escalator, "we're from KMZU radio in Columbia, Missouri and…"

"Ohhhhhhhh," the man interrupted, "I saw your name tags and wondered what they meant. I saw the records too. You guys must really like the Beatles."

Mark continued, "Yes sir, we do." He waited for a response. There was none. "We're supposed to meet someone here and we're wondering if you're the people we're supposed to meet?"

"Sorry," the man answered casually, physically deflating Mark. "We're waiting for a friend of ours."

Mark lifted himself up. "Would that be a Mister Kite?" I couldn't believe Mark had the balls to come right out and ask.

"No, we're waiting for Charles Puckett Hancock, the third."

"Oh. Sorry to bother you." Mark turned toward the escalator. "Let's go."

Beth collected the albums and put them back into her bag. We took off the nametags. We went back to the terminal.

Beth's dorm friends were gone.

We sat back in the chairs where we waited before going to the rotunda. It was obvious everybody's brains were whirring, wondering what to do next.

"Let's page him," I said.

Beth didn't understand. "Page who?"

"Mister Kite!"

Mark hustled to an airport courtesy phone while Beth and I waited, hoping someone would come to us from the rotunda, looking for us.

As Mark came back to us, we heard the page: "Trans World Airlines paging Mister Kite. Will Mister Kite please meet your party in the O'Hare airport rotunda."

We ran back to the rotunda.

"The couple" was gone.

We waited another fifteen minutes at the top of the escalator.

Nothing.

We went back to the courtesy phones. We paged Mister Kite again. And Billy Shears. And Brian Epstein, Sergeant Pepper, even "P. McCartney." We even paged "Charles Puckett Hancock, the third."

None of them answered.

After Mark and I failed in our attempt to go to Chicago to see Steve Handy, we didn't speak to one another most of the way home. This time, the three of us couldn't speak quickly enough or throw out enough suggestions.

"Who else should we page?"

"Should we go back to the rotunda?"

"Should we call the station?"

"Where are the girls from the dorm?"

"Is there another rotunda?"

"Are there clues about anybody named Charles? Or Puckett? Or Hancock?"

"What else can we do?"

It was almost six o'clock. The last flight back to St. Louis was at seven.

Suddenly, Beth gasped. "What? Whatsamatter?"

"I just added it up."

"What? You added what up?"

"My sister does numerology."

Even though we somehow felt connected to Beth's brother from his overseas phone calls, we didn't know her sister and had absolutely no idea from numerology. Beth's family had puzzled us again. "Numerology is the occult study of numbers," she said. "Each letter of the alphabet has a number assigned to it and when you add up the numbers of the letters in someone's name, it tells you something about the person."

"So?"

"So," she went on, her hands shaking again, "I just added up the initials for Charles Puckett Hancock."

"Yeah?"

"The letter C is three, P is a seven and H is an eight. Add them together and you get eighteen. Add the one and the eight of eighteen together and you get..." She choked up. Nobody said anything. We could add one and eight.

We were silent again, overwhelmed by what we knew was happening around us.

"And then when you throw in 'the third,' that's twenty-one and you get three again. Three and nine are the most significant numbers of this whole puzzle, aren't they?"

"Let's go home," Mark finally said.

"I just know somebody would have made contact with us," Beth sneered, "if the girls hadn't been here."

"We don't know that," I answered, trying to make her feel as if our failure wasn't her fault—but all of us knew for certain that it was.

We waited as long as we could before heading to our departure gate. We paced the length of the terminal. We walked the concourse between the terminal and the rotunda. We waited in the rotunda again.

We called Mike Dryden, the station manager, and told him we struck out and that we'd be in Columbia about ten-thirty. He said to come to the station. "We need to talk about this, y'all." His drawl didn't sound so soothing.

The flight was boarding when we arrived at the gate.

If I could see those dorm girls now, I would not tell them "hi."

YOU'D SAY I'M PUTTING YOU ON
BUT IT'S NO JOKE, IT'S DOING ME HARM...
I'D GIVE YOU EVERYTHING I'VE GOT FOR A LITTLE
PEACE OF MIND
(I'M SO TIRED)

Even after we were airborne on our flight back to St. Louis, each of us was still painfully sensitive to the possibility of a "this is it, come with me" shoulder tap. But all three of us also knew anything that might lead us anywhere was totally unlikely. Despite our preparation for and the total expectation of complete disappointment, we were still totally and completely disappointed.

"I want a drink," Mark said.

"Me too," I added.

Beth asked for a Coke. She loaned me two dollars for two little airline-sized bottles of Canadian Club, two cups of ice and a 7-Up. Sitting between Mark and me but without looking at either of us, she asked, "what do we do now?"

I answered first. "I say we try the phone number again this Wednesday morning or Tuesday night or whatever time it's supposed to be."

"I think it's Tuesday night, our time," Beth picked up. "Five o'clock Wednesday morning in London would be ten or eleven Tuesday night, our time. I'm not sure but I'll go to the library and find out exactly when we get back."

"That's during your shift, Mark. Let's find out if Clark Clifton knows anything about the Notre Dame guy."

Mark took a long sip of Tanqueray and tonic from a plastic cup. The cup had a red plastic swizzle stick in the shape of a propeller poking out of it. Neither suave nor debonair (a phrase fraternity rats of the '70s fashionably pronounced "SWAYve and deBONEr" in order to prove their lack of SWAYveness), enough to remove the swizzle stick from the glass, Mark had to avoid poking himself in the eye with the propeller. Finally, he quietly said "Nope. That's not what we're gonna do."

"What then?"

"What we're gonna do," he said quietly, in a way that convinced me that he absolutely accepted the inevitability of his own answer, "is bag it. It's over."

Beth and I each expected the other to argue about how far we'd come and how we couldn't stop now, but neither of us made a sound. No matter how much we wanted the adventure to continue, we both knew the foolishness truly had to end.

Mark continued logically in the kind of calm voice that discouraged argument. "We did everything we could. We did what we were supposed to do. And then nothing happened just like we expected from the beginning."

"Nothing is real," I sighed.

"Riiiiiiiiiiight. How do we know this wasn't just some big joke Clark Clifton or the Notre Dame radio people played on the fools from Missouri? They're probably laughing like crazy right now."

I wanted to tell him how obvious it was that the clues had to point to something real. No disc jockey in Atlanta or any bunch of college boys could have put stuff on Beatle albums. But I kept my mouth shut and twirled my drink in my plastic glass with my plastic propeller.

"The answer is," Mark went on, "that we don't know the question. If it's some kind of prank, then it is what I said the first night on the air, a little ha-ha John Lennon played on millions of people and he's getting his jollies and he'll never know that three assholes from Missouri blew their radio station's budget trying to find out the deep hidden meaning of absolutely nothing.

"If Paul McCartney is dead and has been replaced by a look-alike, then may he rest in peace and my best wishes to the new guy. We'll never prove it's true and we'll never find out if it's false. And the fact is, there's just not a fucking thing any of us can do about it. And that, my friends and traveling companions, is the way it is."

After Mark's little speech, both Beth and I felt put in our place. Beth finally spoke up meekly. "But Maaaaaaaaaark…"

Mark cut her off like a scolding parent. "It's over! I know that I can't afford this financially any more, the station can't afford it and I know Jeffrey can't afford it because Jeffrey never has any money. Beth, if you want to go on then I wish you all the luck in the world and hope you send us a postcard from Pepperland. But I've got classes to go to and a radio station to program."

And that was that.

Feeling the two small airplane bottles of booze, I was sound asleep when we landed. We took the shuttle to the long-term parking lot. Beth paid the fee. The highway was wet but not snow-covered. Before I could realize more than one hundred miles of road had passed beneath us, Mark was shaking me awake.

It was 10:20 and we were parked in a loading zone outside the station. "Who's gonna care about a loading zone on a snowy Sunday night?" Mark hissed defensively. "The campus cops aren't even out tonight. Screw it."

We expected to find a radio station full of people eagerly anticipating detailed descriptions of our journey. But the only ones there were a Sunday night news reader scanning wire copy, a sports guy collecting scores, the chief announcer who was covering my on-air shift and hoping to not have to stay and cover Mark's shift also—he would—and Mike Dryden, the smooth-talking station manager.

"So?" Dryden said as he came out of his office, "j'all have fun?" He was smiling a sweet, sincere, Southern gentleman's smile that held more than a bit of polite curiosity. He seemed to have more interest than anger and that was a relief.

"No," I answered, "we did not have fun."

We went to the office pit Mark and I shared. Mark and I sat at our desks, Beth in a dented old folding chair in the corner. Dryden sat on the waist-high engineering bench, his feet dangling, appearing as casual and as non-intimidating as a management type can look. We told him the entire minute-by-minute story in huge detail, leaving nothing out, making it sound like one incredible adventure on behalf of the station and our listeners.

We told him about the girls from Beth's dorm. He smacked his forehead with his palm and said, incredulously, "Ahhhhhhh cain't believe it, y'all! I jest can't believe they'd do such a thang!" We described "the couple" and explained our attempts at paging anyone who might answer. We even told him about the *Chicago Tribune*.

He looked very impressed.

And then, twiddling a cold soldering iron like a revolver and without ever asking what we thought we should do next, he brought it all into necessary perspective. "It was good hustle, y'all, but Ahm sorry, this is costin' the station way too much monah. You're prolly gonna wanna be reimbursed for the gas, aren't ya Mahk? Hell, ya'll'll prolly want your money back for the newspaypah!"

"No, I don't want to be reimbursed for the gas," Mark shouted angrily. "And I'll pay for the fucking gas!"

"I'll pay you back, Mark," I added generously.

Beth quietly handed him a ten-dollar bill, all she had left.

"I'll pay for the goddam gas," Mark snapped again, pushing away the ten. "And I'll pay for the fucking newspaper, too!"

Amazed and caught too off guard to realize it was inappropriate for the moment, I asked Mark "where are you getting all this money?" Mark rolled his eyes and gave me the finger. Even after his calmness on the plane, it was good to see Mark was still involved enough in the adventure to still get good and mad.

Dryden continued, using a voice of genuine sorrow. "Ah know the list'nahs ate this up, but Ahm afraid it's gonna hafta come to an eeund rahght now." He had already decided how the "eeund" would come. "Mahk and Jay-uff, I want you boys ta record some spots tellin' the listenahs what happened. Go intah as little or as much detayul as y'all want. A lotta list'nahs know what's goin' on. We been gettin' calls from Beth's dorm all day, people askin' questions 'bout what was happnin' and we hadda tell 'em we didn't know anythin'. And now I know why *they* knew so damned much mo' than even Ah did!

"So go ahead on. Tell 'em whatevah y'all want. And then tell 'em it's all ovah."

We agreed to record the tapes.

"We'll run the hell outa 'em on the ayuh tonaght and tomorruh and that'll be the end of it."

We knew arguing with Dryden would do no good whatsoever. We knew that logic, common sense and the firmness of his mind wouldn't get us one more station dollar. No matter how much the listeners—or we—wanted more, our trek into the unknown was most definitely "ovah."

I wrote my tape copy by hand in our office pit while Mark typed his in the newsroom. Out in the hall between us, probably out of habit, duty or obsession, Beth filed records away while we wrote. Then Mark and I took turns recording our little excuses, carefully listening to each other's admissions of defeat.

"Hi, this is Jeff Scott. If you were with us Thursday night, you know we had fun trying to discover clues that substantiated the rumor that Paul McCartney is dead, or at least that something's going on. And it was great. More people came together that night here on KMZU than ever came together before over anything short of a Missouri-Kansas football game. It was a night I'll always remember.

"But at this point, our search has to end. Mark W. Richardson and I are still college students and neither of us can afford to neglect our work any more. We appreciate the support and interest and now we've got to get back to class and get on with our lives."

"This is Mark W. RichardsoNNNNNNNNNN*uh*, KMZU program director and mangler of the heavyweights, eleven to one weeknights on The Great 58. Ever since Thursday night, boy DJ and part-time lump of clay Jeff Scott and I have been totally involved in this 'Paul McCartney thing' and now I'm really sorry to say that we can't continue our search. Our schedules won't allow us to go on and frankly, neither we nor the station can afford it.

"So no matter how much fun we had, I'm sorry but we've got to bag it. Our listeners might be frustrated at 'Paulus Interruptus,' but I hope they'll understand. Keep listening to The Great 58."

We labeled the tape cartridges "Scott-Richardson/Beatles" and noted on the labels that DJs should "play once per half-hour, ROTATE EVENLY."

It was done.

All our discussion about getting back to class and returning to our studies reminded me that I had a test the next morning in my "Life and Literature of Shakespeare" class. Of course I hadn't studied nor was I physically or emotionally capable of pulling the customary pre-test all-nighter. I knew I was in trouble. Had I studied or known the stuff from this particular class, I thought, maybe I would have recognized the chatter at the end of "I am the Walrus."

The next morning, I spent my test time intricately detailing our weekend exploits in my "blue book." I leaned hard on the *King Lear* quote from "I am the Walrus," citing it as a Shakespearean example of great British literature. I figured it was, at minimum, a confident mention of Shakespeare in a context of which I was much more certain than any question asked on the test. I hoped the professor was, at best, a Beatle fan or, at worst, someone who would take pity and give me a chance at a retest. His generosity and sympathy were my only salvations against ignorance.

To fill space in the test booklet, I wrote every event, every clue, every second in exact order. I provided the professor with a death-defying account of our Thursday through Sunday adventure, radio station to St. Louis to Columbia to O'Hare and back. In reality, that retelling may have been more detailed than even this account since I had the benefit of recency. Despite the vividness of my memory now regarding those early days, the years have taken their obvious toll. I wish I still had that "blue book" to check the facts against my memory. For all I know, it's in a dusty box somewhere in my mother's basement or closet, but that's definitely assuming she's kept any souvenirs or record of my existence for all these decades.

What I do remember about that test is what the professor wrote on my lengthy literary copout: "Shakespeare would have appreciated your noble quest. You may take a retest."

If I could see that professor now, I would tell him "hi" and "thanks."

After a full night of cramming for the retest, I got a C-plus.

Nobody cared about grades in Pepperland. Utopia did not function on the curve.

SO LET ME INTRODUCE TO YOU
THE ONE AND ONLY BILLY SHEARS

I spent most of the following summer working in the stock room of the Bee Hat Company on Locust Street in the "garment district" in downtown St. Louis, "manufacturers of fine hats and caps for men and boys." The job paid one dollar and sixty cents per hour.

I couldn't wait to get back to school and back on the air.

Mara spent her summer working in the credit department of a local department store. In that pre-computer age, she sat all day at a little desk in a windowless store basement, writing daily charges onto index cards. At the end of the month, another clerk compiled the charges and typed out customer billings for mailing.

We saw each other four or five nights a week, sometimes just for TV dates at her house. On nights we didn't see each other, we talked on the phone for hours. The calls were glorious, without the onus of unaffordable long-distance charges hanging over our heads. I have no idea what we talked about, but even after all these years I can still visualize myself prone on my parents' dining room floor, my feet up on a chair seat, talking and talking and smiling and smiling.

But through the vacation, I still kept my hand in radio.

KMZU was closed for the summer. There weren't enough summer school students to operate the station and never enough summer listeners in the dorms to justify even a few hours of broadcasting per day.

But every few Saturdays I drove my parents car to Columbia, ostensibly to "check my mail" at the station. I had to go, I told them, "in case something important came."

Of course, nothing important ever came.

At least not in the mail.

The Columbia trips were simply excuses to get back to the radio station, to smell the stale, smoky air, to feel the ambience, to have the station walls surround me, to be in a place where I had some knowledge, comfort and control—to feel the excitement even a closed-up radio station could give me.

On the drive between St. Louis and Columbia, I often thought of the trips made with Mark and Beth.

When I arrived at the station, I opened the closed-for-the-summer building with the keys royally granted to late-night disc jockeys and station mucketymucks. There was always an enormous pile of records and letters the mailman had left waiting inside the station front door.

The packages were ripped open with great vigor and excitement. Even though I couldn't play any of the records on the air until fall, I listened to as many as I could while sitting in the studio, just as if I were on-air and the transmitter was sending out that weak little signal, knowing that when I heard one of them on St. Louis radio, I would know "I would have played *that* one." I was always slow to leave.

After each station visit, I went to the M-Bar. Not a bar at all, but a burger-and-fries joint in the basement of the campus book store, even during summer session it was always crowded and filled with loud music. It was one of the few places on campus where summer school students and faculty could score a cheap, hot, greasy meal.

During the school year, I much preferred to eat at The Shack, an on-campus dive that was exactly what the name described. Low-ceilinged and dark, generations of students had carved their initials and names into the wooden booths and tables. But The Shack was closed for the summer and I had to settle for a meal less kingly than a Shackburger with extra Shack Sauce. I would like a Shackburger with extra Shack Sauce right now. These days, at my current age, I'm starting to believe Shackburgers may have been one of the secrets to eternal youth.

I ducked into the M-Bar after each station visit for a burger and a dessert of pinball. The M-Bar was a serious pinball joint for serious pinballers.

At the beginning of my pinball wizard life, I studied M-Bar pinball pros with an intensity never given to Shakespeare or any other classes. I watched how they stood silently at the machines, shoving their machine with the heels of their hands just enough to direct the balls down the desired slot but never hard enough to tilt the machine. I watched how they caught the ball on the flippers until they had complete control and then, precisely released the button to pop the ball exactly up the 50,000-point chute.

Pinball became almost as important and as addictive as radio.

I adopted a game called "Funland" as my own. Though it mastered the change in my pocket quicker than I mastered it, I got better at it and played as often as I could. Thinking about it now, and knowing what happened literally as I played it and in the hours and days afterwards, I find irony, humor and pain in the name of my favorite game.

"Are you Jeff?" the voice asked as I concentrated on the machine. I didn't reply, waiting to send the ball where it might collect enough points for a free play. "Wait a minute," I answered, as if the Universe depended on what I did with the last ball. The ball didn't fly up the 50-point chute, but bounced around a couple of bumpers and quickly drained down the middle, out of reach of either flipper. "Shit!"

The machine clunked. I hit the match. A free game.

"What did you say?" I asked, turning toward the voice, unsure of either the question or who was asking.

"I said," he repeated, "are you Jeff?"

"No, I'm…" and quickly, I realized that in parts of Columbia, I *was* Jeff. "Are you looking for Jeff Scott?"

He was in his late twenties or maybe early thirties, wearing jeans and a white t-shirt. He obviously wasn't a campus "freak," a real-live, year-round Columbia-dwelling hippie. The freaks would never have set foot in the M-Bar, it was a frat rat hangout. He could have been faculty, I thought, maybe a graduate student. Maybe he was a summer school dormy who recognized my voice from the radio when he heard me talking to the pinball machine.

"Yeah, I'm looking for Jeff Scott," he said. "Can we talk a minute?"

"Sure," I said with the same naïve response I would have given anyone who asked if we could talk. "What can I do for you?"

"Do you still take pictures?"

"Yeah, sometimes. I mean, I can. Why?"

"I need a photographer, my friend, and I'd like to hire you. For money."

"Sure you can hire me," I said eagerly. "For what, for when and for how much?"

I was happy at the prospect of making a few bucks from an old avocation, but I almost never thought of myself as a photographer any more. I was a radio man.

"Can we go someplace quieter to talk?"

"Sure."

Another student stood nearby watching me play the pins the same way I used to watch the experts. I tried to ignore him while I played, the same way my mentors ignored me, following the unwritten rules of pinball etiquette. "You want the rest of my games?" He nodded enthusiastically and quickly slid to the business end of the machine, his hands coolly overhanging the sides so that only his fingertips touched the flipper buttons. Looking up, he saw the number 4 in the little box that showed how many games I had left. He pushed the red button, the machine reset and he started playing.

The t-shirt and I walked out into the muggy mid-Missouri August. I squinted in the sunlight. "Okay, what can I do for you?"

He didn't answer.

I asked again. Even in conversation, I avoided dead air. "Why do you need a photographer? Who put you on to me? Who gave you my name?"

"Let's walk," he answered. "I'll tell you in a minute." We wandered to the Columns at the center of the "red campus." The Columns were all that remained of the original administration building after a catastrophic fire in the late 1800's. Preserved and ivied, they are the quintessential picture postcard symbol of the University.

He introduced himself as we sat down on the grassy hill around the Columns. "Jeff my friend," he said, very cool and calm, "I'm Hancock."

"Who?"

"Hancock. Charles Puckett Hancock, the third."

Little hairs stood up on the back of my neck again. Even though the temperature and humidity were both in the nineties, I was chilled. "Excuse me?" Hoping that by pure coincidence he was someone really and truly named Charles Puckett Hancock who just happened to need to hire a photographer, I tried to hide the fact that my heart was pumping so fast that if I leaned against one of the Columns, the vibrations would knock it down.

"Charles Puckett Hancock, the third," he repeated. When he got no response, he added "O'Hare?" From the look on his face there was obviously total blankness on mine. "Maybe I've got the wrong person," he said. "If you don't know who Charles…"

"No, no, no!" I interrupted, "I know someone named Charles Puckett Hancock, godammit! But maybe you're a diff…"

"This is my favorite part of the job, telling you I'm the same one."

A shot of adrenaline pumped into my stomach.

"You and Mark were absolutely on target. The clues, the lyrics, the…"

"Wait a minute," I shouted. "What the fuck is going on here?"

He smiled. "That's a question I hear in one form or another almost every time."

"Every time what? When? What the fuck is going on here?"

"Paging Mister Kite at the airport is what sold us on you. And the other airport pages too, Sergeant Pepper, Brian Epstein. Billy Shears was a real good lick. That you even paged Charles Puckett Hancock in a public place showed a lot of balls because you knew you were actually paging somebody who just might've answered! When you paged McCartney himself, it showed us you were for real, that you wanted answers."

I sat like a rock, not knowing whether to believe anything this person said and unsure he was even there at all. "I'm sorry but I'm very, very lost here."

He came right to the point. "I know you already know about Pepperland."

"Right. Pepperland. So? What about it? Are you a friend of Mark's? Or Beth? What did they tell you? How do you know them? You know Lou Flowers?"

"Nope," he smiled, "sorry. Never met them. But I saw Mark and Beth at O'Hare with you."

"Then how do you…who are…what do you want?"

"It's not what I want, my friend, it's what you might want. Or, might not want at all. And that, my friend, is okay too. If you want to try for the third plateau, this is it. This is the third plateau, right now. We'll talk a little and if things go right then maybe I'll even ask if you'd like to try for the fourth plateau. Or maybe I won't."

Nothing, truly, can be real.

He found me, but I was very, very lost.

ALL THE LONELY PEOPLE,
WHERE DO THEY ALL BELONG?

He said Charles Puckett Hancock was a made-up "cover." He said he thought using that name would get my attention and he was definitely right about that. When I pressed for more information, he said his real name wasn't Mister Kite or Billy Shears or anything particularly appropriate. "We pulled Charles Puckett Hancock out of the phone book. Each of the three of us found a last name and we strung 'em together. We threw in 'the third' for a touch of class. It's very European sounding, don't you think?"

I wasn't thinking much at all, just sitting with a totally blank look on my face. "What about the numerology thing? If you pulled names out of the phone book, why does it add up to nine?"

It was his turn to look blank. "What are you talking about?"

I quickly explained Beth and her sister's numerology theory. "I still don't know what you're talking about," he said. "If it's some kind of Beatles clue, I don't know about it. But I'll find out what I can if you're really upset about it."

"Yeah. Please. I'd like to know."

"Fact is," he continued, "it's no big deal. What's important is that you found the clues, passed the second plateau and now's your chance to go on if you want." There was another long silence. Finally, he broke the silence again. "That's why I'm here, my friend, to give you a chance to go on. Understand? I'm here to give you a chance to go on."

The realization dawned on me that this wasn't about Beatles trivia. "I'm really confused about all this," I finally admitted. "I know exactly what you're saying and I still have absolutely no idea what you're talking about."

He offered to take me anyplace I might feel more comfortable. I suggested Romano's, an Italian place across the street from the journalism school. It was another dark hangout for J-jocks too SWAYve and deBONEr for the M-Bar. I wanted a place dark and quiet instead of roasting in the public glare of the summer sunshine.

He ordered a beer. I ordered coffee, afraid beer would addle my sensibilities more than he was already screwing with them. "Do you want something to eat?" he asked, making me feel as if I were with my Jewish mother who was always trying to feed and indeed overfeed me. "How's the pizza here?"

"No thanks, I'm not hungry. The pizza's good. It's okay pizza." I didn't feel like giving in-depth reviews of the food at a campus hangout to a stranger.

He ordered a large pepperoni and green olive pizza. "I've had so many pizzas in so many different places. It's interesting how different they are. There's thin crust, thick crust, different sauces, different toppings. You can't get green olives everywhere. Black olives, yes, but not always green ones."

"Yeah, I guess."

"I always get the pepperoni. You can't go wrong with pepperoni. The green olives are a bonus, my friend, a real bonus."

I nodded at his astute analysis of pizza Zen, but didn't give a damn.

"I grew up in Chicago," he rambled, "on stuffed pizza. Have you ever had deep-dish Chicago stuffed pizza? It's the best pizza you'll..."

"Can you help me out here, please?" I didn't feel the least bit rude for interrupting his description of Chicago cuisine. There were more immediate questions than where to find the best pizza. Nonetheless, his words stuck in my mind the way hot mozzarella sticks to the top of the mouth. To foolishly continue the ridiculous pizza metaphor, hot mozzarella burns when it sticks to the top of the mouth and the more he spoke, the more I felt burned and the more I hurt.

The waitress brought his beer and my coffee. "Thank you," he told her, leaning out of the booth to watch her as she walked away. "Nice ass."

"So what's the deal?"

"The deal is this: I work for the Central Intelligence Agency. CIA?"

"Yeah. So?"

"Want some ID?"

"No, that's okay." In retrospect, I obviously should have asked for a badge or a card, but I remember that, at that exact moment, I thought it uncool to ask for ID. In Columbia, the only time you genuinely needed ID was when paying University fees, exactly the time you'd expect people to take your money without question. It never made much sense to me, but such was college life.

As he went on and finally got to the point, no matter what he said, no matter how he explained things, it was still difficult to comprehend. Somewhere in my confused brain, I wanted to think that the CIA wanted to hire a photographer—THAT I could understand. But here was a total stranger out of the clear blue sky, telling me I should be happy because he was from the CIA and offering godknowswhat in godknowswhere.

"What it boils down to right here and right now, my friend, is the third plateau."

"What 'third plateau?' I'm still not clear what we're talking about. Do you need a photographer or not?"

He smiled and shook his head.

The waitress brought the pizza.

He picked up a slice from the platter and moved it to one of two small white plates the waitress brought. The cheese left a long hot strand from the platter to the plate. "Stringy cheese, a sign of excellent pizza." He sprinkled grated Parmesan and cracked peppers on the pizza, picked up the slice and folded it lengthwise, snapping the crust. "The olives and pepperoni don't fall off if you fold it like this."

He took a bite and continued to talk. "I want you to know..." As the stringy cheese ran from his lips to the slice in his hand, he threw the pizza back onto the plate, fanned his mouth with his fingers, made a "hoh, hoh, hoh" sound and took a long gulp of beer, not telling me whatever it was he wanted me to know. "Damn, that's hot!" He took another sip of beer and waited for the pizza to cool. "I want you to know that I've done dozens of these third plateaus and you're the hardest one ever."

"Thank you," I answered. "Now tell me what you're trying to tell me, and tell me straight and tell me so I can understand and tell it to me with no bullshit."

He wiped his mouth, signaled for the waitress and asked for water. I couldn't tell if he was waiting for the pizza to cool or if his delay was for emphasis and drama. "No, I don't need a photographer, that was just to break the ice. We're at the third plateau. You found the clues, you solved the puzzle and now we're here, my friend."

"Where is here?"

"The first plateau was the clues and answering the questions on the phone. Which question did you get? Was it the 'where is Pepperland' question? Or 'who's the walrus?' I always thought that the walrus question was too easy.

"The walrus was Paul. Beth got the 'who is Sergeant Pepper' question."

"Thaaaaaaaaaaaaaaaaat's right. I remember. That's a good one."

"She had to guess."

"And it sounded like guesswork on the tape. Anyway, my friend, the second plateau was the airport. We wanted to find out if you'd really, truly, literally go out of your way to find out what you wanted to know. We needed to know how dedicated you were, how far you'd go. And in your case, four hundred miles was far enough."

"So? We went to O'Hare. Then the station cut us off."

"Yeah, I know."

"How do you know? The station only broadcasts to dorms." Feeling the sudden need to explain carrier current, non-broadcast radio to another one of the uninformed masses, I began the standard definition. "Each dorm has a transmitter. The signal goes through telephone wires until…"

"Telephone wires?" He held his hand to his ear, as if holding a telephone. "Tap…tap…tap…"

The waitress brought the water. He watched her walk away again. "That is still a nice ass, my friend, still a very nice ass." He picked up his pizza again, blew on it and took a large bite, not looking at me. "So you want Pepperland or not? Either way, I've done my job."

"What do you want?" I asked.

"The question is what do *you* want."

"What do you mean by Pepperland?"

"I mean Pepperland, just like in your dreams, like in the movie."

"Pepperland? Are you kidding?"

"Nope, this is absolutely real."

Nothing is real.

"Lots of love, lots of good feelings, lots of music, lots of…"

"You are so full of so much shit, *my friend*." He clearly recognized the sarcasm in my voice. "Just tell me in real terms what we're talking about here and don't give me any line of bullshit."

"A bullshit-free line is the least I can give you. After all, here I am, some guy who interrupts your pinball game to ask if you want to go to Fantasyland. I think it's okay that you ask questions and it's only fair that I answer them."

He waited for another question.

But I asked nothing.

He shrugged and rolled on. "Okay, I'll explain. When the Beatles started selling records by the gazillions, they literally found themselves with more money then they could handle. After all, they were just four young…"

"I understand."

"We're talking serious, serious megabucks here. Not millions, billions."

"Yeah. I got it."

"No matter what regular guys like you and I might think we'd do with that kind of money, it's a lot of responsibility for four young guys in their twenties. So after the records, after the concerts, after the constant attention, they got so tired of the pressure, the fans, the touring, the constant need to be 'on,' they wanted to get away from it all.

"So they asked a guy named Taylor to find them an island. Alistair Taylor, his name was, he was the manager of Apple Corps. Remember Apple?"

"Yessssssssssss, I remember Apple." I wanted to add the word "dumbshit" to my sentence, but managed to hold back my tongue and my emotions.

He took another slice of pizza.

"You sure you don't want any pizza? It's finally cool and it's very edible. It's not bad at all for college town pizza."

I felt a lot of things at that moment, but absolutely no need whatsoever to defend all college town pizza. "No thanks, I'm still full from the M-Bar."

"Just leaves more for me. Anyway, there they were, fed up with the taxes in England, they wanted privacy, they wanted to escape the crowds and the fans, soooooooo, they bought one, my friend. They bought one."

"They bought one what?"

"An island, asshole! They bought a little place off the coast of Greece. Alistair Taylor bought them an island!"

It was amazing to me that for a person I had only just met, he already felt familiar enough to call me "asshole," just like somebody from the fraternity house who had known me for a long time. But I wasn't offended. Despite my discomfort about the subject matter, I was at ease with him as a person.

"Then they got with the Maharishi...you know about the Maharishi?"

This time, his insult felt condescending. If I knew about the Beatles, I certainly knew about the Maharishi. "Yessssssssss, I know about the Maharishi."

"Well," he went on as breezily as if he were talking about baseball, "during the meditation thing, the Maharishi told them they had to create some thing or some place that would cultivate peace, where they could grow serenity like a crop. He told them they should 'plant the seeds of peace' and they bought the idea lock, stock and barrel, especially John and George. Anyway, after the Maharishi, they..."

I laughed out loud.

"What?" He smiled, genuinely interested about what made me laugh while he was in the middle of a big, serious explanation. "What's so funny?"

I felt that his use of the words 'cultivate peace and serenity' were out of character for him, far too hip and way too compassionate. No pizza-eating fraternity brother would ever go into any discussion more esoteric than beer, pizza and the waitresses' ass. When he segued directly to his 'lock stock and barrel' description, it put him back into the dispassionate role I suspected a CIA man ought to play.

"This is getting surreal," I smiled. "We're talking about the Beatles here and this huge thing that people all over the world are going crazy about and you simplify one of their biggest turning points by calling it 'the meditation thing.'"

"I'll accept that. And I'm going to tell you this because I think you're starting to understand here. My training taught me not to believe anything. What you've got to know is that I've seen a lot of stuff in my time with the Company and it's still hard for me to take some things seriously. But this assignment was a big change for me. It's a lot more touchy-feely, not just simple surveillance and then filling out a report. We've got to get into the heads of the people we're watching. Do you know what I mean?"

"Sure. Go on."

"There's not much more. The Beatles bought an island in the Mediterranean and drew up plans for a big hippie resident camp. They started putting clues on songs and record jackets and figured that certain people would figure out what they meant and those were the people who ought to get invitations to be on the island."

"That's it?"

"Hell no," he insisted, "all that's just background. The island thing didn't work." He put his pizza down. "Have you ever heard of Buckminster Fuller?"

"Fuller, Fuller...that's a familiar name. Does he go to school here?"

This time it was Hancock, or whoever he was, who laughed. Sipping from his hourglass-shaped beer glass, I thought he might do one of those Danny Thomas spit-takes and spew a mist across the table. "No, he doesn't go to school here! Since you're from St. Louis, I can't believe you never heard of him."

"Sorry."

"Ya know, you're a real piece of work, my friend, a real piece of work. You're yet another college boy spending his parents' college investment wisely. Fuller developed the geodesic dome."

"Ohhhhhhhhhhhhh! What's that?"

He sprinkled more cheese and cracked peppers onto the last slice of pizza. "I've always liked these little peppers on pizza, but they come back on me later, you don't want to be around. Anyway, the geodesic dome is basically a whole bunch of reinforced metal triangles. The triangles are filled in with glass or plastic and when you fit a whole bunch of glass and metal triangles together, you get a self-supporting dome."

"Okay."

"Once upon a time, Fuller proposed building a huge, mile-wide dome that covered all of East St. Louis, Illinois. Don't you remember that?"

"Oh yeaaaaaaaaahhhhhhhh. I saw it in the papers, but I didn't pay much attention."

"Good. Very good. You're still doing better than most people at this point."

"Thank you." I was flattered with his compliment about my knowledge of current events and happy he didn't ask me about international time zones.

"Anyway, the Pepperland people decided if they built this big, secret Pepperland place on an island, sooner or later some ship would wander off course or a plane would fly over and somebody would ask 'what the hell is *that?'* Plus, anywhere in the Med you've got the Mideast problem just around the corner, the Arabs and the Israelis going after each other for years, and that might create a flyover problem if not worse. So they figured, bottom line, an island off Greece was not the way to go."

"Fine. I'll bite. What'd they decide to do?"

"They kept the basic idea, but threw out the island and decided to 'go under,' to build Pepperland below the ocean."

"'I'd like to be, under the sea, in an Octopus' Garden.'"

"Bingo, bango, bongo! Good work, my friend."

"Wait a minute, wait a minute!" I suddenly made sense of the totally nonsensical. "They built some kind of glass ball in the ocean somewhere?"

"Not exactly a glass ball, a dome. About half a ball, I guess."

"Geez Louise!" I wanted to call Mark immediately. "They're 'fixing a hole,' right?"

"You connect your clues better than a lot of people. Some guys hit the first plateau then they don't go any further. They spend all that time looking at pictures on record jackets, then hang up on the phone call. They sure as hell never get to checkout or to 'the meet.' A lot of people even get to this point and I give up on them—it's up to me to screen you people here at the third plateau. Sometimes, I don't even finish my pizza and walk away hungry because they think all this is just something to pass the time some late night after too much to drink or smoke." His tone was changing quickly. He was sounding much more serious. "This isn't a game, Jeff. We're talking real shit here. You should be flattered that I've almost finished my lunch, it means you've got your act together on this."

"I am. I'm really flattered. So keep talking."

"You'd be amazed how many complete toads are involved in this. All the stuff is right there on the albums that anybody can play. Anybody can find the clues. That was the whole idea. Everything is hidden in plain sight for everybody to see or not see. Of course, we have no idea who's a good guy and who's a toad until the second plateau, until we see them on the checkout in public. Then we do it again here."

My mind raced through clues, trying to come up with other easy giveaway clues that Pepperland wasn't an island but a below-the-surface something. "'Standing on the cast iron shore, Lady Madonna trying to make ends meet.'"

"Very good. You'll meet Lady Madonna if you make it. She's a lovely woman who left four children behind for Pepperland. It wasn't easy for her, but..."

"Wasn't there an 'ocean child' reference somewhere?"

"On 'Julia' on *The White Album*. See? I know my clues too."

"Were the people at the bar—that couple sitting there—were they the ones we were supposed to meet?"

"You were never supposed to meet them," he answered quickly. "They were coy, they were distant and that was their entire assignment. They checked you out and saw what you did when nothing happened. That was their whole responsibility."

"What do you mean they 'checked us out?'?"

"Manohman, you're a real piece of work, my friend. They looked, they watched, they got an overall impression about whether you were serious or just screwing around. We get lots of people, especially college kids, who have too many of Daddy's dollars in their pockets and too much time to kill. They see the clues, make the calls and when somebody calls back to tell them to be someplace, they're more than willing to take an airplane ride just for the hell of it. They're in it for the shits and grins and not for the..."

"Wait a minute, wait a minute!" I insisted, not interested in other people's motives. "If all of this is true, and I'm still not convinced it is..."

"Fair enough."

"Why the fuck is the CIA involved?" While I didn't really feel the Beatles owed me a personal explanation for anything, I did feel the need for more answers, especially when initials like CIA or FBI were tossed out like so much grated Parmesan—initials any '70s-era college student knew were not to be trusted.

"That's a fair question, too." From his tone of voice to his physical mannerisms, it was obvious Hancock was getting down to business. He pushed his empty pizza plate away, leaned forward and spoke in hushed tones. "We got into the whole thing through MI6. The British CIA? You know about MI6? British Intelligence?"

Truth be told, I'd never once heard of MI6, but "British Intelligence" rang a huge bell. "Yeah, I've seen enough James Bond films to know about British Intelligence."

"Good. Even with all the piles of dollars the Beatles made, no matter how pure their intentions, they still couldn't afford a project like this by themselves. I mean this is massive. Even if they could have done it financially, they'd never pull it off without somebody finding out and then the publicity shit would've hit the fan. And of course, they needed tons and tons of technological help to actually build the place.

"So they went to a friend who went to a friend who went to a friend in British Intelligence and it all mushroomed. MI6 came to CIA. We added U.S. Naval Intelligence to the mix because of their experience in the water and obviously because they'd have access to the kind of equipment we'd need down the line. INTERPOL is in because we need them at the fourth plateau."

I stared at him, waiting for more information.

"The agencies agreed to figure out how to find and screen possible residents from around the world, how to build the physical plant and how to keep it going. And because we do what we do, we can avoid the publicity that'll come along if this is ever forced out into the open. We can cover it all with a 'national security' blanket without ever saying 'oh yeah, this is Pepperland and we built it at great expense to the American taxpayer so the Beatles can grow peace and serenity like the Maharishi told them to.'"

For the first time since the conversation turned heavy I laughed again. Hancock even smiled back, almost acknowledging the silliness of the entire situation.

"Obviously, we're interested in the technology to find out if the idea of undersea civilization is possible or even thinkable. That's very important to us. There are all kinds of things that would be valuable to us, all kinds of things we could learn."

"Like what?"

"Ohhhhhhhhh, strategic things. Military basing, space flight..."

"Space flight?"

"You put a whole bunch of people together in a small space, even if it's underwater, and it's got the same effect as a space station or on the moon. It's a closed society, see? Lots of people, forced to live together with no way out and no place to go."

"Yeah, I see."

"We could build our own place and put our own people in it, of course, but it wouldn't be the same as having a bunch of random civilians in that kind of setting, you know?"

"Uh huh."

"Then there's the post-nuclear thing, that's probably the biggest."

"The what?"

"If the Russians start World War III, we've already got data on small group reactions to long-term living in small, enclosed spaces. Like bomb shelters, you know? And as gravy, we've already got a hand-picked group of very cool people stashed away under water, all safe and sound for...for whatever. Now do you understand our interest, my friend?"

"Yeah. I guess I do."

The idea that the CIA would connect with the Beatles in such a project to learn this kind of information totally astounded me. It seemed like the farthest possibility of two inconceivable extremes: creating a place of peace and love as a preparation for war. But Hancock accepted it as normal. "Anyway, after some conversation about what we needed and what they wanted, agreements were made and things started rolling.

"The Beatles agreed to play the 'clues on the records' game and we started doing the nitty-gritty stuff. They've got final design approval, but the technological end is all ours. And like I told you, we also supply certain expertise as far as resident screening, population implementation and other kinds of sociological and biological research—how it works, how people get together in the environment, that kind of thing. We have no interest in the motivation for Pepperland itself. Any motivation for a place like that where we can watch what happens is fine with us. We want to be in on the operations, that's all. How it manifests itself is its own business."

"Okay."

"On some of the later albums, *Abbey Road*, the "White Album" poster, a couple of the boys started getting tired of the whole thing."

"Which ones? Who?"

"I'll ignore that. So we got involved in consulting on some of the clues…"

"I bet it was George and Ringo."

"We were at the photo shoots, that kind of thing, making suggestions. When I was first assigned to this job, I got to sit in on the *Abbey Road* photo session. You'd have liked it, but I didn't care for it myself. The Beatles were argumentative as hell. They thought we were being too blatant about some things."

"28IF?"

"No, that one was theirs. Paul was born in 1942 and the album came out in '69. They made the connection and we liked it. They thought intricate details like that would attract the real maniacs. We threw in the costumes on the cover, but they thought that was too obvious because they did the grave thing on *Sgt. Pepper*. They went along because they knew that when push came to shove, they had no choice."

"What about the songs?"

"I'll tell you what. I'm not going to answer any more questions right now. I've told you all I can for now. If you go with the program, anything you need to know will be answered later. What we have to decide now is if you'd like to try for the fourth plateau."

"And if I don't?"

"Then you can never prove I was here. Only the waitress has seen us together and she must see a million guys a day in here, eating pizza and drinking beer."

Again, there was a long silence. Again, he broke it.

"I have to ask you, it's policy: do you want to try for the fourth plateau?"

"What is the fourth plateau? How many plateaus are there?"

"Getting past the third plateau is just saying yes, you want to try for the fourth. Otherwise, this is the end of our little chat."

"Assuming my simple acceptance gets me past the third plateau, okay. Sure. What the hell? Yes, I'll try for the fourth plateau."

"Congratulations. You just passed the third plateau and are moving toward the fourth plateau."

"Great. What do I have to do now?"

"To reach the fourth plateau, you have to say you're willing to go to Pepperland."

"Okay, and what do I have to do to after that?"

"That's a little harder."

"What do I have to do?"

"To get to Pepperland, my friend, you have to die."

I WAS ALONE, I TOOK A RIDE
I DIDN'T KNOW WHAT I WOULD FIND THERE

"What the fu...?" Dead air. "What the fuck do you mean I...?" Dead air. Finally, I reacted the only way I could react, probably the only self-defense mechanism I had at my disposal to save my own life: I laughed. "Do you shoot me right here right now or do you take me out back?"

"You disappear, that's all. You go away and we cover it up. As far as the world is concerned, you're dead."

Once again, I sat like a rock, and a stupid rock at that. After all, what's the right rejoinder, other than "you're full of shit?" I stared at him. I don't know if my jaw drooped or not. Finally I said the best thing I could come up with. "Now I think I want to see some ID." It was the only thing I could think to ask, or at least had the courage to ask.

He flopped open his wallet to show me a plastic-coated card. He shielded it with his hand to hide it from anyone who might stroll past. It was a bland, greenish, government-issued looking card with a photo on the right side and a signature at the bottom, which I assumed was his. It looked good enough for me. "I guess it looks like all the other CIA IDs I've ever seen." He smiled.

"So where is this place?" I didn't know what else to ask, so the journalism school "five w's" seemed like the right place to start.

"You'll find out when you find out."

"How do I get there?"

"I can't tell you."

"Who's there?"

"Can't tell you."

"Will the Beatles be there?"

"Sorry."

"Mark and Beth?" He sat silently. "Come on, goddamit! You've got to tell me something! You can't leave me like this! You've extended this big, huge invitation thing, Mark and Beth have to be invited too! You have to tell me that at least!"

"I can't say anything more about it, about who might be there, where it is or any more about what it is. At this point, right now, right here, all we're talking about is you."

He explained that confidentiality was routine and required, that secrecy was essential to fulfilling Pepperland's mission, absolutely no-shit necessary to satisfy the needs of both the Beatles and the intelligence agencies. His tone was low and completely, absolutely no-shit serious. "I will never lie to you, but I will only tell you what you need to know, when you need to know it."

"Okay." I was wholly overwhelmed.

He finally explained that each plateau would require a new choice. Each plateau would also provide the opportunity to back out with no problem, no regrets, no animosity and no questions asked. However, he told me, if I dumped out at any time, there would be no trace of provable connection between me and the Beatles, the intelligence community or anybody or anything in the universe except my own obviously overactive imagination.

"Okay. So what the hell do you mean 'I have to die?' Just how the fuck does *that* work?" He shrugged and even gave a small smile. His tone became more hushed and maybe even a bit lighter at this, *the* most absolutely no-shit serious part of the conversation.

"You disappear and they never find a body. We create a cover, you go with us and bingo, bango, bongo, no one ever knows the difference. That's all I can tell you, my friend, that's all you need to know at this time. You disappear. You go away. That's it." He was suddenly and totally dispassionate, as if he were still discussing pizza. In fact, he had more emotion in his voice when he was talking pizza then when describing my death. "It's clean, it's neat, you're gone."

"But come on. I mean, my parents, my friends, my..." I couldn't finish. "I don't understand. What if...how does..." It took a few seconds before I could ask the question I wanted to ask and couldn't even do that very well. "Can I...can...what if..."

"What? Mara? Is she the problem?"

"What do you know about Mara?"

He stared at the tabletop for several moments before he spoke again. "Look, I can tell you her phone number, that the two of you talk almost every night and that the calls are pretty innocuous. When you go out in St. Louis you usually double-date with your buddy Joel. He's a business major at Indiana and his girlfriend Leslie dropped out of IU after her freshman year and now she works at her dad's accounting firm. I know where Mara works, where she goes to school and that she's got a better GPA than you. I can tell you she came to Columbia with you two weeks ago but skipped the two trips before that. Last time she came here you went to the M-Bar, she ordered a tuna sandwich and you got a cheeseburger and played pinball. While you played, she sat in a booth and read *Atlas Shrugged*. She left half her sandwich uneaten. Maybe she didn't like the tuna, that I don't know. Now do you understand that with the exception of whether Mara likes tuna or not, that we have our shit together on this, my friend? Do you understand how fucking serious this is?"

"Yes. I guess so."

"I can also tell you it's a good thing she didn't come with you on this trip, because we've been trying to set up this meet forever. If she came with you this time, we'd have put off contact a couple more weeks. We might have or at least delayed everything until after school started and that would have made it even harder with what, twenty thousand more people around here? Or, we might have dumped you completely." Somehow, despite how objectionable the whole idea of "dying" was, I got a knot of fear in my stomach at the prospect of being left out. "We've been planning a quiet, little meet for you in Columbia for a long time. You're a lot more unpredictable in St. Louis. Here, it's always straight to the radio station, a burger and pinball at the M-Bar, then the drive home. Columbia is easy."

I felt invaded, violated and spied on. I launched a new barrage of questions to find out how deep and how personal their knowledge was.

He apologized, saying he had heard this indignation before at exactly this point in the process. "Listen, we have to know about you before we get to this point so we can set up your disappearance 'cause it's got to be believable and rock solid. We need to know what we need to know, and that's everything about you just this side of how many times you shake it when you take a leak. Second, we have to know this stuff 'cause we're talking about a certain number of people going to a very closed place, we've got to know them inside-out before we make the invitation. I'm sorry, but that's the way it is. Third, our instructions are to 'investigate but not invade'. We work in teams, so there's always somebody to draw the line.

"And finally," he added almost casually, as in afterthought, "*you* called *us.*"

I filled the remainder of the conversation with more dead air.

"Believe me," he assured, "it wasn't a major investigation like we'd do in the real-live espionage business. We just did the easy stuff."

"Like what?"

"You know, we ran 'wants and warrants' on you through the NCIC—the National Crime Information Center. We checked your driving record—too bad about the speeding ticket two years ago, but 49 in a school zone? Shame on you."

"Yeah, yeah, yeah."

He was so casual about describing his prying into my life that I ultimately found it interesting from a purely academic point of view. "Did you follow me? Did you check out my permanent record at school? Put secret microphones in my car? Tap my phone? Record my conversations?"

"Yes, yes, no, yes, no. Yes, we tailed you for about eight weeks. Yes, we checked your school records—which is very difficult, by the way, schools are tougher than the IRS. No, we didn't put mikes anywhere. Yes, we tapped your phones, we listened, but no, we didn't record because that would have been a little too invasive.

"And," he continued, "our people did a full psychological profile to figure where you're coming from and whether you'd fit in."

"So how'd I do on that one?"

"I finished my pizza, didn't I?"

I finally manage to ask the most important question. "What about Mara? Can she come?"

His gaze moved from me to the empty pizza tray. His answer was obvious.

"I don't believe this! Why can't Mara come?"

"She just can't. Those are the rules. If this whole thing was you and Mara finding clues together, if you'd both gone to O'Hare, maybe even if she worked at the radio station in some small capacity, then maybe. But as it is, it just can't be." I felt a thousand pounds of dead weight on my shoulders, making it impossible to rise from my deep slouch. "But I have to have a decision," he hammered. "I know it's hard. If it'll help, I'll tell you I've dealt with this before."

I felt weak, helpless. I thought I might vomit. How could I go without Mara? "If you've dealt with it before, tell me what other people with girlfriends or boyfriends or husbands or wives have done?" I hoped other people could point the direction for someone as lost as me.

"Some go, some stay home. Sometimes I wonder how those guys will be when they're thirty-five or forty, wondering the 'what might have been' question. Anyway, it's all totally up to you. Like I said, there's a decision at each plateau and this is probably the hardest one for somebody in your situation."

"How do I tell her I'm just picking up and going to...?"

He stopped me quickly. "You don't tell her anything at all. That's the hardest part for some people." My emotions had run from hostility to fear to weakness and now back to stunned again, incapable of any emotion except incredulity. "And if we do this, we do it now," he said. "You don't talk to anybody. You disappear today. You die today."

I sighed. "And then I live a new life."

"Very poetic. I heard almost the same words from a kid at Notre Dame."

"Steve Handy?"

"Yeah! How did you...?" Suddenly, he was the one who suddenly looked stunned.

"You don't know how I know?" I felt self-satisfied and amused. "You should do a little more homework next time. What about Handy? Did he go?"

He paused a long moment, wondering how the system had broken down. "Let's just say his situation was a lot different than yours. He was older, unattached, his life was…"

"Did he go? What happened to him after Chicago? What happened in New York?"

"Shit! How do you know all this? You *are* a piece of work!"

"*You* figure it out, genius!" My voice changed from curious to hostile again, not from anger but from the absolute imperative to know. "Did Handy go?"

"His case was different than yours."

"Bullshit!" I banged on the table, demanding answers. "You promised me no line of shit and you're giving me total crap! Tell me what I need to know! If I go along with this, today, right now, how do I do it? How do I die? And then what?"

"Trust me."

My hackles still go up whenever someone says "trust me." Trust should be an automatic, not something gained by telling, asking or begging "trust me." My gut reaction to someone asking for trust is a sign that person isn't trustworthy. Almost anyone who says "trust me" is implying they are probably a liar, or at least easily suspected of being one. "So you're not gonna tell me how I die, are you? You're not gonna tell me diddlyshit, are you?" You haven't even told me your goddam name."

"I'll tell you this much. If we go on, I'll be on you like white on rice."

I smiled, albeit weakly. "At the fraternity house, we'd have said 'on you like stink on shit.'"

"That's what I wanted to say, but I didn't think it was the right time."

I was sitting with a mysterious man who not only violated my life but was offering to end it. He offered both an end of everything and the new beginning of an amazing adventure. But to snatch the golden ring I had to put all my faith in him for no reason except for the pure belief that what he said was absolutely true and the pure desire to see the unseen, to experience the adventure and to know the answers to troubling questions.

But I did trust him, though I still don't completely know why. And I wanted answers more than anything. I thought that sooner or later, if I pushed the issue, they would *have* to allow Mara into Pepperland. I knew they would let her in and that idea satisfied me. There was faith there, too.

And then he finished. "I'll be on you like stink on rice and like white on shit."

"First you'll be the Angel of Death and then you'll be my guardian angel, huh?"

"Exactly. I know it's hard, but you've gone this far on speculation and I know we're asking you to keep going with nothing more than that. If you don't want to go another step, that's fine. I understand. I've dealt with it before."

"Okay."

"Great. You understand. You get it. Now, after building up your confidence in me and in the program, I have to give you a warning. This kind of thing, where you're going—*if* you go—it's never been done before. It involves a lot of new technology. Certainly, if you say yes, you accept a symbolic death. But if the technology doesn't hold up, we could be talking about the real thing here."

"You mean 'dead' in the physical sense? 'Dead' as in *dead*?"

"It's policy. I have to tell you. But I can also tell you there are lots of people involved in this who wouldn't take the risk if they weren't sure about the technology and the idea, and the powers that be wouldn't take the risk with those people either. It seems safe to me. But then again," he shrugged, "I'm no scientist. But I don't…"

His voice tapered off and he hesitated before he became businesslike again. There was no nonsense in his attitude. "So what's it gonna be?"

Shame on me, but my thoughts ran to fun and the possibilities instead of thinking of Mara and the realities. "Pepperland, huh? For real?"

"Just like *Yellow Submarine* but without the Blue Meanies."

"Yeah, yeah, yeah. 'All you need is love,' all that bullshit."

To this moment, so many years later, I don't know how I could have been so cavalier and rude, so insensitive to Mara or my family.

How could I treat them so thoughtlessly?

My parents always warned me not to talk to strangers, much less take Candyland from them.

What did they do that was wrong?

The possibility of a lifetime adventure swelled inside me. And adrenaline.

All I had to do was step outside, I'd be free.

Pepperland.

Leaving home.

Beatles.

The one thing that money can't buy.

Impulse.

"Hell, I don't know the questions, but I sure as fuck want the answers." I had no choice. The possibilities were too compelling. Rejecting the offer was impossible. I captured the moment in my mind as if it were a game-winning jump shot caught on film for my high school paper. I accepted it as an instant that had never happened before and would never happen again. I would figure out a way to be with Mara in Pepperland or wherever.

"Let's do it."

He paid the check.

He's leaving home, bye bye.

TURN MEON DEADMUN, TURN MEON DEADMUN, TURN MEON DEADMUN

Outside, I turned onto the Ninth Street sidewalk and headed for my car. Then I caught myself. "Sorry, I'm going to my...where do you need to go?"

"Right there," he pointed, "that's me right there at the meter."

He pointed to my car, parked in front of the journalism school. Actually, it was my parent's car, a 1961 shit-brown Chevrolet Bel-Air. "No, that's my car," I said, thinking he was confused.

"For now, it's my car too." He walked to the passenger side. Unlocking the door, I apologized for the car's condition. The passenger floor was covered with fast food bags, wadded up gas receipts and a shredded program from *South Pacific* from the last time Mara and I went to the outdoor Muny theatre. "All you do is just drive," my father would have said. "You never take care of the car!" I was guilty of trusting that car maintenance was a father's responsibility. A son's job was to trash it and "just drive."

"You can't clean it out now," Hancock said. "It'd be unnatural. Somebody might think something was up, that you planned this alleged death ahead of time. If your parents have any life insurance on you, they won't collect if there's suspicion of suicide and you don't want that for them."

"No, I guess I don't."

"After you're gone, it'll be harder for your mom or dad to clean it out. They'll realize that even though it's trash, it's *your* trash. But that's the way it's got to be."

I drove south on Ninth, around the block back to Broadway and west to Providence Road and the Interstate. "You better get some gas. You might leave them a trashmobile, but it wouldn't be polite to leave them with an empty tank." With my eight-gallon fillup, I was entitled to a free car wash. "Go ahead," he said, "that'd be a nice touch."

As we turned onto Interstate 70, I realized that even after our conversation, I still didn't know his real name. "You know, with all due paranoia now that you're sitting in my car, I still don't know what to call you."

"What do you call Mara's parents?"

"Pardon me?"

"What do you call Mara's parents? You see them a couple of times a week, you seem to get along with them, they seem to like you. What name do you use when you need to ask them a question or refer to them in conversation?"

"Truth?"

"Truth."

"I don't call them anything. I just say..."

"You say 'your Mom' this or 'your Dad' that, right? If you're talking to them directly, you don't call them anything at all."

"Yeah, but how did..."

"I heard it on the phone tap. Their names are Jerry and Pauline, but you never use their names, you never call them by name. Even though they've told you to call them by name, you just refer to them ambiguously, you work your way around calling them anything. But the amazing thing is that it was exactly the same when I was dating my wife. It's normal for a kid your age. It's a guy thing." I wondered if this was part of the psychological profile or just chitchat. "I just asked to find out whether I was a weird kid or not when I was dating, that's all."

"You're definitely a weird adult."

"Thank you."

"Now tell me," I said, "what do I call you?"

"Call me whatever you call them." He made me smile.

I wasn't at all nervous. His ease and casual attitude gave me a sense of calm and out of sheer innocence—or maybe total stupidity—I believed everything would be all right. Even though I probably had lots to worry about and should have asked a million questions, we didn't talk much. The car was filled with blatant dead air.

Finally, at about Wentzville, thirty-five miles west of St. Louis, I couldn't wait to ask the question I'd wanted to ask for a long time. Sheepishly, I asked, "how do I die?"

"HOLY FUCK!!!" he exploded. "You are a genuine, absolute piece of fucking number one A-plus work! I can't believe it took you this long!" He laughed long and looked genuinely amused. "You take some stranger in the car, believe every bit of bullshit he gives you about how he's gonna arrange for some fake death and it takes you two hours to ask what he's got in mind!" He shook his head. "You're all a piece of work! Every goddam one of you, a real piece of fucking work. You'll believe anything! It's like religion, anything on faith, aaaaaaaaaany damn thing on faith! You're a fucking real piece of fucking work, my friend, and that is the fucking truth."

Nothing is real.

Maybe it was my upbringing as the son of Holocaust-survivor parents that kept me from asking the hard questions, which could also be a problem in journalism school sometimes. Consciously or unconsciously, my parents always taught me not to attract attention to yourself, lest you be noticed—which is, of course, the whole point of behaviors that attract attention to yourself. The consequences of others knowing who you were and where you were was all part of their wartime background. J-School tried to teach me to dare to ask the hard questions and expect answers, but still it was difficult for me. Maybe it was a built-in, genetic survival mechanism. Maybe it was why my father kept telling me I wasn't supposed to grow my hair long or "look like a Biddle."

Maybe that was why I grew my hair long.

Maybe that was why I loved radio, it was an attention-grabber, even though I never saw the people whose attention I grabbed—and maybe I didn't want to. There's probably a shrink somewhere who could make a case against me for craving the attention of strangers that radio brought, but used a fake name on the air when I did it.

But all that's another aside. In my middle age I have developed a preference for the scenic route of tangents to a straight course of conversation.

"Where's your camera gear?"

"I thought you didn't need a photographer."

"Just answer the damn question."

"It's in my room at home."

"Then head that direction."

"And then what?"

"Then you'll find out what you need to know when you need to know it." He read my face. "Look, there are so many opportunities for you to back out, so many chances we'll back out on you, I can't say much until you need to know. It's policy."

"Okay. I can handle that. Fair enough, I guess."

"Good. Let's start with the camera. Tell your parents you've got a photography job, they'll like you making a couple of extra bucks."

"You're right about that, they...okay. Then what?"

"Then come back to the car and you'll find out the next thing you need to know. But before we get to the house, stop at the supermarket at the corner of Hanley and Olive. Once we're there, I'll tell you what to do next."

In the store parking lot, Hancock stiffened his legs and pushed his torso up so his body went straight in the seat. "I've got a present for you." He reached deep into his pants pocket and pulled out a Marlboro box. "Put this in your shirt pocket, and for God's sake, don't smoke what's in there. In fact, give me your cigarettes." Taking the cigarette box he offered, I took an identical box from my pocket and handed it to him. "Can you go ten minutes without a cigarette while you get your camera stuff?" Twisting my face to his scolding, I said, "Yes, I can go ten minutes without a cigarette" in a taunting, childish voice. In truth, I never smoked in my parent's house, naively believing they didn't know I smoked at all. At home, I hid my cigarettes and only smoked away from the house, never thinking they could smell it on my body or breath or when they got into their car.

Smoking is a habit of which I am not proud. I am not proud I still smoke a box of Marlboros every day. There is a Marlboro from a box burning in the ashtray next to my computer right now. The only time I ever quit smoking was during the first days in Pepperland when I was so preoccupied with what was happening around me that I managed to distract myself enough not to feel the urge any more.

But John Lennon had trouble giving up tobacco cigarettes, even in The Onion, and he wasn't the only one. So the Yellow Submarine delivered cigarettes in huge quantities. In The Onion, I switched from Marlboros to *Gauloises Bleues* because that was what John smoked and was the only brand delivered to the Dome. Besides, there was plenty of non-tobacco smoke inside the Pepperland dome.

"This is a transmitter," Hancock said as he handed me his Marlboro box. He opened the lid to reveal a mumbojumbo of small electronics. "The microphone is here on top, in the last 'o' of Marlboro." The usually-red center of the final o was black, the exposed top of the tiny microphone. "I have to monitor you when you go inside." I nodded, absorbing everything he said. "I have to be sure you don't spill the beans, that you don't tell your parents anything. Say anything about this and the deal's off."

"Sorry Mom and Dad, I'm in a rush because I've got to die now and go live with the Biddles in an Octopus's Garden in the ocean. Don't bother waiting up!"

"Very funny."

"And in your case, I also have to listen to make sure you don't call Mara."

I came back to reality quickly. He knew resisting the urge to call Mara would be the hardest part for me, even harder than the prospect of "dying." It hurt me to be unable to share what was happening and the excitement I felt. We shared everything. I would have explained everything to her if I could, the excitement, the quest, how I hoped I would be able to send for her in Pepperland. How could they refuse a request like that, whoever "they" were?

I would explain it all to her right now if I could. I would start by saying "hi" and asking her if she still wears Chanel Number Five.

"Okay," I said, "I won't call anybody." I meant it.

We drove toward my parent's house. At the corner of Midland and Tulane (many of the east/west streets in University City are named after colleges, makes sense, no?), he told me to stop the car. He got out. "Don't screw up," he said as he held the door open, "or I'll be as scarce as hippies at the White House and no matter who you tell you'll never prove anything." He slammed the door and got into a new Pontiac parked along Tulane. It was a car that never would have stood out from any others on the street.

I drove home.

The front door of the house was unlocked, as it almost always was. My mother called to me the instant I hit the front door. "How was Columbia? How was the drive?"

"Fine. Everything was fine."

"The car was okay?"

"The car was fine." I yelled back with pride as I headed toward my bedroom, "I even washed it."

"You did?" She sounded surprised. "Did you clean our your trash?"

"No."

"You should have cleaned the trash. Your father hates the way you just drive."

"IknowIknowIknow…"

"Dinner's almost ready. You want soup? You want fish? We're gonna have soup and gefilte fish. I'll get you soup and gefilte fish if you want. I've got chicken from last night…"

"No Mom, don't get anything for me. I'm not hungry. I ate in Columbia."

"You shouldn't eat in restaurants. You should eat at home."

I could see my father napping in his chair in front of the television.

"No thanks, Mom. I gotta go to work."

"It's Saturday. There's no work today. Have dinner."

Other than overfeeding me, my mother's main job was running my life. The smallest details were not immune. Even as a college man, I always felt her constant babying, never giving me credit for age, brains or sense. Now, years later, of course my strongest feelings about those times confirm that she was expressing her love, concern and caring instead of smothering mothering. I wonder now if I had met Hancock while living away from home during the school year if I would have given more thought to chucking it all for an unknown destination. But because we connected during the summer while I felt constant overbearing parenting, I wonder if my decision to go was colored by my desire to untie myself from home. I leave that to the shrinks.

Because our conversation in the house was being monitored, I chose my words carefully. "I ran into a guy I used to know. He needs a photographer. For money. So I've gotta get my camera stuff and go."

"For money? That's wonderful! How much?"

"A hundred dollars! I can't pass it up."

"For a hundred dollars you better hurry. Dress nice for a hundred dollars, like a professional."

"I will! I will!"

"When will you be home?"

I choked at the question, felt a shot of adrenalin and stopped dead—no pun intended—in my tracks. It was hard to answer. "I don't know." And then, after a beat, I added "don't wait up." Despite my instant and instinctive and perfectly normal post-adolescent resentment of her perfectly natural parental questions, I turned from her as a tear ran down my cheek at my "don't wait up" reply. It hurt to lie to her that way, but I did.

"What are you taking pictures of for a hundred dollars?"

Sucking up the emotion, I answered "his girlfriend."

"She must be pretty for a hundred dollars."

"That includes the prints. I've got to give him a bunch of prints, too."

"You're not going to eat?"

"No thanks."

"You have to eat."

"I caaaaaaaaaaaaaaaaaaan't, Mom! I gotta go. I gotta go!"

"Where are you going?"

"I'm not sure. We're gonna find someplace nice to take pictures, probably somewhere in Forest Park."

"Okay," she sighed, "just be careful." She always told me to be careful, as if the one time she forgot I'd be careless. "Be careful in Forest Park."

"I will. I'll be careful."

I collected my equipment, all thrown together into a fake leather camera bag. Not knowing where I was going, short or long term, I didn't know what to wear. I leaned over and whispered into the top of the Marlboro box in my pocket, thoroughly expecting an answer. "Hello? Hello?" No answer came from the box in my pocket.

I changed out of the jeans and madras shirt I'd worn since morning and put on the straight-arrow, frat rat uniform: blue blazer, blue Oxford-cloth shirt, striped tie, gray slacks and cordovan Bass Weejun penny loafers. If Hancock took me someplace very fancy schmancy, I wouldn't be underdressed and if we went someplace casual I could always take off the tie and jacket. I wondered whether to take anything else. I thought about cramming a fresh shirt, jeans and clean underwear into my camera bag. My mother would be happy if she knew I at least took clean underwear into forever.

But Hancock didn't tell me to bring anything, so I threw my camera bag over my shoulder and started to the front door. I hid the cigarette box in the inside jacket pocket as I left my room.

Turning slowly at the front door, I turned toward the kitchen. "I'm gone." The remark was habit, what I always said when I left the house.

"Will you see Mara tonight?" my mother shouted from the kitchen. "She called you on the phone. We had a nice talk. She wants you to call her. You should call."

"Yeah, I'll try to call her later." I didn't know what else to say. And it was the truth.

Before I walked out the door, I stopped for a very short instant, not wanting to make a big production of leaving and not knowing when I would return. I saw my father snoring in his chair, my mother stirring soup. My parents had, indeed, struggled hard all their lives to get by. They never did anything that was wrong. "I'm gone," I told my mother, what I always repeated when I left the house.

And she repeated what she always repeated when I left the house. "Just be careful."

I whispered it one more time as I walked out the door, not turning back to look again. "I'm gone."

AND IN THE END...

I threw my camera bag into the front seat of the trashmobile and got in. Turning the key, I realized the only instructions I had were to get my camera stuff.

Instantly, the Pontiac drove past and slowed. Without looking at me, Hancock sped up as I backed out into the street. I kept my eyes on his car, not wanting to either lose sight of him and, mostly, not wanting to look back.

We turned right off Delmar onto Skinker, a street name that still makes me smile because it sounds so goofy.

Skinker.

He turned left into Forest Park, a huge expanse of green on the western edge of St. Louis city. He stopped near the golf course and got out of the car, motioning for me to stay in my car. "We're going to the river," he said through my open window. "You know the way?"

"Yes."

"You go first then. If I lose you, park on the levee by the arch and wait. Don't get out of the car, don't talk to anybody, don't do anything but wait. That's it. Nothing else."

"Okay."

"Then roll on out of here. I'll be right behind you."

Again, I wish I could write that I thought of a million clever things or, to the other extreme, that I watched the scenery pass with a gnawing fear of never seeing it again. But again and in complete honesty, I can't say that. I was numb. My mind was blank except for "river," "levee" and "stay in the car." I listened to KXOK radio (it was the station that introduced the Beatles to St. Louis. In fact, KXOK disc jockey Nick Charles was the M.C. for the Beatles' concert at Busch Stadium). Whichever jock was on the air was playing a cover of Joni Mitchell's *Big Yellow Taxi* by a one-hit-wonder group called The Neighborhood, a song I'd heard at the station the month before in Columbia. It was a record I would have put on the KMZU playlist if we were on the air. KXOK called it "hitbound," which meant it wasn't confident enough to make it a true "Pick Hit."

I was too stupid and my mind was too filled with other things to recognize the timely significance of the chorus of the song:

Don't it always seem to go
That you don't know what you've got
'til it's gone?

Or the irony of the near-to-last line:

Late last night I heard the screen door slam,
And a big yellow taxi took away my old man.

(The Neighborhood cover sang it as "*our* old man"). I wasn't in a taxi and to me, at that moment, it was just a cute, fun, pro-clean-earth song. It wasn't until years later that I realized whatever timely significance the "took away my old man" lyrics might have held for that particular moment—if there was truly any significance whatsoever.

Nervously singing along, I was embarrassed when I remembered I still carried the Marlboro box transmitter in my pocket. Tilting my head down, I asked the box "did you like that?" Then I suddenly launched into a high-energy, overly inflated, incredibly sarcastic "Ron Radio" pitch. "That's The Neighborhood on the Great 58 and I'm the late, great Jeff Scott. I'll be taking requests as long as I'm alive, so call that request line fast!"

Very self-satisfied, I smiled and drove on. I tapped my finger on the final o on the top of the Marlboro box about a dozen times. "I hope that didn't hurt your ears!" Of course I hoped it did hurt Hancock's ears just to give me some sort of odd revenge on him for putting me into this difficult situation. I knew Hancock wasn't the one who put me in the situation, I knew that I did it myself.

The butterflies returned when I caught first sight of the Gateway Arch. It stood at the riverfront, only a hundred yards from the rivers-edge levee. For all practical purposes, the arch was my destination. Still, I knew I was closing in on something other than the arch.

Pulling into the riverfront levee parking area, I gave a man inside a glass booth a dollar and he waved me on to a parking spot. I pulled in a waited. I rolled down my window and sat unmoving in my seat, afraid to get out of the car lest I violate the rules. I watched the murky river roll by.

Suddenly, my car started bouncing violently up and down. The jolt scared me. My head darted left to right, trying to discover what else was rocking. I expected to see the Arch itself tumble down from the massive force of the obvious, inevitable "big one." The New Madrid Fault had finally snapped. The unexpected changes in my life weren't the only seismic event of the day.

My head thrashing in every direction, prepared to watch the skyline crumble, I finally caught Hancock with his foot on my rear bumper, his entire body bouncing up and down. He laughed at my panic and surprise.

Schmuck.

Muffled through the closed window, I could hear him say "let's go." Unthinking, I started to get out of the car empty handed. "Bring your camera," he said, pointing to the bag on the front seat.

Walking along the cobblestoned riverfront, he turned to me. "I think it's neat down here, a lotta history. 'Ole Man River, she just keeps rollin' along!' I've seen pictures of steamboats lined up here as solid as Michigan Avenue at rush hour, side by side, all the way down the shore. Have you ever seen those pictures?"

"Sure. In the museum below the Arch."

"Bingo, bango, bongo! That's where I saw 'em too! One of the first days I was in town I did some tourist things. That stuff is interesting to me, real Americana shit."

We walked north for a few hundred feet along the levee in the long shadow of the Arch, and then he stopped. "We're going to the *Admiral*. I want you to hang that camera around your neck and make yourself obvious."

"I can do that."

The *Admiral* was a huge, beautiful, "streamlined" aluminum boat that always seemed to have cruised the Mississippi since just before Pierre Laclede landed and made the first St. Louis settlement. For all I knew, Laclede may have arrived on the *Admiral* itself. Every picture postcard ever sold in St. Louis was a shot of the Arch with the *Admiral* steaming past on the river below.

At one time or another, everyone rode the *Admiral* for proms, anniversaries, birthdays or just a Sunday afternoon or Saturday night entertainment. There was "big band" music on the lower deck for the old fogies and a rock band upstairs for "the kids." No matter how hokey or old fashioned those cruises sound now, it was always a fun ride, a genuine family thing or the kind of date destination people complain is lacking today. Maybe the *Admiral* was the first floating theme park in America.

The *Admiral* is genuinely dead now.

"Okay, I can do that."

"Be obnoxious."

"That I can definitely do."

"Use your flash so people notice you."

"Okay."

"Have you got a couple of bucks for a ticket?"

"No."

"Bingo bango bongo. You are a piece of work, a reeeeeeeeeeeeeeeeeeeal piece of work." He pulled a five-dollar bill from his pocket. "Here. Go crazy."

"Thanks."

"And by the way…"

"What?"

"I'll trade you these for mine." He held out my box of genuine Marlboros. I took it and handed him his electronic one. "The singing was cute by the way, but don't expect to make a career out of it."

Putting my cigarettes and his money into my pockets, I started up the gangplank. Halfway up, I turned to ask him what he wanted me to photograph, but he wasn't there.

I boarded the boat.

...THE LOVE YOU TAKE...

I was Gilligan.

Like the *S.S. Minnow*, the *Admiral* was scheduled for "a three hour tour, a three hour tour." We departed at eight o'clock and would return to the pier below the Arch at eleven. The boat would cruise ten miles downstream, then turn around and fight the current back to the dock. It was a pleasant ride, just long enough for cruisers to have a few drinks, a snack, dance and still have some time left to sit in a deck chair and watch the scenery go past—Illinois on the east side of the boat, Missouri on the west.

But while Gilligan was unaware he would shipwreck, I knew something would happen on my cruise. And like Gilligan, I didn't know if, when or how I would be rescued from my uncertain fate.

I wandered the first deck, taking pictures of dancers and table-sitters, even shooting details of the boat's art-deco details and architecture, a style I've only seen executed as well in Rockefeller Center in New York. But it was hard to concentrate on photography. Even though my camera was focused, my brain was not.

After a few minutes wait, the boat's horn announced we were about to depart.

Seeing couples filling the dance floor put me into a funk, knowing I would rather be there with Mara than with uncertainty. I took more pictures, wide-angle shots of the dance floor at first, then putting on the telephoto for shots of some pretty girls.

After a half-hour of wandering and picture taking, I used Hancock's money to buy a soda and a box of popcorn from a snack bar. I sat down at a table alone.

It was a long day. My feet hurt.

I felt the same emotions I did back at O'Hare, anticipating that something might happen but also feeling the anticipation, fear and unease of not knowing what it might be. Anyone could give me the tap on the shoulder. Based on the O'Hare experience, though, I thought maybe nothing would happen and that it was possible that two months later another stranger would compliment me on the good job I did on the *Admiral* when I didn't know I was doing any kind of job at all.

A waiter asked me if I wanted anything. I told him no.

I listened to the band—no Beatles tunes—and watched the couples. I looked for another "couple" like the one in Chicago whose eyes I could catch and who wouldn't be afraid to hold my gaze, maybe even the exact same two people from the bar at O'Hare. I wished for a nametag or Beatle album I could hold to identify myself to anybody who wanted to know who I was. I wanted to scream "Hey! I'm the guy with the clues! Hancock sent me!" I kept quiet and to myself.

Nothing happened. Nothing was very real.

A girl about my age left the dance floor and sat down at my table. She wore bell-bottom jeans, sandals and a loose fitting, linen "peasant blouse" with embroidery across the top front. She was sweating in a very peasant-like way. Was she the one? She looked the part. "Shit it's hot," she said, looking at me so directly there was no mistake she was talking to me. Even though the *Admiral* was air-conditioned, the summer heat, the tight pack of bodies and the exuberance of the dancers made it easy to sweat. Even though I hadn't danced even once, the idea of talking to a strange woman—under any circumstances, much less these—made my pits drip. I figured she wasn't "the one." She was just a kid like me.

"Yeah, it's hot."

"I saw you taking pictures. Do you work for the boat?"

"No, I just take pictures for myself."

"Oh."

Maybe the main reason I found it so easy to establish a relationship with Mara was that she was so easy to talk with. Her manner, her smile, everything about her was non-intimidating. Most girls scared the hell out of me. Kathy Powell certainly did. Until I had the Beatles to talk to Kathy about, I never knew what to say or do around her. Or most other girls for that matter.

This was another time of big intimidation. It should have been the perfect opportunity to hit up on an attractive girl who had obviously made a conscientious effort to sit at my table next to me. But even if my mind had not been preoccupied with other matters, I still wouldn't have known what to say. "Where do you go to school?" she asked.

"Missouri."

"You in photography school?"

"I'm in journalism school, but I'm not in photo, I'm in radio and TV."

"That's neat. What do you want to do?"

"I don't know. Radio probably. That's what I do now, I'm on radio."

"That's neat."

Then she hit me with the ultimate St. Louis question: "Where'd you go to high school?" For some reason this was the quintessential, definitive question for all St. Louisans, an instant socioeconomic profile of your life. Her asking it convinced me she was just a kid like me.

"U-City."

"Oh yeah? Do you know Bob Rothbaum? He graduated about five years ago."

"No, I don't think I know him."

"Oh."

"But it's a big school, everybody can't know everybody."

She waited for me to ask her where she went to school—I would have guessed one of the snootier Catholic high schools and then maybe St. Louis University—but I never asked and the unfairness obviously upset her. "Nice talking to you," she said as she disappeared back onto the dance floor.

"Yeah, nice talking to you too," I said to no one in particular.

If she was the secret person I was to meet, she was good at keeping the secret. I was glad I didn't ask her about her school.

During the last half-hour of an *Admiral* cruise, passengers usually started to wind down. Tired, hot and feeling their cocktails, most usually savored the final leg of the trip, the end of a voyage on the river with no telephones, no demands, no expectations except having fun.

I reloaded my camera with my last 36-exposure roll of Tri-X and made some shots of the few people who were still dancing, popping my strobe with each one, trying to be obnoxiously obvious exactly per Hancock's instructions.

With only about twenty minutes left on the cruise, I still had made no contact with anyone except the hippie girl whose father probably had enough money to keep her impoverished-looking in expensive "peasant" blouses for a long time. I found an overstuffed, upholstered chair and collapsed into it.

The waiter passed by and asked again if he could bring me anything. Again, I thanked him and told him no.

"How 'bout another soda, Jeff?"

"No thanks, I don't think I want…"

He called me by name.

"Nothing?" he said, "okay. Maybe I can do something for you later." He headed through a pair of swinging doors into the kitchen.

As he left, he tilted his head toward the door to the deck outside. The tilt was so slight I wasn't sure it was a message or even that it was directed at me. I wondered if it was maybe just a tilt of his head and nothing more. But I couldn't discount anything that might be a sign.

I waited a minute, then went out to the deck. It was dark.

Except for a couple making out hot and heavy a few feet away, I was alone.

I stood at the rail for a minute. Then five minutes. Then ten.

Finally, in the darkness near the rear of the boat, I saw a cigarette glowing. The faint tip of the cigarette and the spots of light coming out through the portholes were just enough to illuminate someone in a white jacket. I strolled toward the stern.

The waiter was there.

He held out a box of cigarettes. "Marlboro?"

"No thanks, I've got some."

"They're real. No electronics."

"Yeah. But no thanks."

"Do you want to try for the fifth plateau?"

He asked the question exactly the way the original phone caller asked his to Beth and exactly as Hancock asked me about the third and fourth plateaus.

"Who are you?"

"Hancock. Charles Puckett Han…"

"Shiiiiiiiiiiiiiiiiiiiiiiiiiiiiiiiiiiit. All you guys are goddam comedians."

He smiled and flicked his cigarette overboard. "Splash! One little, skinny butt goes into Old Man River, lost forever in the in the deep, dark water where nobody will ever find it."

"Yeah, sure. Whatever you say."

"Someday soon," he said, "you'll think that's a very funny line." Unable to comprehend the present, much less "someday," I didn't understand any funny or literary references. "Ooooooookaaaaaaaaaaaay. If you're ready, let's get goin.'"

...IS EQUAL TO THE LOVE YOU MAKE

"Follow me." Within sight of the Arch, he led me down some dark back stairs near the back of the boat. In all the times I'd been aboard the *Admiral*, I'd never noticed this stairway. Obviously, because it was so narrow and uncomfortable, these stairs were for crew and working people, not for paying passengers who expected art deco luxury.

We went through a narrow hallway below decks, weaving left and right, following an overhead grid of pipes and tubes. It all smelled of diesel fuel.

He opened a door marked "Engine Room—authorized personnel only."

Charles Puckett Hancock, the third—the second—turned to me. "I haven't waited tables here for a month for nothing. Well, I've worked here for minimum wage plus tips while my regular Company pay came in so it's not such a bad deal, but I've also worked here to find you a hiding place and this is the best one aboard."

I didn't care whether he moonlighted on the CIA or not.

"Come on, come on. Follow me." He hurried on toward what had to be the farthest, most obscure corner of the boat. "Duck." He raised his hand to pound on what had to be asbestos-coated pipes running overhead. After running the pipe tunnel, I crouched to avoid a forty-foot metal shaft that worked back and forth, back and forth. It was the shaft that drove the side paddle wheels of the boat, the wheels that powered the *Admiral* through the water. "Now sit your ass down and don't move until somebody comes for you."

I sat.

"Give me your camera bag."

I gave.

He looked at me scornfully, jabbing his finger toward my face. "Just wait here. And remember that if anybody finds you, you stop being Mister Plateau and you're just a guy weird enough to stow away on a cruise boat that doesn't go anywhere. Then our relationship is over."

"Okay!" I would do whatever I was told by anybody who told me to do anything.

"And whatever you do, whatever happens, keep your ass right here."

"Okay."

"Don't move."

"Okay."

"If Jesus Christ stands at the top of those stairs and calls your name personally and promises your Heavenly rewards, you keep your ass right here."

"Okay."

I was scared shitless.

"Have I made myself clear on this? You stay right here, understand?"

"Yes."

He crouched back under the shaft, ducked under the pipes and disappeared.

I was sitting still but felt I had run a mile. What was happening? What was I doing? Whatever it was, it definitely and deeply involved me—sweet, innocent, never-do-anything-like-this me. I still wondered why I was doing it. How could something as innocuous as being on a little campus rock and roll radio station have led to this? I suddenly became angry with Larry Goldberg for leading me to the radio station in the first place. He was probably spending his summer working for his father, preparing for a life that provided so much security that his biggest fear would be that his father would finally give him some responsibility. I suspected that someday he would tell his children incredible tales about what a wildass disc jockey he was because he played rock and roll records on the radio. I never tell my children anything about the radio, but that's another aside.

Sitting there in the engine room, I thought about the first time I went to the radio station with Larry, how I thought being on the radio was such a fantastic act of trust and how impressed I was that he sat there pumping it out with only the faintest hope anyone was listening. That was faith, I thought then, absolute blind faith. It was the essence of the beauty and magic of radio, talking to unseen people who might or might not have been paying even the slightest attention to someone they couldn't see either. I knew that sometimes there was no connection and the radio was just background noise. But I also knew that sometimes there was also a real connection between the unseen and the unseen, because of the music or the words or the mood.

The engine room of the *Admiral* did not feel like magic or the beauty of radio.

The engine room experience was either absolutely blind faith or total foolishness and probably one of those rare times when the two were one.

Where was Mark? I wanted to go through this with Mark. No one ever mentioned Mark.

Despite my anger and fear, I sat in a ball quietly on the floor in a corner, knees bent, arms wrapped around my legs. I loosened my necktie.

My watch said it was 10:45 p.m.

It had been a very long day. I was hungry, wishing I had accepted my mother's offer of soup and gefilte fish. But eating could wait, I thought, there were other things between my next meal and me. Like death.

Suddenly, a startling noise hit my ears. I jumped, at least as high as I could while sitting curled up on my ass.

It was a klaxon horn echoing piercingly off the metal floors and walls. I didn't know what it meant, only that it was loud and scary. As far as I knew, the noise meant we had hit an iceberg and had to man the lifeboats before the boat sank into the deep. My natural instinct was to run, to find my way out of the below decks hole to fresh air and the clear night. But I sat tight.

It was the "man overboard" signal.

Later, the pilot of the plane that flew the fifth plateau told what the horn meant after I breathlessly described the sound. "It sounded like 'OOOOOO, OOOOOO, OOOOOO, OOOOOO!' And it…"

"Are you sure it wasn't 'aHOOOOO, aHOOOOO, aHOOOOO?' And then it went "MMMMMM, MMMMMM, MMMMMM?' And then it would have sounded like 'aWEEGA, aWEEGA, aWEEGA!?'"

"Oh no!" I insisted, it was definitely 'OOOOOO, OOOOOO, OOOOOO!' And then it…"

He laughed as he flew the plane, looking back and forth from his instruments to his co-pilot, both near tears from laughter. "You fucking people are really something," he laughed, "you know that? You're really something!"

Embarrassed, I wanted to tell him that we aren't "something," we are "a real piece of work." But I knew I had been put in my place and didn't say anything more.

I found out later that the *Admiral* Captain sounded the "man overboard" signal at the insistence of a waiter. Then the captain radioed the Coast Guard.

Most of the crew and as many curious passengers as could pack the rail stood and stared down into the water while the captain throttled the engines down to remain stationary against the upstream current, then watched as the boat drifted slowly downriver with the current, then pushed back upstream again. It was a "search" maneuver. The entire lost person hooha was an unexpected spectacle for the passengers, a free bonus to their evening of entertainment. After taking inventory of their own families and friends to assure everyone in their party was accounted for, the ghoulish spectacle of looking for the lost guy became almost as exciting as a Cardinals baseball game during a pennant race.

Quickly, someone found my camera bag on the deck next to the rail. It held the telephoto and normal lenses, but no camera, no strobe and no wide-angle lens. Those were still hanging around my neck in the engine room.

The microfilmed *Post-Dispatch* article I found just a few years ago quoted "an unidentified young woman" who said the person over the rail "must have been a guy I talked to. He was majoring in photography at Missouri." The article didn't mention my name because I was not officially identified pending notification of next of kin, nor did it correct the error of my college major. It made me even happier that I had not given her the satisfaction of telling me what high school she went to, the idiot.

From below, I could hear it all, from the initial horn to sirens of the St. Louis Fire Department rescue boat, the sound of the *Admiral* ultimately docking and the footfalls of passengers disembarking. Even the sounds I couldn't identify made the whole brouhaha sound exciting. In truth, if I had known what it was, I would have been one of the passengers at the rail, pityingly but ghoulishly looking for some guy in the drink.

Nothing is real.

But it was all over my head, literally and figuratively.

I didn't move.

Contrary to what the waiter had offered, Jesus Christ did not appear and no Heavenly rewards were promised.

When the engines finally shut down, I listened to more muffled activity for about an hour. The St. Louis Fire Department rescue boat rolled through with siren blaring. Another boat with very loud engines cruised past several times—it must have been the local Coast Guard cutter cruising the Mississippi—looking for me.

Then it all settled down. Obviously, all gave up the search quickly, unable to find anything in the wide, dark, fast expanse of river at the Arch or downstream.

And then the *Admiral* got quiet too.

I took off my jacket, folding it inside-out to keep it clean, and draped it across my bent legs. I put my head on my jacket and knees. My watch said it was 1 a.m.

Not even realizing I was asleep, a flashlight beam with the power of the sun startled me. "Wake up kid, it's time." I hesitated getting up. "Come on, kid, you gotta go!" Shielding my eyes with my hands, I adjusted my glasses and looked at my watch. It was 3 o'clock. A hand reached down and grabbed my shirtsleeve, yanking and pulling at me. "We gotta get outa here now!"

I arose, stiff from sitting so long in a corner, knees bent to my chin. A deckhand wearing bib overalls, a work shirt and bright red reflective vest led me back along the same path I followed to get to my corner. We walked quickly, my camera and flash banging into my chest as I ducked to avoid the pipes above. I hurried to stay close.

Once we were up on the deck, I could see the boat was dark and abandoned. I had always seen the *Admiral* as loud and active and its silence was captivating. The deckhand grabbed my sleeve again and pulled. "Let's gooooooooooooooo!"

He led me down the gangplank and shoved me into the back seat of the Pontiac, putting his hand on my head and pushing it down so it didn't bump on the doorway, the same way a policeman would put a prisoner into a squad car.

"Kid," the deckhand said, slamming the door, "you just passed the fourth plateau."

NEWSPAPER TAXIS APPEAR ON THE SHORE WAITING TO TAKE YOU AWAY CLIMB IN THE BACK WITH YOUR HEAD IN THE CLOUDS AND YOU'RE GONE

The car moved out as soon as the door was closed, bouncing violently over the levee cobblestones. My body shook from the vibration, my eyes blurred in their sockets from the pulsing of the stones. All I could make out clearly were the two people in the front seats, both ostensibly named Charles Puckett Hancock, the Third. One Hancock, late of the *Admiral* waiter staff, drove. The other Hancock, the one who so enjoyed watching the behinds of pizza joint waitresses, was in the passenger seat.

"W-w-w-w-w-w-w-w-w-w-w-w-where are we g-g-g-g-g-g-going?"

As we turned south onto the Wharf Street pavement, the first Hancock, the Third, turned around. "Congratulations, Jeff. I didn't think you'd make it this far."

"What's happening?"

"You know, you've cost me a dollar here. I figured you'd try to call Mara or Mark somewhere along the line and that it'd be all over by now."

"What's going on? Where are we going?"

"What's going on is that we're getting the hell away from here." He stopped talking and turned to look forward, then turned back to me. "I don't know how to say this so it's any easier on you, so I'll just say it. About a half-hour ago, a couple of police officers knocked on your parents' door and told them you fell off the boat. The officers told your folks there was a search, that they couldn't find you and that the Coast Guard broadcast an official notice to mariners to be on the lookout for your body in the river. They told your parents that the Coast Guard and fire department will start looking for your body again at first light."

He paused from his brutal description of my death as he turned away, then added a low-key, almost under his breath "sorry."

I felt like total, unadulterated, unpolished, pure, raw shit. I wanted to mourn my own death, but even more I wished I could defend my parents from their obvious pain. And I especially wished I could keep the news and the pain from Mara.

The idea of jumping from the moving car raced through my mind. I thought maybe I could run home and stop it all before it went too far, before it had time to sink in.

The Columbia Hancock spoke first. "Here's the question you've come to know and love: do you want to try for the fifth plateau?"

Grieving me, I neither looked at him nor spoke.

We headed east on the Poplar Street Bridge over the river. I looked down toward the water that had "killed" me but it was too dark to see or feel anything but pure blackness.

He turned back to the other Charles Puckett Hancock. "I may get my dollar back." He turned back to me. "Listen Jeff…look at me!"

I didn't raise my eyes.

"This is the hardest part for everybody. The fun of reading clues on record jackets is all over now and the reality is sinking in. You're still in your own back yard and a million things are running through your mind and you don't know what's going to happen. I know what you're feeling and the only thing I can say is that only you can make this decision. This is one of those places you can back out, just like I told you. Give us the word and we'll take you home or to Mara's or anywhere you want to go. Then it'll be over and nobody's been hurt."

"Nobody's been hurt?" I barked. "Fuck you! Sure as fuck I've hurt my parents! And Mara? Won't she hurt when they tell her, if they haven't told her already? Fuck you! How the fuck do you know what I'm feeling?"

The Hancocks looked at each other as the car reached the end of the Mississippi bridge and swerved south onto the Route 3 exit on the Illinois side of the river.

The driving Hancock answered. "Because we've both been through it."

Before I could ask for an explanation, the other Hancock continued. "This assignment is for keeps, Jeff. This is the assignment of a lifetime for Company guys like us and we couldn't pass it up. You don't take it for the career advancement because once you're Federal Civil Service, that's a done deal. You take an assignment like this because of the challenge and the importance of it, because of the idea of actually doing the job and then finding out what there is to find out. We're here for the same reason as you."

The original Hancock picked up the explanation quickly, as if they'd told this story before and had the timing well-rehearsed. "They told my family I was shot in a gun battle with a terrorist group in the Mideast. My wife and kids had to read days and days of cock-and-bull stories in the newspapers that were all just a cover-up by the Company. The papers called me 'an American businessman.' Then my family buried an empty box. They were told it was sealed, 'government policy.' But that was all part of the plan. I didn't want my family to know anything. I didn't want them to suspect anything. They'll take care of my wife and my kids for the rest of their lives, no matter what happens. They'll be better off than with just my pension, that's part of the deal."

"And I went down in a plane somewhere over the ocean," the other Hancock added. "My parents didn't even get a box to bury."

"Like mine," I sighed.

"Yeah, just like yours. They won't get a box either."

We arrived at Parks Airport, a small civil aviation field just across the river from downtown St. Louis. It was dark and looked closed.

As Hancock Number Two stopped the car near an old hangar, Hancock Number One turned on me again. "I still need a definite answer to the question, Jeff. You're at a critical point here. Do you want to leave the program?" He waited for my response. "Or do you want to try for the fifth plateau?"

"Mara...."

"I'm sorry, Jeff, I need an answer and I need it now. Do you want to try for the fifth plateau?"

I tried to think of all the ramifications of what I had already done, knowing it would be difficult if not impossible to change them. If I backed out and showed up at home, I could never explain what happened, never make my parents understand the impulse that drove me to do such a stupid thing. Mostly, I knew I could never take back the shock and hurt they felt in the hours they thought I was dead.

Sgt. Pepper was the album that changed everything for the Beatles. Indeed, the grave they stood over on the cover symbolized the grave of the "Old Beatles." I had to choose whether to bury the "Old Jeff." But even more, I quickly discovered that *Sgt. Pepper*'s title described that exact moment. This Pepperland business was definitely a club for "lonely hearts."

Staring blankly at the hangar and the idle aircraft on the field around it, I shrugged myself into resignation. I did what I did. I had traveled this far. I wanted to know what would happen next. My stomach fluttered with excitement and fear and possibilities.

"Let's do it."

Faith.

Foolishness.

> **She said, I know what it's like to be dead.**
> **I know what it is to be sad.**
> **And she's makin' me feel like I'd never been born.**

WHAT DO I DO WHEN MY LOVE IS AWAY?
(DOES IT WORRY YOU TO BE ALONE?)
HOW DO YOU FEEL BY THE END OF THE DAY?
ARE YOU SAD BECAUSE YOU'RE ON YOUR OWN?

"If you're ready, Jeff, it's time to move." We got out of the car and both Hancocks walked with me, one on either side. Hancock, The Third—the first—gripped my lower left arm as we walked, prisoner-escort style. I don't know if he held my arm to steer me in the right direction of if he knew I needed the moral and physical support. I appreciated both.

I stopped a few steps from the car. "My jacket! I left my jacket in the car!"

"You won't need it."

"But I want it!" I twisted myself free from his grasp and ran back to the car. The jacket was familiar. It was comfortable. It was mine. "Great. Fine," he conceded. "You want your jacket, have your jacket." I hugged the blazer to my chest like a baby holds a security blanket.

He grabbed my arm again and we crossed the tarmac toward a dark Lear jet. By the light of one solitary bulb outside the hangar I could see the stairs were down on the jet. The Hancocks walked me up three steps to board the plane.

The cabin of the plane was dark. I could see subtle red lights illuminating the instruments in the cockpit. Up front, two pilots used flashlights to see clipboards filled with papers. Both wore casual clothes, not suits. I could hear airplane radio squawking from a speaker somewhere in the cockpit. I didn't understand a word of it.

We stopped at the open cockpit curtains. "Guys, this is Jeff." One pilot, the older one—the one who would later make fun of my ignorance of the subtle nuance of klaxon horns—turned and shook my hand firmly.

"Glad to have you aboard, Jeff. If you don't mind flyin' with us, we won't complain about takin' you where you need to go. Just keep the screamin' down to a manageable level and we'll get along just fine.

"By the way, and I'm sorry I have to ask..." I dreaded yet another plateau question. "You don't happen to know how to fly one of these motherfuckers, do ya?" I managed a small smile, maybe even a chuckle. His greeting was a friendly, amusing and an appropriate mood-changer in the midst of bedlam.

The younger pilot didn't speak at all. He just raised his hand and gave me a finger-wiggle without ever turning around.

Then the introductions were reversed. "And Jeff, these two gentlemen—and I use the term loosely—are your pilots, Charles and Puckett." The Hancocks both laughed, but I didn't smile at their joke. This time, the joke was more an insult than repartee.

The Columbia Hancock asked one of the pilots for a flashlight and he showed me to a seat. The other Hancock stayed up front, leaning against the door. "These guys will take good care of you," Hancock said as I collapsed into the first seat behind the pilots, "and we'll tidy up back home. They know their stuff. You don't have to worry about a thing."

The gregarious pilot turned back to Hancock. "You didn't tell him the FAA revoked our licenses and this was the only work we could get, did ya?"

"He doesn't need that now."

Hancock shook my hand. "Good luck, my friend. Have a safe trip."

The other Hancock came to me, shook my hand and said goodbye.

Then the first Hancock spoke again. "There's one more thing, Jeff. I need your film and your wallet."

"The roll's not done!" It still amazes me that the photographer's instinct still hit me at that exact moment. "There's still got ten or twelve exposures!"

"I promise we'll replace it. I've just got to make sure you don't take any pictures along the way." I rewound the film into the cassette, opened the camera and gave him the film. "Thanks. Do you have any more?"

I remembered the roll that was in the camera when the photo assignment on the *Admiral* began. I took it from my jacket pocket. "This one isn't entirely yours. Do you want it too?"

"Yes. Thank you. And your wallet please."

It was easier to hand over my wallet than my film. I was more protective of my photography than my identity. There was nothing in the wallet, no money, just my driver's license and a picture of..."Wait! I want Mara's picture!"

"Sorry. Somebody might wonder why it's missing." Again, I was hurt and confused by the sacrifice my decision required me to make.

A short time after I arrived in Pepperland, the supply sub brought me an unexpected package. It was my pictures. Included in the stack of glossy prints were shots of dancers aboard the *Admiral*—including the girl in the peasant blouse—and several shots of Mara baking a cake in her parent's kitchen. After staring at them, I realized it hurt to have them. I quietly took them to the trash and watched them eject out of The Onion into the sea. I still don't regret that decision.

After the Hancocks got off the plane, the silent co-pilot came back, pulled up the stairs and locked the door. I watched the Hancocks get into the Pontiac. They sat in the car, apparently waiting for us to take off. "Jeff, you ready?" the older pilot yelled.

"I guess so." My answer was soft-spoken and confused.

I started to mutter that I didn't know what I was ready for, but the pilot shouted again. "I have to ask you, Jeff. Do you want to try for the fifth plateau?"

"I already said yes!" That time, my answer was impatient and angry.

"Sorry, son, but we gotta ask every time. It's policy. If that's what you say, then we'll get on with it. Buckle 'em up!" Quickly the engines revved and after a few moments warm-up we moved out at what seemed like a very high rate of speed.

The airfield was dark. Only the moon and a bright spotlight on the front of the plane guided us. "How can you see?" I yelled.

"Wait a minute! Wait 'til we're at the end of the runway!"

Dark taxiways rolled past quickly as the plane made such fast turns I leaned left or right from the inertia. "Watch this!" the older pilot yelled back. "Look out the front!" I sat straight up in my seat, craning my neck as best I could to look out over the high instrument panel in the cockpit. "Unbuckle your seat belt and stand up for a sec!" I did. "We put the radio on the right frequency, hit the microphone key twice, cross our fingers and it's magic time!" White lights instantly lit both sides of the runway in front of us like an ethereal path so bright it was impossible not to follow it to somewhere. "Now sit back down and buckle it up!" The engine noise grew and we "went into the light."

"Where are we going?" I yelled over the engine noise. Neither pilot answered. I yelled again. Which way are we headed?" Again there was no response. I was still trying to look out the front window and our acceleration for takeoff shoved me back into my seat. I quickly tightened my seat belt. In a few seconds, the plane rose at a steep angle, making a quick and pronounced right turn that stood us on our right wing. My eyes closed, I clutched the armrests, expecting to boomerang to the ground, wing over wing.

After we leveled off and continued to gain altitude, I looked out the window into the night. There were only a few scattered lights from farms and roads. They became smaller and harder to see as we climbed.

"We heard ya' yellin' but couldn't answer your questions there a minute ago," the pilot yelled toward me. "We were in a sterile cockpit up here and that means we're not s'posed to do anything but concentrate on takin' off alive and we can't talk to anybody but each other."

"Oh. Sorry. I didn't know. So, uh, where are we going?"

"You do want us to concentrate, don't ya?"

"Yeah. Please. Concentrate hard."

"Course, concentratin's hard after as many cocktails as we've had." I didn't reply aloud, but the pilot must have known I was smiling again. "So you wanna know where we're goin'?" he added, "We're goin' to the sixth plateau. Past that can't tell you squat. So sit back, enjoy the ride and we'll try to stay awake."

"Good. Awake pilots are a good thing."

"In the meantime, there's a john under one of those side seats there. Just pick up the cushion if you need it. There's some cheese sammiches and drinks in a little 'fridge behind the back seat."

"Thanks."

"Want some coffee? We're suckin' down coffee up here like there's no tomorrow. I sure as hell hope it don't give us the shakes! It's hard flyin' one of these mothers straight and level when you're hands are shakin' so damn bad."

"I'm okay, thanks. And please, see that there's a tomorrow, willya?"

"No guarantees, buddy. Keep your seatbelt on, it might get bumpy up ahead."

FLYING
(AN INSTRUMENTAL)

The sun was up when some sort of meteorological phenomenon thumped the plane down into a deep air pocket. Though I slept only a few hours, the drop flew my butt off my seat and I awoke quickly with a knot in my stomach. It was 6:30. I figured if I could find the early morning sun I could determine which direction we were heading. I moved to the left side of the plane and the bright light hit me squarely. I decided we were flying toward Miami, where planes were loaded with supplies bound for Pepperland.

"We're going south?" I asked. Neither pilot answered so I shouted "hello?" The older pilot backhanded the younger co-pilot on the arm and the both turned to me. I asked again. "Are we headed south?"

"Mornin' sunshine! Actually, we're on a headin' of two hundred eight degrees. That's just about south-southwest. Want some coffee? We just made a fresh pot in the back."

"Yeah, please."

"Well get it yourself bud, you ain't at home and your Momma ain't here."

A box of grocery store powdered donuts sat next to the coffee pot and I took two along with a paper cup of black coffee. A pile of men's room paper towels was scattered next to the coffee pot for napkins. I returned to my seat, realizing that if we were headed south-southwest from St. Louis, we weren't going to Miami. "Where are we going?"

"Not yet Jeff. Just settle on back."

I saw nothing familiar below us. Not knowing how fast a jet like this flew, I knew we could quite literally be anywhere in the world south-southwest of St. Louis.

In the daylight I could see into the cockpit. The talkative, older pilot looked to be in his fifties and his face had a lot of mileage on it, air miles and other kinds. The co-pilot was probably in his late 20's.

"Did you say there's a bathroom back here?"

"Nossir! I did not say there was a bathroom, I said there was 'a john.' Nuthin' fancy, just practical. Lift the cushion on the last seat there on the left side." Underneath the hinged cushion there was a typical airline toilet—an aluminum bowl with a "flush" button on the wall.

"You're right, it's not fancy."

"Hell, if you're self-conscious about it," the pilot said, "pull those curtains outa the wall." I wasn't self-conscious at all. As a fraternity man, I'd urinated in far more public places. "But I don't think you gotta worry 'bout anybody peekin' while you're pissin'," he added, "we're at forty thousand and nobody's lookin' in the windows."

"Right."

"All's I ask is that you try not to spray the wall, the floor or the cushion. That smell's a bitch to get outa the upholstery."

"I can handle that."

I aimed carefully, grateful for a smooth jet stream.

After flushing, I wandered toward the cockpit. Though I knew airplane cockpits were crammed with instrumentation, I was still amazed at the incredibly tight squeeze. There were dozens and dozens of gauges and dials. "We only use two of 'em," the pilot said, "the speedometer and the gas gauge. The rest of 'em are just for looks."

The co-pilot grinned and joined in. "We haven't figured out what all the other ones do yet." It was the first time I heard his voice. He sounded friendly.

We made airplane smalltalk. I asked about flying and they gave me polite, though occasionally smartass answers. "See this little thingy that says 'ALT?'"

"Yeah."

"As best as we can figure, that stands for 'A Lotta Trouble' and I don't know what the hell we're gonna do if it goes up any higher. What do you think?"

"Hey, I'm just here for the ride."

The co-pilot had a map on a clipboard on his lap. I tried to peek at the map to get some idea where we were headed but their maps were meaningless to me, only lines and dots on paper with odd-looking circles. "So where are we going?" I tried to keep the conversation light, hoping to earn a good-natured answer. My tone made no difference.

"I can tell you where we are when we get there," the pilot answered. "But can't tell you squat just now. That's policy. But until we get there, we're just on the way. Sorry."

I tried to change the subject, to continue the smalltalk and to break the loneliness. "Do you guys work for the Beatles?"

"Naaaaaaaaaah, we're Company Men. We work for the same assholes and misfits those other boys work for."

I thought I'd join into the competition of trying to make as much fun of them as they made of themselves, of me and of my situation. "Do you know that one of those other guys made up a story about how he went down in an airplane and he died?"

"Hell, we were flyin' that plane!" They both laughed.

This was a "for keeps" assignment for the pilots too. "That's really reassuring," I said, feeling a kinship, understanding they were making light of their own "deaths." "It was the best damned fatal crash we've ever lived through. Hell, how do you think we got this plane?" I didn't know. I guess I assumed whenever CIA pilots needed or wanted a plane they got one, just like James Bond always got whatever technology he needed to defeat whatever evil he faced. "We used to do a lot of Air America work. You ever hear of Air America there on your campus? Did that come up during all the anti-war shit?"

"No."

"Well you'll prolly hear about it sooner or later and we were it."

Years later, when the Air America story broke and the press learned of secret illegal flights into Cambodia during the Vietnam War, the younger co-pilot was one of their the sources of the story, the leak to the press and Congress.

"Was Air America an airline?"

"Well, we had planes, we had pilots and the pilots flew the planes so if that makes us an airline, that's what we were. Boyyyyyy, I'm tellin' ya, the tales we could tell. But then this assignment came along and that was that."

The younger co-pilot got suddenly talkative. "You know, I've listened to my share of Beatles music, just like anybody. When we got this job and I learned about the whole clue thing, I bought some albums and looked at the covers and listened to the songs more carefully. It was pretty neat. I can understand how so many people could have gotten wrapped up in it like you did. It's crazy, but it's interesting, you know?"

"Yeah. I know."

"Can I ask you a question?"

"Sure."

"On *Sgt. Pepper*, was "Getting Better" just one big clue? I've listened to it a million times and I can't figure it out. When I asked John about it, he said…"

"You asked John? John Lennon?"

The older pilot jumped into the conversation with new energy. "Yeah, we've flown the boys around a bit. John likes to stand right there where you're standin'. I think he likes to keep an eye on us. And dammit, he oughta!"

"Really?" I was actually stupid enough to look down at the spot where I was standing, checking whether John Lennon left any trace.

"In fact, we were on a flight like this one, headin' to…" He stopped and restarted. "We were cruisin' along one day, and he's lookin' at the charts and he was the one who sent us to where we're goin' now. He liked the sound of the place and decided to drop in for a looksee. When he saw it, he decided it'd be a stagin' area for the whole program."

"So where was that? Where are we going?"

"I'll tell you what. You go back and have a sitdown and strap yourself in, 'cause we're headin' there right now."

There was some unintelligible radio traffic after I took my seat and the plane nosed down slightly. We were descending.

Pepperland.

We're there.

No, I remembered, he said it was a staging area.

I looked out the window and saw we were over ground. There was no "Octopus's Garden" near here.

It took another fifteen minutes to descend onto what had to be the most godforsaken airfield on the earth. The plane kicked up so much dust as we landed it was impossible to see anything outside. "Welcome to sunny Meh-hee-co," the pilot shouted as we slowed and made a quick left turn toward a metal shed, the only building in sight.

"Mexico?" I was only a thousand miles and one entire gulf away from my Miami expectation. "Why are we in Mexico?"

The co-pilot answered. "To stretch our legs, change planes, pick up food and another passenger. We'll be up again in an hour or so."

"This is a little airstrip near Aguascalientes," the pilot said, "not close to a damn thing, maybe three hundred fifty miles out of sunny Meh-hee-co City. John picked this joint off the map 'cause he liked the name and so now we always gotta stop here. John figured anyplace with 'Agua' in the name was karma, some kinda sign, someplace symbolic. He was a real bear about it with The Company, insistin' it be on the mix on these flights 'cause it fit with the whole Pepperland thing. When we needed the runway lengthened so's we could land a little easier, the boys even tossed in a few bucks for that.

"It's a pretty interestin' place, with mineral spas and miles and miles of spooky-lookin' tunnels runnin' underneath. Nobody knows where the tunnels came from, but their ancient as hell. Some long-lost civilization built 'em but nobody knows who or when or why.

"When John heard 'bout the tunnels and lost civilizations, he said it was like perfect serendipity. He put them secret tunnels under the ground together with the dome under the water and now almost everybody gets a taste of good old Aguascalientes.

"And that's our little geography lesson for now. I'll bore you again later."

Then the co-pilot asked, "Do you speak Spanish?"

"No, I took German in high school."

"Okay, Aguascalientes means..."

"'Water.' 'Watersomething.' 'Agua' is 'water.'"

Finished teaching his geography lesson, the pilot started his language class. "Right. It means the same thing as the Germans call 'hoches wasser.'"

"Hot water?"

"If you've never been in hot water before, you're sure as hell in Hot Water now, bud! Hot Water, Mexico!!!" Then both pilots laughed as I suspected they laughed every time they used the 'Hot Water' joke on every landing, at least a thousand times before.

FUN IS THE ONE THING THAT MONEY CAN'T BUY
SOMETHING INSIDE THAT WAS ALWAYS DENIED
FOR SO MANY YEARS
BYE BYE

The two pilots inspected the jet while I stood outside by the stairs, mindlessly fiddling with my useless, empty camera. Quickly a man with a heavy Wisconsin or Minnesota accent approached. "Have a good flight Jeff? Everything okay there?" He seemed like an old friend meeting me at the airport.

"Yeah, fine. Thank you." I waited for him to introduce himself, expecting him to say his name was Hancock. He didn't do either. He simply pointed to the pilots and laughingly apologized that I had to "put up with those two characters, eh? So it was a good flight? Good. Very good," shaking his head as he walked away. He never spoke to me again after this exchange, apparently eager to tend to whatever business faced him. Or, I thought, maybe his entire job was to file a report on the quality of my flight, I never knew. Assuming he was another Company Man, the man at Hot Water was the only one I had met so far on my journey who was cold, lukewarm at best.

In fact, the "good flight" conversation was my total, on-the-ground chitchat with any other human while in Hot Water, Mexico, other than very quietly asking the younger pilot if I needed a passport or paperwork to be there. He laughed and assured me I didn't need to worry about passports in some private plane backwater like Hot Water. He said there was nobody around who was legally capable of kicking me out of the country on legal formalities or formal legalities. Then he walked away and that was it.

For the first time since hunkering down in the *Admiral* engine room, I reached into my shirt pocket and took out my cigarettes and matches.

There was only a half-pack of Marlboros left in the box and I thought I should ration them. I put the cigarette back in the box and the matches into my blazer pocket. Besides, for the most part I had lost the compulsion to smoke. I highly recommend dying and flying off to parts unknown with strangers as a method of quitting smoking.

After about ten minutes of waiting for something to happen or for someone to tell me anything, the pilots headed to the metal shed. I followed them if only for the semi-security of being near vaguely familiar people. But they didn't invite me to follow so I kept my distance.

As they went into what looked like the office of the two-room shed, I lingered in the outside "waiting room" area and pretended to be interested in the yellowed sports and flying magazines that had become brittle from the constant sunshine that hit them as they sat on a low table in front of the window, long ignored and unread

Through the door, I could see the pilots sitting in well-worn, green vinyl armchairs snacking at a bowl of grapes, drinking coffee from paper cups and speaking quietly and intently to the Wisconsin/Minnesota guy. I couldn't hear the conversation. It seemed serious, broken by only occasional laughter caused by what I have since learned is typical, private, smartass banter natural among flying men. In the middle of their inaudible chitchat, I was forced to look up from a magazine article that laughably analyzed the negligible pre-season possibilities of a pennant race for Casey Stengel's dismal '69 New York Mets. The loudness of their silence suddenly blared from the office.

The three men were riveted, their ears sitting almost upright like a dog listening to the sound of a familiar car in the driveway. "That's them," the Wisconsin/Minnesota man said, and the three jumped from their seats and hurried from the office.

We stood outside, looking into the nothingness of the ultra-blue Mexican sky. Staring toward the horizon where the pilots watched, I finally saw a tiny black speck in the sky and heard the faint hum of airplane engines. As the dot grew larger and the engines louder, I could see a plane floating from side to side, fighting to move forward like a helium balloon against the strong winds of the flat Mexican terrain.

When the plane landed in another huge dust cloud, I recognized it as an ancient DC-3, a goonybird of a plane that had fascinated me since my plastic-model building childhood because of the stories about it from World War Two—the military called it a "C-47 Skytrain." It was still known as a real workhorse of the air, a legendary plane capable of carrying anything anywhere. Hell, it was a "Skytrain."

The older pilot surprised me when he put his right hand on my left shoulder and said "this is it, Jeff. This is it." Obviously, I didn't know what to expect, had no idea what kind of "it" to anticipate.

The DC-3 taxied toward us and shut down its engines. The propellers took forever to stop spinning. Finally, the door opened and a man in a leather jacket came down the steps, followed by another man in a one-piece jumpsuit. "My" pilots and the Wisconsin/Minnesota man walked toward them and they all shook hands and patted each other on the back the way men of the '70s were supposed to greet one another.

All four pilots walked toward the metal shed and me. "Boys, this is Jeff and he's all right. At least he's all right enough so's that we didn't want to dump his ass out somewhere over Tay-has." The DC-3 men nodded in my direction and all the Company Men went into the metal shed. Again, I was left stranded outside with nothing to do except watch the Wisconsin/Minnesota man drive a fuel truck under the DC-3 wing and gas it up.

So that's what I did.

Ultimately, I sat down on the dusty ground, my back against the metal shed. I got an instant mental image of myself with a serape and stereotypically huge sombrero pulled down over my face enjoying a siesta.

What had it been? Twenty-four hours? Not even that. Twenty, maybe only nineteen hours since my pinball game at the M-Bar. From hot coffee at the M-Bar to Hot Water in Mexico in less than a day. It was the longest day of my life and the first day of my death. I realized how self-absorbed I had become in the events that followed my meeting in Columbia. I hadn't thought of anyone else, I hadn't considered anything, any place or anyone except for myself.

I assumed that, at that exact moment, the Coast Guard and Fire Department were searching the Mississippi River for me as my parents and Mara stood on the riverbank. Maybe they were gathered at my house preparing to "sit Shiva," the Jewish mourning period. I wondered if they would sit Shiva if they didn't have a body. In a way, I hoped they would "sit" because it would help them accept the finality of my loss. But I also hoped some ancient rabbinic law would prohibit it without the certainty of a dead body. I thought Shiva would make what I had done even crueler.

I lit one of my precious Marlboros. Screw quitting. It gave me a definite buzz.

I was alone. The only people I knew were strangers. I wanted to meet another disc jockey, another student, someone to tell me how they got there, how they felt, what turbulence went through their heads while they were flying to Aguascalientes.

Then I decided to put my concerns out of my mind. I was in the middle of something that was not only staring me in the face but also blowing dust into my eyes, nose and mouth, something very real. Even though everyone told me I could turn back at any time, I couldn't. I had to push ahead to wherever I was going. I had no choice.

I stared at the barren desert around me, looking for intricate details. I knew the more I focused on small stuff, the more quickly I'd forget about the big stuff like home.

How could I be certain this was Mexico? There was no way I could prove it wasn't central Kansas, someplace where the prairie grass was burned off in a drought. Maybe we flew in big circles and it was all a sham.

Maybe it was too late to have any doubts.

Hancock bounded out of the shed as wide awake and energetic as anybody I'd ever seen. "You ready to bebop outa here, Bud?" Thinking about that moment and the rest of the trip long after I got to The Onion, I wondered how he could have been so enthusiastic and decided he had to have been taking some kind of serious uppers. I figured some sort of "pep pills" were probably standard-issue Company paraphernalia for pilots on this kind of extreme trip.

I jumped up, eager to admit I was not only ready for whatever might come next, but to change locations and clear my head. I was bored of Mexico. Or Kansas, or wherever we were. "Yes! I'm ready."

"Then let's go." We walked toward the DC-3. "I learned to fly on one of these babies," he told me proudly, "Army Air Corps. And this is one fiiiiiiiiiiiiiiiine aircraft. Hell, I love just lookin' at 'em. Oh, I know you're prolly thinkin' that it's got propellers and it's slow and it ain't worth a shit. But look at the size of those wings! They'll fly in a shit storm. Hell, *one* of 'em could keep most aircraft flyin'! They've put a big mother bladder tank in the back for more range and this baby'll take us anywhere!

"Shit," he continued, "those little jets are fine. You prolly love 'em 'cause they're fast and neat and new and by God there's a place for that. But those Lear jets, a man just sits back and steers 'em. Someday, they won't need pilots at all. But *these* planes son, you don't just steer these planes, you *fly* 'em!" I nodded, agreeable to whatever he might have said. "Well then," he said enthusiastically, "let's fly the hell outa here."

As we walked toward the door behind the left wing, his attitude changed and he held my arm as our walk slowed. "Once more, Jeff, it's policy and I've gotta ask. Do you wanna try for the sixth plateau?"

I kept my stride, looking forward. "Damn right I do."

"That, sir, is precisely what I wanna hear right now, bud. Let's go flyin'!"

We boarded the DC-3 into a very narrow passageway instead of the huge passenger compartment I expected. "Bladder tanks, bud," the pilot said knocking on what sounded like a very flimsy wall. Added 'em for the flight. We need the fuel 'cause it's one longass haul." I followed him up the steep incline toward a small, full-width cabin in the front of the plane. There were only four rows of seats, two seats to the right of the aisle, singles to the left.

Someone was already in one of the front passenger seats. He was asleep, his head against a window, using a small backpack as a pillow. I sat a couple rows behind him.

The younger co-pilot followed us in carrying a bag. He stopped at my seat to ask how I was doing. "Fine," I told him. He went to the cockpit and closed the door without saying or asking anything else.

After a wait, the engines finally started, the huge propellers spinning ferociously, the engines roaring. Like in the Lear jet at the start of the trip in St. Louis, after a few long minutes of warm-up we began to roll. As we taxied, I could see the person in the front row begin to stir. His head came up over the back of his seat and he looked out the window.

I watched the props spin, figuring that if they decided to come loose, they would cartwheel toward the passenger compartment, shear through the fuselage and shred me like so much coleslaw. I reminded myself how this plane is a workhorse, that a plane this old had to have flown a lot of hours and a lot of miles and the propellers probably hadn't yet shredded even one passenger. Then I thought about all those flying hours on the props and figured that one of them was overdue to come off the wing and into the cabin by now.

I thought about coleslaw. My mother made wonderful, creamy slaw, grating the cabbage by hand. "It's no good unless it's got a little knuckle in it," she'd always say. "A little skin always makes it better."

The old plane shook as the engines revved at the end of the runway. Every rivet seemed to rattle as we picked up speed. Once airborne, the noise smoothed and the plane floated reassuringly on those huge wings as we climbed.

Five minutes into the flight, the person in the seat ahead stood and stretched. He looked about the plane and saw me belted into my seat. We made eye contact. He smiled and shuffled sideways past the aisle seat. He came toward me. He stuck out his hand and in a heavy British accent said "Hello luv. I'm Peter. Peter Ham."

I realized nobody on this entire adventure had called me by my real name, only by the name I used on the radio. "I'm Jeff Scott. From St. Louis."

"Nice to meetcha, Jeff. How'd ya get here, eh? Didja follow them bloody clues? Didja read all the jackets?"

"Yeah. I was on the radio in Columbia, Missouri. How 'bout you. Did you follow the clues too?"

"Follow 'em?" He laughed. "Hell no, luv! I *am* a bloody clue!"

DID I HEAR YOU SAY
THAT THERE MUST BE A CATCH?
WILL YOU WALK AWAY
FROM A FOOL AND HIS MONEY?

He looked disappointed when I didn't instantly recognize his name or how he was a clue. He sighed as he sat down on the armrest of the seat next to me. There was genuine puzzlement in his voice but he spoke understandingly, like a teacher trying to show a slow student how to correct mistakes on a test paper. "I thought you said you was on the radio, luv."

"I did. I was."

"'*I was.*' Did you get that clue? The '*I was*' one?"

"That was one of the first."

"Was you a disc jockey? Did you play records?" He called them "rec*ORDS*," not "*REC*urds" as we did in America. I found his accent charming.

"Yeah, I was. But only at the campus radio station." I was surprised to hear myself making excuses for my radio station, downplaying it as "only" the campus station. I felt like I had betrayed an old friend. "But we had a very big audience."

He stared at me, obviously amazed at my ignorance. "Didn't you ever play a Brit group called Badfinger?"

"Of course! We played 'Come and Get It.' It was a good song."

"What label was it on?"

"Apple. I remember it was on Apple and that was why we played it in the first place. We always played anything that came out on Apple."

"You mean you didn't like the song for itself? You liked it just for the pretty picture on the bloody label?"

"No! I mean yes! It was good, but we also figured that anything on Apple was something the Beatles approved so it made the playlist. We figured anything on Apple was hot. We played Mary Hopkin records out the yingyang. I liked 'Those Were the Days,' but could never stand 'Goodbye' 'cause it was goofy. But like I said, she was on Apple so we played anything she…"

"But you did play 'Come and Get It' by Badfinger?"

"Yeah, we did."

"So you didn't get it?"

"Get what?"

"That it was another bloody clue!" He smiled broadly. "'If you want it, here it is, come and get it!'"

"Shiiiiiiiiit! No! We never put that into the mix of the clues because it wasn't the Beatles. Are you shitting me? It was a clue?"

"I'd never shit you, luv, you're my favorite turd." He settled into the seat next to me. "The whole thing was a clue," he went on. "Even the name of the group. *Badfinger*. Get it? It's holdin' up the middle finger and telling everybody 'what you want is right here on these fookin' records, arseholes!'"

"Shiiiiiiiiiit, I can't believe we didn't think of that. I do remember when we first got 'Come and Get It' I played it for my program director and mentioned how much I thought it sounded like the Beatles and we wondered whether it was them singing under another name. I remember that I said it sounded like Paul singing lead, but we never put the pieces together."

"Well luv, here's another clue for you all, the singer *was* Paul."

My jaw physically dropped.

"Are you hungry, luv? I'm starvin'. Where'd you say you're from? Saint Looie? Good blues town, St. Louis. Jazz too, eh?"

"Yeah. Blues. Lots of jazz. Chuck Berry too. He's. St. Louis. He…" I still couldn't speak in complete sentences.

He walked back to his seat and returned with a large brown paper bag. "Got these in New Jersey someplace. After the crossing we stopped at a tiny little airport somewhere to change planes and one of the MI6 boys brought it to me." He took a heaping paper plate of cold French fries from the bag. "I couldn't eat the chips then, luv, but they look good now. There's a couple of cold Wimpys too. If you want 'em, here they are, come and get 'em." It was nine o'clock in the morning and I definitely wasn't in the mood for congealed greaseburgers or cold fries.

As he packed away the "chips," I looked out the window, trying to get a fix on where we were heading. When I saw nothing but water under us, my stomach knotted. Miami? The sun was climbing on the left side toward the back of the plane. We weren't headed east.

"Wish I had a pint to wash these down with, eh luv? But such is life."

"And death," I added.

"Right," he answered. "And death too. Now listen. I advise you to listen now because you obviously didn't listen when the recORD came out."

"Sorry."

"It sounded like Paul was singing lead because Paul *was* singing lead."

"Geez Louise."

"Maybe someday I'll meet your friend Louise, luv, but not now. Anyway, that was the whole thing. Paul wrote the song but John thought if the Beatles recorded it, it would have been too easy. Apple had my group under contract—we called ourselves The Iveys back then—so Paulie brought the song to us and changed our name to Badfinger 'cause it was another clue. He sang lead, we played backup and what happened after that, as they say, is history."

"Shiiiiiiiiiiit."

"Did you see the movie?"

"What movie? *Yellow Submarine?*"

"No, the movie the song came from."

"*Magic Christian?* I loved it. My girlfriend hated it when..." He knew exactly where I was going, to the part everybody's girlfriend hated "...when all those white-shirt-and-tie twits took a walk into the vat of urine and vomit. Do you remember why they jumped into that shit?"

"Of course, after Peter Sellers and Ringo threw money into it."

"All right class. Now it's examination of cinematic literature time. What was the theme of the movie?"

"Um, it was about how greedy people can be, what they'll do for money and..."

"And it was all a clue, mate. The song, the movie, the fact that Ringo was in it, the whole 'anti-Piggy' thing, it's all one bad finger pointed at all the Piggies in the world! It's Pepperland, luv! It's we don't need your filthy money any more!"

It was all becoming more and more of a learning experience. Any trepidation I might have had was overtaken by fascination.

"So how did you get involved with this?"

"We were looking for a label and we met someone from Apple and...hey! That's another clue!"

"What is?"

"Apple! Like in the Garden of Eden, like in the beginning of a whole brand new fookin' world! The apple was the forbidden fruit from the Tree of Knowledge in the whole brand new fookin' world! Eat from the Tree of Knowledge! Taste the apple! Fook the Piggies and understand everything!"

"Shiiiiiiiiiiit."

"You have a marvelous command of the language. If you say 'shiiiiiiiiiiiiit' again I just might, luv. I know that if I'd been sitting someplace looking at recORD jackets and listening to tunes, I'da figured it all out one, two, three."

I pulled a burger from Peter's paper bag. The cold grease coated the roof of my mouth, the bun was soggy and it was good.

Peter pointed to the closed door at the front of the plane. "Are Cricket and Football still flying this leg?"

"Excuse me?"

"The pilots. Did they tell you their names are Cricket and Football?"

"Um, no. These are the guys who flew me from St. Louis. They were introduced to me as Charles and Puckett but I don't think that's their real names. Does the name Charles Puckett Hancock mean anything to you?"

"No. Nothing. Why?"

"I thought it might be another clue that we missed. Your guys must have stayed back at the airport in Mexico."

"Mexico?"

"Yeah, someplace called Aguascal..."

"Aguascalientes?"

"How did you know? I thought you slept through that stop."

"Because during the 'Come and Get it' session, Paulie kept working on a song called 'Aguascalientes.' It had a nice little Spanish rhythm to it. 'AGUAS-cal-ee-ent-ays, in the middle of everything...' But he never could get the tune together."

"No shit?"

"Would I shit you? Fuck yes I would. I'm going back to sleep. We'll talk later."

I still wanted to know how Peter arrived wherever it was we were, how he got from England, what he knew about where we were going, what was going to happen. I wanted to know how he "died."

I only recently learned—and the fascination and stomach knots came back to me again when I heard this—the original name John Lennon wanted to give Peter's group when they signed to record for Apple in 1968. He wanted to call them The Glass Onion. You can look it up.

The whole world is made up of small pieces of the same puzzle that fit together to make something. I suppose we all just have to figure out what our own puzzle is.

OBLADI OBLADA, LIFE GOES ON
BRA
LALA HOW THE LIFE GOES ON

Peter told me he didn't have to "die" to get to Pepperland. But four-plus years after I "died" figuratively and three years after I was figuratively reborn, Peter died genuinely.

He hanged himself in 1974.

Post-Pepperland, inspired by positive experiences and trying to forget the bad ones, Peter returned to songwriting and recording in the UK.

Badfinger issued a few records that broke into the Top 10, including some recorded before Peter disappeared, but after his return it all fell apart.

After Pepperland and after Apple rotted, the band continued trying to create a Beatle-sized smash. The group signed with a new label for a huge amount of cash but went nowhere, man.

In 1972, Harry Nilsson hit number one, went platinum and won a Grammy with a Peter Ham-written ballad that was obviously another post-Pepperland reminiscence, "Without You." Most people probably thought it was a love song, but even with Nilsson's vocal, those of us who knew Peter in the last depressing days of Pepperland recognized his anguish:

> **Oh I can't forget this evening**
> **On your face as you were leaving.**
> **But I guess that's just the way**
> **The story goes...**

After learning of the life and death of Pepperland and becoming intimate friends with the Beatles, Nilsson made the obscure *Son of Dracula* movie with Ringo in 1974. He also became John Lennon's closest confidant and drinking buddy during John's eighteen-month separation from Yoko in 1973-'74 (a time John himself called his "lost weekend"). John produced Nilsson's *Pussy Cats* album during that time. I don't know whether the *Pussy Cats* title referred to what they spent their time looking for or their personalities, but I knew for a fact that John wasn't a pussycat all the time. I knew that sometimes John could be a tiger.

When Harry Nilsson genuinely died in 1994, the *New York Daily News* described *Pussy Cats* in his obituary as "a brooding companion to Lennon's *Rock and Roll* album, a reminder that life isn't always as much fun as it might look." The newspaper left out the fact that fun is the one thing that money can't buy.

Paul McCartney never fronted for Badfinger again, though several Badfinger members backed up the other Beatles, playing with George on *All Things Must Pass* (another post-Pepperland title), with John on "Imagine" and with Ringo on his *It Don't Come Easy* album.

I can only assume that while Peter was creatively inspired by his Pepperland life, he was deeply distraught by its demise. I believe this grief may have ultimately taken over his life and contributed to his own genuine death, but obviously I can never know. The coroner investigating his suicide officially reported it was caused by "personal and professional problems."

In retrospect, I have to think Peter must have put a lot of his energies into mourning the Utopia that might have been instead of writing songs about the life he should have carried on. "Carry On" was another Badfinger song used in *Magic Christian*. Maybe he regretted the possibilities of an unrestricted future put to rest by the unrelenting present, but it's all total assumption on my part. After Pepperland ended, I never saw Peter again and I have no way of knowing what he thought or felt. I only know what I thought and felt in the post-Pepperland times and try to project it onto his artist's sensitivities.

All I know for sure is on that day on a DC-3 flying to somewhere, Peter seemed to be anything but suffering from any type of "personal and professional problems" whatsoever. He looked forward to our arrival and the joy he expected would follow for a long time lifetime afterwards. Utopia was his reward for letting Paul sing lead on "Come and Get It." I told him I thought it was a cheap price to pay for paradise and a whole lot easier than interpreting clues. He disagreed, saying it wasn't so cheap. He said that for a singer/songwriter it might be better to sing lead on a hit record and take a chance on finding his own Utopia, that a hit record might have been Utopia enough.

Peter said he believed Pepperland would be a place to live his music, to play with all the music people he expected would be there. When I asked what he knew about who would be in Pepperland, he clammed up, saying he promised not to tell anybody anything, that spilling the beans might mean revocation of his Pepperland ticket.

Peter was fascinated with my "death" and the rapid-fire events that followed. When I detailed the story that began on the radio and brought it up to that moment on the plane, he listened intently, describing the experience with a phrase that was appropriate for the era but is now hugely embarrassing to repeat, "far out."

We *were* far out.

Compared to a Lear Jet, a DC-3 stands still when it flies. Flying west into an easterly headwind, we averaged only 170 knots and the flight was just plain boring. It was like jury duty, seemingly endless but without the old magazines—I knew we were doing something worthwhile but for an indeterminate stretch of time, aware that at any second someone might tap my shoulder or call my name for something important. If Peter hadn't been on the plane, I don't know what I would have done to pass so many hours.

Peter was my first Pepperland friend and confidant. I told him about Mara, about how I felt terrible for being so selfish to leave her on what seemed like a whim. I described my work at the radio station, my classes and the boring idiosyncrasies of a small Midwestern town like Columbia, Missouri. I compared life in Columbia to a long ride in a DC-3 but with football in the autumn. I told him it was a place where late-night mooing at cows was big fun. He said he thought Columbia sounded very attractive.

He told me about Meg, a London groupie. She was an "Apple Scruff," one of the attractive, hip young women who hung around Beatle recording studios and Apple hoping to meet and/or "make it" (another embarrassing phrase of the '70s), with the band. When they couldn't have the Beatles, they settled for anybody who had anything to do with them and so Badfinger members were more than happy to take up the slack. Besides, Peter said, after "Come and Get It" Badfinger warranted groupies of its own and didn't need Beatle sloppy seconds, even if McCartney was on vocal.

Peter said he was grateful he didn't have to sift through clues. The clues were bullshit, he said, created out of a specific need rather than pure creativity. He said he thought the clues actually took over the Beatles' pure music-making artistry, that it seemed to him they spent as much time creating songs to go around clues as they once spent creating clues to go around songs. And besides, he said, getting to Pepperland would have meant examination by MI6 "and once they get ahold of ya, luv, they're brutal."

"So is the CIA," I countered, lowering my voice. "The people I met were nice enough, but the way they had me down, the way they knew things about me, I felt like a specimen on a microscope slide. Be glad you're not an American."

He quickly challenged me. "Why should I be glad about that? I'd be happy as a fly on shit if I was a Yank!"

"Why do you say that?"

"Shit man, they saved our Brit arses in the War. If it weren't for the GI's, we'd be dishin' up bratwurst 'stead of kidney pie, man."

"But that was twenty-five, thirty years ago."

"Big bloody deal, luv. You're not gonna find a Brit who don't remember what we owe the Yanks. You've got the economy, you've got the jobs. Hell, it's America what determines what's what in music! Like I said, I'd be happy to be a Yank!"

When Peter went to his seat to cocoon, I had plenty of opportunity to wonder again about what I had done. I worried about not having clean clothes. I wished I had packed some jeans. I wanted a shower.

After a long flight broken only by the off-and-on talks with Peter, the pilot opened the cockpit door and came into the cabin. When I tried to stop him hustling down the aisle, he walked past. He pointed as he trotted toward the back of the aircraft, "You're gonna have to wait, bud. Nature's callin' louder than you!" The DC-3 had a genuine lavatory in the back, a typical closet-sized airplane bathroom with a blue-watered flush toilet and real walls and a closeable door.

After a few minutes, the pilot came back to the cabin and sat in the single seat across the aisle from me. "Now," he said, "what can I do for you, my friend?"

"Well, first of all you can tell me who the hell is flying the plane right now!"

"Bruce, my partner, he's flyin'. I 'magine he's doin' just fine, assumin' he's not sawin' logs. He's a smart boy, knows what he's doin'. I might even let him take a stroll to the back when I go back up front." A grin filled his face. "You know, as much coffee as he's been tossin' back since Aquascalientes, maybe Ah'll just keep my butt right here and make 'im sweat. He don't have any empty piddle packs up there and if Ah play my cards right, by the time Ah get back up front he'll be turnin' blue as the water back in the lav!" He laughed aloud at the possibility. "Anyway, we're cruisin' along on autopilot for most of this leg and the old bird's doin' fine all by herself."

Though today I can't remember the day of the week, I still remember what I said back then and especially the significance of his off-the-cuff reply. "I thought you said you had to *fly* this plane and not just steer! How can we be on autopilot?"

"Shit, boy! Don't you believe anything a pilot says! Half of what I say is bullshit and the other half of what I say is meaningless!" Startled by the familiarity of the line, I took what he said as a lesson in both flying and in the Genesis of *White Album* lyrics.

"Are you hungry?" he asked, another person concerned with my dietary habits. "Bruce brought a bag of food aboard, some sammiches, cans of V'eena sausages and a messa C-Rats. Real Mexican food, huh?" I felt like my mother was with me. I expected him to say, "We've got fish, we've got soup…"

"No thanks, I'm not really hungry. Maybe later."

He pushed the button on the armrest of his seat and leaned back. "Well, if Ah ever head back up front and let Bruce come back here to take a leak, Ah'll send him with the bag. We've been eatin' up a storm up there just for sumthin' to do to stay awake." He grew quiet and closed his eyes and I thought he fell asleep. I turned to look out the window. After a minute or two, he pulled the squeaky seat upright again. "Awwww shit! Ah better go. Talk to you later, bud."

He walked back to the cockpit and I realized how tired he must be. He had flown for a long time. He stopped after a few steps and came back to the seat opposite me. "As far as when we're gonna get there, all's I can tell you is we've got a buncha hours ahead of us, depending on the headwind, so just settle back."

"Why didn't we take the Lear Jet? Why did we change planes? I know you love this plane, but I feel like we're crawling."

"Range, bud, *range*. We've got a long way to go, but with them bladders in the back, this pterodactyl's gonna take us wherever we need to go."

"Oh."

"Wish Ah could send some good lookin' stewardess back here with coffee, tea or milk, but me and Bruce and V'eena sausages is all we got. You've always got the longhair to talk to. Like Ah told ya, Bud, settle back." He went back to the cockpit and closed the door behind him.

There was only water below us, all the way to every horizon.

THE DEEPER YOU GO, THE HIGHER YOU FLY
THE HIGHER YOU FLY, THE DEEPER YOU GO
(Come on, hey hey! Come on, hey hey!)

Everyone probably needs a big change now and then just to get out of whatever particular rut they happen to be in at that particular stage of existence.   While fatherhood taught me how young children crave security and routine, the older I get the more I desire and need to escape routine. The most frustrating fact of all is while adulthood is the time we most need to change, it's when we can least achieve it.

Peter Ham must have believed he would find his own way out of his rut of "personal and professional problems."   And then decided he'd never find it.

Maybe this need to de-rut starts as early as high school when the ruts first start to form. It probably gets deeper through college.   Back in the '70s, plenty of people gave in to Timothy Leary's advice to "tune in, turn on and drop out." Maybe the DC-3 trip made me the first in my group of middle-class fraternity rats and U-City eggheads to leave life behind for what I thought was to be for good—and that's "for good" in both the positive and permanent senses.

I wish I could do it again now.

I must be aging more quickly, my digressions here are getting longer and closer together by the page.

Pepperland represented the end of one life, a clean start outside my usual adventureless life.   I welcomed the possibility of something different, of something new. And on that day in 1970, no matter how boring the flight to it, I knew I was going to achieve it. It was coming. I just didn't know when, where or what it was.

Reflexively, my mind turned to home while I sat on the plane. I looked around for details to ponder in order to get the thoughts out of my mind. I couldn't see any parachutes. What if we had to ditch in the ocean? Where were the life rafts? Where were the things we would need to survive?

Maybe we were already genuinely dead and the DC-3 was eternal flying hell.

After a few minutes retrospection about the end of life, Bruce—the co-pilot whose name the pilot leaked on his way to take a leak—came back with the bag he brought aboard the plane. He dropped it in the aisle and hurriedly went toward the rear of the plane. "I'llbebackinaminute!"

I smiled as he hustled down the aisle and slammed the bathroom door.

When he finally came out, he sat down across the aisle and in the same single seat where the pilot sat. "Whew! I needed that!"

"I'll bet."

"Long flight, huh? How 'ya holding up?"

"I was going to ask you the same thing. We can sleep back here, but the big question is how are you guys up front?"

"We're fine," he said. "We get in some sack time in shifts. Julie works, I nap, then I fly and he closes his eyes."

"Who's Julie?"

"Julius, the other pilot. His name is Julius, but we call him Julie."

For the first time since it all began, security was completely breached. I knew the flight crew's names! The gregarious pilot was Julius—usually known as "Julie" and the usually quiet co-pilot was Bruce. I could probably have sold this information to the Russians for a huge pile of money.

"Julie said you were hungry, so I brought out the old feedbag."

"I'm okay." I wasn't hungry, but I was curious. "But tell me what's in the magic bag. Maybe I can get hungry pretty quick."

He pulled out a handful of olive drab aluminum foil bags filled with military C-Rations: beef stew, Spam and packages marked "creamed chipped beef on toast." I thought creamed chipped beef on toast was only a legend, what military people called by the same name we called Mort's fraternity house "mystery meat" dinner: "shit on a shingle."

When he pulled some Snickers bars out of the bag, I took two.

Finally, he reached into the bag again and pulled out a squat, dark bottle. "How 'bout something to wash those down?"

"What is that?"

"Local hootch. The most caliente damn agua you're ever gonna drink! They grow incredible grapes down there and after they do the voodoo that they do so well, they get this at the end." I must have looked blank. "It's brandy! Really, really good brandy! Taste it! Hell, if this program ever ends, Julie and I may keep flying there just to resupply with this stuff. Hell, we may *move* there! We're hooked on this crap! This is the most amazing brandy you're ever gonna have. Try it. Go ahead!"

I knew that too much "local hootch" would put me to sleep. I also knew that sleeping would make the trip go more quickly. I worried about mixing "local hootch" and flying. I didn't want to start looking for a barf bag instead of life rafts and I didn't want to be sick if I actually needed to find a parachute.

But I decided to try the stuff, if only out of the sense of adventure that comes with traveling to strange places. "You gonna join me?" I asked. "They say it's bad to drink alone."

"I'd love to," he answered, "but in the airplane business it's 'twelve hours from bottle to throttle.'" It was reassuring that Bruce separated bottles from throttles so seriously. Since I first boarded the Lear Jet a literal lifetime ago, Julie's jokes about how much he already had to drink haunted me. I didn't know whether to take them seriously and wondered about the people into whose hands I placed my former, current and future lives. That was why I looked for parachutes and life rafts. Bruce's refusal of the shared drink taught me that Julie was right; when a pilot talks, "half of what they say is meaningless." But maybe I shouldn't have believed that either.

I cracked open the bottle, filled my coffee cup and glugged it. True to its origin, the brandy made my esophagus catch fire. Bruce laughed. "Heeeeeey, go slow with that! That's industrial strength shit!"

After my throat recovered, I kept talking if only to keep Bruce in his seat, just for the company and to pass the time. "So how'd you get into this?" He was in no obvious hurry to get back to the cockpit and settled back into the seat.

"I didn't get into this, it got into me."

"What does that mean?"

"A couple of years ago, I was like everybody else, a college kid in Michigan. I was pre-law and that meant what you think it meant—that I didn't know what I wanted to be when I grew up. I didn't know if I'd really go to law school or not but I needed to declare a major and pre-law seemed about right.

"It was just getting ugly in 'Nam, uh, Vietnam, and the draft was hanging over my head so I signed up for Navy ROTC to stay out of 'Nam. You know how that works?"

"I think so."

"They pay for college, send you a couple of bucks every month, you go to class, march around a little and do summer camp, which is actually a lot of fun. At the end, they make you an officer and then comes the payback. You have to do four years of active duty. So my senior year I signed my contract and after graduation there I was anyway."

"There you were, where?"

"Vietnam. They needed pilots. I figured zipping around the sky was better than getting shot at on the ground or on some ship bored to death, so I took 'em up on flight school and they made me a fighter jock. I was hot shit. A Naval Aviator." He pronounced "aviator" in a Red Baron, sWAYve and deBONEr way, "avv-ee-att-er."

"That sounds cool."

"Not if you were there. I flew the standard missions, what you'd expect I guess, bomb runs, that kind of shit." He didn't look at me as he spoke. "After a while, the Company came around looking for pilots to do some things that didn't exactly fit the program. They recruited hard and I bought their line and joined up. Like Julie said, we did some Air America work and...well, I didn't much care for that. We flew some missions, took some low altitude fire, you know, that kind of shit. But I didn't much like ferrying around people without names.

"But after that, I was an official pro-endorsed Company Man. I was grateful they got me discharged and out of country, so here I am, still flying, still a Company Man whether I like it or not. At least you people have names."

I didn't tell him that Jeff Scott wasn't my real name. "That's a helluva story."

"Yeah, it is. But do you know what the shits of it all is?"

"What?"

"Do you remember the draft lottery?"

"Sure. I won. I was number 306. They said the first third of the numbers were as good as drafted, the middle third was iffy and the last third was free and clear."

"Right. Well, I was already on active duty when they made that first draw, so it didn't matter much to me. But everybody in my unit looked up our numbers in the papers anyway, just to see how we would have done."

"Yeah?"

"I pulled 364. I'd be a rich-ass lawyer in Grand Rapids now." He stopped talking and turned to look out the window for a few seconds. Then he stood up quickly. "Shit, I gotta go back up front. Enjoy the hooch." He headed toward the cockpit.

"Thanks."

"But don't finish the bottle. I'd like some after we land."

"No problem. It'll finish me before I finish it."

"Good, 'cause they say 'twelve hours from bottle to throttle, twelve seconds from throttle to bottle.'"

I poured some of the Aquascalientes "hot water" into the coffee cup and sipped it. Sipping turned the throat burn into only mild sizzling as it went down. The trip seemed unending, as is this description of it.

PLEASE, DON'T WAKE ME, NO, DON'T SHAKE ME LEAVE ME WHERE I AM—I'M ONLY SLEEPING

I woke up just in time to see us quickly cross a bit more ocean and fly over a white-sand beach as we landed on another dirt runway that made Aquascalientes look like O'Hare. At least Aguascalientes had a metal shed. This place had nothing.

The Skytrain was pulling into a station.

Peter woke as we slowed. He turned and looked at me over his seatback. I shrugged.

Instead of turning off the runway toward a terminal, the plane rolled straight ahead for the longest time, a forest of palm trees rolling past the windows. Finally, we came to a quick stop and Peter and I jerked forward from the hard braking. One engine stopped turning, then the other, and the plane became incredibly and strangely silent. Even so, I could still hear the hum of the engines in my head and feel the motion in my ass.

My heart raced again. Even if this wasn't Pepperland, it was all still exciting to me. It was another step, another plateau to somewhere I didn't know. Julie came out of the cockpit. "How 'bout that! We made it! Amazin', huh?"

"Yeah, we made it," I answered. "So where'd we make it to?"

He walked quickly to the door behind the left wing. I wondered how many more plateaus were still to come, eager to know where we were and what was about to happen. "You boys glued to them seats?" Julie asked as he popped the door open and lowered the stairs. "Or are you comin' out to see the sights?"

We needed no further invitation.

"Don't expect no kiss and a lei from some hulahula girl boys, this ain't Honolulu." Julie stood in the door, blocking our exit. All we could see were palm trees. He sighed deeply. "Shit, Ah'm tired." He walked slowly down the stairs and hopped down to the dirt below. We followed with energy tempered with fear.

Expecting nothing more than palm trees—marvel enough to a lifelong Midwesterner—when we finally climbed off the plane we could finally see where we were and get a lay of the land. At the end of the runway in front of us, exactly where we couldn't see from the DC-3 side windows, lay a large encampment, a village of crude buildings, large tents, trucks and aircraft beneath the palms.

The buildings were leftover World War II Quonset huts, looking like enormous metal drums cut in half lengthwise. All were painted a puke tan color, their plastic-sheeting windows waving in the light breeze. Two military trucks were parked near the village, both painted olive drab. Neither had any markings.

Two aircraft were parked between our plane and the huts. One was a Sabreliner jet, larger than the Lear we flew to Mexico and the other was a huge, propeller-driven C-119, a "Flying Boxcar," another legendary workhouse of a plane big enough so that any kind of heavy freight would fit inside. During my model-plane building days I built mine so that the enormous cargo door swung open and closed. Both aircraft were the types of planes that could have easily flown crates of supplies from Lou Flowers' Miami airport.

Hello again, Lou.

Overall, the scene was perfect for a model plane building kid: a "Flying Boxcar" next to our "Skytrain," pure airborne serendipity.

It's also time to say "hi" to Kathy Powell again. I don't know if you grew up to be as big an airplane fan as you were a Beatle fan, but you missed two kinds of excitement.

And "hello" to Mara too. Maybe I'll see you soon, but I'm not sure if I can and I especially don't know if you'll ever want to see me.

Like Lou told us, none of the planes had any markings. Except for the jet that seemed so out of place that it must have flown through a time warp to be in the tableau, the whole place looked like tired, old World War Two surplus.

"Welcome to the Jarvis Islands, boys," Julie said with another sigh, "the guano capital of the Pacific."

If my geography wasn't good enough to answer questions about North American locations or British time zones, I certainly couldn't pinpoint the Jarvis Islands. I still have trouble finding them on a globe even though I've looked them up many times.

The temperature was high, maybe in the 90's, but the humidity was low, tropical but tolerable with a light sea breeze.

"You're almost right smack dab on the equator," Julie told us, "right near such luxurious hot spots as Christmas Island, Starbuck Island and the ever-popular Malden Island. In other words, boys, if you ever felt you were no place before, you ain't never been here!"

"What's the guano thing?" I asked, genuinely wanting to know and also trying to make simple conversation to delay facing the feared unknown.

"Guano" is a lovely word that rolls off the tongue in a pleasant way the human mouth isn't used to forming. As easy as it is to say, it's also a pleasant word to hear. As harsh a word as "Skinker" is, "guano" is just as easygoing.

"Bird shit."

"Bird shit, what?"

"That's it!" he explained. "Guano is shit. You've heard of bullshit? Well this is *gull*shit. Americans used to send sailing ships all the way here just to harvest it by the shipload…by the *shitload* I guess. It was hot shit a hundred years ago. They made explosives out of it. It was gen-you-iiiiiine hot shit."

Hot shit.

"Nobody's been here much since they gave up the guano in about 1880. The Brits claimed they owned the place for a time, but then they decided they sure as hell didn't want it. Then the U.S. took over just to expand west. It's been officially listed as 'uninhabited' for years and years and now we're the assholes who uninhabit it!"

We were on a deserted island in the middle of no place, on an island whose claim to history was a harvest of natural shit. I felt like Gilligan again. I thought back to the clues on Beatle records and how they might have connected to this place. I caught up with Julie as he walked toward the village. "Did they ever do nuclear testing here?"

"Nope, not here, bud, not here." he answered. "Hell, if they did nuke testing here, there wouldn't be doodly squat left. It's just not that big a place, 'bout a mile and a half square." It didn't seem to me there was much left anyway, at least without the guano. "Come on in boys. Let's go see the mayor of this little burg."

Julie led us toward the Quonset closest to the runway.

As we walked through the parked planes, I looked over my shoulder to watch Bruce come out of the DC-3. He didn't. I figured he was running a post-flight checklist and couldn't be bothered. He told me later there was no post-flight checklist, that he keeled over asleep during the long flight and the long sterile cockpit of descent, his head thumping into the side window, sawing logs all the way in. Julie landed the plane by himself. Bruce later said such a thing never happened to him before and he was embarrassed at how unprofessional it was. If it had happened during his military days, he said, he would have been court-martialed. But nobody was court-martialed at Jarvis. Bruce's only mission was completing his mission to get us all there alive, which he did.

Before he turned the War Surplus knob on the War Surplus door of the War Surplus Quonset hut, Julie (who had already admitted he was human War Surplus), stopped and turned to us. "Boys, you are about to meet the best damn Company Man this side of Pago Pago, and about this I shit you not."

I quickly tried to add up how many Company Men I'd already met. Five, I figured, maybe six. There were at least two Hancocks, two pilots, the waiter on the Admiral, maybe the deckhand in overalls who pulled me out of the engine room and the Wisconsin/Minnesota man in Mexico. They were all competent and serious about their work but also reasonably personable. Even in light of Julie's low credibility factor, his brief description of the "best damn Company Man" made me expect either a total nincompoop or a somber, all-business type in a suit and tie who was incapable of having any fun, the one thing that money…well, you know.

She was neither.

WHEN YOU FIND YOURSELF IN THE THICK OF IT HELP YOURSELF TO A BIT OF WHAT IS ALL AROUND YOU, SILLY GIRL

"Boys, this is Martha, the head man in charge of this proud and noble Birdshit Bureau of the Central Intelligence Agency. It's a very prestigious assignment in the Company, just eeeeeeeeeverybody's tryin' to get stationed here."

Martha. Mara. The similarity was not lost on me.

She sat at a gray metal desk, an oscillating fan turning back and forth next to her, blowing her hair. She looked like she was finishing some paperwork when we entered and spoke in a calm, quiet voice without looking up. "Fuck you, Julie."

"If only there was no policy, honey, if only there was no policy..."

Martha put her pen down, pushed back the sweaty strands of softly graying brown hair from her forehead, closed the manila folders she was writing in and turned her chair. She was a large woman, maybe five-foot-five, but close to two hundred pounds. She wore khaki shorts and a plain white t-shirt. Maybe forty-five years old, she grinned as she less-than politely asked for some privacy. "Beat it, Julie."

"Yessssssssssss Maaaaaaaaaaaaaaa'am!" Julie clicked his heels to attention and snapped a salute before he pulled a perfect military about face. At the door, he turned back, smiled and asked "And how do you mean that Ah should 'beat it?'"

She held up an arm and pointed to the door. "Out!" Julie scooted a little run to the door, his arms and hands pumping. He slammed the door behind him, making the entire hut vibrate. "I love that guy," Martha smiled. "He's a real piece of work."

I wondered if "piece of work" was an official CIA-issued description.

"But I hope you guys know how damn lucky you are to be alive after flying with that asshole. When he brought me here, he had that DC-3 doing things it was never designed to do and it scared the crap out of me. But the fact is, when push comes to shove, I'd pick him to fly me anywhere, any time."

I never saw Julie again. Even after Bruce showed up at The Onion, he never told me what happened to Julie, always changing the subject in the strongest possible terms. I wondered if Julie genuinely did drop the DC-3 into the ocean. That would have been a waste of a good, kind man who made me feel better during a difficult time and a waste of a legendary aircraft.

"Hi" Julie.

Wiping the sweaty hair from her forehead again, Martha stuck out her hand. "You must be Peter. I like your music a lot."

"Thank you, luv."

She turned to me. "And you're Jeff."

"Yes," I said, waiting to hear there was something about me she liked too.

"Gentlemen, you've passed the sixth plateau. Oops, wait a minute! Sorry. Peter, welcome and congratulations on being here. I think you'll be happy you made the trip. Jeff, you're the one who passed the sixth plateau. So congratulations to you." It wasn't "I like your music," but as a semi-compliment, I took it gladly.

"Thanks."

"And now I have to ask you…"

"I know, it's policy," I interrupted rudely, "and the answer is yes."

She paused a moment before continuing, a small smile betraying her irritation at being interrupted. "You've heard this before, huh? Okay, the question is, do you want to try for the seventh plateau?"

"What the hell do you think?" I was surly out of sheer tiredness and frustration. There was no smile on Martha's face. "I've been kidnapped, died, hid in a boat, then sat on that damn plane so long my butt is legally dead and now I'm in the bird poop capital of…" By the time I started to describe the little I knew about Jarvis Island, her look stopped me the way every mother has "a look" that tells her children she's had enough.

"Anyway," I said, lowering my tone, "you bet I'm going on. Unless you can give me a better option."

I meant nothing more than a weary, smartmouth retort to a redundant question, but her reply was serious and straightforward. "The options are, as always, that we take you home on the next flight out or, if you prefer, we'll take you anyplace you want to go and then you're on your own. But whether you like it or not, I still need a straight answer. Do you want to try for the seventh plateau?" She sounded like a doctor or teacher who had heard it all before and wouldn't let foolishness get in the way of business.

"Yes! Yes ma'am! And I'm sorry. Of course I want to try for the seventh plateau!" I was apologetic and defensive, afraid I stuck my entire foot, calf and thigh into my mouth so deeply a surgeon couldn't remove them or that the teacher would send me to the principal's office. Please just don't call my parents because they'll never understand. I'll be good.

"Good. Understand that I had to ask." Her voice was calm and friendly again. "If that's what you want to do, then you'll both have a couple of days layover here until the…until you reach the next step—the next plateau for you Jeff."

"Okay."

"Peter, you'll find an envelope with your name on it on one of the beds in the next building. Read the information in the envelope and make sure you understand it. Let me know if you have any questions, okay?"

"I can handle that." Peter stood for a moment, waiting for more instructions.

"That will be all, Peter, you may go." She sounded like a Bureau Chief.

"Oh. Okay. Yes mum. Catch ya later, Jeff luv."

"Yeah, later."

Peter slung his backpack over his shoulder and left to discover whatever there was to find. I stayed behind, hoping Martha would tell me to go with Peter. "You and I need to talk," she said. Years later, ages into a long marriage, I learned that when a woman speaks those words it usually means the woman needs to talk and the man needs to listen.

She picked up a file folder from her desktop. "Sit down please." I opened an old wooden, War Surplus folding chair and plopped it down near her desk. She looked at the contents of the folder, then up at me. Her voice was gentle. "How are you doing?"

"Fine I guess. Why?"

"Because I know what's going through your head, believe me. I do. In fact, I probably know what you're feeling and thinking better than you do."

"What then?"

"You know what I'm talking about." She scooted her chair an ootch closer to mine. "I know about you, about Mara, about your parents and how they got here after The War. I know how you were raised in a safe but sometimes overbearing home. I know about your high school and college, that you're a photographer turned disc jockey, that you smoke cigarettes—Marlboros in the box—and I know you've got to be feeling things you've never felt before. They may be feelings you can't even describe, so that's why I asked how you're doing."

"Do you have the profile on me? One of the Hancocks said there was a psychological profile."

"Who? Oh, Hancock, your I.C.A.—your Initial Contact Agent. Right. Yes, I have your profile right here."

"Can I see it?" Journalism school taught me to be aggressive about my right to see documents of public record.

"No, you may not," she snapped. I knew there was no questioning her authority. Obviously, my psychological profile as collected by the CIA was not quite public information.

"Okay then," I wimped out, not having enough confidence or aggressiveness to push my luck, "will you tell me what it says?"

"It says what I told you, that you're someone who left a very stable life behind you, a life that you were used to, a life that you might not have wanted to give up. That's why we need to talk. I need to make absolutely sure that you're okay."

"I'm okay. Really."

"I'm sure you are. But we have to talk anyway."

"Okay. What do you want to know?"

"Let's start off with how you're feeling."

"Tired." I laughed but there was more truth than wiseacre in my answer.

Martha smiled then went on. "I'll give you that one. But what about otherwise?"

"To tell you the truth…"

"That's what I want."

"I feel bad I don't feel bad." I wasn't smiling any more.

"How so?"

I stood up from my chair and started twirling my hair with my thumb and forefinger. "Can I pace?"

"If it makes you feel better."

"When it all started, first in Columbia, then in St. Louis…Geez Louise, when was that? Yesterday? Day before?"

"Something like that."

"Geez it seems like…"

"I'm sure it does. Go on."

"Well, while it was still in the talking stages, I thought about it and worried about it. My parents and Mara were in my head constantly."

"How did you feel about it?"

"I felt terrible! I couldn't believe I was even thinking about leaving them in this huge lie to mourn and cry and think I'm dead!"

"And then?"

"And then?" It took me a long time to build up the honesty to continue. "That's the strangest thing. After it all started rolling, on the boat and on the planes, after it took so long, I started thinking about it less and less. They just weren't in my head any more. I started thinking about what was happening and where I was going and where I was and it all just took over my brain!"

"You were in the moment?"

"Yeah. I'm not sure what that means, but I guess so. I was exactly there, where I was, whatever was happening. It all just seemed so new that everything old didn't exist any more."

"Uh huh. Do you think you'll feel bad again?"

"I don't know. Why? Will I?"

"I can't answer that. But it's my job to make sure we don't have a bunch of unhappy people, that everybody's okay with the program. We want to make sure everybody is in the moment and not somewhere else mentally or emotionally. That's important to success or failure from our point of view. Do you think you can do that?"

"Yeah, I think so."

"Good. But we also know that sooner or later, when you've got time to yourself, those feelings will come back. We know this as a fact. You will have second thoughts. And then you'll have third and fourth thoughts. You'll wonder why you did what you did and about the hurt you think you caused. If you're lucky, those feelings won't last long. But I guarantee you'll have them. We see it almost every time."

"What do I do then?"

This was the first time I ever heard psychobabble and found it interesting. I would hear it again years later from a therapist to whom I could never be totally honest, could never tell the full extent of my history and experience lest he think I was truly crazy. "We'll work with you and try to help you deal with your feelings," Martha said. "I know that if it gets that bad, you might even think about going home, so that's why the seventh plateau question is so important to everybody."

"Uh huh."

"But you also need to know that once you're at the destination, once you're finally part of the program…"

"Yes?"

"You can't go back."

"Right." That was all I could muster.

"But this is all very normal. We've been able to deal with all of the 'what have I done' problems so far because we did such a good job of selecting our people."

"Okay."

"But we have to talk about this and settle any old issues right now. This is the make-or-break point."

I gave real consideration to the seventh plateau question and then, feeling I had no other choice, made a command decision. "I'll be okay. Really. I mean, this is such a drastic change I don't think there'll be a problem. It's such a whole, clean start-over. Do you know what I mean?"

"Sure I do. There have been lots of people with situations like yours back in The World. Most of them never even got the initial contact. To be honest, there were a few who got all the way here who had so little remorse they didn't go any further either, we never even asked them about the seventh plateau. But it's part of my job to give the final evaluation, to worry about the things the other operatives might not think about."

"Okay."

"Then I'll finally ask you. Do you want to try for the..."

"Yes! Definitely, yes!"

"Good." She scribbled inside the folder, then closed it. "I expected you to say that. So now you do what Peter did. There's an envelope with your name on it on a bed in the next hut. Read it, relax and enjoy yourself while you're here."

"Thanks. Are there showers here?"

"Not in the hut, they're in the lolly next door—that's the bathroom and the showers. But shower fast, the water's solar heated, it's not that warm to begin with and once the sun drops it cools off pretty quick. And even when there is warm water, there's not much. So you better get used to the idea of quick, cool showers."

"Okay."

"And Jeff, I have one favor to ask."

"What?"

"Get rid of that goddam tie." Martha smiled broadly. "There's no use for neckties except to keep necktie-makers rich. When I was married, I bought ties for my husband and that was the part of the marriage I hated most. Among other things."

My necktie was loosened hours before my meeting with Martha and, quite frankly, I forgot I was wearing it. No matter how much I hate wearing ties now, it was different then. While I knew some people who adopted the "hippie" role full time who wore neckties only as headbands, I also knew others—especially the frat rats—who gladly wore coats and ties, not always needing any occasion any more special than wanting to wear them. They were raised in a necktie culture and the "traditional look" was part of their wardrobe. For me, tying a tie was an unnatural act, wearing it a sin. But I got used to it as a fratboy and did what I had to do. This is one of the greatest embarrassments of my admission that I was a fraternity man, confessing that I knew necktie people. It is also one of my proudest confessions that I am not now, nor have I ever been, a voluntary necktie man myself.

I pulled the knot of the tie until it untied itself. I straightened it out, folded it and put it into the pocked of the blue blazer I carried off the plane.

Martha smiled. "Isn't that better?"

"Yeah. Lots."

"Is there anything else?"

"Just the big questions, like am I close? Where are we going? How many more damn plateaus are there? What's going to happen next? I know neckties are a pretty pressing issue, but could I get some answers to the other questions too?"

"You've earned some truth so I'll give you some. You're within a hundred miles of where you're headed and once you leave here it won't take long to get there. But I can't tell you where it is, how you'll get there or what you'll find when you get there or what will happen after you arrive. Fair enough?"

"No, but I'll deal with it." I was trying to be "in the moment."

"Excellent. Enjoy yourself while you're here. Read what's in your envelope. Meet the others who are waiting with you. You'll get more information along the way and you'll find out everything soon." She stood up from her chair and walked me toward the door and out of the hut. "Is your camera empty?" I had carried the Pentax off the plane.

"Yes. Hancock took my film."

"May I see?" I opened the camera to reassure it was empty. "Any more film?"

I patted my blazer pockets. "No. No more."

"Good. Go to the hut and keep reminding yourself that the hard part is over."

"Thanks."

"You're very welcome. Now have a good time."

Appropriately social worked, psychologized, profiled and photographically purged, I walked away from Martha's hut wondering whether she meant I should have a good time at Jarvis or at wherever I was going later.

I didn't know what to do. Though the DC-3 was still parked outside, Julie was gone. I hoped to find Peter's familiar face but he was gone too.

The second Quonset hut had cots pushed against both outside walls. Most were covered in sheets and green army blankets (more War Surplus), and tightly made. A few were unmade and looked as though they were slept in for many rough nights. At least two of the beds were shoved together to make a double, very unbarracks-like. There were maybe twenty cots in all.

Between each bed were crudely made wooden storage cubbies. They not only looked like War Surplus, they were so rickety they looked as if the soldiers who made them must have been ordered to build them during the heat of battle. Like the tables at the Shack, the cubbies were covered with graffiti and carved-in initials.

I found the bed that held the envelope with "Jeff Scott" typed on it. I sat on the bed, noticing Peter's backpack on the adjacent cubby. The pseudonym would, I supposed, go with me for the remainder of my Utopian eternity. I was still proud that they were, at least, my real initials.

I noticed that more than initials were carved into the cubbies. Mine also held such appropriate markings as "I Was" and "28IF." Under the latter carving, someone penciled in "And I was 24 IF." Someone else drew the name "Joe Jake" followed by a question mark, all in the shape of a left-handed guitar.

I examined the envelope. There was a series of numbers written in the lower corner on the back, but the numbers meant nothing to me and I would not learn their significance until Pepperland fell. The numbers were the Social Security number I would be given in my new, reestablished life, the Social Security number I still use.

I ripped the envelope open, dropping the shreds on the floor.

The top sheet of many papers inside the envelope was a hand-written letter on deep blue stationery. There was an odd design atop the letter. I recognized it as a John Lennon drawing in the style of *In His Own Write* and *Spaniard in the Works*. Above the design was a horizontal line. Below that line was an arc-up semicircle with another horizontal line closing it off beneath. It looked like a line drawing of a sunset. Inside the semicircle was a dove flying in front of what I thought was the setting sun. I had to stare at the dove before I realized it had a fish tail. I'd never realized how much fish tails and bird tails look alike.

Shortly after, I learned it was John's simple graphic concept of an undersea dome filled with love and peace.

The letter was written in ink, by hand:

> *Dear Jeff:*
>
> *Welcome to the Revolution.*
>
> *We know this has been a difficult time. Travel is hard under the best circumstances, and it's no fun at all unless you are with people you love.*
>
> *And soon you shall be. And soon it will be.*
>
> *Please know that you have been chosen as part of this little experiment in a new society, as has everyone you shall meet. We look forward to having you in the group. It will be just like starting over. All you need is Love. And soon, you shall have that too.*
>
> *Don't be afraid of the dark.*

The letter was signed "John," "George" and "Ringo."

The absence of Paul's signature was blatant. Maybe he simply wasn't there when the letter was written, I thought. Instinctively, I wondered if it was another clue but I quickly realized that the time for clues was past. This was the real thing.

At the moment, not knowing what joy and disappointment were to come, I was pleased to have officially been welcomed to the Revolution—the one with a capital R.

SOON WE'LL BE AWAY FROM HERE
STEP ON THE GAS AND WIPE THAT TEAR AWAY
ONE SWEET DREAM, BE TRUE TODAY.
BE TRUE TODAY

The envelope held a number of printed information sheets behind the cover letter. One explained how Jarvis was an orientation to the program, the people and the time zone. Another page explained how medical, dental and psychological personnel would be available whenever anyone needed them. Another sheet was about how we were welcome to raid the Jarvis "dining/supply" shed for food or drink at any time on a fix-it-yourself basis. The same page also explained how appropriate clothing was available for those who didn't bring their own and included a request that all swimwear taken from the supply shed be returned to a laundry hamper before departure.

Still another page emphatically said each person was responsible for cleaning up his or her own messes in the Quonset and dining huts, the lolly and outside. Already, I thought, Utopia was not as perfect a place as I imagined it would be. Somehow, I never thought I would have to pick up after myself in Utopia. I collected the shreds of torn envelope from the floor and put them in my pocket.

Though I didn't notice it at the time, many years later I realized I never signed any documents waiving legal liability for my health or safety. Either the Intelligence Community didn't care about those things or 1970 was simply a much less litigious time. Probably both. Such was the Revolution with a capital R.

Below the information sheets was a map of Jarvis Island. It didn't show much, just the landing strip, two Quonset huts at the end of the runway, an adjacent building marked "LOLLY-LOO" (toilets and showers)" and a square representing "dining/supply." A line leading away from the village was labeled "path to beach" and next to the beach was another large Oceanside area printed in bright red capital letters: "DANGER—OFF LIMITS!"

I was immediately lured to the beach. As a landlocked Midwesterner, it held great curiosity and huge attraction for me. Plus, I needed to find other people who were also insecure and uncertain about their present and their futures and I figured the beach would probably be where to find them.

I wished I'd brought swimming trunks. Based on the information in the envelope, I hoped to find what I needed at the supply hut. But I tarried, thinking about sleep.

And on top of it all, I was afraid again.

I tarried because I wanted to put off going yet another place where I had never been, following a map to someplace I didn't know, to meet more people I'd never seen.

And then, like one of those stupid and unbelievable scenes in a bad movie when a character experiences an epiphany and the plot pulls a one-eighty toward the happy ending, I realized the stupidity of my fear. I wasn't the same fearful person I was before. I was suddenly and remarkably fearless. I had already made the biggest decision of my life by deciding to die. I flew thousands of miles alone. While others helped me along, I made the choices and acted on my own. In all these miles and hours, I'd grown up into myself. I traveled a lifetime away from who I was before.

Stashing my filmless camera, useless jacket and ridiculous tie into my cubby, I walked out of the hut. As a mental compromise to my fear, I skipped the supply hut and went straight to the beach wearing the slacks, shirt and loafers from my comfortable former life. I wasn't dressed for the beach, but I was making it there on my own.

The walk seemed longer than the map indicated. Outside the clearing of the village, the palm trees became so tall and thick I could only see the sky in small, waving, sunlight dots as the fronds swung in the breeze. I constantly hoped to hear reassuring voices as I drew closer to the beach. Dots of sunshine dappled the path.

There were no voices.

Only the sound of my own footsteps on the dirt and birdsong in the trees.

I began to become afraid again.

Still, I marched forward down the path.

And then, like a movie soundtrack, music quietly snaked in under the sound effects of wind through the palms. Faint at first, it grew louder with each step. I ran toward it. Through my cigarette-induced huffing, I finally recognized it as "Soft Parade" by the Doors. Not a Beatle song.

Can you give me sanctuary?
I must find a place to hide.
A place for me to hide.

I went toward the music, alternating fast walking with running. The music became louder and more distinct. I began to hear the ocean.

Unexpectedly, the darkness under the trees opened up the way Oz revealed itself when Dorothy opened the door of her house after the tornado. Everything was incredible color. I wasn't near Kansas any more.

The sea was phenomenally blue, exactly the same color as the stationery of the letter in my envelope from John, George and Ringo. The waves were unthreatening and inviting. The sky was a bright red-orange with clouds streaking in front of a setting sun. It was more of a postcard picture than I'd ever seen on a picture postcard.

Five people sat clustered on the beach, three men and two women. The music boomed from a portable eight-track tape player on the sand.

As the group watched, a man stood alone, chest-deep in the surf, looking over his shoulder and out to sea as his body faced the beach, waiting for the next wave to break just behind him. With the wave, he dove headlong toward the shore, caught the curl and rode and rode and rode, his head rising above the water, gulping for breath (even landlocked Midwesterners knew about surfing and "catching the curl" from the main sources of American oceanographic culture, the Beach Boys and Jan and Dean).

He bounced along with the wave, arms forward, riding on his stomach like Superman on water. When he neared the beach, I saw his pale bare butt shining brightly as it bounced with the surf. After his ride, he ran legs-high back into the water to catch the next perfect wave for another ride into shore.

As I stood in the clearing that led from the path to the beach, the naked man in the surf noticed me and waved. "Jeff!" he cried. "Come on down luv! Come on! Get your anti-American, Commie-pinko arse down here!"

YES WE'RE GOING TO A PARTY PARTY
I WOULD LIKE YOU TO DANCE
YES WE'RE GOING TO A PARTY PARTY
TAKE A CHA-CHA-CHA-CHANCE

His genitalia flapping, his legs splayed apart to reduce the possibility of testicular injury, Peter jogged out of the water and on to the shore. He stopped at the group on the beach, picked up an olive drab War Surplus towel and wrapped it around his middle. I walked toward him quickly. My shoes quickly filled with fine sand. I took the loafers off my feet and yanked off my socks, barefooting it toward Peter.

Striding toward him, I could see Peter pick up a large blue can the size of a tomato juice can. He took a long drink and even though I couldn't hear it, I knew there was probably an audible "ahhhhhhh" following the long slug. He pointed toward me and the others all turned to watch me approach.

My fraternity pledge days taught me many important things besides urinal cleaning: how to say the Greek alphabet three times while holding a lighted match; how to identify every sorority pin at a glance; the names, hometowns and college majors of everyone in my fraternity house; and, for purposes of both pledge rush and house security, that new people are to be met with an outstretched hand and an introduction that included my name, hometown and major. With no apparent need for recitation of the Greek alphabet and since no one was wearing an unidentified sorority pin, I met the group with "Hi, I'm Jeff from St. Louis." I omitted my major, deciding it was irrelevant.

One of the men stood and shook my hand but didn't tell me his name (much less his hometown or major), before Peter cut in. "What the hell took so long, luv? I told these people to expect you and I've been havin' to make excuses for you!"

"Well, I was…"

"I don't give a pile a' guano where you been, luv! Meet the crew, every one of 'em a true lover of the sacred bird shit."

He introduced me to Jacques and Susanne, a French couple who spoke no English. Jacques was the one who first shook my hand on the beach. He didn't answer because he didn't know how. The other two men were Dan from Sydney, Australia and Stanley from Winnipeg, Canada.

Winnipeg.

There's no way to say it slowly. It must be pronounced almost monosyllabically. *Winnipeg*. It comes off the tongue almost as nicely as the word "guano."

The other woman was Judy from Jersey. Peter made a big point of how she really wasn't from Jersey but was from *New* Jersey, one of the colonies near *New* York. He hocked on and on about how Americans weren't clever enough to think of names for places, that all they ever did was add "New" to the names of old places. He claimed that Elvis, Coca Cola and Edward R. Murrow were the only original things the U.S. ever exported to the U.K. Taking a line from toilets manufactured by the Kohler Company of Kohler, Wisconsin that labels its ceramic products "K of K/USA" we soon started calling Judy from Jersey, "J of J/USA."

Everyone but Peter wore swimsuits from the supply shed, some more ill fitting than the others. Peter said he was too impatient to make a supply hut stop so he wore "the togs I came with." I admitted I was also too impatient to stop, but I added that I didn't think I'd wear the same swimsuit as Peter.

"Fostah's?" Dan asked, picking up a tomato juice-sized can like the one I saw Peter drinking.

"What is that?"

"It's lagah, mate. You know, *beah*! It's Aussie beah! We know how to drink this shit, and it's not out of them little pussy bottles!"

I smiled, enjoying his accent and thinking it much sharper than Peter's. "Ey, Jeff! What's the similarity between American beahs and makin' love on a boat?"

"I don't know, what?"

"Theyah both fuckin' neah watah!" Dan roared with a delightful hardeharhar laugh and his laugh made me laugh. "Ain't you been ta the supply hut, mate?"

"No, I came here first."

"Then ya still don't know what good cah they takin' of us heah, eh mate? I figgahed thah musta been a Yank comin' when I saw that watery Boodweisah! It makes sense if you're from Saint Looie! That's Boodweisah country, ayn' it? It was another bloody clue! I shouldn've guessed thay'd be a bloke from Saint Looie!"

"Great," I said, though I didn't really mean it. Not only did he offend me—albeit with great charm—by calling my hometown "Saint Looie" (locals never call it anything but "Saint Louis"), I just wasn't that much of a beer drinker. Besides, I thought of the brandy I had on the plane and remembered another fraternity house lesson: "beer on whiskey, mighty risky. Whiskey on beer, you're in the clear." While I didn't know if brandy was considered "whiskey," I knew it was in the same league and worried about getting puke drunk sick if I topped it with the "lagah."

I thought about Mara's ability to make one small drink last an entire party, how she nursed it even while others around her chugged away.

Mara.

In the moment. In the moment. In the moment.

I took a giant can of "Fostah's" and Dan opened it with a "church key" he wore around his neck the way other people wear religious medals. "Want anothah? Take two, they're small!"

"No thanks."

"Two beahs or not two beahs? That is the question." Dan laughed again, hardeharhar.

Dan did teach me how to drink in The Onion, at least how to drink with great quantities of both "lagah" and laughter.

Jacques and Susanne, the French couple, apparently didn't understand much of the conversation on the beach, but they smiled and nodded lot.

Both a few years older than me, Susanne had an incredibly wide, oversized, overtoothed Mary Tyler Moore/Carly Simon/Jennifer Garner smile that seemed to supplement the light lost by the setting sun. Jacques was a nice enough fellow, especially for someone I couldn't understand.

Judy explained that she spoke a little high school French and managed to combine it with hand gestures to learn Jacques and Susanne were from Paris. Jacques was a house painter, she said, and Susanne was a writer for European music magazines. Judy said Susanne told her that she and Jacques deciphered the clues while she was working on a magazine story about the rumors.

In fact, I wondered whether Susanne's story in that European magazine may have inspired the American newspaper story I read in Columbia, the one headlined "Rumors of Beatle Death Rampant in Europe," the one I took to the radio station, the story that started the whole thing for Mark and me so many months later. I wondered if Susanne's story was what killed me and put me on the beach at Jarvis.

I wondered again why Mark and Beth weren't there with me, what they did wrong to keep them off the plane.

In the moment. In the moment. In the moment.

Blonde, muscular and tanned, Dan explained he was a charter fishing guide in Sydney. About 25 years old, he said he spent a lot of time listening to reel-to-reel tapes of Beatle music during his fishing trips at sea. He said he felt both curious and foolish when he heard "all that boolshit" about Paul's death. But since he spent so much time on the boat, he said, he started keeping a list of clues and sharing them with the people on the charters. Obviously, he shared with the right people because two strangers took his clue notebook from him when he left Wollengong.

I made him repeat the name of the city again, just to make sure I heard it correctly. I laughed at the sound of it but he didn't understand where I found the humor. It was as awkward to pronounce as Winnipeg was easy.

Guano.

Winnipeg.

Wollongong.

If nothing else, Pepperland promised to be a feast for the ear and the vocabulary.

Stanley from Winnipeg never said much of anything except that he was headed to Pepperland "for political reasons." His head-down manner was so curt, I didn't question him further. He seemed a year or two younger than me. What I had in skinny, he made up in rolls of baby fat. He wore the baggiest swimsuit I ever saw, almost long-legged, covering his knees. He wore black high-top basketball shoes.

Judy from Jersey was red-haired and a few years older than me, maybe in her mid- twenties. Single and plain looking, though not unattractive, she was a junior high school English teacher. She admitted being such a consummate Beatle fan that the rumors of Paul's death became a genuine concern. She said she became obsessed with the clues out of fear they were true. She naturally made me think of Kathy Powell. I wondered if Kathy did the same thing and I got a swell of anticipation when I considered if the clues would also lead her to the beach at Jarvis or to Pepperland.

I plead guilty to charges of thinking of Kathy Powell. It was, after all, being in the moment.

Jacques and Susanne said they'd been at Jarvis for five days, Judy for four days and Dan for three. Stanley surprised me when he said he was there more than a week, that until Jacques and Susanne arrived he was alone in the Quonset hut.

Even though we'd all just met, we seemed to be natural friends and acted like old pals who hadn't seen each other in ages. Our conversation was fun and animated, mostly about such important issues as weather and body surfing and how our flights were and the tiredness of our pilots. No one ever mentioned fears of the future. There is not only physical safety in numbers, I guess, but also emotional security among people who understand they might also share great physical danger.

Our first stop after the beach was the "dining/supply" hut. The "dining" part was small, about the size of a two-car garage, filled with a few small tables and chairs. One wall held a large, institutional, stainless steel refrigerator.

The "supply" side was much larger. It was filled with huge rows of metal shelving holding clothes, building material, more canned food than a Christmas "help the needy" campaign and sealed wooden boxes that I immediately assumed came off unmarked planes that were loaded at Miami.

I found some swimming trunks and an olive drab towel. Holding the trunks against my body, I was afraid they might be too tight. But better too tight, I figured, than so loose they pulled off in the waves.

All the clothing in the supply hut was exactly alike. There were hundreds of pairs of jeans and blue denim work shirts, all stacked in no seeming order. After searching, I managed to find some that fit.

After exploring the "supply" side, we all went to the "dining" side and straight to the refrigerator. Behind one door, there was nothing but beer, soda and small airline-sized splits of wine. Behind another door were cases of military rations, including more "shit on a shingle." The third door held treasures of fresh fruit, vegetables and meats.

Stanley grabbed a small box of steaks and started rummaging around the stove. "I was a short order cook in a former life," he announced as he hung a white apron around his neck. He plopped the steaks into several frying pans and lit the burners of two propane camp stoves.

Dan was very pleased with the high life. "See how they feed us, Jeff? Steaks! I told you they'ah takin' cah of us!" He pulled another huge can of "Fostah's" from the 'fridge, leaned back on the legs of his chair and took a long slurp like a man on vacation, someone without a "cah" in the world.

As the luscious, greasy smell of frying meat filled the room, we were all slipping into our own reveries, some fearful and others fanciful. I broke the silence. "I fell off a boat into the Mississippi River." I grinned as I said it, almost cheerful and certainly mischievous, as if I was the coolest person on earth.

There was more silence as everyone looked at me, waiting for the rest of my story. "Yeah?" Stanley asked. "So?"

"That's how I died to get here. What about you guys? How did you die?"

Dan answered first. His death came easy, he said, and was uncomplicated. He took his boat to sea one morning, telling friends he was running engine tests, then he was helicoptered off. The boat was empty when the Aussie Navy found it, turning wide circles in the ocean, engines running full bore.

After Dan's story, Judy admitted she was still uncomfortable with her death. She had to write a nebulous, non-specific goodbye note, then her initial contact agents—her I.C.A.'s—left her note on a bridge. She said she felt guilty, that she never gave anyone the idea she might become a suicide and she feared her friends and family would always wonder why. She also said the religious implications of suicide haunted her, that taking her own life would keep her out of heaven. I tried to convince her it had nothing to do with heaven since she wasn't really dead, but she said it went beyond theory for her, that she was afraid that even faking suicide might be a mortal sin. But, she shrugged, it was the plan they came up with and she had to live with it. And die with it. Besides, if all worked out well, it would take her to a Beatle-based heaven sooner than later.

I remember being impressed with how many water related "deaths" there were. While I know they were done for simplicity's sake—it's hard to find a body in deep or fast-moving water—I also thought it appropriate to our destination.

Stanley said he simply told some people he was "going underground" and didn't need a contrived appearance.

With some difficulty, Judy translated Jacques and Susanne's story about how they told friends they were following an investigative magazine story about something called "Air America." Their families were told their plane was shot down somewhere in Southeast Asia and they did not survive. I assumed Bruce and Julie were the unlucky pilots on that "fatal" plane crash.

All of them thought my "death" on the historic Mississippi sounded romantic. Dan started singing "Old Man River." I pooh-poohed the idea of romance, claiming death is death and none is any more romantic than another. There are no romantic deaths, I said, no matter what the cause or motivation. Any death leaves too many people behind for there to be romance. There was only death and then there was only mourning. I said that since each of us gave up our former lives for something unknown, for an adventure, all our deaths were equally intriguing and interesting but none, I added, carried even the slightest aura of romance.

Immediately, the conversation dwindled until the steaks were ready.

After food and a tiny bit of another enormous can of Foster's, I admitted I was more tired than inspired and needed to rest. Stanley volunteered to clean the kitchen if we all agreed to take our turn next time.

I went to my cot alone, emptied my pockets of change, keys and handkerchief, took off my watch and put them all atop my cubby. I threw my clothes on the floor and fell into bed.

During the night, I was awakened by the sound of Jacques and Susanne making love in the two pushed-together beds. After a minute of voyeuristic listening with my eyes closed, I opened my eyes and tried to peek through the darkness. Unable to see anything, I fell back on my pillow.

Peter took me aside the next morning and asked if I heard them. He said Stanley speculated co-ed living was part of the orientation process to get us used to men and women living together, to living with the inescapable idiosyncrasies of total strangers. Stanley thought they wanted to make everything from public lovemaking to defecation absolutely no big deal.

As I listened more attentively to Jacques and Susanne the next night, my hormones and imagination raging, I started envisioning, wondering, hoping that someday I might be one of the people keeping others awake in some dorm living situation.

In the moment. In the moment. In the moment.

Okay, ahead of the moment.

But give me that. It was a long trip and I had a new life ahead of me, one that for the time being, I could only imagine.

IN THE TOWN WHERE I WAS BORN LIVED A MAN WHO SAILED TO SEA

I was the alone in the Quonset hut when I awoke. We agreed no one would wake anyone else and that we'd all meet on the beach.

I knew a hot, soapy shower would be my first taste of heaven after death, a clean start for a new person living a new life in a new place.

Pulling up my supply hut jeans for the walk to the lolly, I reconsidered my new life. After only an instant's thought, I dropped the jeans, peeled off my underwear and strutted my stuff toward the door in the same uniform Peter wore on the beach. I felt like a bad boy exposing himself without shame. I knew I never would have paraded my skinny, pale, naked body in public before, but this wasn't really me, it was someone else.

In the moment, in the moment, goddammit.

But at the door, I went back to some other moment and wrapped my rough, War Surplus towel around my middle for the walk to the lolly.

The sun was still relatively new to the sky so the water in the solar-heated shower was tepid, hardly steamy, but comfortable. With a breeze blowing over the short wooden lolly walls, my shower was cool and quick, but entirely satisfying and truly cleansing.

Back in the hut, I put on my swimming trunks and left behind all traces of yesterday when my troubles didn't seem so far away. Remembering to clean up after myself, I picked my clothes up off the floor and crammed my slacks and shirt into the tiny cubby with my jacket and tie. I stopped short when I got the coins, useless keys and my watch in the heap atop the cubby. The keys were to my parents' house, the trashmobile and the radio station. Each one unlocked a different part of my life—my former life.

The watch was a gift from Mara. When her cousin visited Switzerland a few years earlier, Mara asked her to find a reasonably priced but high-quality watch for me. It was intended as a Chanukah present in December, but the cousin didn't go to Europe until January so it became a timepiece that didn't come on time. It was a beautiful and different kind of watch, an unknown Swiss brand, local to wherever her cousin visited. I loved it because it was unusually shaped, a gold square with a black leather band. "I wanted something unusual," Mara told me on that Chanukah night in January, "because it would match you." I quickly forgave the gift's tardiness because it was so beautiful in and of itself. And because it was precious for other reasons.

Holding the watch for a moment, turning it and feeling the gold and leather, I toyed with the idea of burying it on the beach or tossing it into the ocean as another way to cut myself off from home, a gesture that would leave the past behind. But I couldn't do it. The watch meant too much. I put it into the pocket of my blazer, folded the jacket and carefully put it into the cubby.

Alone in the hut, after decisions about watches and loose change, I surprised myself when I began unconsciously humming Simon and Garfunkel's "Overs," a song I played often on the radio from an album I overplayed in my room on days when I suffered from serious non-Mara melancholia.

> **No good times.**
> **No bad times.**
> **There's no times at all.**
> **Just the *New York Times*.**

Starting at that moment, with my decision to keep the watch as a reminder of the past, times were suddenly different. I understood the vagaries of time, the literalness of "living in the moment." The moment here and now was the only moment. All past moments were gone, future ones not yet arrived. Time and moments did not exist anywhere but where I was and when I was. I thought it was a very Pepperland kind of philosophy.

I thought about other "time" songs. The first was another Simon and Garfunkel lyric: "Time, time, time, to see what's become of me as I look around for my possibilities."

"Shit," I thought, "another inappropriately appropriate song."

Then I started thinking about the rest of Simon and Garfunkel's *Bookends* album, a record probably every college kid in the world owned at the time. I played it so often I knew every note and every word and realized it was filled with perfectly appropriate time references, starting with the very first song, the "Bookends Theme":

> **Time it was and what a time it was**
> **A time of innocence.**
> **A time of confidence.**
> **Long ago it must be,**
> **I have a photograph.**
> **Preserve your memories,**
> **They're all that's left you.**

This moment was all that was left of me.

From "Fakin' It":

> **When she goes,**
> **She's gone.**
> **If she stays,**
> **She stays here.**

If I had stayed, I would have stayed there. But I went and I was gone. And I was definitely "fakin' it."

Geez Louise, I thought, even the first words on the first full song on the album were on target. From "Save the Life of my Child":

> **'Good God! Don't jump!'**
> **A boy sat on a ledge.**
> **An old man who had fainted was revived.**
> **Everyone agreed it would be a miracle indeed**
> **If the boy survived.**

At the end of the song, the boy "flew away." Then they sing, "Oh my grace, I got no hiding place..." I flew away and I was about to get a hiding place.

Maybe Simon and Garfunkel were building their own Utopia and put clues on *their* albums too! Maybe they were working with the Beatles!

Maybe they were in competition with the Beatles! There were clues that could prove it all!

Even though I was alone, I was embarrassed for even thinking any of this.

Happy birthday to you,
Happy birthday to you,
Happy birthday, dear Jeff,
Happy birthday to you.

Yes! Yes! I had been reborn! It *was* my birthday!

Bullshit.

But such was the mindset. Since that first Thursday on the radio in Columbia, everything was suspicious, everything led to something and everything was subject to interpretation. "Help, help!" I said aloud to no one but myself, "the paranoids are after me!"

I still get that feeling sometime, so many years later, that everything is a clue that actually means something else.

Another personal aside. Sorry.

I tried to think of Beatle songs about time. There weren't many. "A Day in the Life" and "When I'm 64," but not many more.

"Shit," I said aloud again, "there was a damn 'Sea of Time' in *Yellow Submarine* where everybody got younger. They became children in the 'Sea of Time!' Then, as they left it, they got older again! Damn…"

I was being completely absurd.

Months later, a group of us in The Onion all literally rolled on the floor with laughter thinking about songs by other artists that might have been Pepperland clues. "How 'bout *See you in September*?" someone joked. "Maybe the Happenings were in cahoots with the Beatles. "I'll be alone each and every night, while you're away don't forget to write." Then we all sang together "Bye-bye, so long, farewell. Bye-bye, so long farewell." Someone dampened the mood when they reminded us that the spirit of that particular song was that the boy singer was telling his girlfriend to enjoy her summer vacation, that they'd be back together in the fall, that he'd "see you in September." And then everyone was quiet. That was being in the moment for that moment.

"Hey! Hey! How about 'Does Anybody Really Know What Time it is?' Even the name of the group is a clue…it was '*chic*' some time '*ago*!'" That lighthearted stupidity brought us back.

"And 'Monday, Monday?' I died on a Monday, can't trust that day!"

Obviously, I wasn't the only paranoid interpreter of odd musical literature.

We managed to interpret Pepperland clues from virtually every popular song of the 1960s, from "Satisfaction" to "House of the Rising Sun," from "Ferry 'Cross the Mersey' all the way to "Do the Freddie." Maybe it was the gasses that were allegedly pumped into The Onion that got us so silly, maybe it was some Company drug experiment, but those moments at The Onion were particularly memorable.

But back to the moment of the moment.

The general tone on the beach was more subdued than the day before. Talk was mostly innocuous discussion of the warm, green water, friendly waves and tips on riding the surf on outstretched bodies. There was noticeably less loud camaraderie than the day before. Jacques stayed close to Susanne, Peter hung with me while Dan, Stanley and Judy all kept to themselves. It was hard to tell what moment anyone was in at any given moment.

Near midday, after a few "Fostah's" and some allegedly watery "Boodweisahs," we were all on the beach when an olive drab, War Surplus jeep fishtailed toward us at high speed, spraying a wave of loose sand behind it. Martha was at the wheel, alone in the car. She stopped just short of us. "So how is everybody?"

"Fine." "Yeah, fine." "Okay." "Mahthah, how 'bout a bloody Fostah's?"

"Maybe later. I just wanted to tell you that we just got word that your ship is about to come in, if you know what I mean." We had no idea what she meant.

While we questioned Martha about what was about to happen—and while she steadfastly refused to give any answers—Judy tried to translate Martha's news for Jacques and Susanne. It was obvious from the head shaking and hand waving that she had trouble getting them to understand. "I can't figure out how to translate an idiom like 'your ship is about to come in.' I keep telling them 'your big boat is about to arrive' and they say they don't have a boat, they've never had a boat and would never have a boat! I tell them it's a figure of speech and they yell something about the yacht-owning bourgeoisie!"

Martha stepped toward Jacques and Susanne, speaking fluent French. They listened closely, smiling and nodding. When she stopped, Jacques and Susanne looked completely satisfied. Martha turned to Judy, said something in French and Judy slapped herself on the forehead and smiled. She turned to the group and said, "she told them we leave here tomorrow."

We pounced on Martha for more information, but she disclosed nothing more. "You'll find out what you need to know when you need to know it."

Six voices continued slinging questions.

"Where are we going?"

"How will we get there?"

"Are Julius and Bruce gonna fly us?"

"How much longer?"

"Ah we takin' the Sabahlinah?"

"Oh shit, I hope it's not the DC-3!"

"Is this more plateau bullshit? How many plateaus are there?"

Finally, Martha had taken enough badgering. "Look, people! People! Please!" There was frustration bordering on anger in her eyes. Like good Scouts seeing the troop leader hold three fingers in the air, we fell silent. "I can't tell you any more. You leave here tomorrow. I can't tell you where you're going, how you'll get there, how you'll travel or with whom. I've told you everything I can tell you for now."

Then   her   face   brightened   and   her   voice   lightened. "Buuuuuuuuuuuuuut, I can tell you that you are all invited to dinner at my hut at five o'clock." She looked directly at me. "Black tie is neither required nor optional. In fact, anyone wearing any form of neckwear runs the risk of being turned away at the door." I smiled at Martha, recognizing our quiet connection. She half-smiled back as she continued talking. "That's all I can tell you now, there ain't no more and goodbye. See you at dinner. And clean yourselves up! I don't want any more damn sand in my hut than is absolutely necessary!"

After repeating the invitation to Jacques and Susanne in French, both nodding appreciatively, Martha drove off at high speed in the direction from which she had come, fishtailing the jeep left and right as she raced away. If there had been pavement under her, she would have "laid a patch." Since there was only beach, she sent a high spray of fine sand high into the air.

"How the fook are we gonna know when it's five o'clock?" Peter asked.

"We go when it's the moment to go," Judy said. Everyone laughed.

Stanley grimaced into the sun and speculated it was a little before noon. Dan, the seagoing man, speculated it was a bit after twelve, maybe as late as one. Jacques and Susanne started a back-and-forth conversation that made Judy laugh. "They're arguing whether they should go back now since Jacques always takes so long to get ready. He says there's plenty of time but she says 'non,' they need to go back now. Isn't that the cutest married-people thing?" Jacques looked as if he didn't appreciate the cuteness. He looked like a grown man being mothered and nagged.

Ultimately, after more talk and a lot of gesturing, Jacques and Susanne did go back while the rest of us stayed at the beach. Jacques turned and shrugged to us over his shoulder as they walked toward the village.

The four of us who stayed at the beach spent the day doing nothing more productive than sitting, sunning, body surfing and sunburning in the Pacific perfection. As the landlocked Midwesterner, I wanted to spend more time genuinely romping and gamboling in the water, appreciating the novelty of the ocean, but held back to give an impression of oneness with the others and also because I was just never much of either a romper nor gamboler. Judy maintained a polite distance from the water and especially from the men on the beach. Occasionally, inconspicuously, I shot a glance toward her to stare at her body as she lay on a towel.

After approximately three-point-two-five million inconspicuous glances, she felt my stares and walked over to me. Thinking she would accost me for visual intrusion, she asked me to rub a thick coat of Coppertone on her back. As geeky as I felt around women, I built up my courage and testosterone and said of course I would, as if rubbing suntan lotion on female flesh was something I did all the time. The creamy lotion was warm from the sun as it poured from the bottle onto my palm. I rubbed it onto her shoulders and back, honestly enjoying the process and the contact. With newfound chutzpah, I asked her if she also wanted me to rub lotion on the front of her body, hardeharhar. She brusquely said she could handle the front quite well and had for years, thank you very much. As she walked away from me, I could smell the fresh Coppertone, but it was mixed with a barely detectable trace of another light scent that I recognized immediately: Chanel Number Five.

She returned to her towel, acting as if I had done nothing more than rub suntan lotion on her back. I felt something more happened, that there was a connection, but maybe suntan lotion makes connections too slippery to take hold. And maybe the faint bouquet of Chanel made my mind wander to places it shouldn't have gone.

This beach nothingness—save the sunscreen episode, which, in my head and fantasy life at least went far beyond nothingness—went on for several hours. Then Peter, naked again and sunburning parts that would be very painful the next day, sat up absolutely straight. "Bloooooooooooooooooooooody fooooooooooooooooooock!" We all turned to look at him. "What the blooooooooody fooooooooooock is that?" He was staring wide-eyed out to sea.

Coming directly toward us, just off shore, was a boat very low in the water. As it moved closer, it rose higher.

A submarine was surfacing from the sea.

Visibly attached to the front deck and riding high was a small, cigar-butt-shaped appendage. It didn't look long enough to be truly cigar-shaped, it was just a stub.

The stubby cigar butt on the submarine deck, whatever it was, was bright yellow.

I still have Mara's Swiss watch in a box in a dresser drawer.

...AND HE TOLD US OF HIS LIFE
IN THE LAND OF SUBMARINES...

We watched the submarine sail toward us and down the coast toward the area that was in red on the map and marked "DANGER."

"Bloooody foooooooock." It was all Peter could say, over and over, each repetition longer than the previous one. "Bloooooooooooody foooooooooook! Bloooooooooooooody foooooooooooooooooooooock." To hear him, we might well have sighted the Loch Ness Monster riding a UFO with Bigfoot, not simply a submarine in the middle of the ocean.

"Yeah," I agreed, without the overemphasis of vowels. "bloody fuck." I made no attempt to mimic his accent, only his sentiment. "Bloody fucking fuck."

Later, among a group of Brits, Aussies and New Zealanders at Pepperland, Peter told me that my chosen words stuck in his mind. He taught me, to the delight of the real "English speakers," that "bloody" was the British equivalent of "fucking," therefore "bloody fucking fuck" was a triple redundancy. "That's the problem with you Yanks," he said. "None of you can speak bloody fooking English."

Why we never suspected a submarine, I can't even speculate. But it was such a non sequitur, such a surprise, it amazed each of us long after we thought we had experienced every possible everything.

As the sub disappeared down the coastline, Peter wrapped his towel around his middle and chased after it. He came back quickly to report he discovered a tall fence with a locked gate further down the beach, running from inside the jungle to deep into the water. The fence, he said, was topped with razor wire.

As composed and calm as we all tried to be, each of us also knew there would be no more beach time, no more worrying about whether we would be early or late for dinner. We all quickly snatched up our things and hustled back to the village.

We raced toward quick showers, knowing but not caring about the possibility of the shortage of warm water. Sand sprayed from the crotches of our swimsuits onto the floor all around our bunks as we raced to be the first to the tepid showers.

But as the burst of energy caught up with us, and as some of us— me—recognized the nakedness of the moment, we—I—slowed down and covered. "J of J/USA" had the same thought at the same time and modestly turned her back to undress, quickly pulling up her jeans and putting on a long-tailed work shirt.

Peter, of course, felt no embarrassment and was the first one out of the hut, bounding toward the showers, his genitalia flapping again, his legs apart again to avoid injury. I pulled my supply hut jeans up over my damp, sandy ass.

We met Susanne and Jacques heading back from the showers, knowing Susanne had been right. If we started back to the hut when she insisted Jacques leave the beach, we'd all be done already.

Judy tried to explain to them what we saw, but said it was difficult because she didn't know the French word for 'submarine.' With many hand motions, deep knee-bending demonstrations and glugging sounds, Jacques and Susanne's eyes finally grew wide and they seemed to understand. They turned and scurried to the hut.

At the lolly, we found Peter already holding his head under a weak stream of water. "There's room for one more," he said, pointing to the adjacent shower stall. All three men offered to let "J of J" go first—who says chivalry is dead?—but she declined, whispering she'd rather take her chances on ice cubes pouring from the shower than share the lolly with Peter.

When he finished, the rest of us let Judy shower alone as we waited outside. Dan's eyes and an elfin head waggle suggested we should all peek over the low lolly walls. I'll admit I was tempted to sneak a quick look. Still feeling chivalrous, none of us did.

By the time it was our turn to shower the sand and sweat off our bodies, the water that was left was cold. The tanks on the roof were nearly emptied and stood waiting for the next day's rains to refill and warm in the sun.

In the end, we went to Martha's dressed in the only available clothing, blue work shirts and jeans. I couldn't help but notice that Judy smelled of Chanel Number Five.

"You know what you look like, luv?" Peter asked.

"No, what?"

"You look like bloody George on the cover of *Abbey Road.*"

We looked around and saw that everybody looked like bloody George on *Abbey Road.* We all wore the only wardrobe available from the Jarvis supply hut, the denim work shirt "gravedigger" costume. "Fuck a duck," I said. "Everything in the whole goddam world is a fucking, goddam clue!"

Hearing our voices as we neared her hut, Martha stuck her head out the door and left no doubt that she was pissed. "It's only three o'clock! Go home!" Slamming the door, she quickly reopened it, coming back with two decks of cards and a Scrabble game. She tossed one deck to Dan, the other to Peter. She handed Judy the Scrabble set, adding "you're the school teacher, use this if you want. But don't lose the tiles! It's not easy to get new ones out here! And don't come back for two hours!" She slammed the door again, the hut shaking from the force of the slam.

We skulked back to our hut like children banished to their rooms. I took my watch from my cubby and looked at it, not so much to know the time since the watch didn't reflect the local time anyway, but to know when two hours was over. Picking up my blazer to get the watch, my Marlboros fell onto the floor.

It was the first time I realized I wasn't smoking. I didn't miss it and wondered whether the only reason I smoked at all was to give myself something to do. I was tempted to wad the butts up, but played safe and put them back into the cubby. I was "in the moment" and there was too much to do. The moment was more important than cigarettes. Besides, saving cigarettes was an insurance policy against uncertain moments of fear or anxiety in the future.

There is a Marlboro burning in the stinking ashtray next to me as I type right now.

"Pookah?" Dan asked, tossing the cards in his hands. "How 'bout a game?"

"What'll we bet, luv?" Peter asked. "You gonna wait for treasure to wash ashore? Shells? Sand?"

"We bet infahmation, mate," Dan answered. "Money's no good heah, this is a place for wot's inya head, not inya pocket. We bet clues!

"Ya lose a hand and tell a clue. And nothin' obviooooous. You ante with somethin' like 'one from Sergeant Peppah.' If you lose, you amaze and astound the winnah with somethin' from that album he or she didn't know befoah. Sound fah?"

We happily played cards for the next two hours, swapping clues that led us to this particular card table—actually a card bunk. It was the first time since the fraternity house that I'd gone over the clues so meticulously in my head or aloud.

I won a moral victory when I bet "one from the White Album" and scrambled to come up with "trying to make a dovetail joint" from "Glass Onion." I told the group that on the radio in Columbia we figured a "dovetail joint" was a shareable marijuana cigarette. Stanley, sounding most experienced at all types of joints, pooh-poohed it as a clue and as a bet, claiming a "dovetail joint" was a way to hold parts of wooden furniture together. "Aha!" I jumped in, "in this context, what's the difference between true sharing and 'holding together?'" My logic and defense of the lame clue received respectful applause from the other card players.

I even bet my ridiculous Simon and Garfunkel clues for a few hands and then, coming up empty, other players called my bluff and said no way. Everybody laughed.

Time passed quickly.

After an hour and fifty-five minutes, I looked at my watch, announced it was time to go and the game ended instantly.

After waiting a few minutes at the same spot from which Martha shooed us before, she opened the door and almost obsequiously let us in. "Now you may enter."

The War Surplus hut was elegant. Four long tables were set up, each with crisp white linens, fine china, silver and crystal. A jazz record played low from a small record player in the corner. Martha wore a blue dress and low heels, nothing too fancy for a formal dinner in a War Surplus Quonset hut on a deserted, guano-saturated island on the equator in the middle of the Pacific Ocean in the summer of 1970.

It all seemed absolutely natural.

Even after all these years, having attended many fancy-schmancy dinner parties in tuxedos, my strongest memory of that party is clear that it was no less elegant.

Standing behind Martha were four naval officers in uniform, each holding a crystal cocktail glass. "Ladies and gentlemen," Martha began, "I want you to meet our hosts for this evening, the command staff of the American submarine *Scorpion*."

Judy reacted to Martha's announcement with an audible gasp, a gross over-reaction I thought. Martha hesitated with her introductions, nodded at Judy, then slipping into fluent French for Jacques and Susanne. The two looked pleasant and accepting as Martha spoke to them, smiling and nodding toward Martha and the uniformed strangers.

But suddenly, as Martha continued, Susanne's eyes grew big. She looked shocked. Still and again, Martha smiled and nodded.

Turning to the rest of us, Martha translated her French into English, explaining how she told Jacques and Susanne that if they had arrived only a few days earlier, they would have also met some of their countrymen from the French submarine *Minerve*.

Martha calmly explained to the rest of us that Judy, Jacques and Susanne reacted so strongly because they remembered that the *Scorpion* and *Minerve* were both sunk in 1968.

SO WE SAILED OFF TO THE SUN
'TIL WE FOUND A SEA OF GREEN
AND WE LIVED BENEATH THE WAVES...

The animated Beatles movie *Yellow Submarine* came out in 1968.

Otherwise, 1968 was a very bad year for real submarines.

Under the heading "submarines" in the 1968 *New York Times* microfilm index, there are stories about four—count 'em, 4!—subs lost that year. *The Times* made a point of using the word "lost" instead of "sunk" or "destroyed." The paper said they were *lost*, as in "damn, where the hell are they?"

Truth be told, The Company knew where each submarine was every second.

The Company took each boat and crew for "Project Number Nine."

On January 26, 1968, the Israeli submarine *Dakar* was reported missing in the eastern Mediterranean with a crew of 69 aboard. *Dakar* was a diesel-powered, World War Two-era sub built for the British navy. After its disappearance, British, Greek and American planes joined in the search.

Only two days later, the small French submarine *Minerve* also disappeared in the Mediterranean with a crew of 89. Its last reported position was one thousand miles west of the last reported position of the *Dakar*.

At the end of May, 1968, the "Skipjack" class U.S. nuclear attack submarine *Scorpion* was reported "overdue" at Norfolk after a three-month training exercise in, what a darn coincidence, the Mediterranean. The U.S. Navy launched a massive and frustrating search that stretched across the sea and sky from Virginia to the Azores.

Three days after the *Scorpion* disappeared and as the search began, just as families of the 99 *Scorpion* crewmen held a vigil for their loved ones, hopes were raised when no fewer than six ships and one search aircraft reported monitoring a radio message that used the *Scorpion*'s top-secret code name: "Brandywine." After a thorough investigation, the source of the transmission was never located. The Navy publicly determined the message and transmission of the submarine top-secret code name was a hoax. The Navy never explained how hoaxers might have gotten access to a submarine top-secret code name.

It was only searching through the *New York Times* microfilm index for information about the Pepperland Project (and finding nothing), that I learned the full story of the *Scorpion*, including the code name and story of the false radio message. It broke my heart, knowing the heartache I'm sure it caused.

The boat's code name reminded me of the DC-3 ride and how the Aguascalientes brandy burned my throat. As I read the microfilm so many years later, I felt a lump growing in my own throat, probably much like the ones the families of the "Brandywine" crewmen felt as they waited for their men to come home. I thought about how the lumps in their throats must have grown after reports of the "Brandywine" radio transmissions and how the lumps must have grown again after the U.S. Navy declared the very real transmissions a fraud. I was sure they were the same lumps Mara and my parents felt as they endured the fraud of waiting for my body to wash up on the Mississippi shore.

I'm getting those same lumps in my throat right now.

Martha was right. It's definitely still possible to have "second thoughts" about what I did, even so many decades later.

I knew the *Scorpion*'s code name was probably chosen at random from the entire glossary of the English language, but few words could have been more bittersweet for me than "Brandywine." While my throat was burning from Mexican brandy, the American nuclear submarine "Brandywine" was fixing a hole in the ocean. "Make a hole" is submariner jargon for "get out of the way."

On June 5, nine days after it first made headlines as "overdue," the *Scorpion* story was knocked off the front pages by the assassination of Robert F. Kennedy. That same day, *The Times* reported on an inside page that the government officially declared the *Scorpion* "presumed lost" with all aboard. Submariners refer to their fellows who are lost at sea as "on eternal patrol." Like the *Dakar* and *Minerve*, the *Scorpion* and its crew were officially gone forever.

Me too.

Like all the people at Martha's party.

An East-Coaster, Judy remembered the *Scorpion* story and reacted appropriately at Martha's introduction of the crew. Jacques and Susanne remembered *The Minerve*.

I didn't know or remember the original news about either submarine.

In October of 1968, *The Times* reported yet another lost submarine.

It was a small, deep-diving research submersible called *Alvin*. According to *New York Times* reports, it sank while it was being winched aboard another boat, hatches open. A cable broke suddenly and it dropped into the sea. The newspaper reported the boat flooded through the open hatches and went down quickly as the boat's three-man crew scrambled to safety.

The submarine *Alvin* was painted yellow.

AND OUR FRIENDS ARE ALL ABOARD
MANY MORE OF THEM LIVE NEXT DOOR.
AND THE BAND BEGINS TO PLAY

Martha continued making introductions. "These men and their ship…"

"Boat!" one of the older officers shouted. "It's a boat! How can I make you remember that a submarine is not a ship, it's a boat?"

"These men and their tiny little sardine can…" Martha nodded toward the officer and smiled as she continued, "…will take you to your final destination tomorrow morning. But they have chosen to spend this evening with us. Please make yourselves comfortable, enjoy the party and I hope you all have a pleasant trip."

Stanley held his hand up meekly, hoping to be recognized without being too conspicuous. Martha's eyes darted to the rear of our group. "Stanley? Yes?"

"Excuse me, but are we going to go on the submarine?"

"Indeed you are," Martha smiled. "And I can tell you, it's the thrill of a lifetime."

More talk about lifetimes. The thrill of which lifetime?

"Can we talk about this?" Stanley asked.

"Certainly. Later. First we have some lovely hors d'oeuvres and a beautiful dinner, all prepared by *Scorpion*'s superb galley crew. Feel free to begin."

As we attacked the munchies, Martha stiffened her body and her attitude and walked straight to Stanley, catching him as he reached toward a plate of crackers with something brown on them. Without breaking her steady stride, she grabbed his arm with a firm clutch and led him directly out the front door. From the angle of Martha's knuckles as she dug her fingers into his arm, I did not suspect Stanley felt the same reassurance I felt when Hancock held led me to the jet the same way back at Parks airport. She closed the door quietly behind them. The hut did not shake.

Those of us left behind looked at one another, once again unsure about what was happening.

The individual naval officers introduced themselves to us, shaking hands and welcoming us to this phase of the program. When one of the younger officers tried to break the ice and good-naturedly made an innocuous remark about Peter's long hair, Peter took the offensive and started a downright hostile, squinty-eyed, in-your-face counterattack. "At least I'm not a baby-killing, bald-headed…" I grabbed his arm and walked him toward the food. "In the moment, Peter, in the moment. Nothing to get hung about." The officer seemed genuinely embarrassed and surprised, though not angry.

"I'm in the bloody moment," he said, calming himself with a mouth full of crackers and cheese. "I'm in the bloody 1970 moment and he's in the bloody dark ages with that stiff-arsed military shit."

"But what about how the Yanks saved Britain during The War and all?"

"This is *this* bloody moment," Peter growled, walking toward the bar.

Aside from that brief incident and Stanley's unceremonious departure, the cocktail hour was pleasant.

After about twenty minutes, Martha returned to the party. She was alone.

She walked to one of the officers and took him to an unoccupied corner. They returned after a minute, arm in arm. I wondered whether they discussed Stanley or some other pressing issue, or—from the way Martha held his arm—whether they possibly discussed the idea of pressing more than issues. "Please take a seat everyone," she announced. Her demeanor was not as pleasant as it was when she invited us into the hut, before Stanley said anything about the sub. She was much more businesslike.

Like some Grand Dame from an old black and white "high society" movie, she rang a small bell indicating it was time for the meal to begin. Two men wearing starched white jackets came through the back door carrying huge silver trays, each with an enormous, golden turkey. It was a

Norman Rockwell moment. After displaying the birds to everyone, the officers applauding and the rest of us awkwardly joining in, the waiters put the trays on a table near the bar and disappeared back through the door. They quickly returned with trays filled with bowls of stuffing, cranberries, potatoes, green beans and melon. They put those trays on the table and began carving and serving, officers first.

"It must be Thanksgiving," I whispered to Peter.

"It must be, luv," he answered calmly. "And by the way, what's Thanksgiving?"

Seated at the next table with two officers and Judy, Dan turned to me. "Wot's happened to Stan? Weh is he?"

I shrugged. "I don't know. He'll probably be back in a minute."

Dinner was excellent and Peter ultimately even managed polite conversation with the officers at our table. When one asked him about Badfinger, explaining how he enjoyed *Magic Christian*, Peter's attitude turned and, in Peter's eyes, the officer turned from fascist to fan. While Peter talked about the band and the movie, the other officer at our table asked where I was from. When I told him I was from St. Louis, he said (in yet another broad accent), that he was from Tennessee and told me how he had spent a few summers visiting relatives in the Lake of the Ozarks region. He said his Tennessee family sent him there reluctantly, worried about Missouri "hillbillies" while his Missouri family was always skeptical of Tennessee "white trash." He said neither branch of his family was either hillbilly or white trash, but to avoid ending up being thought of as one or the other classification, he fled to the Naval Academy to become "an officer and a gentleman."

Martha rang her bell again after dinner. "This meal is for our friends who have come to see us and our friends who are about to leave," she announced, her stiffness and formality reminding me of Margaret Dumont in all the Marx Brothers movies, "to give them a happy sendoff and to introduce them to the people who will take them on."

Then she stopped being Margaret Dumont and once again became the no-nonsense Company Man. "You will be awakened tomorrow at oh-six hundred hours—6 a.m. At oh-six thirty, you will board a truck to take you to Secure Harbor, that's the area in red on your maps. You will depart from there. Let me emphasize the importance of staying on schedule. If you're late, you wait. The next ship, uh, *boat* will leave here in twelve days and while we enjoy your company it's our job to get you the hell off of my island. Questions?"

We exchanged glances, almost afraid to ask questions lest we be escorted out of the hut like Stanley.

The officer who corrected Martha when she called a submarine a "ship," the one with whom she shared "a moment" as they walked together, raised his hand and spoke aloud, as if he knew he didn't have to wait to be recognized and as though he knew he ran no risks by saying anything, no matter how glib or smart-alecky. "Are we going to go on the submarine?"

"Yes, Captain, I'm afraid you are." Martha smiled at him warmly. "Any more questions?"

Judy raised her hand without a hint of insecurity. "How long will it take?"

The captain stood to answer. "I'll take this one, Marth. At a normal cruising speed of 25 knots, it'll take about six hours. Transfer and docking take another ninety minutes or so, all in all. But don't worry, we'll take good care of you."

Peter whispered to me again, "that's what I'm afraid of, luv."

"Shhhhhhhhhhh."

Martha continued, still very official. "As of one hour after dessert, people, you are all confined to quarters. Everyone is to be where they are supposed to be. No moonlight swims, no supply hut runs, no lolly. So go easy on the coffee and other liquid refreshments and make sure you take care of any bathroom business before you turn in tonight."

I raised my hand, asking the same questions I'd asked since the beginning. "Where are we going? What's going to happen?"

"Those are fair questions, Jeff, and as always they will be answered on a 'need to know' basis and not before." Not surprised by Martha's answer, I accepted it completely.

After pastries, exotic tropical fruits I had never before seen and after coffee poured from a silver service, Martha said it was time for the party to end. "One hour, people, then it's in the racks. Early start tomorrow."

Many years ago, I was roaming the produce department of a supermarket with my youngest daughter who was then five years old. She asked me to buy some zucchini. I was surprised at her request, but she explained she had snacked on it at a friend's house and enjoyed it. My mother's son, the boy who was raised never to be hungry, bought her the zucchini. My daughter was tremendously upset when I sliced it open at home. She wouldn't eat it. After some cross cross-examination, she told me it didn't look right.

Weeks later, she sheepishly sidled up to me. "Daaaaaaaaaaaaaad?"

"Yes?"

"'Member when we were at the store and bought some 'chini?"

"Yes."

"'Member how you were mad when I didn't eat it?"

"Yes."

"I 'member now."

"You 'member now what?"

"I didn't eat 'chini at Becca's house, I ate kiwi."

Laughing at her mistake, her mix-up reminded me of that final night on Jarvis, the first time I ever ate kiwi fruit. The next day I took her back to the supermarket and we bought kiwi. It was the first time I had eaten it since Pepperland and it was still luscious, as were most of the memories of the places I first experienced it.

After the party and Martha's announcement of our incarceration for the night, we returned to our Quonset cell. Almost everyone made a conscientious and elongated stop at the lolly.

Stanley was sitting on his bed when we arrived. Peter sat down beside him. I followed. Everyone else went to their own space, trying not to intrude, probably feeling Stan's dilemma was none of their business. Besides, everyone knew they would hear the story from Peter or me sooner of later. "What the bloody hell happened back there, luv? Why didn't you come back? You missed a great pahty!"

Stanley reached his hands up and put them on his forehead, supporting the weight of his entire down-turned head. "I can't do it, man. I know I just can't do it!"

I jumped into the interrogation. "You can't do what?"

Without ever designating official roles, Peter naturally assumed the "good cop" part. "Come on, luv, talk to us. We're the only friends you've got here."

After all the miles, all the time waiting for this moment to arrive, Stanley said the journey was over for him and began to cry. "I can't go on any fucking submarine."

"Why not?" I asked, being the "bad cop." "What's wrong with submarines?"

Stanley began sobbing. I never heard a man cry so hard before, though I have heard it many times since. "Submarines are closed up. They're below the water. I'd feel I died and was in the coffin with the lid locked and buried. I can't do it!"

"Come on, luv, it's a boat! You've been on boats before!"

"Open boats! Canoes, motorboats, sailboats! A submarine is all closed up! I can't ride elevators without being afraid. I can't stay in small rooms or stand big crowds. I don't even like riding in cars, for Chrissake! The only way I made it here on the plane was because I dropped acid and was so fucking wasted that I didn't give a shit!"

Figuring it was time to take the "good cop" role, I jumped back into the conversation, shocked to hear my own suggestion. "So just drop acid again!"

"They took it from me," Stanley sobbed.

"Who, luv? Who took what from you?" Peter moved closer to Stanley.

"The fucking Company assholes took my whole stash, all my shit— my acid, my 'ludes, my weed. They said they couldn't let me be 'out of control.' I told them I could control it and they said that wasn't what they meant. They said they didn't give a shit if I dropped acid all fucking day but it had to be *their* fucking acid. All I know is that I can't go on any submarine and I sure as hell can't be locked in someplace under the fucking ocean! I'll just fucking die, man!"

"What did Martha say?"

"Shit, man, she was mean as shit. She said if I wasn't willing to be on the boat at six fucking o'clock I'd be on a plane at six fucking fifteen."

"What did you tell her?"

"I told her I was gonna fly."

"Where will you go, luv? You gonna go home?"

"I'm not sure. But not home, not back to Winnipeg. Fuck this shit, man. Fuck 'em all."

Stanley would be the first Pepperland casualty I saw, the first one unable to take the pressure.

He wouldn't be the last.

Pepperland itself would be the last.

WE'D LIKE TO TAKE YOU HOME WITH US
WE'D LOVE TO TAKE YOU HOME

Peter and I tried to comfort Stanley for another hour and worked hard to make him change his mind. We failed at both. By the time Stanley told us he needed to be alone, I could see Jacques, Susanne and Judy were already asleep. Dan lay on his cot with his head and shoulders up on his pillow, sipping a final "Fostah's" of the day. The proud size of the Aussie "beahs" quickly haunted him. He realized he couldn't make a lolly trip and solved the problem by standing on his bed and using a window. "Didn't even drip on the pillah" he boasted in a loud whisper. "You know what they say in Australiah, don'tcha, mate? 'No mattah how hahd ya hop oah how hahd ya dance, the last few drops go inya pants!' It's a damn good thing I'm not wearin' any pants!"

With my head on the small, mushy War Surplus pillow, I had time to start having second thoughts. I again questioned the wisdom and reinforced the stupidity of what I had done and the prospect of what was going to happen. I thought maybe I should fly away with Stanley. I thought that the best thing I could do would be to stop it all now.

What time is it at home? What are they doing? Was I 'OPD' yet, "Officially Pronounced Dead?" Was the search on the river still going on? I hoped it was over. Had Shiva begun? Would they even sit Shiva without burying a corpse first? Would I fear the submarine just like Stanley?

"Peter? You awake?" I whispered. There was no answer.

Like it does almost every night in tropical climates, it began to rain.

It was still dark when I was shaken from deep sleep into semi-consciousness. I could still hear the rain. The scent of Chanel Number Five was hot in my brain. Only partially awake, I had no idea whether it was a wonderful dream from my subconscious or a nightmare. Judy's hand rocked my shoulder as she sat on my bed and whispered into my ear, "Jeff! Jeff, wake up!"

"Go color the balloons," I told her.

"Balloons? What balloons?"

"You know exactly what I mean. Go color the goddam balloons!"

Speaking nonsense is a genetic trait for anyone in my family when we are awakened from a sound sleep. We speak nonsense so convincingly, at least to ourselves, we are absolutely certain of our sincerity.

Crap, another tangent.

"Jeff, wake up! You're not making sense!"

I slowly woke up enough to realize where I was. "What'd I say?"

"Don't worry about it. It's Judy."

"Jude...um...what...Judy? Oh. What? What's happening?"

"Nothing's happening. Everybody's asleep. I just want to know what you think about this confined to quarters business. What do you make of it?" Despite having put on perfume a few hours earlier, before dinner, I could still smell Judy's faint Chanel Number Five. Who knows? Maybe I had just been trained by the scent of so many of Mara's letters.

"The conf...? The...? Ummm, I don't make anything of it. Maybe it's another test or something. Why are you waking me? What do you want?"

My hormones suddenly told me I should be alert, that something important might be about to happen. "What's the matter Judy? What can I do for you?"

I could see her face in the light of the few bulbs from outside that spilled into the hut. "I just want to know if you think everything is going to be okay," she said. "How are you with all of this?"

"I'm fine. Why wouldn't I be?"

"I don't know. I was worried, that's all."

"Yeah, it'll be fine I think. We get on the boat, we get off the boat and we're there. Isn't that what we've all wanted?"

"Yeah, I suppose."

"Then what are you worried about?"

"Nothing, I guess. Thanks. Goodnight. See you at six."

She went back to her bed.

Absolutely nothing else happened.

End of hormonal anticipation.

My imagination sprinted with the possibilities of what might have been with Judy there on my bed, the same way it ran after the suntan lotion incident.

The next thing I knew, Martha was standing at the door banging a metal garbage can with a metal rod. "It's been fun, it's been real, it's been real fun, but now it's time to say goodbye to all our company! It's six o'clock! Rise and shine! Up and at 'em! Time to get up and get out, boys and girls!" She even sang as she banged her way down the row of beds. "Oowee, oowee baby. Oowee, oowee baby. Wontcha let me take you on a—sea cruise?"

As most of us jumped from our beds and began to dress, she put down her steel gong and knelt at Stanley's bedside. She whispered to him on his pillow and he nodded, never looking at her directly. He turned to watch her walk away and slowly rose and pulled on his jeans and buttoned his shirt.

She continued her announcements from the doorway. "It is now oh-six-oh-two. In twenty-eight minutes there will be a truck outside. You will board it without speaking to anyone. Good luck to you all!"

She smacked the garbage can a few more times before she left.

Peter and I headed to Stanley. "You're comin', aren't ya luv? You're gonna do it, ain'tcha?"

Stanley shook his head. "I can't, man. I'll die in that submarine."

"You won't die, Stan," I told him, "we'll be there with you."

"You don't understand, man. If I go on that boat, I'll fucking die for real. I can't do it. She said there's a jeep for me outside. I'm supposed to get in it." He tied his shoes. "I gotta go, man."

He stopped to say a quick goodbye to Dan, Judy, Jacques and Susanne. He turned at the door of the hut and looked at Peter and me. "Good luck, man. Think of me." As he opened the door, he held up two fingers. "Peace, man." And then he left.

Even though none of us really connected with Stanley, we were sorry to see him go. His departure was a loss for all of us. His departure *was* all of us. We knew we were all afraid, still not knowing what might become of us as the uncertain mystery continued to unfold.

We heard a jeep drive away outside the hut. After a few more minutes, as we collected our things and our thoughts, we heard the Sabreliner take off over our heads. We all stood still until the sound of the engines disappeared in the distance.

"Hi" Stan. Peace, man.

You missed a helluva trip.

LET ME TAKE YOU DOWN
'CAUSE I'M GOING...

There wasn't much to pack for the trip. Peter had his backpack—which, as he dumped it on the bed to repack, I could finally see contained only a couple of shirts, some underwear, a toothbrush—the kind of stuff I thought about packing back home.

I had nothing worth taking. With no need for the trappings of my old life, I left the jacket, slacks and necktie in my storage cubby. Maybe the next person could use the tie as a headband for their long hair.

But I lingered over my camera and strobe. They were useless since I had no film, but they were expensive items, a high school graduation gift from my parents. How could I leave them? I realized my whole being was tied to making and/or saving money and that attitude was making the camera decision more difficult. I realized those attitudes were part of my old life. In the moment, in the moment. I put the camera and strobe into the cubby.

"You ready?" I asked Peter.

"Hell, I've been waitin' for you, luv."

I put my hands into the pockets of my new jeans and we walked through the door. "Wait a minute!" I ran back to my cubby. I took Mara's gift watch out of my jacket pocket and strapped it to my wrist. Since I hadn't wound it in two days, it had stopped dead. Out of habit, I started to twist the stem but caught myself, content to leave the watch as dead as my former life. "Look," I said, holding my wrist up to Peter. "It was running fine when all this started and now it's dead too."

"Yeah, sure," he answered, without consideration of either the symbolism or the sentiment. "Let's go for a boat ride, luv."

We walked to the door.

The rain had stopped.

I expected hubbub outside, lots of people moving around preparing for the mobilization, but all was calm.

As promised, a truck arrived just as we left the hut. It was one of those olive-drab War Surplus troop trucks that should have had—by the accounts of all the military movies—a canvas cover over metal struts, a motorized Conestoga wagon.

According to all the movies, there also should have been a wizened old sergeant bellowing for us to "mount up." He would offer us chewing gum as we sat on the truck benches, haunted by our fears and dreading our uncertain futures. He would tell us not to worry and would tenderly call each of us "trooper."

There was no canvas cover over the truck, no benches, no gum, no wizened old anybody. It was an old, dirty truck with an open back end, the tailgate hanging down.

We loitered near the truck, wondering if we should climb aboard or simply hang out. We decided on the latter since it was less uncool than taking the initiative.

After a few minutes, Martha came out of her hut as cheerful as anyone who had a full night's sleep. "Glad you could all make it to the show," she said, shaking a huge, institutional-sized bottle of aspirins like a maraca. "Anybody feeling ill effects from the party? Anyone?" She shook the bottle again. "It's not good to go on the submarine feeling the effects of overindulgence. No one? Good. Then let's load 'em up." She wasn't quite a wizened old movie sergeant with an unshaven face and dirty uniform offering Juicy Fruit, but she and her bottle of aspirins would do for the moment.

Peter and I climbed onto the truck first. Jacques offered Judy and Susanne a boost. Neither of the women needed help, both were perfectly capable of climbing up on their own, but Jacques was being polite. Maybe that's why well-traveled women say they like French men better than American men, because French men have manners and consideration. At least, I suppose, when it comes time to climb onto a truck.

As we climbed on, two men dressed identically to us—in denim work shirts and jeans—came out of Martha's hut. "More gravediggers," I thought. The only thing that set us apart from them was their white "sailor hats," the brims turned up.

They climbed into the cab of the truck as we all stood casually in the benchless truck bed as if it was an extension of our on-the-ground loiter. When Martha banged on the back of the truck with her open hand, the engine revved. "Good luck," Martha said, "maybe I'll see you soon!" She slammed the tailgate closed and the truck pulled out.

The forward lurch set us all off-balance and sent us dangerously toward the rear of the truck. For an instant, I thought we'd lose Judy as she stood alone by the tailgate. Still Mister Polite, Jacques jumped quickly and grabbed her arm to keep her from falling. He said something to her in French and they both smiled. Judy moved forward and we all sat down as a close group in the truck bed.

We rode down a gravel road and away from the village, quickly reaching a gate in a high fence that ran across the road. The fence and gate were topped with razor wire. The sailor riding shotgun in the cab of the truck got out, opened a large padlock and walked the gate open for the truck to drive through. As the truck pulled through the gate, he stopped at the back of the truck. "Y'all doin' okay?" We all nodded or yelled in the affirmative. "Good deal. We don't wanna lose any of y'all this close. Hold on now!"

This close.

He climbed back into the cab and we went on.

After another short rumble along, Jacques stood up and pointed to the front. He yelled something that from his voice sounded like the French equivalent of "holy shit!" Shakily, we all fought the motion of the truck and tried to stand to see what astounded him so.

There were another half-dozen half-barrel shaped huts, a lot of trucks, jeeps and an old Sikorsky "Skycrane" helicopter (I'd built a model of one of those too), all forming an entirely different village on the seaside just up from our beach.

Sitting half out of the water were not one, but two submarines. We'd already seen the larger of the two, the one with the small yellow cigar butt on the deck. The smaller sub was similar but quite not the same, not as round or sleek.

We all felt a new rush as we realized what lay before us.

From the truck, seeing the big sub from much closer than the day before, we saw clearly that the yellow cigar butt on the deck of the big boat was a bloody fucking fuck real, live, holy shit, honest-to-God yellow submarine.

Everybody near the boats was dressed as a gravedigger. I knew they were dressed like sailors, but I was unable to get gravedigger imagery out of my head. To this day, when I see someone in a blue work shirt and jeans I never think "sailor." I still think "gravedigger."

Congratulations, me. It's been a long time since the last aside.

The truck stopped and both men got out of the cab. The driver walked away without ever saying a word to us. The drawling shotgun rider came to the rear of the truck and answered our questions before we could ask. "The one on the left's our 'Merican sub, the *Scorpion*. The little thing on the deck is a real piece of work called *Alvin*. It's 'Merican too.

A real piece of work.

"The other one there belongs to the Israelites."

It was the *Dakar*.

"She ain't goin' out for a few days yet. Got some engine trouble."

I wished I had my camera.

Five men approached the truck, three in gravedigger outfits, two wearing khaki uniforms. The two khakis were officers from the party. Each man carried a manila folder. As if it were a practiced maneuver, which it probably was, one walked directly to each of us, shaking our hands and introducing himself. Two spoke French to Jacques and Susanne. Then, as if it was drilled and practiced, which it probably was, they separated us, turned and walked us in five different directions. I looked back in alarm when I heard Jacques's panicked voice call Susanne's name. Each of their men patted them each on the shoulders, obviously reassuring both that everything would be okay.

"They'll be fine, Jeff," my gravedigger said to me. "This pre-boarding briefing will take just a couple minutes then they'll be together again. You'll all be together. This'll only take a minute.

"I'm Kenny," he added as we stepped away from the others, "and I'm your escort for this leg of your trip."

"Hi."

"How 'ya doing?"

"Fine."

"Good. You know the question I have to ask..."

"It's policy, I know. Yes, I'm ready to try for the, the, what are we up to here? The seventy-third plateau? Ninety-fifth?"

"Martha made a note that you got hostile at the question, but I'm afraid it's only the seventh. Do you want to try for the seventh plateau?"

"I'm just ready to be finished, ready to be wherever it is we're going."

"I understand."

"Yes, I want to try for the seventh plateau."

"Then welcome aboard."

He explained that after we boarded the sub we'd go to the "Officer's Mess" until our next instructions. He said the walk would be tight, the ceiling low, so I should watch my head. The room would be small, but he sounded proud when he explained how they once successfully made the same trip with eleven people packed into the same small space. "You'll find everything you need there. Someone from the galley will bring you meals, there'll be coffee, cold drinks, a head..."

"A what?"

"A head. A bathroom."

"Oh."

"Are you gonna be okay in the boat? I know one of your friends had some trouble."

"Yeah, sure. I guess I'll be fine. I've never been in a..."

"It'll be just like being at home but without Mom or windows. You won't feel the motion. You'll hear a little drone from the screws—the propellers—and that's it."

"Okay."

"I'll have to be at my station while we're underway, but if you need anything, there's a button you can press for help."

"Okay."

"Then let's go."

"There's just one thing."

"What's that? Is there a problem?"

"Why don't they clean up after themselves?"

"Pardon me?"

"The Officers Mess...why don't they clean up after themselves?"

"Ha ha. Big joke. I've *never* heard that one before. Ha ha. Now let's go."

It was stupid, I know, but the tension of the moment made it seem like the stupidly right thing to say, hardeharhar.

Jacques and Susanne were already together on the road, holding hands as Kenny and I rejoined the group. Dan and his man joined us next, then Peter. J of J arrived last. Her escort smiled and proudly proclaimed she had just set the Jarvis Island record for consecutive questions. "I was concerned about the nuclear reactor on the sub," she said with calmness and concern. "I don't trust it."

One of the khakis finally said, "as they say in the railroad business, 'all aboard'" and he led us toward the boat. Hardeharhar.

Most of the *Scorpion*'s workingmen stopped what they were doing to watch us pass. As we walked up the gangplank we heard distant voices yelling at us. It was a group of green-clad sailors from the *Dakar* waving both arms. "They're saying hello to the ladies," one of the khakis said. Susanne and Judy waved back, obviously feeling a combination of embarrassed and flattered.

The Captain met us at the top of the gangplank. His tone was warm and sincere, as it had been the night before. "Welcome aboard, Jeff, we're glad to have you." He welcomed everybody, one by one, remembering each name from the party.

We walked a few feet along the deck until the khaki leading us pointed to a hole. "As they say in the bartending business, 'down the hatch.'" Hardeharhar.

We looked down into the submarine and one by one climbed down a ladder to board the "presumed lost" nuclear submarine *Scorpion*.

Maybe Stanley was right.

I squeezed the ladder rungs tight, but my hands trembled a bit as I climbed down. I was afraid I was going to hyperventilate before I hit the bottom rung.

No hardeharhars. None whatsoever. There was nothing funny about this whatsoever.

AND OUR FRIENDS ARE ALL ABOARD

The "Officers Mess" was a fine place to spend a windowless, abnormal cruise to an impossible, unimaginable destination. It had a large table set amid a wood-paneled room. The chairs were comfortable, the lighting was bright and it was clean.

I assumed the only difference between the times the room was used by officers and when we used it was the hand-written label someone taped to the wall next to a doorbell-type button. The label read "panic." I assumed that for all the buttons aboard a nuclear submarine, the Navy discouraged officers from pushing one marked "panic."

"Bloooody fooooook," Peter reveled. "I never fooooooooooking thought I'd be on a bloody fooking soobmarine." I was thrilled he was thrilled but didn't share his excitement. My hands still shook and I was a little lightheaded. I asked no one in particular if there was any coffee, not only to calm me but also out of simple morning habit. It was still early and our stomachs were still empty.

Dan wasn't concerned about food or caffeine. "Wondah if theah's any beah."

Judy seemed concerned about my feelings and pulled a pot from a coffee maker that was built into a wall. It steamed as she poured a cup full of coffee into a white porcelain mug. I wrapped my hands around it. The warmth from Judy's coffee felt good.

Though we were eager to depart, it was probably two more long hours before we left the harbor. I can't be sure of the delay since my watch was stopped, but two hours felt about right. And it felt long. Emotions were taut, everyone complained about everything—the temperature, the humidity and the cramped quarters. Often during the wait, someone crept around the table to push the button. Each time, men came to the door and asked what we needed or what they could do to help us. Would we be leaving soon? (Yes). Could we see the rest of the boat? (No). Where was the bathroom? (The head? Behind that door). How much longer? (We already told you, soon).

I tried my best to be "in the moment," but the moment was oppressive.

To relieve the tension, I shared my "Officer's Mess" joke, bragging about how I pulled it on the officer who was my escort. Nobody laughed at it in the officer's mess then either.

Dan snooped through the room, opening drawers and cabinets. He found china and silverware, including a fancy silver coffee service—which he pretended to stuff under his shirt—table linens, a few magazines stashed under some tablecloths in a drawer and, most important, decks of cards and a rack of well-used poker chips. We tried to resume the poker game from before dinner the night before, using real chips intended to be bet instead of information as wagers, but the game wasn't nearly as inspired as before.

We finally felt gentle vibrations and heard the engines. There was tension at first, each of us wondering again where we were headed. Then as we sensed the boat starting to move out, there was relief. We cheered and applauded.

We all sat quietly for a few minutes, appreciating our moment and our movement while listening to the smooth hum of the screws. The talk was sparse, mostly limited to platitudes like "this sure is neat" and "I don't believe it" and "blooooody foooooooook."

Then, after the initial awe of being in motion, Peter returned us to our normal abnormality when he picked up the cards and began to shuffle. The game resumed with a new vigor, no one caring if they tapped out of worthless plastic chips. When anyone found themselves chipless, the winner of the moment shared their swag, tossing a handful of chips to allow the loser to stay in the game. The no-losers wagering became another important symbol. Whenever anyone gambled and lost, somebody else jumped in to cover them. When I admitted I thought this was quite a generous and sharing "moment," there were groans and catcalls from the others. Several threw poker chips at me. Because of their rude chip-throwing response, I announced I would "see your groan and raise you some pissed-offedness." They threw more chips. When two chip-throwers tapped out to my superior bluffing ability, I held my loot close, threatening not to share until they appreciated my fooking soobmarine spirituality.

After an hour, some crewmen brought trays to the door. "You guys ready for some chow?" We devoured scrambled eggs, bacon, sausage, toast and sweet rolls. With the food, the atmosphere in the Officer's Mess became genuinely festive. I think it was probably release, like college freshmen after successfully making their way through their first finals week. We were finally going where we thought we wanted to be.

For me, it had all started that moment a few days—a lifetime and a million years ago—at an M-Bar pinball machine when someone asked, "are you Jeff?"

I put my faith and trust in strangers.

I betrayed everyone I most dearly loved.

I died.

I flew thousands of miles to an unknown destination.

I met new people and started a new life.

I surrendered everything, absolutely everything, for this precise moment.

After all the hours on the radio pretending to be someone named "Jeff Scott," I finally *was* Jeff Scott, a fictional character living a fictional life after a fictional death.

It was just like starting over.

EIGHTY THOUSAND LEAGUES BENEATH THE SEA IT LAY
OR LIE
(I'M NOT TOO SURE)

Not many books assign homework to readers. Most authors probably figure that reading their book is enough and are appropriately grateful for the eyeballs on their efforts. But I've invested this much effort on the memory dump and I think many readers desire more active involvement. Besides, "interactivity" is as big a buzzword as "Obladi Oblada" once were—and both mean "if you want some fun."

So here we are, cruising page after page down the "information gravel road," so let's go interactive and make a reader participation assignment: go out and rent a movie.

While it's untraditional for book writers to encourage the film rental business—if all book writers did that, nobody would ever have time to read books, leaving book writers in a heap of trouble as if they're not in a big enough pickle as it is just because they're book writers—but it's essential at this point in the telling of the tale.

This is your assignment: watch *Yellow Submarine*. Buy it if you want, you might even find it used at Amazon.com or on ebay. Get it from Netflix or a Red Box or a Blue Box or a Purple Box, watch it on YouTube, I don't care. You may have trouble finding it since not all rental stores carry it and especially since there are so few movie rental stores left. Do whatever you think is best. I recommend you make a few calls first, just to save yourself the mileage and time.

Then watch it.

Stop reading.

Now.

Go get the movie.

I'll wait, even as long as it might take to get it delivered from Amazon.com or Netflix or ebay. I'll wait.

They've been showing a digitally restored version lately on select big screens. I went to see it recently, even took the grandchildren figuring they'd enjoy it as a cartoon if nothing else. But once it started, I couldn't bring myself to watch and walked out after the first ten minutes. Afterwards, when the grandkids asked why I waited for them in the lobby, I couldn't explain. I told them I was getting sick. And I was.

So get on with it. Find the movie.

No kidding. Get the movie.

I knew you should have called Blockbuster before you went schlepping all over the place.

It's okay. I'm still waiting. It takes a long time to get and watch a movie.

Okay.

Readers who actually watched the movie probably had a wonderful time. You didn't miss anything here, I waited for you like I promised. I appreciate your ability to follow directions.

Wasn't that a great movie??? It still holds up despite the passage of time and changes in attitudes. While there are places I remember and some are gone and some have changed, *Yellow Submarine* remains alive and kicking and gorgeous just the same.

Unfortunately, I'm certain some readers skipped the assignment and jumped ahead to here where this story starts again. Shame on you for not doing what you were told by a book writer and conspiracy-revealer! You're only hurting yourselves by not keeping up with everyone else. Now I have to spend valuable time recapping the film for you. I swore I wouldn't, but I'm far too easy a touch in my old age. Those who followed the assignment and watched the movie will just have to be patient while the rest of the group catches up.

Okay. Here we go: *Yellow Submarine* was an incredibly vivid animated film about an imagined Utopia of perpetual love and beauty called "Pepperland."

The original subtitle of the movie was—and this is a real, genuine piece of completely trivial Beatles trivia—"Nothing is Real."

Nothing is real.

The film was released in 1968, the same year as the losses of the *Scorpion, Dakar, Minerve* and *Alvin*.

The first words of *Yellow Submarine*—the only words in the entire movie spoken by a sweet-voiced narrator in a slow, gentle, soft British accent—describe Pepperland: "Once upon a time, or maybe twice, there was an earthly paradise called Pepperland. *Eighty-thousand leagues beneath the sea it lay.*" How about that, sports fans? "*beneath the sea.*" And then, to add a touch of cleverness, class, irony and humo*u*r (definitely spelled in British and not the u-less American style), after a beat the voice adds: "or *lie*...I'm not too sure." Maybe the addition of "lie" was still another clue. I'm not too sure.

The Pepperland in the movie is an incredibly verdant, lush, mega-colorful pop extravaganza filled with beautiful flowers, bizarre animals, serene butterflies and content people dancing to music of all kinds, from classical string quartets to songs from the local star attraction, a familiar, colorfully-clad foursome called "Sergeant Pepper's Lonely Hearts Club Band."

The movie's eighty-thousand leagues beneath the sea animated Pepperland is attacked by dastardly Blue Meanies who take away the music and the beauty, leaving Pepperland gray and bleak and desolate. Those who actually watched the movie know this meager description is woefully short of true Meanie meanness. These movie watchers are quite aware of the fiendish flying Glove, evil Butterfly Stompers, vicious Snapping Turtle Turks, unfeeling Apple Bonkers and horrendous Hidden Persuaders (the guys with guns in their shoes). They know how the callous and pitiless Meanies show no mercy and experience no joy. They are very mean Meanies. They will never take "yes" for an answer.

This simple description is perfectly adequate to bring those who did not fulfill the assignment and keeps them abreast of the story without giving them the pleasure and luxury of the lush colors, songs by the Beatles and a magnificent, under appreciated instrumental score by Sir George Martin. It's all they deserve.

Anyway, in the film, the Lord Mayor of Pepperland dispatches a wrinkled Young Fred to find rescuers to rid the land of Meanies. Fred recruits the Beatles after he travels to Liverpool in, of all things, a yellow submarine. While the Lord Mayor refers to his messenger as "Young

Fred," the Beatles refer to him as "Old Fred." It's all in the mind, you know.

And after arriving in besieged Pepperland, the Beatles save the day and with Love which is, of course, "all you need."

Get this: the liner notes on the original-issue, vinyl *Yellow Submarine* soundtrack album describe Pepperland as "a beautiful pleasure dome." A dome. A goddamn DOME!!! *It says it right there bloody fooking fook in print on a record jacket sitting for all these years on people's shelves.* It's right there to read over and over. *"A beautiful pleasure dome." "Eighty-thousand leagues beneath it lay. Or lie. I'm not too sure."*

The complete solution to the entire "Paul is dead" mystery could not have been more blatant. It was all right there on the album and in the movie. Everything was right out there in the open.

Almost nobody read it.

Almost nobody got it.

Almost blooooooooody fooooooooooking unbelievable.

> **There's nothing you can know**
> **That can't be known.**
> **Nothing you can see**
> **That isn't shown.**
> **Nowhere you can be**
> **That isn't where you're meant to be.**
> **It's easy.**

By showing Pepperland on a big screen in bigger-than-animated-life to moviegoers, by admitting Utopia and by openly calling it "a beautiful pleasure dome" that was built "eighty-thousands leagues under the sea," the Beatles said outright "if you want it, here it is, come and get it." They could not have been more blatant. But exactly because they were so obvious about it, most people didn't come to get it and almost nobody got it, even the ones who wanted it. Most people considered the movie *Yellow Submarine* a simple pop-art vision of Fantasyland.

They said it was a fucking "beautiful pleasure dome" you blind assholes! And I include myself in that category. They said "under the sea it lay. Or lie." We were so busy confirming that "one and one and one is three" from "Come Together" that we never added "pleasure dome" and "under the sea" to get Pepperland. You've GOT to be kidding me.

Perhaps if Pepperland never existed there would still be crackpots and loonies who fiercely argue that it did exist and that was being covered up, which it did and it is. There is nothing more real than those who believe in disbelief, nothing less real than not seeing what's right in front of you. "Nothing you can see that isn't shown."

If nothing is real, maybe real is nothing. Back in the Officer's Mess of the *Scorpion*, that kind of bullshit philosophy would have absolutely earned me a poker chip shower.

Mostly what readers need to remember from *Yellow Submarine* is how bright and colorful and perfect it all was until Blue Meanies came and how beautiful it was again after the Blue Meanies were conquered.

Readers need to know Pepperland was Utopia.

Readers need to know how beautiful it was, to recall the colors and feel the feelings. Readers need to know the perfection and simplicity of it all.

Readers need to think of how the Beatles and music and Love saved everything.

And readers need to know the real Pepperland wasn't anything like that at all.

A BEAUTIFUL PLEASURE DOME

I am not someone who understands technical things. I can neither totally comprehend nor relate the design or construction of Pepperland. Its architectural and engineering subtleties were lost on me. It was dry and warm and a lovely imperfect attempt at a perfect idea. And it was home for a time. That was all I needed to know.

Now that I need to know about the technical aspects, it cannot be done.

Whatever information I relate here is based on my memory from several conversations in The Onion with a Company Man who wanted to explain it all to me in intricate detail. Unfortunately, I did not want to hear even the slightest bit of his story at the time, even though he desperately wanted to share his expertise and kept collaring me to brag, so I was helpless.

But I cannot prove any of this with any official documentation.

The United States government denies the existence of Pepperland. Any documents showing specifics of the place or CIA involvement are not available, no matter how aggressively a former journalism student tries under the Freedom of Information Act. My inquiries have received no support from the Central Intelligence Agency, the Department of the Navy, a number of members of Congress or the staffs of the Bush I, Clinton, Bush II or Obama administrations.

All categorically dismiss me as a crackpot and loony.

I did, however, discover that near the end of 1993, the Navy did release a twenty-five year old top-secret report on the loss of the *Scorpion*. It claimed the boat was lost in 1968 when it "shot itself with its own torpedo."

For all I know, the *Scorpion* did sink itself with its own torpedo, but definitely not in 1968. I was aboard *Scorpion* in August of 1970 and again in the late fall of 1971.

Starting in 1968, the *Scorpion* was used to build, populate and maintain Pepperland. So were the other submarines lost that year: the Israeli *Dakar*, the French *Minerve* and the Woods Hole Oceanographic Institute's *Alvin*. The CIA and other intelligence agencies commandeered all for the project, as were a number of surface ships that were ostensibly assigned to routine sea duty.

People at the U.S. Navy, Woods Hole, the Israeli and French embassies all dismissed me as a loony crackpot.

I must believe that the documentation, plans, budgets, reports, follow-ups, any and all paperwork relating to Pepperland and its connection with any or all formal governmental agencies truly don't exist any more.

I must assume that all Pepperland documentation was destroyed at or about the same time Pepperland was blown to smithereens and scattered on the seabed one hundred miles east/northeast of the Jarvis Islands in the Pacific Ocean.

In 1971.

By a torpedo from the *Scorpion*.

Pepperland was designed and built between 1966 and 1970 by contractors of the United States Navy. They did not create their sections on-site, one hundred miles east/northeast of the Jarvis Islands in the Pacific Ocean. They built their subcontracted sections in industrial cities like Neenah, Wisconsin and Gary, Indiana and Memphis, Tennessee and Long Beach, California. None of the fabricators knew what they were building to such exacting specifications except that it was "for the government" and that their modules would be blended with pieceparts from other manufacturers to assemble some kind of top-secret military project.

The contractors did not know they were creating parts for "a beautiful pleasure dome" that might have been the basis of human guinea pig research about post-nuclear survival, life in space stations or undersea civilizations. Nor did they know they were working on a place where a group of disillusioned, idealistic and allegedly dead people hoped the Beatles would entertain them forever.

Some manufacturers built ultra-high-tensile aluminum tubing with odd ridges on the ends. Others created five-inch thick, high strength, non-distorting, triangular Lexan panes to fit inside the steel tubing that was made somewhere else. Still others made huge pumps, some for air and others for water. Even more unsuspecting workers at companies happy to have government contracts created interior facilities and furnishings, from the frameworks of the terraced housing levels to built-in bed frames for individual rooms, from kitchens and baths to public gazebos and administration office areas. Some made artistic wooden, concrete or steel benches shaped in the words "LOVE" and "YES" and "KNOW." Those who watched *Yellow Submarine* understand the meaning of these.

As specified by government contract, all manufactured pieces were shipped in solid-sided wooden crates via flatbed railcars or truck to a military depot near San Diego. The crates were addressed to "Project Number Nine." No matter which individual person at the depot actually received the shipments, all receipts received the rubberstamped signature of a low-grade Army officer named "Lieutenant Pepper," newly promoted from sergeant to avoid suspicion.

The crates were loaded onto ships and taken to Jarvis where hollow sections of aluminum were assembled, floated and towed to their destination. Then the small sections were mated with larger sections as the dome framework was completed. The specifications called for "dovetail joints" to fasten the sections together, not because of any "Glass Onion" lyrics but because government engineers determined them tò the best way to withstand pressure and prevent leakage. After mating the tapered male and female joints, they were welded over by U.S. Navy Seabees to create a solid, waterproof seal.

Finally, each hollow-tubed section of framework that would ultimately become "a beautiful pleasure dome" was flooded with seawater, gradually sunk and taken to its position and attached to a foundation on the ocean floor by a submarine with robotic arms.

Once under the surface, divers added the Lexan to sunken sections using robotic arms from the submarine *Alvin* and a crane from a ship anchored overhead.

Some of this undersea assembly was done in cooperation with NASA as astronaut training, teaching construction in near-weightless conditions in preparation for Space Shuttle and Space Station travel planned for the near and distant future. The Company Man who told me about Pepperland construction said all three Apollo 11 astronauts practiced weightless construction and repair by adding their two cents to the creation of Pepperland.

Once the outside shell was finished, air was pumped into the water-filled dome under high pressure to purge the sea from the interior.

There were crossed fingers all around, my Company Man said, because no one was completely sure the dome would hold. Since there had only been on-paper and mock-up testing, there were still doubters who didn't believe the dome could withstand the water pressure. Obviously, the skeptics were wrong.

The overall design was based on the original concept created by Buckminster Fuller. Like Charles Puckett Hancock said, Fuller envisioned his biggest dome would cover all of East St. Louis, Illinois, to create what he called a "community of the future."

I doubt Buckminster Fuller ever called his design a "Glass Onion" or a "Hole in the Ocean."

In reality, the name "Glass Onion" originated with Ringo, coming to him as he made a pot of soup at his home. After months of planning, the design for Pepperland was finally approved and the project began. Shortly afterward, as Ringo sliced vegetables, he noticed a leftover heel of white onion on his cutting board. Putting his eye down to board level, he announced, "that's wot it looks like! It's an oooniooooon. It's a goddam glass oooooooooooooonion!"

Wide, flexible "lifelines" ran from the oooooooooooooonion to the ocean surface for air intake and exhaust. All were connected to huge electric pumps that exchanged the air inside The Onion with air from above. The inlets and outlets were camouflaged with floating blue-green baffles to conceal them from overflying aircraft. Usually, though not always, Navy surface ships cruised the nearby area on "training maneuvers" and several hundred square miles of ocean above the dome was effectively blockaded to all other maritime and air traffic. Even though they were on "maneuvers," these ships were absolutely forbidden to fire guns or use undersea weaponry as part of their "training."

Electricity inside the dome was provided by generators and batteries that were somehow charged by seawater. Of all the technical aspects, of this I am most uncertain except that the generators vented into the water outside the dome. Once, there was a tremendous to-do about whether we were polluting our own environment with the venting, but the environmentalists lost the argument to those of us who enjoyed having light and air inside. Besides, most of us inside enjoyed watching the huge, fine, Alka-Seltzer stream of bubbles rise outside the glass like the aeration of a huge aquarium.

All sewage and trash was vented directly into the sea. When the visible pile of debris became an issue, the environmentalists did win a round with the Meanies when it was agreed the trash would be scattered across the ocean floor by the *Alvin*'s mechanical arms instead of piled up on the seabed outside The Onion glass, visible to everyone inside.

Once the water was blown out of what would become the "beautiful pleasure dome" and the place became habitable, Navy divers were replaced by other military construction people who built the inside guts of the place where Pepperlanders lived under the sea, in an Octopus's Garden in the shade.

Pepperland was declared habitable on March 2, 1970.

The first group of visitors included representatives of the CIA, U.S. Naval Intelligence, British MI6 and Beatles Lennon, Harrison and Starr. They were accompanied by businessman Allen Klein who had just prior been appointed manager and financial savior of the Beatles.

Beatle McCartney was not there because he was finishing his first solo album.

The three Beatles and Klein stayed at the nearly-vacant Pepperland for more than a week. When they left, they gave their approval to the place by spray-painting a message on a support beam near the village. The message was "Love is all you need."

The first permanent residents arrived a few weeks later. The population grew until October, 1970 when capacity was reached.

Shortly after the Beatles' original visit, Paul McCartney released his first solo album.

On April 10, 1970, Paul publicly announced the official breakup of the Beatles.

April 10 is Mara's birthday.

WE ALL LIVE IN A...

The *Scorpion* leg of the trip was another tedious stretch of travel with
nothing to do but wait for someone to tell us we were finally where we
wanted to be. After the card game petered out, we all fell into a subdued
eating/drinking/sleeping/waiting routine.

I spent a large chunk of the time talking with Judy and discovered she
was a delightful and intriguing "older woman" with a good and kind ear.
When I told her about Mara, Judy said Mara sounded like a fine person
and she knew how difficult my decision was. But she was adamant that I
should realize Pepperland was our destiny, that we were intended to be
there and that everything before was simply the path that led us to where
we were at that moment. Kindly, she even added that she believed Mara
would agree I had to go. I appreciated her understanding and wisdom,
even the spirituality of her feelings about everything in our lives leading
to Pepperland. I always figured my being on the *Scorpion* was a
combination of chance, dumb luck and coincidence, certainly not destiny.

Sometime during our conversation, JofJ stopped looking as plain as I
thought she looked that first day on the beach and became a much more
attractive woman. She may not have had a classic "sorority girl" look but
she carried a stylish confidence and it gave her a look of her own. I
found her deeply attractive and very comfortable to be with and for those
feelings I have no apologies. Once again, she smelled faintly of Chanel
Number Five, which consciously or subconsciously churned my emotions
even more. After we talked for a while, my nose was working like a
bloodhound on a trail during the whole conversation, I finally relaxed
enough to mention the perfume and the Mara connection and how much
I liked the scent for godknowshowmany reasons. She reached into her

purse and showed me a small black spray bottle. "As of this morning, it's officially gone," she said. "It's all gone."

"Just like us." I muttered.

"Hi" Judy.

Maybe what I experienced there with Judy was one of those research projects graduate students do in singles bars where they learn that people who are unapproachable during the evening begin to look more attractive as closing time approaches, but I truly think Judy looked better because she finally opened up emotionally. And because of the scent, of course. There on the submarine she started to literally look physically friendlier and more attractive. When she revealed her smile, she revealed herself.

Ultimately, she took her turn and told me she was in the oldest of three daughters of a laborer father and a housewife mother. She said everybody thought she was the independent, responsible "first child," but she knew better. There were times she couldn't face the expectations, she said, and days when she simply stayed in bed. There were days in high school when she sat in a restroom stall all day rather than show up for classes unprepared.

I told her I thought it was amazing how people could share such intimate secrets after knowing one another for such a short time, telling things to strangers they wouldn't have told people they'd known for years. But such was the immediate intimacy created when everything was left behind, the nothing-to-lose attitude created by traveling under the ocean in a long-lost submarine to an unknown destination we could never leave.

"Hi" again, Judy.

"Hi" again to you too, Mara. I don't know why I still feel so guilty about talking to "another woman" so many years ago, but I still do. Perhaps it speaks to the depth of the relationship you and I had back then. I always told you everything and there I was, replacing you with Judy. Later, I watched Judy replace me with someone else.

As we neared our destination, the captain knocked on the wall outside the Officer's Mess to tell us what would happen next. "We'll take a few of you at a time to the front of the boat for transfer to the *Alvin*, the small submersible on the deck. It will take you to the dome. Questions?"

Dan stupidly repeated the stupid question I asked on shore. "Cap'n sir?"

"Yes, Dan?"

"Cap'n, sah, why don' the officahs on this heah ship, uhhhhhhh, *boat*, why don't they clean up theah own mess?"

"Dan?"

"Yessir, Cap'n, sah?"

"You'll be in the first group."

"Aye aye, Cap'n sah! No worries, Cap'n sah!"

The captain turned toward the hallway. "Mister Ackerman?"

A voice answered with a crisp "sir?"

"Get this man off my boat."

"Aye aye, sir!"

Mister Ackerman stuck his head in the door and motioned for Dan. He was the same Navy man who took Dan aside before we boarded. "Let's go, Dan." As they walked down the hall, we heard Ackerman say "the Old Man is pissed. What the hell did you do?"

Then Peter's on-shore man came to the door and motioned for him to follow. Peter picked up his bag, smiling as he walked out. "Meet you later, luv."

After a moment, my escort came in. "How 'ya doin' Jeff?"

"A little claustrophobic, but okay. I'm ready."

We walked through the narrow gray passageway as he repeated what the Captain told us before. He'd take me to the *Alvin*, it would take us to the dome. "I'm ready," I said.

At the end of the hall, we came to a closed metal door marked "Forward Escape Trunk." He told me to watch my head as I passed through the hatch. But he didn't open the door. "I've got to ask, Jeff…"

"Yes! Yes! Yes! Whatever plateau it is, I want to do it! I'm ready!"

"No, that's not it."

"What then?"

"A minute ago, you used the word 'claustrophobic.' Were you serious?"

"I don't know. Why?"

"Because if you've got problems now, they're going to get worse. *Alvin* is a lot smaller than this boat and there might be a problem in the dome itself."

"No. No problem," I said, "it was just something to say."

I didn't tell him how I felt when I first boarded the *Scorpion*. If he hadn't noticed my shaking hands, I wasn't going to tell him. As far as I was concerned, it was officially a manila folder problem and not important any more. Besides, it was just nervousness. I was fine.

"Okay, then now it's time to ask you if you want to try for the eighth plateau."

"Gee, let me think this over."

He smiled and opened the door. "Every one of you assholes is a comedian."

"Yeah," I smiled, "you've gotta be a piece of work for this, a real piece of work."

The Forward Escape Trunk was a very small compartment with gauges and dials on the walls. "Climb up the ladder," my khaki said. I could see another small room on the other side of another hatch in the ceiling. "Keep going!" he said softly, his voice rising through the hatch. "Climb the other ladder and go through the other hatch!" I could see lights and hear voices coming down from above, so up I went.

My hands didn't shake as I pulled myself up through the second hatch. I was almost there. "Keep going," I thought, "just keep moving." Peter and Dan were already aboard the *Alvin*, a real, live, honest-to-God yellow submarine.

The space inside was no bigger than a kitchen table—without leaves— and three of us were packed inside.

Make that four.

"Everybody in?" a voice asked from behind Dan and Peter. As small as the space was, I still couldn't find the source of the question. "I'm at the flotation panel!" Peter and Dan were scrunched up in the tiny area, both standing hunched over, so tight we all became human sardines in a yellow metal can.

"Excuse me. Duck around please," the voice asked. Dan and Peter split as far apart as they could, which wasn't far, and a third man balanced his way around the open hatch in the floor, carefully trying to avoid

falling down into the Forward Escape Trunk of the *Scorpion.* "Welcome
aboard. It's tight, but we'll get you out of here as quick as we can." Then
he shouted through the hatches, "I'm sealing 'em up!"

A voice came from below. "Sealing 'em up! Aye aye, sir! Have a safe
trip."

He slammed the hatch on the big submarine with a chonnnnnnnnng.
Then the *Alvin* man chonnnnnged the hatch in our floor, making the
available floor space seem like Alaska. Plus Canada. We spread out as
much as possible, which still wasn't much.

The *Alvin* man worked his way toward a control panel at the front of
the boat. "Gentlemen, whaddya say we shove off?" An electric motor
began to hum and metal clanged as the boats separated. The *Alvin* man
manipulated some levers and we felt the boat point up at a steep angle.
We leaned back against the rear wall. After a few minutes, we could feel
the boat heading down. "Twenty minutes for the trip, ten up, ten down,"
the *Alvin* man said, "then fifteen minutes to blow the dock and then I
head back for another load."

No matter how smart-alecky any of us felt at other stages of the trip,
there were no sounds on this leg but electronic blips from the controls
and motor hum.

Finally, the *Alvin* man spoke again. "Number Nine, this is *Alvin.*"

A voice squawked back on the radio. "We've got you *Alvin.*"

"We're five minutes from home."

"Five minutes. Roger. You got the guidance plane?"

"Affirmative. And visual, number nine."

"Front door's open, *Alvin*, come on in."

The *Alvin* man concentrated intensely as he watched a screen on the
control panel and looked out the small windows on the front of the cabin
at the same time. "Are we there, luv?" Peter asked. "Not now, please!"
the *Alvin* man barked. "Sterile cockpit," I assumed.

Finally the motor revved hard, we jerked backward, jolted downward
and settled. The *Alvin* man hit a red switch and the motor stopped
humming. "Now we wait." It was incredibly quiet inside and no one said
anything as we listened to the silence.

I don't know how we spent the half hour it took to "blow the dock,"
whatever that meant. I simply blanked out, mindlessly staring at the silent

control panels and the other silent faces around me, but I don't remember waiting more than what seemed like a flash before a most welcome message came over the radio. "*Alvin*, welcome home."

"Thank you Number Nine. I'm popping the top."

He pushed his way through the three of us and reached above his head to pull down a metal ladder. He climbed up, turned a wheel and a hatch opened over our heads. He ducked as water dripped in. It wasn't a high-pressure gush of ocean, just the dripping residue of what was left on top of the boat.

There was dry, open space above the hatch. "Gentlemen, this is the place. Welcome home."

For an instant, Dan, Peter and I threatened to pull a Three Stooges, each telling the other "after you," "oh no, after you!" I was afraid we would all suddenly make a grab for it and jam up in the hatch like Moe, Curly and Larry.

Finally, I hit the ladder while the others waited.

The climb up the ladder must be what a baby must feel like being born. I knew something waited outside, but I didn't know what and wasn't sure I wanted to go.

At the top rung I stopped climbing and stuck my head outside.

I looked around.

"Keep in goin' luv! We're waitin' down here!"

"Get a move on, mate! We wanna see it too!"

The entire universe above us was blue-green triangles. It was the ocean, backlit through triangles of thick plastic.

A Beautiful Pleasure Dome.

We were in an undersea dry-dock, a room slightly bigger than the *Alvin*, maybe twenty or thirty feet of clearance all around, an underwater glass garage. The *Alvin* man had parked his long-lost submarine in an enormous steel and rubber cradle that held the boat up from the concrete slab floor.

A ladder ran down the outside of the boat.

I couldn't stop looking up through the glass.

Sunlight was visible overhead. It looked as if we were in a huge aquarium, but we were inside the fishbowl and the fish were outside. It was spellbinding.

"You gotta see this!" I yelled to Dan and Peter.

"We'd like to fookin' see it!" Peter yelled back. "Hurry up, dammit!"

Climbing over the side and down the ladder to the floor, my eyes riveted up, incredulous at being under the ocean, I was startled when I heard a round wheel turning on a metal door on the solid-side wall. As the seal broke and the door cracked open, a man was yelling. "Jeff! Jeff!" the voice cried. "Jeffrey! This is it! We're here!" At the last turn of the wheel, the door flew open and the man ran through.

It was Mark.

BECAUSE WE KNOW WE CAN'T BE FOUND

Mark and I hugged the way macho men were not supposed to embrace in 1970, the same way sensitive guys of the twenty-first century hug to prove how sensitive and non-macho they are. It was a full-armed, I'm-so-glad-to-see-you-now-that-we're-dead-ohmygodwhathavewedone hug. By all standards of the times, we should have punched each other in the arms in a manly-man way. But it was much more meaningful than that. I was a *real* hug. Okay, I'll even admit I cried, though I turned my head so Mark wouldn't notice. That was the manly-man, macho thing to do at the time.

When we spoke recently about our meeting at Pepperland's front door, Mark was embarrassed to admit that moment is one of his strongest Pepperland memories. And, he's told me since, he cried too. But he turned his head so I wouldn't notice.

"This is it!" he shouted, grabbing my arms. "We were right!"

"I know! I know!" I started jumping up and down, holding on to Mark. We must have looked like schoolgirls or cheerleaders or simply the geeks that we actually were, but there was no self-consciousness about our geekiness, only honest emotion.

"We don't want to interrupt this ecstasy and passion, luv, but could you boys have your reunion elsewhere so's the rest of us can get through the door?"

I felt self-conscious and geeky.

Quickly, I dragged Mark to meet Peter and Dan. "This is Mark! Mark W. Richardsonnnnnnnnnnnnnnnnnnnn*uh*! From Missouri! Mark, this is Peter!

Peter Ham!" It seemed Mark wasn't nearly as excited about meeting Peter as I was to introduce them, but he smiled back and shook hands warmly.

"Welcome, Peter," Mark told him. In reality, Mark was excited but acted cool because he had already met stars whose constellations shone much more brightly.

"What, no hug, luv?" Peter asked.

"Peeeeeeeeterrrrrrrrrrrrrrrrr   Haaaaaammmmmmmmmmmm," I repeated, slower and louder so Mark would get the message.

"You didn't know who I was either, luv," Peter reminded me. "And you didn't even give me a hug."

"Peter's the lead singer with Badfinger, Mark. Remember when 'Come and Get it' came out, how we thought it sounded like the Beatles? It was! Paul was singing lead! That's why Peter's here!"

Mark smiled again and told me to slow down. "I know who Peter is. I know about Badfinger. I've been here a while. I know lots of things you don't know yet."

"How long have you been here? How did you get here? What's going on? What's it like? What do you know?"

"And you must be Dan," Mark said, ignoring my questions. "It's good to meet you too." Mark put his arm over my shoulder to lead me away from the dock, motioning to Dan and Peter. "You guys come with us, I'll show you around."

I talked and talked and talked as we walked, looking at everything at once, asking everything, wanting to know and do everything. "How long have you been here? How did you die? Are the Beatles here? Is Beth here?"

"You'll get it all sooner or later," Mark said. "There's plenty of time."

"Dammit, Mark!" I pulled away from him. "I'm fucking sick and tired of waiting!" Mark started to sing. "So tired, tired of waiting, tired of waiting for yooooooooooooouuuuuuuuuuu."

"Fuck you both, godammit!! I'm tired of not getting information and I'm tired of going from place to place without knowing what's next! I'm goddam sick of goddam plateaus! How many more goddam plateaus are there, anyway?"

Mark shook his head, looking placid and under control, just like he always looked at school when he knew he had the right answer. "Asshole."

"What? Asshole what?"

"What plateau do you think this is?"

"Shit, I don't know."

"Number nine, number nine, number nine…" His eyes got bigger as he lowered his voice an octave to the perfect level for telling ghost stories around a campfire. "Number niiiiiiiiiiiiiiine. Asshole! I told you! This is it!"

"Oh. No shit?"

Peter jumped gleefully at the chance to torment me in my ignorance. "Your friend's right, luv. You are an arsehole."

Mark looked at Peter and smiled. "I've known him so much longer than you, but you're perceptive enough to really describe him perfectly!"

"Thank you, luv."

I stopped talking and began seeing what I only looked at before.

It was not the Pepperland in *Yellow Submarine*. There were no "cellophane flowers of yellow and green, towering over your head." Exposed pipes and ventilation shafts ran higgeldypiggeldy above, blocking the top of the dome in places. Steel and concrete framing was scattered everywhere. Brown grass grew here and there, with no lush landscaping to speak of and it was definitely not filled with multihued flowers like in the movie. In some areas of the ceiling, light from above was blocked with huge triangles of blackness that cast dim triangular shadows on the floor. "The dome leaks a little," Mark said. "As soon as the water starts to drip in—or spray—divers come in and close it up pretty quickly. It's a big party when they swim over."

It was all too real, not the cartoon perfection I expected.

Truly, many things were painted in bright colors like in the movie, but the entire place had an overall industrial feel and an ambiance of unusual brightness. Years later, I felt the same frigid high-tech coldness while visiting a large research laboratory.

Which is exactly what Pepperland was.

Had it been true to the film, Pepperlanders would have worn outrageous, brightly colored costumes. Everyone I saw wore denim work shirts and jeans.

Peter and Dan fell behind us as we walked.

"Why does it look like this, Mark?" I finally asked. "This isn't what it's supposed to look like."

Mark shrugged and sounded embarrassed and apologetic, as if my disappointment was his fault. "I know, I know. Everybody has the same reaction. It's not what we saw in the movies or inside our heads but this is the way it is. You'll get used to it. Once you're here, you won't notice how grody it looks and you'll even start to think it's pretty pleasant. All I can tell you is that you'll get used to it."

"How long have you been here?"

"I'm not sure," he answered. "Four weeks maybe. Six? Since late May."

"Mark, it's August. You've been here more than two months!"

"Riiiiiight. There's no time here, no real days, no real nights. You establish your own time. You make your own schedule. You'll get used to that too."

Data-gathering experiments in Circadian rhythm, the way the human body naturally establishes a day/night timetable without external stimuli like clocks or sunlight, must have been another Pepperland mission. In retrospect, I think The Company wanted to know how we adjusted during twenty-four hours of artificial light with no easy reference points to tell us when it was time to get up or go to sleep. It would have been valuable research for space travel or survival techniques underground or undersea or perpetuation of the species after a nuclear holocaust.

"This isn't the Sea of Time like in the movie," Mark went on. "Actually, it's a Sea of No Time."

"No time at all, just the *New York Times*."

"Riiiiight." Because he was a radio man, I thought Mark would catch the reference and I was disappointed. "But we don't get the *New York Times* here. What I'm saying is that minutes and hours don't exist any more, at least not here. Neither do weeks or months, probably not even years. The lights are always on out here, it's always day. There are Diachronic filters on the fixtures to make the incandescent bulbs the same color as daylight. You decide for yourself when to be awake, when to sleep.

"If day or night is important to you, The Onion will tell you." Mark pointed up, as if to indicate that everything came from above. "It's light, it's dark, whatever it is. The curiosity wears off pretty fast after the neck strain sets in," he explained, "only the druggies keep looking up. Plus, it doesn't really matter if it's day or night. It's always the same."

Neck strain or not, we ultimately did establish our own rhythms, timeframes and schedules. While we stayed awake for what must have been days at a time—then slept for what must have been days more—we did create personal Circadian rhythms that were close to whatever normal schedules our brains and our bodies needed.

"The druggies? Is there a lot of dope here?"

Peter jumped into the conversation. "If you want it, here it is, come and get it."

"Riiiiiiight," Mark answered. "There's a guy everybody calls Lucy, as in Lucy…"

"…in the sky with diamonds." Because I was a radio man, I caught the reference. Actually, almost everybody in Pepperland and most everybody else in the universe would have caught the reference, radio men or not.

"Lucy is one of the Company Men and he's got more shit than Roto-Rooter. They keep bringing in more stuff with the supplies. You ask for it, you get it. But I don't think that's your style. You were never attracted to those people when we were in Columbia."

"So?"

"Well, *I'm* attracted to those people, luv," Peter said. "I'd like to meet Lucy."

Dan spoke up. "Me too, mate!"

Mark shrugged. "If you want it…" Mark waited for Peter to finish the line. He didn't. Instead, Peter just looked at Mark and said "Arsehole."

"You know, Peter," I chimed, enjoying the opportunity, "I've known him so much longer than you, but you're perceptive enough to really describe him perfectly."

"Thank you, luv. And you're an arsehole too."

It's old news that the CIA tested LSD and other hallucinogens during the '60s. With recent revelations of CIA and military experiments that injected drugs and diseases into human guinea pig subjects, it should come as no surprise that they also distributed test drugs to a seemingly unending supply of volunteers in Pepperland.

There were also times when almost everyone in The Onion got giddy all at once, even if they weren't "using." We attributed the giddiness to the general atmosphere of the moment and to some degree we were probably right. But knowing what I know now about CIA involvement in drug experimentation, I also believe Company Men often pumped some type of gas into The Onion atmosphere to test its effect on a large number of subjects.

It wasn't until some years ago or so when I saw a Mel Gibson/Julia Roberts movie called *Conspiracy Theory* that I learned about a CIA mind control program from the early 1970's called "MK-Ultra." Apparently it was a real *Bourne Identity* kind of thing involving hypnosis and drugs, the stuff of *The Manchurian Candidate* to use yet another pop culture reference. Based on what I can find on the internet about that program, I think it would have been far too brutal for Pepperland, but obviously I can never be sure.

We continued walking and Mark kept giving us his orientation. "The time thing is the hardest to get used to." Then he leaned close and spoke to me in a whisper. "But it's not the only thing."

"Like what?"

"I'll tell you later."

"No, tell me now."

"I can't. Sometimes things come back."

"What do you mean they 'come back?'" Mark shushed me and put his hands to his ears as if he was eavesdropping. "Are you saying the place is bugged?" I whispered back to him.

"I didn't say anything."

"Are you saying this is a terrible place, that it's not what we imagined?"

"I'm not saying anything. Just that there are things I didn't expect."

"Like what?"

"Hell, young Jeffrey, maybe you'll think everything's fine and dandy. That'd be great as far as I'm concerned. But you should find out for yourself." Mark's face brightened. "Hey, listen!"

For the first time since we left the dock, I heard music. "You'll like this." Mark led us through The Onion more quickly. "You'll like this a lot."

We arrived at a wooden gazebo beneath the very center of the dome. The gazebo looked as though it belonged in some small town square or 1890's park. Six musicians rehearsed, plinking away at an obviously incomplete song. They stopped occasionally to try a phrase again or experiment with playing it a new way.

I recognized only one person in the gazebo. "Hoooooooooollllllllllllyyyyyyyyyy shiiiiiiiiiiiiiiiiiiiiiiiiiit!"

It was George.

Harrison.

The Beatle.

There was no crazed mob of screaming fans surrounding him, only a hundred or so people listening quietly. A few danced to the music, but many weren't even paying attention and carried on conversations or slept on the ground or on benches around the gazebo. Some blank-faced people stared up to the sea above. At least one man and one woman were bare-chested as they explored each other, oblivious to the crowd around them, the crowd oblivious to them.

Almost everybody, save the bare-chested couple, wore denim work shirts and jeans, including George, the original gravedigger.

"Hoooooooooollllllllllllllly shiiiiiiiiiiiiiiiiiiiiiiiit," I said again, unable to take my eyes off of George.

Harrison.

The Beatle.

Playing a concert right in front of me.

"Hi" Kathy.

"Hoooooooooollllllllllllllllllllllly shiiiiiiiiiiiiiiiiiiiiiiiiiiiiiiiiiit," I said again.

"You got that right," Mark answered. "I had the same reaction when I saw one of them here the first time. Everybody did."

After a few minutes, George looked up from his guitar. He noticed Peter in the crowd and came down the stairs toward us.

George Harrison.

The Beatle.

"Peter!" he said gladly. "Good to see you!" George hugged Peter the same way Mark and I hugged at the dock, the way '70s men weren't supposed to hug. Neither hit the other on the arm. Peter hugged him back, unembarrassed.

They made smalltalk about Peter's trip and yakked about nonsense like whether Martha treated us as poorly as she did everyone. Then Peter made introductions. He introduced Dan first, apologizing for being prejudiced toward people from the Colonies who "speak almost the same language." When he finally got around to me, Jeff Scott from Missouri, I got instantly and totally stupid.

George held out his hand.

I gushed. "I love...I...I...we...I've got all your albums," I said, my face blank and my mind equally vacuous. It was all I could think of in the moment and ever since I have felt it eternally untoppable in dumbness, triteness and ridiculousness.

"Well thank you, luv," George said, "none of us would be here without people like you." He smiled as he said it and his sincerity was obvious. Still, I shrunk inside.

I still don't know what I *should* have said or even what I *might* have said at that moment that would have been correct, and God knows I've thought about it for all these years. But I'm still convinced that "I have all your albums" wasn't the best, most perfect thing. Maybe a simple "hi" would have been best.

I wish I could say "hi" to George now. Sorry George. I was the dumbass who couldn't think of anything better than "I have all your albums."

Peter explained that George was the producer on several Badfinger albums and after each session everyone went to a nearby pub to decompress. "But it was hard to go out, luv," George said, looking at Peter, "the birds kept flocking all over him."

"I have all your albums." Hooooooooooooooly shit.

Peter explained to George we just got off the submarine and were still finding our way around. George said there would be plenty of time to play later. He'd be in The Onion for some time before he went back to "the World."

"You remember Jimmy?" George asked as he introduced one of the other gazebo musicians. It was Jimmy McCulloch, a guitarist for Thunderclap Newman. Their one big hit was "Something in the Air." Mark and I played it on KMZU, never recognizing the lyrics as another clue in the Beatle mystery:

> **Call out the streets and houses,**
> **Because there's something in the air.**
> **We've got to get together sooner or later,**
> **Because The Rev-o-lu-tion's near.**
> **And you know it's right.**

Mark and I always thought Thunderclap Newman was an individual, one person singing about The Rev-o-lu-tion.

Missing those clues seems almost as dumb as saying "I have all your albums" to George Harrison.

The Beatle.

"Something in the Air" was the closing theme music of Ringo's movie, *Magic Christian*. Badfingers "Come and Get It" was in the movie too.

Now I know why.

"I've got all your albums." Stupid, stupid, stupid.

Two bootlegged George Harrison albums came onto the underground market long after Pepperland died and before George did. The first is called *Somewhere in Utopia*. The other is *All Things Must Surface*. Go figure.

IN OUR LITTLE HIDEAWAY
BENEATH THE WAVES

When George and Jimmy went back to the gazebo, Mark recommended that he and I should push on. He said we could come back but we needed to settle in. "There'll be time," he told me, "lots and lots of time."

"Are the others here?" I asked, looking back toward George as we walked. "John? Paul? Ringo?"

"They're in and out. Ringo was here, but I don't know whether he's still here or not. He might be someplace. All the Beatles are here one time or another."

"Hooooooollllllllllllllllllllllllly shiiiiiiiiiiiiiiiiiiiiiiiiit," I exhaled again, amazed at the possibilities of actually being so close to the gods.

"They come and go whenever they want," Mark said off-handedly. I was amazed at his casualness, his nonchalance. "After all, it's their place."

The gazebo and George seemed like the midpoint of our hike. "It can be a long walk," Mark said and we all agreed. "Somebody said it's fifteen or eighteen acres or something, and that can be a long walk sometimes. There are bicycles around if you don't want to hoof it. You ride one and leave it. But they're in pretty high demand. I think some people hoard them in their rooms."

Still flushed from meeting George and from my accompanying stupidity, I felt it important to get back to reality. "How did you die, Mark?"

"Ohhhhhh, there was a terrible fire," he grinned. "Remember the Ford?"

"Sure."

"Burned to a crisp. They told my folks nothing was left of me but a briquette."

"I fell off a boat into the Mississippi."

"Right. That's good," he said, "but not the best."

"Oh yeah? Who's the best?"

"A guy from Montana we call Pop. They put him in an enormous avalanche, buried him in snow on a ski slope, his body was lost and he's out there frozen forever."

"Why do you call him Pop?"

"As in 'Popsicle.' Another guy, from London, they made him cut out letters from a magazine to spell out his own ransom note from kidnappers. I think it was pretty cruel, making him do it himself."

"Hell, we all did it ourselves, Mark," I said.

After long consideration, Mark finally answered. "Riiiiiiiight. I guess so."

"They're all cruel to somebody," I said. "There's no easy way."

"I guess not. But the end justifies the means."

"Shit, I don't know, at least not yet. Anyway, how did you know I was coming?"

"They post a list. I knew there was a chance you'd change your mind, some people do, but at least I knew you were on the way. The last report we got was that you were on the *Scorpion* so I figured I'd meet you if you got off *Alvin*. When I heard your stupid voice yakking at the dock I knew you didn't chicken out."

"I thought about it, I really did."

"Everybody thinks about it. Are you still with Mara?"

"Not any more."

"Riiiiiiiight."

"Is Beth here? Is she on some list?"

"No. She's not coming."

"Why?"

"There was a boyfriend back home and that was the end of that."

"Really?"

"Really. I don't know if she would have fit in anyway."

"What's that supposed to mean?"

"Nothing," Mark defended, "it's just that she didn't find the clues and she didn't go about all this with the kind of passion we had. She was just the one who answered the phone, that's all. I don't know that she was really into this like we were."

"Shit, Mark," I said as we walked. "I feel bad we're here and she's not. She helped us, she answered the questions, she went to…"

"Riiiiiiiiiiight. I know. I was there." I had nothing further to add to the conversation.

After a lollygagging stroll, we finally reached the side of the dome opposite the dock. Ahead of us were tiers of walkways and doors, rows of cliff-dweller Pueblos one atop the other, level after level, all cantilevered under the contours of the dome so the top row extended far above the bottom row. "This is the Village," Mark explained. "Dan and Peter, you guys are on the second row, tenth or twelfth room from the right, I'm not sure. Your names are on the door."

"Wot, luv? We share a room?"

"That's the way it is," Mark said. "You share a language, you share a room. At least to start. Some people just spend all of their time out in the dome and never go into their rooms at all. It's up to you."

Peter looked genuinely indignant and upset, as if no one in his position in the music world should ever be required to share a room. "Wot if I bring a bird up?"

"You wouldn't be the first. You'll work it out. The stairs are there." Mark pointed to an open-frame metal spiral staircase in the right-center cluster of rooms. "Jeff, they made the Missouri connection, so we're rooming together."

"What if I bring a bird up?" I asked.

"There aren't any canaries here."

"You know what I mean."

"I've known you long enough to know it ain't gonna happen any time soon. So all I can tell you is that if and when it does happen, we'll deal with it then."

"Oh yeah? We'll see."

"We're on the top level, left side."

We climbed the spiral staircase to the top tier, five or six levels up. I huffed and puffed. "You'll get used to it. You still smoking?" I nodded. "Asshole."

"I haven't smoked very much since I left home."

"Good. But you're still an asshole."

I stood aside, waiting for Mark to unlock the door, but he just opened it up. "No locks here, there's nothing to steal. Besides, where would a thief go? Everybody's cool. Except you, of course."

"Of course," I answered. "And I don't trust you either."

"Of course not," he responded.

"Asshole," I retorted wittily.

"Prick," he cleverly replied, thinking he was depleting the bulk of the remaining anatomical insults. But I didn't agree. "Schmuck." Except for that one. "Putz." And that one.

We went into the room.

My eyes were immediately caught by the room's primary architectural feature, the angled walls: thick plastic triangles filtering blue-green sunlight from above. The see-through walls contoured along the curve of the dome from the ceiling above, rolling down past the floor below and all the way down past what was below our level to where the dome finally met the ocean floor. Our biggest wall was a complete window to the Octopus's Garden. We knew we could not be found. It was a genuine "hideaway beneath the waves." It was a true fishbowl, viewed from the inside-out, one of those walk-through aquariums almost every city has nowadays, but that comparison doesn't do it justice if only because this was now our home and not just a place to visit.

The rest of the room was simple, dim but not dark. The only lighting came from outside the glass and from small fluorescent fixtures over the beds for use when the sea was dark. The sidewalls were stainless steel, the furniture more War Surplus.

The closet was a series of hooks on the metal walls. Mark's hooks held a few denim shirts, a couple of pairs of jeans and several olive drab towels. There were empty hooks on the opposite wall. "That's your closet," Mark said. "You're not gonna need much storage space here. It's like a commune. Nobody owns anything, everybody shares."

The room felt more comfortable than the Quonset huts at Jarvis, though more hospital-roomish. Except for the incredible drama of the outside wall, it wasn't much, I thought, but it would be easy to get used to, especially with the view.

"The bathroom is mid-tier," Mark went on. "It's co-ed, so forget any inhibitions about showering or taking a dump in private."

This made me stop staring out into the ocean and start paying attention again. "Okay."

"The crappers are salt water, so don't worry about wasting water and always give the next person the courtesy of a flush."

"Of course I..."

"But fresh water is rationed, which means quick showers and fast tooth brushing. We're the 'blue group.' When they turn on the blue light, it's our turn to shower. But keep it short. There was one day I soaped up and the showers shut down on me."

"Okay."

"That's why the grass is so brown and the plants all died, not enough fresh water. In a while, I'll take you to the meal area and supply. Are you hungry? We can go now."

"No. I'm okay. Thanks."

"Riiiiiiight. No problem."

We sat on the beds, alone for the first time. I was excited that the end of the end had finally come, that I'd reached the true start of a new beginning. Looking at my friend and not to the outside world, I asked Mark what should have been a yes/no question: "is it fun here?"

He hesitated before answering, looking down at the floor and his boots. "Fun is the one thing that money can't buy."

POWER TO THE PEOPLE
POWER TO THE PEOPLE
POWER TO THE PEOPLE
POWER TO THE PEOPLE
RIGHT ON

Fifteen, twenty years ago or so, by nothing more than chance and sheer curiosity, I spent five bucks for a beaten-up, used, hardback copy of *The People's Almanac* (Doubleday, 1975), by David Wallechinsky and his father, Irving Wallace.   It is a wonderful compilation of wonderfully unimportant and lovingly irrelevant information, from the biography of Snoopy the comic strip dog to how to handle emergency childbirth.   In other words, it's a classic bathroom book, one to pick up and open to any page for as long as you need to amuse yourself.   After I scanned the book and read a few sections, I put it away and never picked it up again.

And then only a few years ago, looking to pass some time, I pulled it off the shelf.   As I grabbed the three-inch wide binding, the book fell to the floor.   All by itself, it opened to page 1435, almost at the end of the book, a section I had never read before.

It was "The *Almanac's* Exclusive Symposium on Utopia."

Wallechinsky and Wallace polled famous people about their visions of Utopia, asking them all the same questions.   Included were Buckminster Fuller, father of the geodesic dome, and John Lennon, former Beatle. They were interviewed separately.

Here are some excerpts from their answers:

What would the physical environment of your Utopia be like?
FULLER: As near perfect as possible.   Man would have as much control over his environment as possible—controlled climate.   There

would be no nations, no borders, no government as we know it, no wars, no fierce competition. Everyone would be a world citizen, a born student of life and nature, a comprehensivist, uninhibited, appreciative of himself and others.

LENNON: Typical.

What family structures would be used?

FULLER: Since people would interact freely without inhibitions, their children would be exposed to many diverse individuals and spend much time away from the family without difficulty. The roles of husband and wife would be limitless, without personal strictures. Members of the family—individuals in general—would no longer "belong" to each other.

LENNON: Any

How would government be organized?

FULLER: What government?

LENNON: Toss a coin.

How would work and goods be divided?

FULLER: Naturally, since cooperation and efficient technology will have replaced competition and low-yield production, there will be enough wealth and goods for all to have a high standard of living. Work will no longer be a drudgery or a necessity. Everyone will spend most of his time doing what interests him.

LENNON: Color of eyes.

*What would be **your** role in this society?*

FULLER: I would first be a consumer, enjoying life to its fullest. Like everyone else, I would be a world citizen, learning, traveling, creating and contributing, if possible, to the world's knowledge.

LENNON: Heavenly.

Why isn't life like this now?

FULLER: We are basically ignorant, still governed by old reflexes. Technologically, our old, political, religious and economic systems are obsolete, yet we cling to them. Our whole system of "rationality" needs revision.

LENNON: Isn't it?

As I read this section of *The People's Almanac*, I found each answer incredibly eerie. That the authors included these two men in their interviews was just another piece of the Pepperland puzzle.

Buckminster Fuller, a man who inspired it physically but probably never knew of Pepperland, saw his Utopian dream as a pure ideal. John Lennon, a man who saw modern society's most viable attempt at Utopia, never referred to it.

I believe John's answers were terse primarily because that was how he always answered questions but also because he feared that giving more complete answers would reveal the truth of Pepperland, a bitter truth he was afraid to disclose.

That *The People's Almanac* fell open to page 1435 on that day a few years ago was what convinced me to write this book. After all those years, I truly believe that something other than gravity made it fall open to those Utopian pages.

As a final irony, another piece of the mystery, I notice that Wallechinsky and Wallace also polled themselves as part of the Utopia symposium. Irving Wallace's statement on the subject begins this way: "As you know, 'utopia' means 'nowhere...'"

Nowhere.

Man.

HOW DOES IT FEEL TO BE
ONE OF THE BEAUTIFUL PEOPLE?
(WHAT WOULD YOU LIKE TO BE?)

Unaccustomed to seeing Mark in an emotional dumper, I was more interested in him than Pepperland. Hell, I didn't even know he "died." What a lousy friend I must be. There would be time to explore Pepperland, forever as a matter of fact.

"What's going on?" I asked him. "Except for when you first met me and you had a little excitement in your voice and some color in your face, you look like an underweight version of death itself. What's happening?"

He considered his answer carefully. "Look, I don't want to spoil your arrival here 'cause this ought to be a great time for you. You deserve a great arrival. You ought to have the most fun of your life, right now. I had that kind of first impression when I got here and you deserve it too."

"Thanks. I appreciate that. Now tell me what's going on."

"And I also know what you're going through, Jeff. I did it too. I left my life and now I've had some time to think about it."

"The world-famous 'second thoughts,' huh?"

"Riiiiiight. I guess Martha gave everybody the same speech. It's just that I'm not sure what's happening here, but I know it's not what we expected it to be, it's not…"

"What? What is it then? What *isn't* it?"

"I don't know what it is or what it isn't! Plenty of people here think that it really is heaven, that it really is Utopia. Talk to the Popsicle man from Montana. Hell, talk to Steve Handy!"

"From Notre Dame? Holllllllllllllllllllly shiiiiiiiiiiiiiiiiiiit!"

"Riiiiiight. He thinks I'm full of holy shit. When I asked him about that whole airport thing—seems like a million years ago, doesn't it?—he jumped down my throat like I said Knute Rockne was a communist."

"Who?"

"Never mind."

"So what's the problem? What's the problem, dammit?"

As usual, he considered his answer carefully. "There's a feeling here, at least I get a feeling that..." He stopped again and looked out through the ceiling. "Look, it's not fair for me to spoil your arrival here. Nobody spoiled mine and it was the best time I ever had. Intellectually and emotionally, I don't want your ideas ruined by a malcontent."

"I'll worry about that. Go on."

"Well, it's just that when I saw your name on the list, I decided it's not fair for me to pollute your feelings and now here I am, doing exactly what I told myself I wouldn't do. You're gonna have to decide for yourself if you made the right decision. Maybe you'll think this is what you expected and not a..." He stopped.

"Shit. Will you keep talking?"

"I'm beating you over the head like a Chicago cop here. You should feel glad, welcome, you should be happy to be here, ecstatic! Go nuts! We worked hard to get here and now you deserve to enjoy yourself. Talk to people, talk to the ones who got here first. There were lots of people from the first waves who feel completely different than me. Make up your own mind. I don't want to talk about it any more."

Neither of us spoke for a time. "Isn't that what it's supposed to be about?"

"What?"

"Deciding things for ourselves. Isn't that what it's all about?"

"Riiiiiight. That's what it's all about."

"So what's it all about?"

"Alfie."

"Yeah, what's it all about, Alfie?"

I shuffled my feet, figuring I had asked the wrong question, questions too personal for Mark to answer. Finally, he gave in. "Do you remember how we had these visions of how Pepperland would be some place of perpetual love and harmony?"

"Sure."

"How we figured the Beatles would play together all the time? 'Sergeant Pepper's Lonely Hearts Club Band,' all that shit?"

"Yeah, I remember."

"Riiiiiiight. Well, they're never here together. John is never here with Paul, Paul is never here with John, and if George and Ringo are here at the same time it's a miracle. I know the place is supposed to be more than one big concert, but once and a while you expect...you...you know...you expect *something.*"

"I suppose so."

"Then there are the Company Men."

"Yeah?"

"Most of 'em are pretty cool, but there's a few that we call 'Meanies.' But not to their faces, of course." I laughed at the nickname. "Those guys, they're so...wait a minute!" Mark's eyes grew with his volume. "Let me show you around! That's what you're here for, not to sit in a damn room!" His attitude brightened. I figured it was a false front he put on to dispel whatever gloom may have further darkened the dimly lit room, but it was a welcome change nonetheless.

"Okay. Sounds good to me."

As we headed for the door, he stopped yet again. "This is the last thing I'm gonna say about it."

"You know, you keep saying you're done talking, then you keep talking."

"Riiiiiight. But it's like, I think, my problem is...I wonder if it was all about the chase. You know, the quest? The pursuit? I wonder if the important thing was finding out what was going on, what the clues meant and solving the puzzle. And now we're here and...shit! I don't know. It's over. It's sort of a letdown."

"Okay."

"We didn't know what we were chasing, but we went after it anyway. And now that we've caught it, it's no big deal. And that's the last thing I'm gonna say."

"I doubt it."

"You're absolutely, positively, definitely still an asshole." Mark paused only a second after saying he would say no more before he said something else. "And sometimes, it's just plain boring."

"I knew you'd say something."

"Riiiiiiiiight. You win, asshole. Now let's see what there is to see."

He pushed the room door open and in an instant, all the terrible things he hinted at were forgotten, all shadows of doubt obliterated by the light. My excitement was suddenly overwhelming.

Music began just outside the door. It came from everywhere, every pore and cell and atom of the place, not too loud and not too soft. It was more visceral than auditory, felt all the way down in the marrow of my bones more than heard with just my eardrums. All of a sudden, the entire Onion sounded and felt as if it were playing "Wouldn't it be Nice" by the Beach Boys, a song about young people yearning to be together forever.

Mark saw my reaction, smiled and understood my euphoria. "It's a Defense Department thing," he said, "Project Sanguine, they call it. They transmit ultra-low frequencies straight through the earth from Wisconsin or Minnesota or something. There's a receiver in The Onion and the sound carries through the metal in the dome, just like we used to transmit at KMZU through the walls in the dorms."

I didn't care about the technicalities, only that the music went all the way through me. It was wonderful, almost sexual.

"George must be finished," Mark added, matter-of-factly with the same kind of "so what?" attitude he might give "the sun came up today." If Mark ever noticed that the sun came up.

"Sometimes they play rock, sometimes classical, sometimes when George is here they play really shitty sitar music. I've really gotten into Indian flute—that's American Indian, by the way, not India Indian. It's beautiful. It really gets inside your soul."

One of the dictionary definitions of "sanguine" is "confident, optimistic." That's how the music coming through The Onion made me feel and how the Indian flute made Mark feel. That's American Indian, by the way, not India Indian.

I was captivated. The place was alive. Beach Boys harmonies gave me good vibrations all the way through my being.

Just as our *Scorpion* conversation made Judy more attractive, the way her smile brightened her being, The Onion looked better too when it had a sound track filled with music. But Mark was unimpressed. More than once I once caught him mouthing the lyrics to some of the old songs we played on radio, but he still seemed down. All I could think of was how animated and full of adventure he was when we went through clues on the air and in the days after.

He took me to the supply area and I picked up some towels, a few shirts, a pair of jeans, some underwear, socks and a pair of brown leather, rubber-soled, high-ankle "Chukka boots" to replace my loafers. The shoes were the kind of boots developed for British soldiers when they occupied India—that's India India, by the way—and exactly the shoes that completed George's "gravedigger" costume on *Abbey Road*.

Then we went to the dining area, an area of tables on the dome edge. Just walking the distance was enough to work up an appetite. Since there was no time in The Onion, there were no designated meal times, Mark said. We could eat whenever we wanted.

There were always C-Rats and any time I wanted to eat from a package I could drop in and grab some. There was also fresh fruit, vegetables, drinks—including liquor, wine and beer—whenever we wanted them. It was like raiding the 'fridge at home, Mark said, but better supplied. Hot meals were available whenever anyone was ambitious enough to cook for themselves or others and also willing to clean up after themselves or their group. Occasionally, our group feasted on steak or chicken banquets, but as time passed the frequency of the feasts decreased.

We rotated KP, our turns indicated by colored shower lights set on "flash." Like the way we cleaned ourselves, we cleaned the dining area as the blue group. It was no big deal. Since all meals were served on paper plates with plastic cutlery, KP meant only wiping down tables and pushing chairs underneath. There was minimal dishwashing, just pots and pans, though some cooks were sloppy and the work became more difficult.

Mark showed me the small infirmary run by a Company doctor and said sooner or later I'd be called in for a physical. He warned me about the doctor. "He's a real Meanie sonofabitch. I think he took this assignment because it was the only way he'd ever get patients to come to him." Then Mark explained the suspected purpose of the physical. "They do a bunch of tests, take some blood and they talk a lot. It's got to be more psychological testing."

"Manila folder time."

"Riiiiiight. I guess they want to see if you've gone nuts or not. Or, in your case, whether you're still nuts."

"Thank you."

"The only medical problems so far," he said, "are a few reactions to Company drugs, bad acid trips and stuff. One guy tried to fly off the top of the village and broke himself up pretty bad."

"Geez Louise."

"There's a couple of pregnant women here, probably more of 'em sooner or later. You can get pills or rubbers whenever you want, just stop by the infirmary."

"Okay."

"You don't want the pills."

"Thank you. I know."

Our tour took us through the rest of The Onion, with another stop at the dining area for Mark to get potato chips and soda. He introduced me to more people from around the world with strange and wonderful names and accents.

He showed me the exercise area with weight-lifting equipment, a basketball court and a large open area with green shag carpeting. "Ringo's a football nut—soccer. Games last for days when he's here. The field used to be grassed, but they carpeted when it browned out. They brought in squares of carpet because the *Alvin* couldn't handle rolls. Everybody was here one day, on hands and knees, putting in hunks of carpet like pieces of some huge puzzle. It was a big happy carpet party."

Another large area had easels and potters wheels and other art supplies. "John spends lots of time here," Mark went on. "He does all this shit. There, that's one of his over there." On a shelf was a sculpture of two hands clasped together in a handshake. Though I knew I'd never seen it before, it looked familiar. "It's from *Yellow Submarine*," Mark said. "There was a huge one of these in the movie, it was the Pepperland centerpiece. John saw it and wanted to make one for real. Then he just left it."

Somewhere in mid-tour, we ran into Judy, Jacques and Susanne, just arriving from the *Alvin*. They were still looking at everything at once, trying to see it all, just as I did. Our reunion was as happy as if we hadn't seen each other in years.

"Hi" Judy. "Hi" Jacques and Susanne. Haven't seen you in years.

I introduced Mark all around, explained my vast knowledge of Pepperland excitedly, and told them I wanted to show them around after they were settled. As we separated, Jacques reached into his pocket and pulled out a deck of cards he liberated from the *Scorpion*. "Play pooker?" he asked proudly. "Later," I told him, "we'll have the first Pepperland poker championship!" Judy translated and he smiled broadly.

Still a newcomer and untainted by Mark's feelings, I was completely enchanted by all of it. Asking him about it recently, he said that until I arrived, he was rife with doubts and seriously questioned his decision to try for the ninth plateau. He said that until my group arrived, he had too much time and too many second thoughts. He refused to be "in the moment" and admitted he often wished he could go back to The World, which is what Pepperlanders called anything outside The Onion.

I learned years after Pepperland that "The World" is also what prison inmates call anything outside their own closed walls and locked doors. I suppose there are many people who would scoff at our "in the moment" idea of life in The Onion, calling it nothing more than a different kind of prison.

Mark would learn to love Pepperland.

In the meantime, I loved Pepperland from the beginning.

BABY YOU'RE A RICH MAN,
BABY YOU'RE A RICH MAN,
BABY YOU'RE A RICH MAN TOO

I adapted quickly.

Pepperland was a permanent vacation without the threat of ever having to go back to work or school. We were all totally out of whatever routines and ruts we might have had in our lives before and deeply installed into a new routine and/or rut of fun and games and laughter and music and friendship, if you can call that a rut. And sex. That played a big part too. But even in my old age I still have trouble talking or talking freely about it so I won't, despite the fact that I know that steamy undersea sex scenes increase my chances of this book succeeding. But figure it out. Like Pepperland itself, the imagining is probably better than the reality anyway. Imagine, a bunch of young, inexperienced kids with carte blanche to…well, figure it out. Despite my own embarrassment and a personal resolve to be a gentleman and not to do it and tell, I will do the best I can to explain the situation later in this book.

We played constant poker, using M&Ms for chips. Brown M&Ms were $1, yellow ones $5, red ones $10 and tan ones $20. The idea of actual money was, of course, as worthless as our debts and winnings, but the idea of winning huge sums of chocolate was as delectable as the M&Ms themselves. We never bet green M&Ms, by the way, because Jacques insisted we give them all to him. He nearly force-fed them to Susanne because of their reputed aphrodisiac qualities. Jacques said they worked. Susanne denied it.

Quickly, the cards Jacques liberated from the *Scorpion* became ratty and chocolate-covered so we requisitioned a few new decks from the Meanies. Soon, the *Alvin* delivered forty-four cases of new decks and card games of all varieties became an Onion-wide passion. For a while, a mini-Las Vegas thrived on the bottom of the Pacific Ocean with M&Ms the currency of choice. Big winners showed off their prowess by rubbing chocolate all over their faces and wearing it as primitive body paint to display the success of their hunt. M&M wagering went on during games of poker, gin, sheepshead, bridge and "go fish."

After a time, however, most people lost interest in cards and went back to the same old sex, drugs and rock and roll.

Our dedicated group even bored of cards after a time and decided to play Scrabble, so we asked for a set. *Alvin* quickly delivered five cases of Scrabble games, plus additional cases of Monopoly, Life, Easy Street, Parcheesi, Sorry and Ouija boards.

After Judy pushed for a Scrabble tournament, someone still retaining their idealism explained why the games got so little use. "There's no use for competition here," she said, "nobody cares who's better than anybody. There's no need to do anything as crass as beating somebody." All this empirically proved that Buckminster Fuller's *People's Almanac* prediction was absolutely right, that in Utopia "efficient technology will have replaced competition." Our group played Scrabble anyway because it made sweet, even-tempered Judy happy to mercilessly crush us so harshly and my apologies are extended to Mister Fuller.

Jacques and Susanne learned English quickly, though they often had vocabulary or syntax problems. During a poker game, a down on his luck Jacques once threw his cards into the air and announced he was "tired of being slobbered." Even today, I tell my card buddies to prepare to be "slobbered." I tell them it's a phrase I picked up from my kids.

Movies played constantly in those pre-VCR days. Films were projected in 16-millimeter and were probably rented from some film supply house that had no idea their films weren't being shown in some school auditorium except that it took longer than usual for the films to be returned. The films ranged from *Hemo the Magnificent*, a grade school level instructional film about human blood, to reasonably new theatrical releases, from travelogues to classics. Sometime before the film, especially before the classics, someone gave a brief talk to explain what we were about to see. After, there was discussion, though no one was required to make "in-class contributions" toward their grade.

Of course, Beatle films were shown to great audience amusement and great embarrassment to any of the participants who were present.

When *Hard Day's Night* was shown, an interesting mood fell over the crowd. When we all first saw it in theatres at home, it was a delightful romp, a fun look into what we thought were Beatle private lives and a chance to see how clever and funny they were individually and together. But in The Onion, knowing what we knew about Pepperland's origins, it was uncomfortable to watch. We could see the pressures the Beatles felt. We knew the difficulty we ourselves created for them simply by loving them.

Filmmaking became another activity for many people. Super 8 cameras and film were available from the art area and many people became involved in movies, even though their casts and certainly their filming locations were limited.

It was a slow and difficult process. Exposed film had to be sent outside via the *Alvin* to be developed. Editing was difficult (such was the nature of tiny Super 8 film), and sound had to be recorded and mixed on a separate reel-to-reel tape recorder so most of the films were "silent" movies with only a music track, though some of the more ambitious producers tried for "talkies." The lack of synch between the audio track and the film was a great source of amusement at the beginning but was quickly forgiven when we became fascinated with the idea of seeing ourselves on screen. No matter that the simple, little films were just a touch more sophisticated than home movies, minus the waving and camera mugging, once we understood the difficulty of making them and appreciated the art that went into them, they were just as enchanting as anything Hollywood ever produced.

I don't believe any of the completed films ever made it out of The Onion at the end, but from the style and content of several post-Pepperland films that came out over the years, I suspect there may have been more than a few people involved in the Hollywood and British movie industries who got their start in Pepperland. I can't know for sure, since I didn't recognize their names on the credits because the names on the credits were not the names I knew.

Since there was such a timeless opportunity for recreational and educational reading, the small library in The Onion was well stocked and the inventory was rotated in and out. While there was a problem with people keeping books in their room or simply leaving them in public places, The Onion library probably had fewer theft or overdue problems than the average public library.

There were no magazines or newspapers to tell us what was happening in The World. The Onion was our world. Some people complained about this shortcoming, but the Meanies never satisfied our desires for timely periodicals.

Sometimes, our group would raid the Costume Area and play "dress up."

Whoever decided there should be such an area in Pepperland was a genius. Maybe the costumes were another Company experiment, just to see what alter egos we would create, but that seems irrelevant. The area was much used and hugely appreciated.

There were hundreds of outfits. The place gave the feeling that an entire Hollywood wardrobe department had been shipped in or that an ancient Broadway theatre had moved to The Onion. We could be whatever we wanted. We loved the cowboy and Indian costumes, the cheap plastic space suits, friar's robes, white dinner jackets, formal dresses, medieval squires and ladies garb, military uniforms, surgical scrubs, priests vestments, wedding gowns, tuxedos, long black Hassidic rabbi coats, a complete collection of bright uniforms from some long-ago high school band and hundreds of hats of all types and styles. Literally, just putting on a new hat could change a person into the fireman or jockey or cop or baseball player whose hat they wore. As George said in *Yellow Submarine*, "it's all in the mind you know." Maybe it's just atop the head.

We wore costumes for endless games of make-believe, creating characters and situations to fit our personalities and moods, usually creating new moods and characters. We carried these personalities for days—if there had been days—transforming ourselves into different selves for as long as it took to bore ourselves of our new selves. Then we changed costumes or hats or personalities again.

There were salt water sprinklers to run through—exactly like the sprinklers the kids in my childhood neighborhood ran through—except in The Onion, nearly everyone was naked.

It was total, uninhibited childishness.

And that was Pepperland's reality: uninhibited childishness.

For others, Pepperland's reality was unreality.

Drugs were plentiful and easy to get. Most of our group stayed away from hard stuff, favoring silly fun, goofy games and all-purpose general kid stuff. We usually limited our chemical indulgence to alcohol and interrupted the foolishness only when the booze or lack of sleep kicked in and we fell asleep or simply passed out. Certainly, we were all polite enough to take hits from any community joints passed through the crowd at gazebo concerts, but for the most part we could see what happened to the druggies and preferred consciousness to the pharmaceutical cornucopia the Meanies offered.

I do not include this information to prove we were goody-goodies, it's just part of our particular side of the story.

In truth, nobody ever pointed fingers or wagged tongues unless someone was in obviously serious life-threatening jeopardy or put someone else in danger. Neither the druggies nor the straights cared what anyone else did or didn't do and that's part of the story too. "Do your own thing" was not only a saying, it was a way of life.

There were, of course, plenty of people who took full advantage of the Company-sponsored opportunity to live in Pepperland completely and permanently stoned. In return, I'm sure they provided The Company with all kinds of interesting data about drug use and addiction.

All that was needed to get drugs was a quick visit to the infirmary and a signature. It was as easy as checking books out of the library. I always found it ironic that we could get drugs at the same place we went when we were sick or wanted birth control. I found it interesting that the infirmary could cure a problem, prevent a problem or create one. Occasionally, rumors of "some new shit" swept through The Onion and the druggies flocked enthusiastically to the infirmary, eager to become guinea pigs.

I'd love to turn you on.

Overdoses were rare since the infirmary Meanies carefully regulated the flow, quality and amount of drugs given to any individual. Problems only occurred when one druggie gave his share of the shit to another and that one person ingested quantities designed for two or more. Drug theft was a medium-sized problem, one with which I never had to bother myself.

I only remember a few times when there was a negative community reaction to Company experiments, including one hairy incident when a druggie started whapping at the dome glass with a metal chair. A minor panic swept through everyone straight-headed enough to understand the threat a glass-whapping incident represented. The druggie was quickly wrestled away from the glass by a group of straights while a large crowd of his peers stood by and watched, enthralled by the possibility of watching the sea rush in to scuttle the dome and kill everyone instantly.

Like drugs, sex was plentiful and the Company saw that any undesired results of love under The Onion would be dealt with quickly, safely and without moral judgment.

Most sexual relationships were purely hormonal, one-on-one quickies (and occasionally, two-on-one, six-on-five, four-on-eight and any other mathematical combination possible). Other relationships were more significant, lasting either any amount of time longer than a quickie or an expected lifetime.

Love is all you need.

For all the casual sex our original group was involved with, as far as I know, none was intra-group except for Jacques and Susanne who were intra-ing long before they were in the group. Sex inside the group would have seemed nearly incestuous.

Peter was the most blatantly promiscuous, continuing to draw so many groupies that we told him he should change his name from Peter Ham to Peter Man.

I'm sure Company Meanies monitored and made note of all sexual behavior in Pepperland though no one knew for sure and few seemed to even give a damn about the possibility. It would have been useful information for the Company to have to apply to space travel and dandy data about perpetuation of the species after a nuclear holocaust.

Despite what we did individually, our original group stayed close, continuing to function as a solid group. We played, we ate, we listened to music, we frolicked together the way fate put us together at Jarvis. Individual but inseparable as a unit, we passed time any way we wanted with no responsibilities, timetable, deadlines or restrictions. For us, this was what Utopia was all about. It's probably most people's definition of Utopia today, though I'm not sure it would be correct.

Fun is the one thing that money can't buy.

Peter made music often in the gazebo when he wasn't making someone someplace else. Maybe it was the only real time he found stardom in his own right and not as a Beatle protégé. He made music with professional musicians and with pan banging, drugged out rhythmizers. I think he felt the place originated with music and that music was the main purpose of the place. He made it one of his goals to see that purpose was fulfilled and it made him very happy.

This may have been why Peter had such a difficult time readjusting to life in The World. He went back from pure music-making art at Pepperland to the commercial averageness of life in The World and he wasn't happy any more.

And happy was another definition of Utopia.

God, I was happy at Pepperland.

Mark wasn't happy.

AND THE EYES IN HIS HEAD
SEE THE WORLD SPINNING 'ROUND

Very soon after my arrival, Mark and I developed very separate schedules. Sometimes I was just getting to bed as he arose and vice versa. It was the same relationship he created when he shared the apartment with Edward Abbott in Columbia, without the having to go to class part. Ed worked the morning shift, Mark closed the station in the wee hours.

Often, Mark stayed in bed for what would have been days (had there been days), reading book after book, surviving only on candy bars, potato chips and Dr. Pepper after Dr. Pepper. The trash from wrappers, bags and bottles filled the floor of our room. Sometimes I picked up, but often I angrily kicked his trash into a heap on his side of the room. More often, I shoved it off to the side quietly.

Despite Mark's early disparagement of the druggies, he began dropping acid regularly and this worried me. I feared that if he had a bad experience, nobody would be there to help him. I feared he would try to fly off the top tier of the village.

Our on-and-off schedules can't be blamed on differences in our Circadian rhythms, they were because of his heaviness and my lightness, pure and simple. I feared his attitude would rob from my pleasure and, in fairness, he couldn't stand being around anyone so cheerful.

We became estranged and worked hard to avoid each other, like an old married couple that can't admit divorce is the right thing to do.

A few times, I genuinely tried to get him to join the group for poker, costumes, exercise sessions or general loitering and fooling around, but he always refused. Sometimes, I saw him around the gazebo, listening to whoever was playing, but he was always alone. Often he lay on his back, staring up into the outside.

The separation created obvious tension in our room, but we both pretended not to notice and never spoke of it. In fact, we never spoke at all.

And then one day it changed.

Just like that.

It was a new "moment."

Nothing is real. It's all in the mind, you know. Fun is the one thing that money can't buy. Blahblahblah.

The group was playing cards on the soccer carpet—as comfortable as if we were sitting on the grass in Central Park—and working hard to keep the M&Ms out of the shag, when Mark suddenly sauntered up as if all was right with the world. Smiling, he hunkered down and said, "Deal me in." I remember wondering what kind of drug he was using at that exact moment and wished he had more of it.

Handel's *Water Music* was playing, a grossly cruel inside joke one of the Musicmasters loved to play on the people who couldn't identify it. Whenever I hear *Water Music* now, I still think about when my friend Mark came back to us. For once, Beatles music was inconsequential. It was George Frideric Handel who wrote the soundtrack for that perfect, elegant moment.

Positioning himself between Dan and Judy, he asked for a stake of M&Ms. It was obvious he wasn't there for cards, that he was there for company. It was more than apparent that specifically, he was there for Judy's company. While six or seven people played cards, another game was being played in the same spot that involved only two.

I couldn't tell if Mark was stoned shitless or not, but I don't think he was. He was as lucid and clever and quick-witted as he ever was on radio, putting on the best show of his life for an audience of one. He had even showered and shaved, the former of which he had taken to doing only irregularly, the latter nearly never.

And Judy was an attentive and appreciative listener.

Frankly, I felt slightly jealous and jealously slighted. No matter how funny or clever I had ever been, Judy and I kept a platonic, proper, group relationship and despite any sexual tension—at least *my own* sexual tension—our relationship never went any further. While I could have developed feelings toward Judy, certainly lust, she telegraphed nothing but sisterhood in return.

But the telegraph between Judy and Mark was busy with electricity.

And in truth, I was truly glad for both of them.

Mark joined our group more and more often, but their two-person subgroup grew within the larger dynamic.

With some difficulty, Mark and I readjusted our schedules so we were awake, active and alive at the same time. We began to talk again, not about anything important, just normal guy bullshit. Somewhere amid the bullshit, he told me he was attracted to Judy from the beginning, from when they first met as the group arrived. After all this time, he said, he decided it was time to stop being such a chickenshit and do something about his attraction, at least try. He said he was tired of being alone and thought Judy was his best chance at a relationship with another human. Besides, he said, he saw The Light. "I took some kind of shit, I don't know what, and washed it down with a lot of rum and Dr. Pepper. I was on my bed, looked up, and I swear to God, a huge Jesus swam by."

I tried to stifle my laughter, but the image of a huge swimming Jesus was damned amusing to me.

"Fuck you, asshole!" Mark shouted. That out of his system, he went on as if there was nothing unusual. "Jesus said if I kept doing all the shit I'd die here, and soon. And that's exactly what Jesus said, if I kept doing *'all the shit.'*"

"Doesn't sound like Jesus to me," I told him. "Mike Nelson from *Sea Hunt* maybe, but not Jesus. But then again, what do I know?"

"That's right, you don't know shit, so double fuck you, asshole. All I know is that it scared me. I want to live. It's time to get straight."

He had pulled himself out of his funk and joined our card game. He said his decision to live—and subsequently Judy—literally saved his life.

I knew this was good, but adjustments had to be made.

A towel on our doorknob became the signal that Mark and Judy wanted privacy. At the beginning of their relationship, I often slept on a bench somewhere in The Onion, but after waking up sore and stiff in every part of my body, I started sacking out in unoccupied beds in neighboring rooms. Ultimately, I stayed in Judy's empty bed whenever a towel was on my doorknob. Her roommate, a brilliantly blonde Swedish woman, came to expect me in Judy's bed more often than Judy.

For a brief time, I hoped the Swedish roommate and I might establish a relationship along the lines of Mark and Judy's. It would have been a fair deal. But when I clumsily tried to put the moves on her, she proudly announced she was a lesbian.

Nothing is real.

I settled for sleeping space in her room and nothing more than heterosexual fantasy. But there were also times I found a towel on her doorknob too.

While the Sexual Revolution raged in The World and even though The Onion may have been the front line, for a long time I remained an unwilling conscientious objector to it all. Some of this reluctance to jump into any Sexual Revolution skirmishes that did arise may have been from some sort of continued, conscious or subconscious loyalty and fidelity to Mara. Most of all, though, I truly think my own innate, deep and long-standing fear of women kept me alone in my bed or on my bench at the beginning of my stay in Pepperland. I simply didn't know how to talk to or deal with women in anything but a goofy, platonic, humor-as-defense-mechanism way. I didn't know how to flirt or how to do the dating things that my relationship with Mara never required me to learn or practice. And I still don't, for that matter.

But slowly, in time, as my new life grew and my old one fell further behind, as moments became more momentous, even I ultimately came close to learning what others seemed to know.

During one heavy-drinking, heavy dope concert at the gazebo, the excitement and exhilaration of the music caused almost everyone to find someone. Even me. People began to sway and dance in small groups and in pairs. Many, many stayed together to pair and sway and dance long after the concert ended.

So I did manage to have several relationships in Pepperland—that is to say that I finally got laid, proudly hanging a towel over the doorknob and requiring Mark to find alternate sleeping arrangements. But when those in-the-moment relationships quickly and awkwardly ended, I always thought of Mara and wondered how things might have been if she were in Pepperland. I wondered whether that was why those relationships never solidified for me and I wondered if she and I would have stayed together under The Onion or whether the open, uninhibited environment would have changed us.

Buckminster Fuller was absolutely right when he told *The People's Almanac* in his ignorant-of-Pepperland interview: "...people would interact freely without inhibitions...members of the family...individuals in general—would no longer 'belong' to each other."

In fact, Mark and Judy's monogamous relationship was one of the rare ones in The Onion. When we evacuated Pepperland at the end, Mark made a bold stand, announcing he would not leave without Judy. The two gave The Company Men no choice and they quickly rescheduled Mark and Judy's departure times and covers for the afterlife.

After we found each other decades after Pepperland, Mark told me he and Judy were indeed covered and relocated together and they were married.

The marriage lasted six years.

Mark said their marriage failed because Judy decided he "wasn't the person she first met."

Of course he wasn't.

By then, we were all somebody else, in name and in history and in personalities.

He's told me that the last time he heard from Judy was in the late 1980's when he received a Christmas card from her. It had no message and was just signed "Jude." He doesn't know where she lives. He doesn't even know if she's still alive.

Hey Jude, take a sad song and make it better.

The pregnant woman in The Onion gave birth to a son.

There was some discussion that she might give birth in the gazebo, making childbirth just another concert, but she delivered in the cleanliness of the infirmary.

She named the baby Paul George.

She named him after her grandfathers. Some coincidence, huh?

I DON'T REALLY WANT TO STOP THE SHOW BUT I THOUGHT YOU MIGHT LIKE TO KNOW

There were three hundred and fourteen people in The Onion, counting defected Company Men (of both sexes), and the Meanies who carried out their assigned duties and kept the place running day-to-day, ordering supplies to be delivered by the *Alvin*, regulating the systems and, presumably, keeping the records and filing reports that would ultimately be destroyed in Washington. Other Company Men showed up occasionally to do whatever they did and then left.

The Beatles came and went at will, sometimes bringing outsiders with them. Sometimes we knew the others, sometimes not.

The Company did a good job in seeing that the Pepperland population was a mix of people, a mix of ages and types and backgrounds and ideas. It was not all students or loafers and ne'er-do-wells who could afford to or wanted to or needed to pick up and leave home. The Company certainly didn't want a Hoboville under the sea. It was a mix of musicians and artists, teachers and scientists, students and druggies, professionals, amateurs and working class heroes. It was full of people who, back in society would have created—a society.

Here are the names of some of the others:

Donovan Leitch: The Scottish singer was there from almost the beginning. Unlike most of us, he could have left at any time but he chose to stay. Like Peter, he was a special invitee. He met the Beatles in India as they studied with the Maharishi.

He played often in the gazebo, usually with others but sometimes alone. Even when not playing, he almost always wore a harmonica on a harp around his neck.

He told me that when he first learned of plans for Pepperland, he sat down and wrote "Atlantis" in five minutes, later adding all the spoken mumbo-jumbo at the beginning for the recording. The real song is simply the repeated words "'way down, below the ocean, where I want to be." It was his last top 40 hit.

After Pepperland, he published a book of poetry called *Dry Songs and Scribbles*. None of the poems were about Pepperland but the title was clearly a reference.

Bruce the co-pilot: He arrived very shortly after I did. He said he needed a break, that he was tired of literally holding other people's lives in his hands.

Even though he was a Company Man, he quickly became a true Pepperlander, spending most of the time stoned, drunk or both. When the end came, he was evacuated with the rest of us without ever assuming his Company role again. I always wondered whether he was given special treatment because of his background, or special mistreatment for the same reason.

John Taichert: A wannabe Nashville "picker," he found his way into honkytonk beer bar gigs in west Texas that specialized in country music and fistfights. He played pedal steel guitar with a country swing band at a bar called "Carol's Corral." Since there were no pedal steels in Pepperland, he borrowed a regular guitar whenever he played in the gazebo. He played reasonably well and we took his word that he was equally good on steel. We also took his word about his proficiency in the fistfight part of his claim and never asked for proof.

In The World, he supplemented his band income by working in a used record store and discovered the clues after a customer asked for Beatle records to "figger out all this bullshit I've been readin' 'bout."

He disappeared while on a camping trip/retreat in the New Mexico desert. He hiked out alone to "find himself," but several weeks after his disappearance he was determined lost. Only traces of his torn clothing were ever found. Instead of "finding himself," it was assumed he was found by wild animals, which dragged his body away.

Clark Clifton: The Atlanta disc jockey Mark and I called the first night of our quest. He apologized for how little information he gave us that night, but he feared that telling us more might have jeopardized his own departure to Pepperland.

The night after our call, he told us, he put on the 17-minute side of Iron Butterfly's "In-a-Gadda-Da-Vida" album, phoned his station manager and announced he was resigning. Clifton said he left the phone on the counter so the manager could hear the studio door slam. He said he was sorry he never got the satisfaction of knowing whether the boss had listened to the phone long enough to hear the end of the record side or whether he heard the turntable needle hitting the record label over and over and over and over on the air.

Sexy Sadie: A secretary at Apple. Despite her complaints about the lousy hours, she answered the phone Wednesday mornings at five o'clock.

Arnold Fenton: Perhaps the person least expected at Pepperland, he was a stereotypical Irish dirt farmer. He was proud of his roots, both his familial ones and the ones he maintained in the literal dirt of his farm.

I suppose I considered him "least expected" because almost everyone else seemed to come from deep inside some cultural middle class, mostly educated and involved in popular culture. But Arnold didn't fit that mold and, fortunately for all of us, never tried to change. Everyone else adjusted to him because of his honesty and earthiness and our adjustments were made without condescension. He was a much-loved, colorful character and kept the place a democracy of varied cultures and backgrounds.

He said he "never gave two runny shits 'bout them Beatle boys" until he overheard people talking about the clues in a pub. Arnold convinced them the clues were real, he said, out of sheer meanness and a crazy desire to start any argument whatsoever with two "fancypants boys" who had the nerve to visit *his* pub. He told them he knew for a fact that "Paulie" was dead and even boasted that he had seen the body, "jest don' ask me where 'cause you don' need ta know!" He challenged the strangers to prove Paul was alive and gave them a week to prove it. When he offered to wager they couldn't prove it, they took him up on the bet, he said, out of sheer callousness toward an old man.

He admitted he barely knew who "Paulie" even was, but after sobering up he began his own investigation out of fear of losing a one hundred pound wager he could not afford to pay. He had to prove Paul was dead.

Everyone adopted him as a very special Pepperlander, especially the person he always called "Dead Paulie."

His wife, "the old woman," was accustomed to him walking into town for an evening at the pub and not returning for several days, but he was presumed dead a week after he staggered out of the pub the night he collected his wager after the "fancypants boys" could not prove Paul was alive. It was assumed he fell into one of the surrounding bogs. Neither his body nor his winnings from the bet were ever recovered.

Robert Hahn: A writer from New Zealand who said he once toyed with the idea of attending Missouri's journalism school. We spent hours talking about J-School, him telling me how sorry he spurned the opportunity to attend and me assuring him he didn't miss much except the Shack, the M-Bar and Romano's.

Robert, Mark and I actually published a one-page, mimeographed newspaper called *The Onion Skin Paper* ("all the news that fits, we print"). There wasn't much news at Pepperland, of course, because everything was constant, so we gave minor stories big headlines and raked muck big and scandalous. We issued an "extra" when new varieties of military rations showed up in the dining area, headlining the story "Rats Invade Onion!" Sometimes we blatantly made up stories that were such major lies they went out of the realm of journalism and became parody: "Martha elected President of U.S., Vows to make Onion 51st State!" For the most part, the paper was a way for people to share poetry, song lyrics or whatever creativity they wanted to exchange in print. And it was fun, another game to pass the time and amuse us. It lasted as long as it took us to get bored, then a few other people took over. Then they got bored too and the paper died.

Robert fell into the clues while writing for a New Zealand newspaper syndicate. INTERPOL agents contacted him after he called the *Magical Mystery Tour* phone number and tried to pry information from Sexy Sadie, which was impossible.

To get him to Pepperland, he was admitted to a hospital for some minor ailment, where Company doctors administered drugs that slowed his body systems. He was declared dead of natural causes. He left a will donating his body to science and it was quickly taken from the hospital in an unmarked hearse.

I was always surprised he didn't write this book before I did. I'm certain he would have done a better job. I have no idea whether he is connected to the online newspaper, *The Onion*, but I doubt it since he's far older than the average dot-commer.

Allen Williams: A Welshman, he ran the Jacaranda Club ("The Jac"), in Liverpool and was the Beatles' first manager. It was Williams who sent them to the Cavern Club in Hamburg "for seasoning" in 1960 and warned Brian Epstein not to manage the group, "Don't touch them with a fucking bargepole," he advised, "they will let you down."

The Beatles brought him to Pepperland out of gratitude for what he did for them.

He wrote a book after Pepperland, a memoir called *The Man who Gave the Beatles Away*.

Yan Chu: I always pretended to forget his name just so he could repeat it and I could say "gesundheit." He never once got the joke but I always thought it was the funniest damn thing I'd ever heard or said.

A Taiwanese college student, The Company arranged employment for him on a fishing boat so he could fall off. After rescue by a submerged diver, he became one of Pepperland's leading "druggies."

Katherine Powers: She was the radical activist wanted by the Feds for her part in a 1970 Boston bank robbery and shooting that killed a police officer. She was on the FBI's "Most Wanted" list for many years, but they never found her.

The CIA did find her, however, at John Lennon's insistence. Though Company Men protested the Beatles harboring a Federal fugitive, John was adamant she receive sanctuary in Pepperland, claiming it was a protected place "for religious reasons," the same way a church was a safe haven from the law.

Katherine once gave me the same chills up my spine that I felt the night of our original radio program. She said that years before, after she placed just inside the top ten of a national achievement test, her friends at Marycrest High School in Denver nicknamed her "Number Nine."

When she turned herself in to Federal authorities in 1993, after a long time underground that followed a short time underwater, she admitted that she led her new life by assuming the name of a child who died about the same time as her own birth. In truth, the child's name was the cover The Company gave her at the fall of Pepperland.

At the end, we were all covered with names of children who died about the time we were born and afterward we lived the lives they did not live themselves. I always thought that was the final irony of the place, so many more lives used up.

These covers were all researched and created by The Company even before initial contact was made with any of us. Even before the first person arrived at Pepperland, they knew what lives we would lead after the lives after our original deaths failed. They knew who we would become before we even became those new people. It was all developed as part of a Company escape plan for when, not if, Pepperland failed for whatever reason.

None of us knew about the pre-existing covers until we got them.

They gave us names we weren't born into, histories we didn't live, even college degrees and resumes we never earned.

Katherine Powers never told where or how she received her cover.

Until now, nobody has.

WE'RE SERGEANT PEPPERS LONELY HEARTS CLUB BAND
WE HOPE YOU HAVE ENJOYED THE SHOW
WE'RE SERGEANT PEPPERS LONELY HEARTS CLUB BAND
WE'RE SORRY BUT IT'S TIME TO GO

The Beatles were at Pepperland too, but as Mark warned, all four of them were never there together. Like the clues on the album jackets said, they were "Beatles," not "*The* Beatles." The only time I ever saw all four Beatles together was at Busch Stadium in St. Louis in 1966. That was another time, a time when there was time, and another life before.

When I first met John, Paul and Ringo at The Onion, I resolved not to be stupid again, not to gush, not to say, "I have all your albums." But despite my Revolution Resolution, it was difficult for me as I'm sure it would have been for most anyone. As it turned out, I was only occasionally dumb and only marginally stupid.

George and Ringo came to The Onion separately, but were often there at the same time. Whether alone or together, they almost always jammed in the gazebo with the other musicians, including Peter.

In a great piece of interactive concert showmanship, George once called for the crowd surrounding the gazebo to sing at the same time, "sing all together now," he laughed, and then played the simple opening guitar riff of "All Together Now." The song took over. Musicians filled the gazebo to overflowing while the rest of us banged chairs, smacked pieces of metal or just clapped hands in an intense, driving, tribal rhythm. People danced everywhere, singing and yelling new lines and verses: "One, two, three four, I want to go to McDonald's store!" "A, B, C, D, won't somebody sleep with me?" "Cold beef stews, hot dog wienies, we all love the Company Meanies!"

It was forbidden for music to be louder than a certain level for fear of the vibration damaging the structural integrity of The Onion. There was a volume meter on the gazebo and an alarm blared when the maximum level was exceeded. During that "All Together Now" mega-concert, someone smashed the meter just to shut the alarm up. Everyone constantly looked upward as the volume swelled, afraid the sky would fall and we would all die again, this time for real. But if the sky fell and we were all crushed by the Pacific Ocean fixing its own hole, it would have been a perfect time and a perfect way to go.

It was fun.

Fun is the one thing that money can't buy.

Ringo organized soccer games that drew more players than his carpeted sward could handle. We surrounded the field, taking turns in and out of the game as energy built and waned. Ringo stayed in most of the time. They were co-ed "shirts and skins" games, one team wearing work shirts for uniforms, the other team bare-chested, including the women. Ringo's team was always "skins."

When he wasn't playing soccer, Ringo was just like every other Pepperlander, eating C-Rats, drinking beer and holding court in the dining area. He even took KP.

Conversations with Ringo were always fun and seldom serious. Once though, I was in a discussion with a small group of people that included Ringo and he surprised everyone when he sided with people who believed Vietnam was an empire-building war that the U.S. kept escalating to continue some self-perceived westward Manifest Destiny. Simply the tone of the conversation and his arguments took me by surprise. Ringo was supposed to just smile and toss his moptop, not discuss foreign policy.

During one visit, Ringo boasted he was the biggest Beatle backer of Pepperland and he had convinced the others, especially Paul, that they were the only ones who could pull off Utopia and that they had a responsibility to the world to do it. John felt strongly about the project, Ringo said, and George's agreement followed soon after. But he also said Paul fought it until the last instant before he reluctantly agreed to participate.

Ringo was the only Beatle present in the dome when the end was announced. His presence was no accident. He said he felt a personal responsibility to be there.

George taught Transcendental Meditation in the dome, which almost everyone attended. The Musicmaster turned off the music during classes and the lights around the gazebo were dimmed as hundreds of us sat in a circle surrounding it. The place was absolutely silent but for the sounds of our bodies and the ocean around us. I truly believe I could hear my soul in the silence. I can honestly say it was the most spiritual experience I ever felt, before or since.

I wish I could get it back.

George promised that one day we would work on levitation. We never had the chance.

Paul's visits were the most spectacular, the most star-like, always with an entourage. Even when he wasn't performing, he was always "on" and his high spirits kept everyone around him laughing and cheerful.

When he played in the gazebo, Paul was always sided by Jimmy McCulloch, the Thunderclap Newman guitarist I'd met on arrival. Years later, I wasn't surprised to see McCulloch became part of McCartney's group Wings.

One visit, Paul gave us a preview of the songs from his solo *McCartney* album. He said one song was based on people he met in The Onion:

Man we was lonely,
Yes we was lonely,
And we was hard-pressed to find a smile
Man we was lonely,
Yes we was lonely,
But now we're fine all the while.

Most of us thought the song was sweet but innocuous.

There were several photographs inside the original *McCartney* vinyl album jacket that Linda Eastman took while the two waited for the submarine at Jarvis. Those photographs were not transferred to the always-lacking CD cover art.

But of all the Beatles, I was most drawn to John, just to linger in his magical aura. His visits were the most eclectic, electric and most unpredictable.

They were the most fun.

They were the least fun.

Sometimes, John was fast and funny and never stopped talking. He could ad lib in the nonsense syllables and gross interconnections as if non sequitur were his native language, the way he wrote in *In His Own Write* and *Spaniard in the Works*, or with the same monosyllabic smartass attitude as in *The People's Almanac* interview.

When he was like that, he was the most charming man I've ever met.

But at other times, he brooded and didn't speak to anyone. For long periods, he isolated himself in the art area, making clay things then abandoning them or squashing them after they were formed. He would draw pictures and tear them up, both simple ones and complex ones.

During those visits, he was unapproachable.

Once, John carried a cardboard box to the gazebo and several of us helped him assemble a plastic Christmas tree. Not having a calendar, I couldn't be sure but I felt Christmas was long past. He insisted the date didn't matter, that Pepperland gave us "a happy Christmas" always. He led a bunch of us in a dance around the decorated tree, a dance he claimed was an ancient Druid ritual. Afterward, panting and tired, I told him that if that was the kind of fun Druids had, I wanted to be one. He said, "That's funny, you don't look Druidish."

I loved being around John during his *In His Own Write* moods.

But there was also the other John.

The biggest mistake I ever made involved "the other John."

Lennon.

The Beatle.

Me, schmoozing with John Lennon.

Nothing is real.

The incident taught me in very real terms that Mark was right from the beginning. Something was genuinely amiss in Pepperland. Something was happening there that never should have happened.

Because the Beatles were always dressed for the equatorial climate of Jarvis when they arrived in The Onion, it was impossible to tell from their clothing what season it was in The World. But because of John's deep tan, I assumed it was summer.

Later, I figured out it was summer, 1971.

Paul released his solo album a year before and announced he would never play again as a member of the Fab Four. The Beatles were over.

We never got word in The Onion.

All we knew were rumors. Because they never came to Pepperland together and because they never played together as a group, word spread that the Beatles were feuding, especially John and Paul.

Investigating old rumors got us to Pepperland. New rumors would take us out.

The new rumors hinted John was angry with Paul for a lot of things, including Paul's disinterest in Pepperland and lack of support for the project. Too often, the rumors said, Paul sided with The Company in policy that didn't reflect Pepperland's objectives of peace and love.

We couldn't know how ugly the feud was. In The World, we would have known the extent of the bad blood since it was so highly played in the media. But sequestered in Utopia, where no one feuded and we were all together now, we were part of the unreported disagreement. In Pepperland, we were sheltered from information the way overprotective parents shield their children when they think the truth or news might be painful or hurtful or difficult to understand. Certainly, to know what was happening would have been all of those things for all of us.

On the outside, we would have known Apple was rotting.

We knew nothing.

In exchange, The World didn't know that one of the reasons Apple was collapsing was the financial drain of Pepperland. Apple, as in also-played-a-role-in-the-end-of the Garden of Eden.

Pepperland was supposed to be a release from tension for the Beatles, a place where they could get away from being Beatles. Instead, it intensified the problems among them.

I already admitted that my biggest personal mistake in The Onion involved John.

This was the mistake: I asked John if the Beatles would ever play together at the same time, in the same place.

I asked if they would ever play together in The Onion.

He exploded like dynamite.

He screamed at me that it had been more than seven years since the Beatles were first successful and the statute of limitations was over. He never had to play with the others ever again.

When I innocently added that "we gave up everything for the Beatles..." he went from dynamite to thermonuclear, ranting and yelling. As he screamed, he kicked a hole in the wooden lattice around the gazebo. "If you think you're here for Beatles, you've been wrong ever since you got off the fookin' submarine!

"You didn't give up shit for Beatles, man, you gave it up for fookin' Utopia. You gave it up for fookin' peace and love and harmoony and that's what you fookin' got! You're fookin' fed and clothed and fookin' play your little games and have no troubles or worries in the whole fookin' world! This is heaven, man! It's fookin' heaven! Beatles aren't fookin' Utopia, man, *this* is fookin' Utopia! Beatles aren't fookin' real! Beatles are fookin' *noothing!*

"Nobody's tellin' you what to do, where to go, who to be! You got no fookin' job, you don't fookin' work, you don't make fookin' noothing! You got all the fookin' drugs you can eat so what's the fookin' problem?! It's fookin' *Alice in Wonderland*, man! It's fookin' Oz! 'Ding-dong, the witch is dead,' and so are fookin' Beatles!

"All you do with your whole fookin' life is eat and sleep and fook and shit and you're in the fookin' little womb while the rest of the world is outside worried they're gonna get blown up by a fookin' atomic bomb!"

I was literally stricken into shock by this point, violently and loudly humiliated by one of my idols, in tears, embarrassed and shrunken into a heap on the ground by the wrath of a god. A crowd gathered to hear John's tirade and to watch me berated and belittled.

By John.

Lennon.

The Beatle.

"Fook, man! Enjoy what you can while you can!"

He sat down on the gazebo steps for a moment and then came to my side. He put his hand on my shoulder and apologized "for the fookin' tantrum." Then he walked away.

Mark and Judy heard the commotion and came to me. Mark asked if I wanted anything to ease the pain. I said no. I wanted to be alone.

And through it all, even though he hurt me, I absolutely still loved John.

Lennon.

And the Beatles.

And I still fookin' do.

WE'RE SERGEANT PEPPERS LONELY HEARS CLUB BAND
WE'D LIKE TO THANK YOU ONCE AGAIN
WE'RE SERGEANT PEPPERS LONELY HEARTS CLUB BAND
IT'S GETTING VERY NEAR THE END

After the Company investigated potential residents of Pepperland, it created psychological profiles of each person who might be chosen. Once Pepperland was completed and occupied by those finally selected, Company Men continually updated those profiles whenever we met with a doctor for scheduled and required checkups. We also suspected that Company men were observing us at all other times, making discrete notes in our folders indicating whether we were stable or unstable, doing well or appearing depressed. Sometimes, the more paranoid among us thought that there were Company operatives living among us who were passing as normal residents. They were probably right.

The profiles not only explained who each of us were, they anticipated and projected how we might act and react in Pepperland and how we would fit in.

Charles Puckett Hancock explained all this to me at the beginning. Martha repeated the explanation during our "in the moment" interview on Jarvis.

No one ever told me that the only people on whom The Company did *not* create manila file folders or profiles were John Lennon, Paul McCartney, George Harrison and Ringo Starr.

There was no need, I suppose. Even if their profiles turned up horribly negative, the four Beatles were the source of the project and despite what John bellowed at me, they were exactly and precisely what attracted everyone else to the Pepperland experiment, even more than the dream of "fookin' Utopia." It would have been impossible to keep them away from Pepperland no matter what their profiles said, had there been profiles.

But if Company men had investigated the Beatles the way they investigated everyone else, which they were never going to do, questions might have been raised. They would have learned that by 1968, when the Beatles were with the Maharishi and while Pepperland was still in the conceptual stage, tensions were beginning, especially between John and Paul. The death of Brian Epstein while the boys were in India just made matters worse and more confusing.

If Company Men had created profiles on the Beatles, perhaps they would have learned that as early as 1967, the Beatles wanted to get away from being Beatles. They might have discovered that the Four had asked Alistair Taylor to buy them an island, somewhere they could escape the pressure of being Beatles and relax, to just be four regular humans instead of cultural phenomena. All four, in fact, went to Greece in 1967 to look for an island where, according to one report, "they could build a little utopia." The Company could easily have learned that in 1967 John actually did buy his own island, Dornish Island off the coast of Ireland, but never used it as the getaway he had hoped for.

The profiles might have shown that by 1969, when Pepperland was on top-secret government drawing boards, the Beatles had long stopped touring and, thanks to multi-track recording, didn't even play together in the studio any more.

If Company Men had truly learned everything there was to know about the Beatles, even half as much as they had learned about the rest of us, they would have known that by 1970, when Pepperland was almost completed and Paul announced the end of the Beatles, the Four met at Apple Corps offices and decided that despite mounting personal and financial pressures, Pepperland had gone too far to be cancelled.

The Beatles decided that no matter how they felt about one another—as people or as Beatles—Pepperland must go on. If any Utopia in the history of humankind had a chance, Pepperland would be the best opportunity.

Who could argue with Utopia?

Who could let file folders get in the way of perfection?

Who could let psychological profiles come between ignorance and data gathering?

At that Apple Corps meeting, the Beatles decided Pepperland would be a final act of possible reconciliation. If they couldn't get along among themselves in Utopia, they decided, they wouldn't get along in The World. They decided that if they couldn't get along in Pepperland, it would be all over.

It was. The profile-less Company never saw it coming.

THERE ARE PLACES I REMEMBER
ALL MY LIFE
THOUGH SOME HAVE CHANGED

Martha first came to The Onion more than a year after I arrived, in what I would later learn was November, 1971.

She arrived on the *Alvin* with several new Company Men and Ringo. A soccer game began immediately. Ringo's team was "skins" just like always.

Martha was cheerful, saying she was glad to visit. Since literally everyone in The Onion had passed her inspection and examination, she knew everyone, if not by name then by face and probably by background and potential emotional and mental problems.

Though she slept in the Administration area with the Meanies instead of in the Village with the people, she circulated and made herself available to everyone.

It was a quite a while after their arrival before we knew why she, the other Company Men and Ringo came for a visit.

At once point during her stay, she sidled up to our group as we played high stakes M&M poker at a table in the dining area. Everyone liked Martha and we were glad she joined us. She asked to be dealt in and we staked her with a fresh bag of candy all her own. She played several hands, engaging in the kind of card table banter that could have been expected from anyone on holiday with nothing to lose but M&Ms. And she did lose all her M&Ms. She was the worst card player we ever saw. We were relentless in the hard time we gave her. But she was a good loser, the kind every card shark hopes to find.

Declining another chocolate stake but watching the game a few hands more, she and I made eye contact and she leaned over to ask, "can we talk?" Afraid I had done something wrong, I fearfully agreed, promising to rejoin the game as quickly as possible.

She asked if I'd take a walk with her. "Okay with me," I said, standing up from the table.

She started the conversation simply. "It's been a long time."

"Yeah," I agreed, "a long time. How have you been?"

"That's what I was going to ask you."

Her response wasn't surprising. In fact, I would have been surprised if it had been anything else. I knew my condition was what interested her from the beginning. "I'm okay. I'm really okay," I answered. "It's been an interesting time."

"Have you had fun?"

I started to give her Mark's standard "fun is the one thing..." answer, but since I didn't think Martha was a radio man and expected she might not catch the reference, I restrained myself. "Yes."

"Good. I know you and Mark had problems between the two of you, but that seems worked out."

"Yeah, it's been worked out for a long time."

"Good. No girlfriend?

"Nope. Sorry to disappoint you. No girlfriend."

"That's okay. No problem. I was just curious and looking out for you."

"Thanks."

We continued walking. Finally, I built up my courage and asked a question that had bothered me since my arrival. "Why didn't you tell me Mark was here? Back on Jarvis, why didn't you tell me what was going on with him? And for that matter, why didn't you tell me what was happening with the Beatles. Didn't you know?"

"Yes," she offered without breaking stride, "we knew. I knew about Mark's unhappiness and I knew about the problems between the boys. I didn't tell you about either situation because I couldn't. This was supposed to be a good experience for you and I wanted to help make it so."

"Thank you," I answered, genuinely accepting an honest admission. Then she admitted she also had things to ask me. "Those were your questions, now it's my turn."

"Shoot."

"Can you live in the moment?"

Her question made me laugh out loud.

"Do you mean am I over Mara? I suppose absolutely yes and absolutely no. I mean, I'm having a spectacular time here. I've had real, live, genuine fun. But to be completely honest, there have been moments I wasn't so happy and wondered..."

"Do you mean the 'John thing?'" she asked, hearing exactly the message I was sending without saying the exact words.

"Yeah, the 'John thing.' I'm over that too, I guess."

"Good. I'm glad you can be in the moment. It's important."

And then, without even saying goodbye, she turned and walked away.

At first, I thought we were having a friendly, personal, one-on-one conversation about meaningful things. Then I realized we were having another manila folder analysis.

A short time later, notices appeared all around The Onion. In three sundowns, the notices said, there would be a mandatory meeting at the gazebo for everyone. We were expected to keep our heads up toward the top of The Onion and count sunsets. The notices asked everyone to wake roommates, neighbors and anyone who might be sleeping at the time of the third sunset.

It was the first time anything at Pepperland was "mandatory."

Between the posting of the notices and the meeting, Lucy closed up shop and the drug supply dried up. Some serious druggies went through withdrawal and some became hostile. Some went to the infirmary and a few went out under sedation on the *Alvin*.

Rumors were rampant.

Some rumors said the meeting was to deal with "the drug problem," to announce Prohibition was about to catch up with Pepperland. Some people said the meeting was to quash rumors about the Beatles feud. Still others spread word the meeting was simply to dispel any rumors about Prohibition or problems between the Beatles.

None of us expected Martha's real announcement: "Ladies and gentlemen, we are going out of business."

SOME FOREVER, NOT FOR BETTER
SOME HAVE GONE
AND SOME REMAIN

I've repeated over and over, nothing is real.

And sometimes, reality is nothing.

"Pepperland is a fortunate experiment that unfortunately has run its course and failed," Martha announced. "We have made arrangements for everyone to leave and go back to The World. I'm sorry people, but it's over. We're all going home."

A roar of hundreds of argumentative voices was raised, shrieks of disbelief and grief, but Martha would not give us the answers we wanted.

"You promised us Utopia!" someone shouted.

"And you got it! Hasn't this been something you would never have gotten otherwise?"

"You promised us forever!"

"Nothing is forever!"

Nothing is real.

The voices raised again, hundreds of emotional, angry, hurt people crying foul, feeling they were cheated out of their pasts and now the promise of their eternities too.

"People! People!" Martha shouted over the din. "It's been agreed by the Beatles and The Company and it's unchangeable policy! It's impossible for anyone to stay! You cannot resist the move!"

There were more loud shouts, more hoots, voices raised in protest and voices raised in the pain created by fear of losing the comfortable and familiar. And there was also the audible panic of facing another unknown future.

"I can't allow any discussion and I won't take any questions. The decision was made by people higher than me, including the Beatles, and that, my friends, is that."

The hoots died down slowly as the announcement settled in. But the anger remained. One of the druggies ran to the edge of the dome and started banging the glass with a bench—how he picked the heavy thing up is still a mystery to me. The echo resounded over the silent Onion. He was quickly hauled away by residents and Meanies.

Martha continued. "You'll be taken out the same way you came in. The *Alvin* will take you from here and transfer you to larger ships, uh, boats. They'll take you to Jarvis then very quickly you'll be flown out or taken by British or American surface ships to your individual destinations. Unlike when you came here, there will be minimal lag time on Jarvis on the way out, no fun and games on the way home.

"Even though we've increased the number of submarines and aircraft for the evacuation, we still anticipate it will take six to eight sunsets to evacuate fully."

Martha knew sunsets were the only measure of time in The Onion and she told us to start looking up to relearn about the passage of real time in the Real World. Re-teaching us "real time in the real world" might have been the final Company experiment, if only to see how quickly we could re-establish normal Circadian rhythms.

But none of us could establish anything normal. Nothing was normal and normal was nothing. Everyone's internal rhythms were either standing at flat zero or running at ten thousand miles an hour.

Besides, looking up through The Onion was more than a way to keep time. It was also symbolic. We were not only looking up, we were looking out.

Finally, Martha dealt the lethal blow. "And after six to eight sunsets, after everyone is evacuated, The Onion itself will be destroyed."

While most people stood silently in acceptance, there were scattered shouts that claimed that destroying Pepperland would be like killing our own mother or, at minimum, destroying something important. "Leave it alone!" "Let it stay for history!" "Maybe people can come back some day!" "Leave it! This is our home!"

There is a deeply ironic fable called "The Scorpion and the Frog" that I once heard relative to a specific corporate executive for whom I once worked. When I first heard the tale, I immediately thought back to that moment in Pepperland: a scorpion and a frog both lived on a small piece of land. One day, fierce rains came and as the water rose, the scorpion asked the frog to carry him on his back to safety. The frog, of course, was skeptical and feared the scorpion would sting him. The scorpion denied the possibility, admitting that it was obvious that if he stung the frog, neither would survive the rising flood. Out of compassion then, the frog finally agreed to carry the scorpion to dry land.

But as the frog swam through the rushing floodwater with the scorpion on his back, he felt a sting. Quickly becoming groggy, the frog looked to the scorpion and asked, "Why did you sting me? Now we both will die."

"Why did I sting you? Because I'm a scorpion. It's what I do."

Martha told the crowd that after evacuation, when Pepperland was abandoned, the American nuclear attack submarine *Scorpion* would fire a torpedo into The Onion, destroying it forever.

All nuclear attack submarines are scorpions. It's what they do.

Give peace a chance.

There was nothing more to be heard from the crowd but the din of hundreds of people in silence. It was the same eerie silence I felt at the beginning, the same helpless quiet I felt at the revelation of each obvious clue.

"After evacuation, you'll have the option of going back to wherever you were before Pepperland or The Company will relocate you."

The shouting began again. "How can we go home?" "They all think we're dead!" "We can't go back!" "You promised us forever!"

It's all up to you," Martha answered. "You can go back to where you were before the project or you can start over with new identities we will give you and then you can live in the places where we settle you!"

Martha called Pepperland "the project," like some sort of science fair exhibit. But to us, Pepperland was home. Pepperland was where we were meant to be.

I knew I couldn't go back to my parents, to Mara. None of us knew what we would do or where we would go. We only knew we couldn't stay. We would soon be true nowhere men and nowhere women, lost forever in the Sea of Future.

My decision to die and leave my life behind was irrevocable. I hurt people and knew there was no hope of a happy reunion. I resigned myself to accept the cover and go wherever The Company took me. So did almost everyone. Each of us started new lives once and hoped that maybe the second time would be easier, that maybe the new lies would be simpler to live with than the ones we told before.

We lost each other after resettlement, of course. We all were covered under the blankets of our new identities. All contact with one another was lost, never knowing where, or who, the others were.

In 1975, I read a small news item that Peter Ham of the rock group Badfinger ended the life he resumed as Peter Ham of Badfinger.

In 1993, Katherine Powers was captured by the FBI and revealed her cover in a courtroom. She spent twenty years as a suburban housewife.

Martha explained how we would be evacuated by shower groups. Yellow would go first, then red, blue and then white. We were to watch the colored lights to tell us when to go to the dock.

Six to eight sunsets.

I didn't want to go.

I didn't want to leave home again.

ALL THESE PLACES HAVE THEIR MOMENTS
WITH LOVERS AND FRIENDS
I STILL CAN RECALL

I quickly found Mark, as if some internal homing mechanism drew me toward him through the crowd. He and Judy were holding each other tightly and with heads on each others' shoulders, comforting one another the same way victims of crime, natural disaster or some shared community tragedy hold each other, the way families and friends embrace after a funeral.

As I stood next to them, looking lost, I put my head on Mark's shoulder. Judy pulled me into their clutch. The three of us held each other for the longest time. After a few minutes more, Jacques, Susanne, Dan and Peter joined us in a group clutch. As they joined our huddle, I began to weep openly. So did everyone else in the group.

My tears turned to sobs when Martha came to us. She was crying too. Even though she was the official ogre of the moment, I still felt a bond with her—maybe she became a mother figure, who knows?—but I reached my arm out to pull her into our group. She accepted the offer and returned the embrace.

Suddenly, Dan stepped back and boldly announced he would not leave, that he would die with Pepperland. It was home, he exclaimed, familiar surroundings where he was comfortable for the first time in his life. "You can't make me leave," he insisted, separating from the group and standing alone facing Martha, fists clenched.

"Dan," Martha pleaded in her most understanding tone, "it's over."

"NO!" Dan stood firm. "If thah gon' ta take Th' Onion, they'll haf ta take me too!"

"If you resist," Martha said calmly, "there will be Company Men who…" She stopped in mid-sentence and wiped her tears, straightening her posture and regaining her professionalism. "There will be Company Men with infrared sensors who will find you wherever you hide, even in the dark. They will hunt you down and shoot you with tranquilizer guns and put you to sleep. They will physically carry you to the submarine and take you away." Then Martha excused herself and took herself away from us.

Tranquilizer guns.

Nothing is real.

They would hunt us down and put us to sleep like elephants efficiently scheduled to be transferred from one zoo to another.

To The Company, Pepperland had become a white elephant.

The Meanies in the movie *Yellow Submarine* lost the battle for Pepperland to Love, which is "all you need."

Did the plan for Pepperland include the idea that we would all grow old and die there, new generations of Pepperland-born children repopulating the place over and over? We certainly didn't know what the Meanies might have had in mind for the future and we never considered the possibility ourselves, never worried about it, never thought that far ahead or spent a second concerned about old age. After all, we were young and immortal. We were Pepperlanders. We lived in the moment. If Blue Meanies come to Pepperland, they would be run out by Love, which is all you need. Oh what joy, for every girl and boy, knowing they're happy and they're safe.

But in the fantasy reality of Pepperland, the Meanies won.

Despite the Love, the Meanies destroyed Pepperland.

Love was not all we needed.

Love was totally inadequate.

SOME ARE DEAD AND SOME ARE LIVING
IN MY LIFE
I'VE LOVED THEM ALL

We had six to eight sunsets before the blue light was lit for our turn to go.

In a *Yellow Submarine* Sea of Time where time was nonexistent, time suddenly took on new importance.

When time is endless, it is meaningless. But time passes quickly when every moment is precious and when all of time adds up to only a few more sunsets.

We spent much of our remaining time looking up, dreading the disappearance of the brightly backlit blue-green in the triangles above The Onion, dreading the darkness each sunset brought.

There is a rhetorical/sociological/psychological question people ask sometimes when they want to know more about a person or create conversation or controversy: "What would you do if you found out you only had a few days to live?"

The question is not rhetorical.

I know the answer.

Some people do absolutely nothing. They drug out our drink, spending all their time in a stupor, oblivious to the present—ignorant of the moment—and ignoring the future. When the future is omnipresent, others become acutely aware of the moment.

We did everything.

It would have been easy to sit Shiva for Pepperland before it was genuinely dead and before we had a body. It would have been understandable to have given in and mourned our loss.

But we didn't.

Over the days we waited for our own sunset, as groups of three and four and five people went into the dock and disappeared onto the *Alvin*, those whose time had not yet come always went to see them off. Even people we never really knew or loved in The Onion gave and received warm hugs and kisses to and from everyone.

Goodbye.

No hello.

And then the blue light was lit.

BUT OF ALL THESE FRIENDS AND LOVERS
THERE IS NO ONE
COMPARES WITH YOU

Over the years, Paul McCartney and Ringo Starr have drawn enormous crowds playing live concerts all over the world. I read that on at least one occasion, Paul played Busch Stadium in St. Louis, just like the good old days when I saw all the Beatles there.

Most of the people in their audiences were Baby Boomers wanting to hear the music, see the gods and recapture a piece of their youth. They went to the shows just to be in the presence of someone who played such an important part of their lives. Many of the fans took their children to the concerts, children who were raised by parents who instilled Beatles in them the same way they taught them religion or family recipes or their bad habits. There are Beatle-people grandchildren who are being raised as third-generation Beatle people. I know this because I have some, God bless 'em.

In the past years, the Beatles as a group have actually made more money and sold more albums than they did when they were new, more than when all four were alive and well and working together, before anybody shot any of them or stabbed any of them and before they were stricken by cancer and before any of us finally hit old age.

Paul has played especially active tours, making much more of a splash than Ringo, whose "All Starr Bands" are still newsmakers nonetheless.

But Paul outsells Ringo by far. His tickets are more expensive, his crowds more enthusiastic, his albums better received.

The dead man still turns them on.

.no meht snrut llits nam daed ehT.

After each of the concert tours, Paul has issued a "live concert" album.

The album after the 1993 tour was called *Paul is Live*.

The album cover shows him walking his dog across Abbey Road. There is no minister in the photo, no undertaker, no gravedigger. Just Paul and his dog.

There are cars in the background of the cover photo.

One of the cars in the background is a Volkswagen Beetle.

The license plate on the Volkswagen Beetle reads "51 IS."

AND THESE MEMORIES LOSE THEIR MEANING

As I near the end of this tale, I confess my guilt of spending far more pages explaining the process of getting to Pepperland than explaining the actual being there.

Maybe it's because the timeless time in Pepperland became one constant, long experience in my memory, one quick unbroken moment uninterrupted by seconds or minutes or days or weeks or months. There was no time there. It was all one time. No time at all, not even the *New York Times*. During the travel days—when time was attached to my wrist in Mara's lovely square Swiss watch, waiting for me to witness it pass one second at a time—time lasted forever.

No watch, no clocks, no time.

Or, maybe I've simply repressed what happened and what we did in Pepperland, forgotten it, put it somewhere in my memory where I can never reach it simply because the end of the story makes it too painful to remember.

Maybe it was like a wonderful love affair, all caught up in itself where everything is glorious and runs together and seems perfect until it goes to pure shit.

But now I'm getting sappy and stupid.

Readers need to know the many details involved in getting to Pepperland.

Readers need to know there was only one detail while there: the one thing that money can't buy.

Or, maybe it was all described best by what Mark said when I first met him at Pepperland: maybe the quest was most important, the adventure and the challenge of getting there were more significant than being there. Maybe the Utopian ideal is all about the quest. Buddhists believe that there must be a lengthy physical and personal journey before arrival in Shambhala, a Utopia of beauty and peace. Islam has flourished for a thousand years in a remote, impossible-to-get-to place called Hunza in the mountains of Pakistan, said to be the model for Shangri-La. Christians and Jews believe in the Garden of Eden and that Adam and Eve were exiled from that Utopia for tasting of the forbidden fruit. The forbidden fruit was an apple.

Our quest took us to Pepperland. Shambhala. Shangri-La. All courtesy of Apple.

Once, during Mark's bad times in Pepperland, he was in bed riding out a bad LSD trip. I put wet towels on his forehead and held his hand. It was all I could do.

He started to recite dialogue from *The Wizard of Oz*, yet another story about yet another seeming Utopia.

There were no VCRs or DVDs then, no movie rental stores, no Netflix, no YouTube and no streaming video. *The Wizard of Oz* was shown on network television only once a year. It was a major event in most American homes.

But somewhere inside his brain, Mark had already recorded the movie from those network showings. Every frame was stored in his head like videotape or a computer file ready to be played or pulled from memory.

He recited parts of the movie dialogue perfectly, word for word. I was astonished and amused at the same time.

In retrospect, I remember his delirium as not only an amazingly perfect transcription of the movie, but perfect for my current feelings about Pepperland and what we did and what happened to us after.

He even tried to click his heels together as he tossed and turned under his War Surplus army blanket. In a light voice that didn't sound like Mark, deep throated rock and roll radio man that he was, this is what he said: "If I ever go looking for my hearts desire again, I won't look any further than my own back yard. Because if it isn't there, I never really lost it to begin with."

Now it's Mark who's getting sappy and stupid and he's not even telling this story.

I totally forgot that silly incident until many, many years ago when I was watching a video at home with my children.

We were watching *The Wizard of Oz*.

In 2003, a lifetime away from Martha's announcement in The Onion, I was sitting in the gate area of a major American airport.

As I mindlessly glanced up from my *USA Today* to watch the crowds go by in the concourse, my eyes made contact with the eyes of one of the many gray-haired, briefcase-toting men passing by.

I don't know why I glanced up. I don't know why I glanced up at that exact second. I don't know why I glanced up at that exact man in that exact crowd at that exact second.

I didn't know who he was.

He didn't know me.

He walked on.

He was no one.

I was no one.

We were merely two of the thousands of people in an airport concourse.

I didn't budge.

As soon as the man passed out of my sight down the concourse and into the crowd, the part of our subconscious that gives no explanation for what it makes us say, that part that stores dialogue from old movies for recitation later, made me literally stand up and yell in the midst of a crowded airport.

"Maaaaaaaaaaaaaaaaaaaaaaaaaaaaark!"

An excited and clearly audible voice shouted back from down the jammed concourse.

"Young Jeffrey!"

WHEN I THINK OF LOVE
AS SOMETHING NEW

Pepperland did not stop being Pepperland.

The Beatles stopped being Beatles.

The pressure of the Pacific Ocean did not crush Pepperland.

The pressure of being Beatles crushed Pepperland.

Besides every conceivable stress that could have been put on the most popular musicians in history (someone once even called them "more popular that Jesus Christ"), the money, secrecy and espionage trebled the pressure that crushed the Beatles.

The end of the Beatles ended Pepperland.

Pepperland ended the Beatles.

I wasn't the only person to ask when the Beatles would play together again. Millions of Baby Boomers wanted to see and hear them again. An entire generation yearned for a Beatle reunion.

We wanted their music, of course, but we also wanted more.

Just as the Beatles shaped the Boomer's music with an upbeat, sassy, hair-tossing attitude, they made our generation upbeat and sassy too. They taught us to grow our hair and then let it down.

The Beatles set the tone for all of us.

They didn't just make music during our youth, they *made* our youth *itself*. They were the soundtrack of our very best years, the years when we defined and defied the world.

They defined our youth itself.

They were the thread that connected our childhood to our adulthood, they were the constant through the best years and remain so now into our later years. Relationships, jobs, health and youth have all come and gone, and as we've entered our sixties the Beatles still provide the music and the words and the spirit.

I feel sorry for the Baby Boomers who have lost that ideal and that sense.

We didn't just want Beatles.

We didn't just want Beatle music.

We *all* wanted Pepperland, whether we ever knew Pepperland existed or not.

The Beatles *were* Pepperland.

When my children were small, I read to them from a beautifully illustrated, vintage book called *Stories that Never Grow Old*. Sometimes they asked why I sounded "so funny" when I read one story in particular. Once, as I read, my youngest asked why there was water in my eyes.

The story is "The Pied Piper of Hamelin."

The Pied Piper told the people of Hamelin, "I have a musical charm by which I can make any living creature follow me."

So did the Beatles.

The Beatles were the Pied Pipers of our generation.

With his charm and enchanting music, the likes of which no one had ever seen or heard before, the Piper freed Hamelin of rats by leading the rats to the river and drowning them in the water.

Charm and enchanting music also led me to drown in a river.

Then, according to the story, the mayor of Hamelin refused to pay the Piper the one thousand guilders he promised. So the Piper began playing music again. This time, all the children of the town followed him.

For a few short years in the 1960s and '70s, the world's children followed the Beatles.

As the children of Hamelin followed the Piper, they disappeared through the doorway of a secret, magic mountain cave and were never seen again by their mothers, fathers, or the people who loved them.

Just like we disappeared into the secret, magic Onion.

The story tells of a little lame boy who couldn't keep up with the procession of children following the Piper and was left behind, the only child who remained in Hamelin. He was sad at being left behind, he says, because the Piper promised that if the children followed him they would see the most beautiful sights of all. The child says the piper's music itself said he was leading the children to "a joyous land where there are fruits and flowers more wonderful than anyone in this world has ever seen…and everyone is happy and well."

In that 1938 storybook anthology, a book that I still treasure, and in the telling of a story that spans multiple generations, the boy describes exactly the music and promises that led us to Pepperland.

For the majority of Boomers, Pepperland was an imaginary place from an animated movie that promised fruits and flowers more wonderful than anyone in this world has ever seen, where everyone was happy and well.

For a tiny minority of us, Pepperland was real, a joyous land where we did find fruits and flowers more wonderful than anyone in this world had ever seen, where everyone was happy and well.

In either case, all of us wanted the same thing: we wanted the soundtrack of our youth to play for us just like always. We wanted John, Paul, George and Ringo to continue piping. We wanted them to keep breaking new ground, to keep defining fashion and style and our ideas and our politics and our dreams, to tell us how and what we and the world should be. We wanted them to be the thread that stitched the seamless connection from our teens and twenties into the rest of our lives.

Certainly the CIA could have kept Pepperland running without the Beatles, but there would have been a mutiny at sea. We were not there for the CIA. We were there for the Beatles.

Once the Beatles were gone, Pepperland was gone too.

A Beatles reunion would have reunited us with our own youth.

A Beatles reunion would have made us young again.

When the Beatles weren't the Beatles any more, we were officially not young any more.   Certainly, we weren't "grownups," we were a generation in confusion. Not young, not grown up. We were the Beatles generation.

In *Imagine*, a documentary about John Lennon, an old piece of film shows an excited fan in absolute euphoria when he sees John on a New York street. The fan gushes stupidly, stopping just short of the ultimate stupidity, "I have all your albums."

Despite the fan's honest excitement, John puts him down, taunting "I bet you still like *Hard Day's Night*!" The gushing, idiotic fan admits he does and John walks away in disgust.

I still like *Hard Day's Night* too. When it was released on DVD in 2002, it sold millions of copies immediately, to us and to our children.

What that fan, and most of the rest of us, never realized was how much happened to and with the Beatles, how much good and how much bad. He and we never acknowledged that the Beatles *had* to be put to rest. Beatles *had* to put the Beatles behind themselves and behind us. The real hard day's night was all too much for everyone to take, too intense to last.

All of us had to grow and change, whether we wanted to admit it or not.

The breakup of the Beatles taught Baby Boomers that no matter how much we tried to maintain our youth, no matter how powerful a generation we were and no matter how much we did change the world, even if we wanted the Beatles to last eight days a week, the Pipers could, indeed, be silenced by the Sea of Time.

And they were.

And we had to grow up.

The music ended the instant the *Scorpion* fired a torpedo into the glass domed Onion that was Pepperland.

And so did the short-lived Utopia of three hundred and fourteen people.

Any final hope of recovering the magic was lost forever when Mark David Chapman pulled the trigger that killed one of the Pipers.

And so was our youth.

It could never be rebuilt.

Only remembered.

Paul, George and Ringo once announced that bygones were bygones and they recorded several new Beatle tracks along with old John Lennon solo tracks. A new era of Beatlemania began when *The Beatles Anthology* was one of the biggest events in television history. The Beatles *One* set sales records all over the world.

But it's not the same.

Pepperland is gone forever.

The Beatles are a marketing tool.

A Hollywood director recently said the reason so many new movies are remakes of old TV shows is because of my generation's lingering fantasy with our pasts and our willingness to pay to see it updated. "If I could make a Beatles movie today," he told a news magazine, "I'd make a Beatles movie."

The "Pied Piper" story ends with a description of a group of strange old men and old women who suddenly came "out of the earth" and walked into Hamelin. They are "people different from everyone else." These strange men and women, different from everyone else, moved into the homes where the children of Hamelin once lived. But the children themselves never returned.

The children of Pepperland also went home as strange, wizened, men and women.

"And wherever it was—that wonderful land—no one in Hamelin ever learned."

The children kept the Piper's secret forever.

THOUGH I KNOW I'LL NEVER LOSE AFFECTION FOR PEOPLE AND THINGS THAT WENT BEFORE

While I can't remember what happened this afternoon, I know exactly where I was in the waning hours of December 8, 1980.

I was thirty-one years old.

The TV had been off in my home for quite some time and my wife flicked it on as we crawled into bed. Out of habit for almost a year, she turned on *Nightline*, a still-new program that captured the country's interest after Americans were taken hostage at the U.S. embassy in Iran.

But Ted Koppel wasn't talking about the Ayatollah or Tehran or hostages.

He was talking about John Lennon and New York and bullets.

He said Lennon was shot outside his New York apartment "by a crazed fan."

John Lennon.

The Beatle.

Dead.

The "crazed fan" was Mark David Chapman.

Like everyone else, I reacted with shock and loss.

I mourned.

Then, by now understandably I hope, I wondered if it was true.

I wondered if John had dreamed it all up, just as he dreamed of a perfect Utopia for more than three hundred of us, "a hole in the ocean" where "love is all you need."

I wondered whether he created a fictitious public death for himself the way so many other fictional deaths were created so that we, and he, could live without pressure.

I wondered if John found his Utopia someplace where there was no knowledge or memory of Beatles, of Pepperland, somewhere there were no "crazed fans."

And then I decided.

John is dead.

Genuinely dead.

John was genuinely gunned down on December 8, 1980 by Mark David Chapman.

I genuinely mourn his genuine loss.

But Mark David Chapman was not merely a "crazed fan."

I believe he was an operative agent of the Central Intelligence Agency, U.S. Naval Intelligence, British MI6, INTERPOL and the Worldwide Intelligence Community.

I believe John Lennon was about to go public with Pepperland.

He was going to ease the plague on his soul and tell the world the truth about Pepperland, about the other Pepperlanders who "died" but lived and were reborn in the identities of other people. He was going to spill the beans about billions and billions of dollars spent on a foolish experiment and in an impossible effort to reconcile the Beatles.

John knew he would not be dismissed as a crackpot or loony.

When Mark David Chapman shot John Lennon, the files and documentation about Pepperland were destroyed in Washington and London and everywhere else.

John Lennon is genuinely dead.

So is Pepperland.

Nothing is real.

Nothing is.

I KNOW I'LL OFTEN THINK ABOUT THEM
IN MY LIFE
I LOVE YOU MORE

Once there was a way, to get back homeward, once there was a way to get back home.

"Hi" Mom.

The long and winding road that leads to your door, will never disappear. I've seen that road before it always leads me here, leads me to your door.

Mara, "hello."

It's been a long time, now I'm coming back home. I've been away now, oh how, I've been alone.

Blahblahblah.

This child of Hamelin has returned.

AND IN THE END
THE LOVE YOU TAKE
IS EQUAL TO
THE LOVE YOU MAKE

It all boils down to this: in the spring of 1970, construction was completed on a steel and glass geodesic-domed Atlantis on the floor of the Pacific Ocean. It was fully pressurized to sea level and located approximately one hundred miles east-northeast of the coast of the Jarvis Islands, south of Hawaii, almost on the equator. Because it was built on a volcanic shelf on the seabed, the highest point of the dome was only fifty feet below the surface of the water.

And then, it was successfully occupied by humans for more than eighteen months.

It was conceived, planned, authorized, constructed and populated under the auspices of the Beatles.

The dome was Pepperland. An *Octopus's Garden*. It was "the Glass Onion." It was a genuine place of perpetual love, music, serenity and beauty. It was Utopia. It was Shangri-La

It was Pepperland.

And after all these years, I'm tired of being dead.

ACKNOWLEDGMENTS

This book was actually written many years before this publication. In that period of time, many people read the manuscript, including a number of literary agents who took passes or, like most books from most authors, ignored it completely.

My three daughters, of course, all read it because they had an obligation to read it and I am grateful for the loyalty they have to their father and to the novel. I am equally grateful that they and their children are all Beatle fans. Or would have been.

Many others also read the manuscript and none of them used the phrase "it sucks," which I consider to be a very polite bit of amity and generally positive reviews. I thank them for their interest, their friendship and their eyeball time.

I'm also extremely grateful to my friend Paul Fiddick, a genuine, down-to-the-marrow-of-his-bones radio man whose connection to this story goes indescribably beyond his encouragement, expertise in detail and nit-picky copyediting.

The background cover art and graphic are by Carol Carter (carol-carter.com), a St. Louis-based, internationally acclaimed watercolorist and friend whose wonderful work very often features water. She was, therefore, the natural person to ask to paint a cover about a place under the sea. The cover itself was designed by Cindy Kalman of Kalmarx Design (kalmarx.com), in Boulder, Colorado. I thank them both for their help, talents and cooperation.

I also thank any and all readers who share a love for the Beatles and who may or may not have lived through the time when we all thought "Paul is dead" or might even remotely, possibly be. It's all in the mind, you know.

In an effort to minimize the chance for any and all possible unpleasant and/or ugly communication, I acknowledge that I am well aware that the original title of the song on the Beatles' *Abbey Road* Album is "Octopus*'s* Garden" (with a second *s* after the apostrophe), so please don't write me about that. With all due respect to the composers, it just looked better on the cover without the second letter *s*. Thank you.

And I thank John, Paul, George and Ringo for changing the world. Mine at least.

ABOUT THE AUTHOR

Since starting his broadcast career as a disc jockey on the campus radio station at the University of Missouri and subsequently fooling the world-renowned Missouri School of Journalism into awarding him a diploma, Aaron Mermelstein has been a semi-professional journalist for more than forty years. While he has occasionally dabbled in radio and has even dipped his toe into newspapering back when newspapers still existed, he is, for the most part, a television man.

He lives in St. Louis.

Made in the USA
Charleston, SC
06 June 2014